THE ROYAL CITY

By Les Savage, Jr.

THE ROYAL CITY
SILVER STREET WOMAN

THE ROYAL CITY

Les Savage, Jr.

Friends-of-The-Palace Press
Santa Fe, New Mexico

New material copyright ©1988 by Museum of New Mexico Foundation
All rights reserved
Published by the Friends-of-The-Palace Press
Palace of The Governors
P.O. Box 9312
Santa Fe, New Mexico 87504-9312

First Printing

Library of Congress Cataloging in Publication Data

Library of Congress Number 88-080571

Savage, Jr., Les
  The Royal City

   This is an unabridged reprint of the original 1956 edition,
published by Hanover House, with new notes and foreword.

ISBN 0-941108-01-5

IN APPRECIATION

The Friends of the Palace are grateful to the Museum of New Mexico Foundation for supporting our efforts on behalf of the Palace of the Governors, Santa Fe.

We also wish to express our appreciation to the Museum of New Mexico Press for its valued contribution and assistance. Special thanks to Charles Bennett, Curator of Collections, the Palace of the Governors, for his background notes. Also, our deep appreciation goes to the widow of Les Savage, Jr.

ABOUT THE AUTHOR

Les Savage, Jr. wrote *The Royal City* with rare understanding. His descriptions of characters and events reveal careful research into the early history of Santa Fe and the Spanish borderlands. The author wrote twenty-two novels, two of which were adapted for motion pictures. Aside from *The Royal City*, his most famous novel was *Silver Street Women*, a story about life on the Mississippi River. A prolific writer, Savage published several books under the pen-name Logan Stewart. The author died in Santa Monica, California, in 1958 at the age of 35.

COVER ILLUSTRATION: José Cisneros, El Paso, Texas.

BACKGROUND NOTES

When the Spanish conquistadors arrived in the Southwest, they named the Indians who were living in small adobe villages the Pueblos ("pueblo" means "village" or "town" in Spanish). The term was originally used to distinguish the settled Indian farmers from their nomadic neighbors. Later the term was applied to the Indian people who lived in "pueblos" along the Rio Grande River in northern New Mexico: Tesuque Pueblo, San Juan Pueblo, Taos Pueblo, and so on.

The various Pueblo Indians did not share the same language. Those differences were apparent to the Spaniards, who laid out church and civil districts according to the language spoken. West of the Rio Grande lived the Hopi, Zuni, Keres or Keresan; to the east, the Tiwa, Tewa, and Towa spoke related languages, now called "Tanoan." The author refers to the pueblo groups by the name of their village and by their language.

At the outset of the novel, on the eve of the Pueblo Revolt of 1680, the Pueblo Indians had suffered eighty years of Spanish oppression. The Spanish system of *ecomienda* had awarded the conquistadors large parcels of Indian land. Under *repartimiento*, natives were forced to work for their landlords as slave labor. Finally the Pueblo Indians rebelled against the abuses, drawing strength from their traditional way of life.

FOREWORD

In the late summer of 1680, the Pueblo Indians of northern New Mexico united in revolt against the Spanish who had settled among them. The revolt was the most successful Indian rebellion in North American history. Some one thousand Santa Fe settlers escaped death and fled south. The novel's hero stayed behind in hiding. Thirteen years later, newly appointed Governor and Captain General Diego de Vargas led the exiles back from Mexico City to the New Mexican territory, where they laid siege to Santa Fe, eventually defeating the Indians during the waning days of 1693.

Through this eventful historical landscape wanders a fascinating fictional character, Luis Ribera. He opposed the mistreatment of Indians, was left for dead during the revolt, and later nursed back to health by Indian friends. He made his way to Mexico City, only to be jailed by the Inquisition. Rescued by General Vargas, he takes the dangerous journey north to participate in the reconquest of New Mexico.

This historical novel is a window through which the reader can experience the triumphs and conflicts of the early Spanish settlers as they struggled to survive in a parched land. This vivid account of the Pueblo Revolt and its aftermath will appeal to aficionados of Southwest history. Descriptions of Indian life in the pueblos, and Spanish society in colonial Mexico City, add an even richer texture to the story.

As an historian and director of a venerable history museum, I welcome the republication of *The Royal City*, because so much of the action occurs within the walls of what is today the Palace of the Governors. Built in 1610, the Palace is the oldest public building in the United States. After the Pueblo Revolt, the Palace—then called *The Presidio Real*—was occupied by the Indians. Later it was the focus of the Spanish siege of Santa Fe, as the bastion of the Indian defenders. Throughout the period of the book's story, the Palace served as the seat of government. Even the Indians tried to govern from this tough adobe fort.

The Royal City is the first publication of The Friends of the Palace. Read the book for enjoyment. Ideally that joy will entice you to visit the Palace of the Governors and learn more about the remarkable history and culture of the City of Holy Faith.

Thomas E. Chávez, Director
Palace of the Governors
Santa Fe, New Mexico

CHAPTER ONE

THEY were the Mountains of the Blood of Christ. All day long the two riders had labored upward against their ancient buttresses until late afternoon when they emerged from a high pass and looked down into the valley of the upper Rio Grande a full mile below. The men began their descent through the bedizened glitter of a million trembling aspens, and sunset turned their horses red with the calvary glow that so often stained the mountains at this time of day, at this time of year. It was August 6, 1680.

When Luis Ribera reached the road at the bottom of the valley he checked his horse and glanced southward. Nine miles in that direction lay Santa Fe, the capital of the Spanish province of New Mexico. To the west, half a mile beyond the road, was the Indian village, Tesuque. It was masked by the dense cottonwood grove, but the yellow haze was visible above the trees. Only a big crowd in the plaza could make so much dust.

"What passes?" Luis asked.

"A race or something," Bigotes said.

"A race in this heat?"

"I think we should go on to Santa Fe."

"I think we should go over there."

Bigotes put a hand on Luis's arm. "*Patrón*, I think we should go on to Santa Fe."

Luis glanced sharply at the man. Bigotes flushed and let his hand drop off. He had a Mongoloid face, broad, flat, with slanted eyes and a thick-lipped mouth that looked bawdy no matter what shape it assumed. Bigotes was a full-blooded Pueblo, a native of Tesuque. These Indians were village dwellers, farmers, a people whose forty-six adobe towns were scattered along the Rio Grande for the whole length of New Mexico. When the Spaniards had come north from Mexico City more than eighty years ago they had made the Pueblos vassals to the king of Spain. For generations the Franciscan priests had been establishing missions at the villages, converting the Indians, giving them Spanish names, teaching them to speak Spanish as fluently as their own languages.

"Bigotes," Luis said, "if there is something wrong you will tell me."

"Nothing, Don Luis, for God, nothing wrong."

But Bigotes still peered apprehensively at the younger man. Luis, at twenty-two, had a lean face, distinctly Spanish, the tilted cheekbones, the hollow Iberian temples, the hooded black eyes. He was tall for a Spaniard, shanked as lean as an alley cat, with a seat so relaxed in the peaked Moorish saddle that it made his shoulders look stooped. He wore a coarse wool shirt, rawhide knee breeches, a black deerskin jacket stained and bleached by wear. The only thing that marked him as a nobleman was the handsome serape over one shoulder and the glazed yellow hat of vicuña skin.

Even this late in the day the summer heat was like a brittle and trembling pressure. Drying lather made scummy stripes against the black hide of the horse, and gnats from the irrigation ditches were beginning to hum about Luis's face. He slapped irritably at them and touched spurs to the nervous Arab, trotting it across the road. Bigotes followed, and as they passed through the cottonwoods the feathery tufts of the shedding trees showered them like a snowfall. Ahead lay the terraced mud buildings gathered about the central plaza, seeming to rise from the earth, a part of that earth, the same shade, the same texture, beaten by sun and wind and storm to the color of faded buckskin. Shaky cottonwood ladders led from ground level to uneven roof tops, and chimney pots breathed dinner smoke against a sky so blue it made the eyes ache. The crumbling church stood at one side of the square, facing the sunken *kiva* within the plaza. The round edge of this subterranean ceremonial chamber projected sullenly a few feet above ground level, and the ladder poles slanting from its hatch led down into secrets the church would never know.

Luis rode into an alley between two of the communal buildings. He could see the whole village population gathered in the square or lining the roof tops. Jet hair and faces shining like old copper in the sun, the men naked to the waist or wearing long-tailed shirts of white cotton, the women shrouded in their black mantles. Luis saw Catua standing on the roof directly above him.

"*Qué pasa, amigo?*" Luis asked. "What passes?"

The young Indian glanced down at him, eyes opaque, resentful. Luis was not used to such insolence from these people. For three generations his family had held Tesuque in *encomienda*. As reward for meritorious service, the king could commend any Spaniard a stated number of Indians. By labor and by an annual tax these allotted vassals supported their *encomendero*. In return he provided them with his patronage and military protection.

Luis flushed, realizing he was not to be answered, and reined his horse to the end of the alley. The main crowd was gathered around the *kiva* in the plaza. There was something sullen about their unintelligible muttering, their restless movement. Above the black Indian heads Luis could see the sharp points and hatchet blades of halberds, and knew that Spanish soldiers must be in the crowd.

At the edge of the throng, holding a nervous Barb on a tight rein, Luis saw Toribio Quintano, the sheriff for the Holy Office of the Inquisition. He was one of the few *mestizos* to reach any eminence in the official circles of New Spain. From the story of this half-breed's remarkable rise, Luis had gained a picture of a clever opportunist whose driven ambitions seemed fed by the fires of contempt and prejudice for his mixed blood.

He had the body of a Spaniard—slender steel in a velvet sheath. But his face was a curious mixture of both races. The cheeks had a ravaged look. Marked deeply by the pox, they were drawn and sunken. Beneath the primitive slope of his brow his eyes were deep set, hungering. Luis had never seen him smile.

"*Buenas tardes, le de Dios, Don Luis,*" he said.

"*Hola,* Toribio. What are you doing here?"

Luis saw the man's eyes flicker at the rough greeting. But he took delight in ignoring the complex formalities so traditional in this land. Without answering, the sheriff glanced at the crowd. They were stirring up a fog of pale dust, and he brushed it impatiently from his clothes. It was palace gossip that he dressed himself from the wardrobe of the heretics whose property was confiscated by the Inquisition. His shirt was of the finest Rouen, his serape must have been worth two hundred pesos, the golden buckles at the knees of his black velvet breeches were as big as cups. He wore them all with the air of casual arrogance he thought befitted the aristocrat he would so dearly love to be.

With his affected Castilian lisp he said, "As you know, Don Felipe Manzano has been accused by the Holy Office of Lutheranism. I arrested him two days ago, and we are confiscating his property."

"Before the trial?" Luis asked.

Toribio's pinched nostrils made him look supercilious. "Everything will be impounded till the verdict. But the sheepshearing must go on. Manzano's own field hands have fled to the hills."

The crowd had shifted so that Luis could see the soldiers now. They were a squad of the Inquisitional guard Toribio had brought north with him. With swords and halberds they were pushing and poking at the massed Indians, separating the strongest young men and herding them together.

"Toribio," Luis said, "could this be *repartimiento?*"

Color stained Toribio's ravaged cheeks. Luis knew he had struck the truth. The system of *repartimiento* had been established to fulfill the general labor needs not provided under *encomienda*. It permitted the drafting of ten per cent of the men of any Indian village for work at the mines, at harvesting, or other seasonal labor. But the Crown had repeatedly denied the use of *repartimiento* to any government official or ecclesiastical institution.

Luis said, "I thought the Inquisition's function was the punishment of heresy—not the illegal impressment of loyal subjects."

"There is nothing illegal here!"

Toribio pulled his reins so sharply that the Barb tossed its dished head, squealing and fighting the bit as he whirled it to trot toward the other mounted man. Luis saw that it was Matarife, the sergeant of Toribio's guard. He was a Tlascalan Indian from Mexico, a strange twisted man, humped, gnomelike. Despite the heat he wore his leather *esquipile*. A sleeveless quilted doublet, two fingers thick, it was patterned after the *ichapilli* the Spaniards had found the Aztecs wearing over a century ago, so serviceable against arrow fire that it was now a standard part of the Spanish colonial uniform.

"Get them moving," Toribio told the sergeant.

The Spaniards grew rougher, kicking, using the flats of their swords. One of the Indians resisted, dragging back as they tried to herd him from the mob. Luis recognized him as Omtua, a slender youth he had known since childhood. The struggle drew a wail of protest from the crowd. As Bigotes joined him, Luis looked vainly for the Indian governor.

"Where is Don Felipe . . . the war chiefs?" he asked. "If somebody does not stop this——"

"*Patrón*—this is not your concern."

Luis glanced at Bigotes, remembering his reluctance to enter the town. "You knew about this."

"No . . . I swear——"

Omtua's struggles had carried him against Toribio's horse. The excited Barb reared, almost unseating the sheriff. With a vicious curse he quirted Omtua across the face, knocking him away. Other Spaniards were rushing in to help subdue the young Indian. Luis made a soft sound of outrage and pulled one of the firelocks from the pair of holsters at his saddles. It was a big pistol, ball-butted, chased in silver. He checked the flint, poured in a measure of powder. Bigotes was sweating, froglike eyes bulging grotesquely.

"*Patrón* . . . to this day it is a mystery why you have not been excommunicated or hanged in the plaza. But this is not just missing confession or insulting the governor or making a fool of your grandfather. Job's boils! This is the Holy Office."

Luis rammed the ball home, primed the firelock. The shouting swelled sharply, wild, outraged. Luis saw that the soldiers had knocked Omtua to his hands and knees and were kicking him and slamming him with their halberds. Luis shut the pan cover on his gun and struck sparks with flint and steel. When the match caught and began to smolder he spurred his horse through the crowd to the soldiers.

"Let him go—get away from him!" he said.

The soldiers backed away uncertainly, looking at the gun, at Toribio. The sheriff shouted something, but he was too far away for Luis to understand it in the tumult. Omtua got up, dazed and bleeding. Though linked by a common culture, the Pueblo tribes spoke several distinct languages. The people of Tesuque were Tewas, and Luis called to Omtua in that tongue.

"*An yugi ho'o vi ka'a tuye* . . ." Omtua wiped blood from his face, eyes filmed, uncomprehending. Again Luis called, gesturing toward the others for emphasis. "Quickly now, you with them, walk quickly . . . to your houses."

Omtua looked at the soldiers. He wheeled and stumbled through the crowd toward the terraced buildings on the south side. The corporal in command started after him. Luis swung his firelock to cover the man.

"I will shoot the first man who tries to stop them."

The corporal halted, gaping bucolically at Luis. It started the rush. The other young Indians broke through the handful of soldiers holding them and ran toward their homes.

"Stop them," Toribio shouted at Matarife.

As the sergeant wheeled his horse to obey, Luis swung the firelock to cover him. Matarife checked his horse. Toribio shouted at him again but he would not move. His hump gave him the look of a vulture, sitting with his head thrust forward at a grotesque angle, his eyes fixed on the gun. The other soldiers, cowed by the threat, took their cue from their sergeant and made no move to stop the scattering Indians. Toribio was so dark with fury that the pockmarks looked like a chalky stippling in his haggard cheeks. He spurred his horse toward Luis, pulling his sword.

Luis swung the gun farther in its arc, till it covered the sheriff. "The first man . . . Toribio."

Ten feet away, hand pinned to the hilt of his half-drawn sword, Toribio brought his horse to a halt. At first he could not seem to trust his voice. Finally he said:

"You are insane."

"It is my *encomienda,* Sheriff, and there are many witnesses."

The half-breed took his elegant gloved hand off the hilt of his sword. Touching his Barb with a heel, holding it under close rein so it would make no sudden break that might startle Luis, Toribio moved the animal slowly forward till he was two feet away.

"You have a chance to reconsider, Don Luis."

Luis smiled recklessly. It infuriated Toribio. For a moment Luis thought the man would spur his horse directly into the gun. Then Toribio emitted a vicious sound and gave a savage jerk on his reins. The Mameluke bit dug in, the horse squealed and whirled and galloped across the plaza. Luis looked at Matarife. Surprisingly, the man was grinning. It was idiotic, meaningless, a monkey's grimace.

Matarife gestured at the soldiers, giving them a casual order. They got their mounts from the horse holders at the edge of the square and swung into their saddles. They sheathed their swords, shouldered their halberds, and followed Matarife out of the village in a rough line. Their dark peasant faces turned toward Luis as they passed, but they merely looked tired and dusty and indifferent to what had happened. Bigotes joined Luis. He sat with his stirrups flapped out wide, wiping his sweating jowls and shaking his big head. The yellow pony fiddled beneath him. It looked like a crotchety little old man, with the bristly whiskers, as coarse as tail hair, parted in a mustache over its sneering upper lip.

The crowd of Indians had scattered with the younger men, but many of them were banked up against the house walls around the plaza, watching the soldiers leave. There was something ominous about the complete silence of the whole town, after the noisy demonstration. Still Luis could not see the governor.

"Where is Don Felipe?" he asked.

Bigotes sighed. "Well, you had better not worry about him. You had better go and make peace with your grandfather. You will have need of him now."

Luis snuffed the burning match, unloaded the pistol, and put it back into his holster. He wanted to hold onto his reckless mood. But only a fool would be blind to the implications of what he had done.

"I suppose you are right," he said. "You will come with me?"

"With your permission, *patrón*, I will stay here."

They had been away three days on the hunt. This was Bigotes' village, and it was logical that he should want to stay. Yet something made Luis hesitate. He could not forget the Indian's reluctance to enter Tesuque. Why should it give him this feeling—some corner of Bigotes cut off from him, some door suddenly closed? He had come up against it before, the depths of the Indian mind that no Spaniard could hope to penetrate. But with Bigotes it had always been different.

In their attempts to keep the Indians subject, the Spaniards by law had forbidden them the use of firearms or horses. Bigotes was one of the few privileged to ride. Since boyhood he had worked in the Ribera stables. His talent for horses finally gained him a position as *amansador*, breaking and training the finest Ribera stallions. It was natural that Luis should gravitate toward such a man. Luis's grandfather objected. It was not fitting that an aristocrat's closest friend should be an Indian servant. But he had been unable to prevent it and finally gave in.

Bigotes touched his hatbrim. "Go with God, *patrón*."

Luis nodded and put a heel to his horse. He rode through the narrow alley between two terraced mud buildings and passed into the shadowy grove of cottonwoods. But he was not satisfied. Where were the old men?

The Spaniards had established a government in each Pueblo village, the Indians electing annually a governor, lieutenant governor, and other officials from among their own people. Yet the real power remained with the traditional rulers, the council of elders, the war chiefs, and above all the *cacique*, the high priest who attended to the spiritual needs of his people and was their archruler. That none of these men had been present was unnatural.

On a strong impulse Luis turned back. He came across no Indians till he entered the plaza. The crowd still surged restlessly back and forth across the square and along the parapets of the buildings. But now, Luis saw, there were men coming out of the underground *kiva*, climbing through the hatchway on the ladder and descending the mud steps into the square. He recognized the Indian governor, Don Felipe, and the half-dozen white-headed ancients who made up the council of the elders.

The last man to climb out was big for an Indian, almost six feet tall. He wore a Navajo blanket like a poncho, its folds hanging slack against the stooped gauntness of his body. He had the tortured, hieratic face of a man dedicated to self-flagellations, fasting, visions, and other esoteric disciplines. The bony cheeks were slanted, and the lidless eyes were slanted and hidden in the shadows of their sunken pits. It was the face of an Oriental idol sculptured in anger by a cruel god.

Luis recognized him as Po-pe. He was a mysterious and controversial figure, a *cacique* who had been ostracized from his own village of San Juan (some whispered for witchcraft) and who now lived at Taos, the northernmost of the *pueblos*. He had a dreamlike bearing, and the Indians moved away from him as he descended to the plaza.

Before Luis could go to the *kiva*, Bigotes disengaged himself from the crowd and crossed the plaza. He stopped his yellow horse in front of Luis.

"They were in there all the time?"

"It appears."

"Does your governor not care if his young men are carried off like slaves?" Luis asked. Bigotes did not respond. Luis leaned forward, studying the Indian's face. "We were away three days. You could not have known Toribio was here with the soldiers."

Bigotes pulled uncomfortably at his mustache.

"Did you know Po-pe was here?" Luis asked.

Bigotes stirred restlessly in his buffalo saddle. "*Patrón*, perhaps I can go into Santa Fe with you after all."

Luis did not answer. He knew that many things went on among these people which a Spaniard did better not to meddle in. He had always respected their privacy and had gained their friendship by it. Before wheeling his horse to leave he looked past Bigotes at the Indians. The governor and the council were arguing among themselves. Po-pe stood apart, silent and aloof.

He was looking across the heads of the crowd at Luis.

CHAPTER TWO

THE capital of New Mexico lay three leagues south of Tesuque. With their penchant for grandiloquence the Spaniards had called it *La Villa Real de la Santa Fe de San Francisco de Assisi*—The Royal City of the Holy Faith of Saint Francis of Assisi. As much as he loved the town Luis had always thought the name a pathetic pretension. This frontier outpost whose population rarely exceeded a thousand souls. This primitive mud village straggling along the miniature Santa Fe River on a plateau seven thousand feet above the sea. This handful of adobe buildings crouched at the base of the Mountains of the Blood of Christ as though seeking protection from the frightening vastness on every side.

It was a provincial capital formidably separated by time and distance from the rest of the world. Three months' journey by oxcart to the south lay the mother colony of New Spain and its capital, Mexico City. Connecting it to Santa Fe was the slender life line of the Camino Real —the Royal Highway—a road running for fifteen hundred miles through a land of inimical desert and hostile Indians.

Southeast of Santa Fe were the warrior Comanches of Texas; to the west were the dread Navajos of Arizona; east and north lurked the Yuta, the Apache, the Pawnee. The Spaniards were constantly fighting to protect themselves and the Christianized Pueblos from the endless raiding and looting of the nomad tribes that had threatened the existence of the province from its very beginning.

Luis was aware of this isolation. Yet it could not change his feeling for the town. There was the first sight of Santa Fe from the north.

The Camino de la Canada winding down through the gentle hills, the junipers standing like the cones of a thousand Spanish ovens on every brick-red slope, the haphazard checkerboard of flat roofs abruptly coming into view below. There was the sound of the vespers bell at twilight and the sight of people kneeling in the plaza and the fading light turning the earth to a cape of dark velvet threaded with the silver glitter of irrigation ditches. And most of all there was the *enebro* smoke breathed from the red and blue chimney pots of every house. The center of town was surrounded by an adobe wall with but one entrance, where the Camino de la Canada entered from the north. The gates were open, and the sentries passed Luis and Bigotes through without a challenge. The huge hand-carved *vigas* that supported the flat roofs protruded through the walls at ceiling height. The houses were built flush to the curb, turning the streets to narrow chasms that rang loudly to the echoes of galloping hoofs. As Luis neared the plaza a coach rolled swiftly around the corner. Both Luis and the coachman had to pull their horses to a rearing halt to keep from colliding. Dust settled in a silvery haze about the slender-spoked wheels. Luis saw that the driver was Cruz, the deaf-mute *zambo*—half Indian, half Negro—who served the Condesa Verónica de Zumurraga.

The Count of Zumurraga had died six months ago in Mexico City, and the Countess had come north alone to settle in his house at Santa Fe. The stories soon followed her north. She had not been the Count's wife, but his mistress. Before that she had been a notorious courtesan. It was even rumored that she was a *morisco*—one tainted with the forbidden blood of the Moors—and that she had fled Mexico City to escape the fires of the Inquisition.

Bigotes hung back as Luis sidled his horse up beside the coach. The Condesa's face appeared in the window; narrow, haughty, illusory, it left him with the familiar impression of never really knowing whether she was beautiful or ugly. There was a sallowness to her skin. The clever use of cosmetics only partially altered it, and even the intense blackness of her hair could not make it seem white.

He touched his hat. "Condesa."

She smiled in greeting. But she was looking at his dusty clothes. Her black eyes were a little too narrow, set too close to her nose, so brilliant they looked almost metallic. They were speaking the lisping Castilian, the official tongue of all the Spanish world.

"You look rather travel-worn," she said, "for the guest of honor."

"The what?"

She glanced toward the palace. He could hear the distant strains

of a violin, could see the brightly lit windows, and knew a *baile* must
be in progress. A gust of impatience entered the woman's voice.

"Visit me instead, Luis. I have such loneliness. Defy Don Bernabe
once more. She is an empty, shallow little vessel."

He was puzzled by her talk. She had never shown jealousy of his
wenching before. Which one did she mean now?

"My fate is that I must see my grandfather and cannot accept your
invitation, Condesa. Accept mine instead and accompany me to the
ball?"

"Companion."

The tone of her voice was chiding, maternal, making him realize
that she was a woman eight years older than he.

"Thousand pardons, Condesa. The thought of shocking them has always amused you before."

The delicate nostrils of her imperious nose seemed to flutter. She
was not looking at him, she was looking straight ahead into the shadows of the coach, and he knew what she was thinking. With her past
and the rumor of Moorish blood, such a woman could be nothing but
an outcast in a town as narrow and provincial as Santa Fe, never invited to the parties, snubbed by the women of the finest families,
forced to make her life on the shadowy fringes of society.

"Forgive me, companion," she murmured. "I suppose I just have a
mood today." She had been holding her opened fan just beneath her
chin. She closed it with a soft click. It gave him a tantalizing glimpse
of her breasts swelling against her brocaded gown, a sense of the body
below that, vital, mature, dedicated to the rites of Venus. She looked
at him, opening the fan again and lifting it so that he only got a hint
of her smile before her mouth was hidden. She said, "Perhaps, after
facing the formalities at the palace, you will decide I am right about
her and will visit me after all. I have learned some new *villancicos*.
I will play them for you."

She rapped on the ceiling with her fan. Cruz flicked his whip and
the coach lurched into motion, clattering across the plaza toward the
Alameda. Luis watched her go, thinking of her loneliness, saddened
by it.

Bigotes joined him. "What was she saying?"

"Some girl . . . fate, I do not know. Maybe she is jealous."

"Could it be Barbara de Cárdenas?"

It made Luis think of the quarrel he'd had with his grandfather,
Don Bernabe. He and the old man were always clashing, but lately
it seemed worse. Don Bernabe was trying to get him to settle down,

get married. The old man had brought up the name of Barbara de Cárdenas at every possible occasion. Such an illustrious family, such a fine match. Bowels of Judas! Luis threw back his head and laughed.

"I will see you at Nazario's. Do not give that yellow horse all the wine, Bigotes."

He turned to canter down San Francisco. Ahead of him the plaza was a gray rectangle of earth. At the east end of the square the twin towers of the church were fading silhouettes against the darkening sky. On the south side stood the houses of the aristocrats. The scrolled posts supporting second-story balconies looked as slender as silver matchsticks in the dusk. Edging the north was the royal quadrangle of the *presidio*, two blocks long and a block wide. Within the walls completely surrounding it were the royal houses of the governor general and other officials. An integral part of the quadrangle, fronting on the plaza, was the Palace of the Governors.

At either end of the building were the square and massive towers. Between them, running the width of the front, was the *portal*, a covered arcade whose roof was supported every twelve feet by immense columns of unpeeled pine posts. The adobe walls of the palace were four feet thick. Sun and wind and water had weathered them to the faded yellow of old buckskin. Arrows had scarred them and they bore the random pox of bullet holes. For seventy years the building had stood there, the seat of administration for the province, dominating the square, ruling the town.

Luis knew that most celebrations in the palace were of an official nature, and his grandfather was sure to be invited. A dozen handsome coaches were drawn up before the building, the armorial ciphers of the finest families in New Spain gleaming on their lacquered panels. An army of coachmen and servants filled the twilit square, lounging and smoking around the gibbet, gambling on the ground under the *portal*.

A pair of Ribera servants came to help Luis dismount. One was Ignacio, Don Bernabe's personal retainer. A dwarfed, bowlegged Pueblo, he shared his master's chronic disapproval of Luis's escapades and did not bother to hide it. Luis stood restlessly while the other man squatted to remove his spurs. It always made him uncomfortable to be served.

"*Gracias, hombre*," he said. "Thanks, man."

There was but one entrance to the quadrangle, a tunnel-like *zaguán* large enough to permit the passage of carriages and carts. A sentry stood to one side, cuirass unbuckled, leaning on his halberd and peering inside at the aristocrats. Luis doubted that the man even saw him pass. Beyond the entrance was one of the dozen patios, large and small, that were cupped within the walls of the quadrangle. It was filled with people. Light from a hundred wax tapers glittered against silver jewelry and inlaid sword hilts, satin dresses and brocaded waistcoats, excited black eyes and white shoulders. At one side were three long tables heaped with food. The air was honeyed with the scent of brandy and local wine simmered in an earthen pot for a day with spices and sugar. Enchiladas were stacked like blue dinner plates beside deep Talavera dishes from which steamed the New Mexican smells of chile and onions and melted cheese. The musicians stood near the tile-roofed well —a violin, a guitar, a *vihuela*—their faces gleaming with sweat as they picked out the intricate rhythms of a saraband. Beyond them Luis saw Governor Otermin and two of the councilmen talking with Don Melchor Cárdenas, the *visitador* from Mexico City.

Governor Otermin's stubbornness and lack of diplomacy had created enemies for him in the province. Many thought his Indian policies too complacent and vague. He was always clashing with the priests and their accusations had piled up in Mexico City until the viceroy felt called upon to authorize a *visita*. He had commissioned Don Melchor de Cárdenas, an eminent judge in Mexico City, to conduct the official investigation. Don Melchor had already interviewed many witnesses and collected a mass of testimony. The fact that the visitor had brought his family north gave substance to the rumor that, should the evidence prove Otermin incompetent, Don Melchor was commissioned to replace him as governor. It cast a cloud of stiff reserve over any meeting between the two men and over any public function they attended.

Governor Otermin saw Luis. He murmured something, excusing himself, and left Don Melchor. Luis waited for him near the entrance, trying to judge by the expression on his face whether the news about Tesuque had reached him yet. But Otermin's heavy black brows were drawn so low over his eyes that he always seemed to be scowling anyway. He was originally from Spain, and wore court dress rarely seen in this frontier town. His suit of yellow Castilian satin was slashed over blue Italian velvet, the matching stockings and garters glittering with bullion. But no amount of tailoring would hide the shape of his torso, thick and solid as a Roman Centurion, and his protuberant rump always wrinkled the coat across the rear. He made none of the usual punctilious preamble, speaking with his characteristic bluntness.

"What is this thing about Tesuque?"

Luis smiled. "Apparently you already know."

"Excellency."

"Apparently you already know, Excellency."

"And I did not ask for insolence," Otermin snapped. "One of Toribio's soldiers said something. But it was garbled. The truth of it now, quickly."

As Luis told him, Otermin's scowl deepened. He pulled irritably at his collar and Luis could see how the stiff Dutch cambric was rubbing his thick neck raw. Lifting his arm drew the sleeve back and revealed a bristly black mat. The man shaved the hair off his wrists so it would not show beneath his cuffs. Catching Luis's glance, Otermin flushed, dropping his hand.

"Young fool!" he said. He glanced toward Don Melchor. "Am I not having enough trouble? I have no doubt that you deliberately chose this particular time to defy the Holy Office."

"If you will not give the Indians proper protection——"

"I had no knowledge of this."

"Nor of the hundred other times the Indians were taken illegally to work?"

Otermin's feet scraped angrily against the hard-packed earth. The muscles bulging in his thick calves made the rose-colored silk stockings look ridiculous. Before he could speak, Luis said:

"There is something you should know. Po-pe was there."

Mention of the San Juan *cacique* checked Otermin's rage for a moment. He frowned at Luis and absently reached up to ease his collar again. The jeweled rings looked out of place on his blunt, knobby fingers.

"It means nothing," he said.

"They were hiding him in the *kiva*. They would not come out until Toribio had gone."

"Naturally. Was not Po-pe one of the priests Governor Trevino imprisoned? He barely escaped hanging."

"That was five years ago. A man does not hide unless he is doing something wrong. He was seen at Cochiti two weeks ago. And at Isleta before that. Why should a Tewa priest go to a Keres village?"

"Are you trying to divert me from your own crime?"

"I am trying to show you where your blindness is leading——"

"Enough!" Blood had crept like a vivid dye into Otermin's face. It darkened the bluish stain that clung to his square jowls no matter how carefully he shaved. "Do you recognize no authority? Do you think there is any other man in Santa Fe who dares address his governor in such a manner? It is you who defied the Holy Office, not I. It pleases me to think that this outrage will be your last escapade. I have every confidence that you will be sent to Mexico City in chains. And should you persist in this foolishness about Po-pe I will gladly add a list of complaints to the Inquisition's file that will most certainly assure you of excommunication and perpetual banishment, if not the flames of the *quemadero* itself."

The governor turned and stalked away.

Luis became aware of another man standing nearby at one of the tables of food. It was Andres Rodrigo. Twenty-three, scion of one of the oldest houses in New Spain, his face was a history of inbred aristocracy. A waxen monument of a brow, a nose like a supercilious beak, the mouth of a licentious Nero—gaping now in tipsy amazement.

"Luis, companion," he said. "If I could speak to them like that once . . . just once." He was already drunk, flushed and swaying. "I was beginning to think you had struck your colors. They are already taking bets on how soon the banns will be read."

Luis was still watching Otermin. "Banns?"

Andres brightened. "You mean I will win my bet? Your family did not really go to the Cárdenas household with the letter?"

"What letter?"

"The letter asking that Barbara be given to you in marriage."

Luis stared blankly at Andres. He knew now what the Condesa had been talking about. But it was inconceivable. It simply had not entered his head that Don Bernabe would go this far. Andres saw the surprise on Luis's face giving way to rage, humiliation.

"You really did not know?" Andres asked. He began to laugh. "By the Five Wounds—that is almost as bad as being made cuckold."

His laughter ceased quickly. He looked beyond Luis, swaying, and quickly excused himself. Luis turned to see his grandfather crossing the room toward him. Don Bernabe Nicolas de Pacheco y Ribera was sixty-eight years old, tall, gaunt, all sinews and knobs. He had the face of a conquistador, highborn and intolerant. His eyebrows were fierce tufts of snow overhanging a pair of piercing eyes. His cheeks, ravaged by time and the fires of his own domineering nature, bore the sucked look of senility. But there was nothing senile about his walk. Despite a pronounced limp, he stalked across the room like a hungry lion. As he reached Luis, the young man said:

"I understand you called upon the Cárdenas family."

The ancient cheeks quivered. "Forget you to whom you speak?"

Luis was adamant in his refusal to honor the old man with the tradition of formal greeting. "Can I give respect for humiliation?"

Don Bernabe gripped the hilt of his dress rapier. His knuckles strained against the yellow flesh in great bluish knobs. In a brittle voice he said:

"We will discuss the Cárdenas matter when you explain these wild stories I have heard about Tesuque."

"Then it is true. You did take the letter to Cárdenas—without even consulting me."

Don Bernabe's breath rattled in his throat. He wheeled, walking a pair of steps away, turning to limp back. He suffered from a wound he had received in the right leg thirty years before. It ached so constantly that he could not stand still long and he was always moving around, seeming to take great delight in making his accouterments rattle as much as possible. His hand opened and closed on the hilt of his sword. He looked at the floor.

"Very well. It is true. I have asked that Barbara de Cárdenas be given to you in marriage. Don Melchor was most gracious. I take this to indicate that the evidence he has collected could mean that he will replace Otermin as governor. Under those circumstances an alliance with the Ribera family would be to his greatest advantage. Our answer should come very soon."

Don Bernabe seemed to have gotten himself under control. He walked to a nearby table, picked up a bottle, and very carefully poured wine into his glass. With his back still turned he said:

"Now, you will observe the formalities. You will go over there. . . . You will ask the permission of Doña Piedad Cárdenas. . . . You will dance with the girl."

Luis looked across the patio. On rude benches against the white-washed wall sat a whole line of duennas and their charges, aunts, grandmothers, mothers, all standing the never-ending watch over the young girls. He saw the women of the family the visitor had brought from Mexico City. Doña Piedad, his wife, was a tall woman, white-haired, grave as a nun. The shadows in her patrician face were turned an ashen violet by the Mexican white lead used as a cosmetic. Beside her sat Barbara.

She was barely seventeen. At that age most girls had already bloomed in this land, their breasts an impudent invitation. But she still seemed a little girl, painfully young and fragile, her slim body hardly giving shape to the gown of black satin she wore. Her enormous black eyes seemed too big for her face, lending her a gamin look. Birdlike, they kept darting around the room, and he realized that she was trying almost frantically not to look at him. Despite his own anger he felt pity for her. She was caught even more helplessly than he in this situation. To a girl of this land the dictate of her parents was irrevocable law.

He saw Don Bernabe's hand tremble, spilling some of the wine. "Luis," the old man said, "if you do not do as I command immediately I will have you taken home, I will have you tied to the corral fence, I will have you flogged like a common slave."

His pity for the girl had brought Luis close to the point of relenting. But the blind tyranny in the old man's voice brought his rebellion back with renewed force. His mouth pulled down into a savage shape. He turned and stalked out of the patio.

CHAPTER THREE

THE Church of Saint Francis had been built on an elevation at the east end of the plaza. That evening at seven its two square towers and the wooden cross between them were gilded by the light of a rising moon. That evening at seven Toribio Quintano paced restlessly across its cloister, awaiting the arrival of Fray Juan Bernal.

Toribio had made a mistake and he knew it. It was the first time in many years during his long and bitter climb that he had blundered so badly. Despite his anger at Luis he would rather have forgotten the incident at Tesuque. But he knew it would be all over town by to-morrow, and he had to reach the commissioner first with his carefully prepared version. He stopped in the arch of the corridor flanking the open patio. He rubbed sweating palms together. He heard the rustle of feet, the opening and closing of a door.

An image formed in the shadows, the tall stooped figure of Fray Juan Bernal, superintendent of all the New Mexican missions as well as commissioner for the Inquisition in the province. His face, a thing of knobs and bones and sunken hollows, made Toribio think of El Greco's burning-eyed saints.

"May God give you good evening, my son. How goes the work at Rancho Manzano?"

"It goes not at all, Father. Thirty thousand sheep to shear . . . all the peons fleeing to the hills as soon as we arrested Don Manzano. I had to get labor elsewhere."

The priest's eyes flashed. "My son . . . do you speak of *repartimiento?*"

Toribio moistened his lips. Why did he always feel at such a loss before these men of God? "Father, in Mexico City it is done all the time—"

"A thing forbidden by law?"

"Is not the Holy Office a law unto itself?"

Fray Bernal wheeled and paced away from him, his rough cassock whispering angrily against stringy calves. "The Holy Office of the Inquisition was established for one purpose—to keep the Faith pure. Not for simony, not for nepotism, not to enrich itself on the confiscated property of those poor misguided heretics, not to use illegal Indian labor for its own profit—"

He broke off, as though realizing the danger of expressing such opinion to an underling. Many in the Holy Office, from the *Suprema* on down, held that there was no validity to the laws excluding the Inquisition from the right of drafting Indians. As Toribio had said, it was an established custom in the capital to ignore the decrees. And the people were in such terror of the Holy Office that few dared complain or investigate. With the inquisitor general himself giving unofficial sanction to the practice and most of the Tribunal in agreement, the priest who had the temerity to speak out against it was imperiling his career.

Toribio bowed his head. "My zeal to serve overcame my prudence, Father."

"Do you serve the Holy Office . . . or yourself?" asked Fray Bernal. Toribio glanced up sharply. The priest's face looked gaunt, haunted. He said, "The *corregidor de los Indios* tells me that most of the Manzano wool is in the storehouses . . . that there is no shearing left to do at Rancho Manzano, and little other work."

A faint sickness stole through Toribio. He wondered if a thief felt this way on discovery.

Fray Bernal continued. "I know you got your appointment to my staff through Don Gómez Gallegos in Mexico City—who has a brother up here, the Marqués de Gallegos. This family for generations has been one of the most fanatical opponents of the Crown's policies concerning the Indians. I would hate to think that you were sent north to further their aims in this province."

Toribio flushed. "I came north only to serve you, Father. It is not just a matter of the Indians. The Holy Office has been offended."

He told Fray Bernal about Luis. As he had hoped, it diverted the man. Deeply disturbed, Fray Bernal said:

"Was Don Luis not simply defending his *encomienda?*"

"Would the inquisitor look upon it that way?"

The priest bowed his head. Toribio could see the conflict in his face. Defying the Holy Office was ranked with heresy, and more than one man had died for it. To the members of the Tribunal who sanctioned the use of Indian labor Luis's action would be unjustifiable. To allow such defiance to go unpunished would cast dangerous reflection on the jealously guarded authority of the Holy Office.

"That young fool," the priest muttered. "Why did he have to make such an issue? I have tried to overlook his escapades . . . a harmless young rebel . . . stamping his feet and pounding his chest. . . ."

"Now no longer harmless. The story will reach the Tribunal sooner or later, and if we have not sent them the denunciation . . ."

Fray Bernal locked his hands behind his back and began to pace again. He looked like a man wrestling with his soul. Toribio pitied him his conscience. To the Indians under his jurisdiction Fray Bernal's discipline often seemed severe. But that was only because he was convinced of its righteousness. When doubt hung over the decision on a man's fate, there was underlying compassion in the priest that brought torture. To Toribio it was a weakness.

"If it were only a clearer heresy, Judaizing, Lutheranism——"

The man's doubt gave Toribio a sense of power. He could afford to soften his voice now, show servile respect. "Can you split hairs now, Father? No matter what the circumstances, the fact remains that Luis Ribera defied the Holy Office. To let him go undenounced would be a defiance of the Papacy itself. Is there not the bull of Pius the Fifth? *Si de protegendis* . . . providing the pains and censures for all who impede or offend the Inquisition."

The priest raised his head, apparently surprised. But it was not erudition in Toribio so much as a lifetime of watching and listening and carefully storing away any scrap of material that would further his rise. When Fray Bernal finally spoke defeat rusted his voice.

"Very well, my son. A courier will go south tomorrow with the denunciation." He paused. His eyes seemed to burn into Toribio, into his heart, his mind, all the dark corners where he himself was afraid to go. In a changed tone, Fray Bernal said, "Only remember you this: Ambition is a two-edged sword—it cuts both ways, and it cuts grievously deep."

The plaza was dark when Toribio left the church. The hot smell of parched earth still hung in the air. He tried to shake off the sense of guilt he always felt after leaving a priest. It was even hard to feel any triumph over Fray Bernal's decision. Against his will he had always liked Luis. He had never met the contempt in the young man that he found in most aristocrats. It was a rare thing in this intolerant age. Luis seemed to accept all men at their face value—as much at home with a beggar as with a king. But now Luis had humiliated him before his men. Memory of it brought back the cold fury he had known at Tesuque.

Matarife waited at the corner of their church with the horses. He was a black and grotesque shape in the darkness.

"You will put Luis Ribera under constant surveillance," Toribio said. "If he attempts to escape the city you will arrest him."

The sergeant nodded. "*Si . . . hermano.*"

"Do not call me that. Do not call me brother."

The vicious whip of Toribio's voice made Matarife gape in surprise. He backed away, mouth twitching into its spastic grin.

"Matarife," Toribio said.

His voice was softer. The hunchback stopped, moistening his lips. Leading his horse, he returned slowly. Toribio put a hand on his twisted neck.

"How is it? Much pain?"

Hesitantly Matarife said, "Sometimes . . . in the night."

"This Dr. Roybal . . . perhaps he will have something that will help," Toribio said. He paused, looking deep into the man's eyes. He murmured. "You understand me, Matarife. Could any brother have done more? Can it simply not remain between us?"

The hunchback nodded his head, eyes fixed glassily on Toribio. Toribio lifted his hand off. He watched Matarife cross the plaza in his peculiar, sliding walk. Why did a man have these chinks in his armor? Why could he not hate the world enough to stand completely alone, devoid of feeling?

Morosely, Toribio looked toward the Palace of the Governors. Lights glowed from the slotlike windows; he could hear the twang of a guitar and the laughter of women. He knew his position would give him entree to their party. He could claim a dance with their women and drink their wine and talk their politics and play the brittle part of belonging up to the hilt. But it would be the usual bitter sham, with the contempt so thinly veiled behind their polite greetings, the casual indifference with which they included him in their conversations, the disdain they managed to convey with their slightest gesture.

He did not think he could bear it tonight. They were all Creoles up here—Spaniards of pure blood born in the New World—provincial, narrow, backward. He hated them. How could he despise them all so much and spend his whole life struggling so bitterly to be one of them?

He mounted his Barb and crossed the plaza, a man cut off from his fellows by his ambition, his blood, his very profession. Vanity and an avid need to rise would not let him consort with those he thought beneath him; his hatred for his Indian blood made him avoid the men of his own caste. Yet that same blood had denied him entree into the aristocratic circles he coveted. His position as sheriff of the Holy Office seemed the final irony. While it gave him some of the power he sought it removed him even further from people, making him a pariah, feared and suspected by all classes.

Moonlight shimmering on distant movement in the northern hills caught his attention. It was a coach, coming down the Camino de la Canada. He glanced quickly at the coaches gathered before the palace but could not see the Gallegos coat of arms among them. If the late arrival was the Marqués, Toribio wanted to see him. He met the coach as it entered the town, hailing the driver to stop him. He swung his horse broadside to the door. Inside, alone, he could see Don Desidero, the Marqués de Gallegos, one of the richest landholders in the province.

At forty-one the Marqués was a classic picture of the Spanish don. His arrogant face with its waxed mustache and graying goatee made Toribio think of Seville, Granada, the distant music of a plucked guitar. The man's greeting was a gem of traditional courtesies. But it was a frigid gem. Toribio thought that out of habit he would probably employ the same punctilio in greeting a dog.

The Marqués leaned closer, managing to give the impression that a vast gulf still separated them. "Is this not a little public?"

"I thought you had better know as soon as possible," Toribio said. "I could not get those Indians for you at Tesuque."

"I heard of your trouble." The Marqués frowned irritably and stroked his goatee. "I must have more Indians. The Holy Office puts the Manzano wool up for auction soon, and I need a hundred bearers to carry it to Mexico City."

"What about the Indians of your *encomienda*?"

"They are busy shearing my flocks. Why not try Cochiti?"

"Those thirty men I brought you last week were from Cochiti. And Fray Bernal is beginning to suspect."

"Let him. If he complains loud enough it will reach the ears of the Tribunal. There are enough who do not share his philosophy. It could well mean his transfer. This incident at Tesuque might even be turned to our profit."

"The Ribera family is powerful," Toribio said. "The arrest of Luis will raise a storm here."

"It will also put an unholy fear into the people. Think you anyone else will dare impede you? You can draft every Indian in the province without a whisper of exposure or reprisal."

Toribio felt a touch of excitement as he realized the possibilities. With an official investigation threatening, these aristocrats could not be so flagrant in their abuse of the Indians. But the Holy Office was a different matter. Even so eminent a man as Don Melchor de Cárdenas would hesitate to pit himself against the Inquisition.

The Marqués put a hand on the window, a conspirator's huskiness in his voice. "My brother said you were an audacious man seeking to climb high. Would not the next step be sheriff of the Holy Office in Mexico City itself?"

Toribio did not smile, but a deep flush darkened his ravaged cheeks. He touched his hatbrim. "Tomorrow I will get your Indians."

The Marqués nodded, rapped on the ceiling, and settled into the shadows of the coach. As it rolled away, heading down the Royal Street toward the party at the palace, Toribio backed his horse away to avoid the dust. Sheriff in the capital of New Spain itself! The thought filled him with a cruel exaltation. He was swept with a gust of impatience for the clumsy machinery of the Inquisition. The power of the commissioner was jealously limited; he executed orders, took testimony, and reported, but was forbidden to arrest unless there was imminent danger that the accused might escape. Under ordinary circumstances the commissioner requested a notary to make up a report, including the articles of accusation and the names of witnesses, which was sent by courier to the Tribunal in Mexico City. Such defiance as Luis had committed would certainly bring an order of arrest from the Tribunal. The whole process would take months. And yet Luis's fate was inevitable. With his rash act he had set into motion the machinery that had crushed countless men in far higher places than his own.

The Barb stirred beneath Toribio, transmitting its restlessness to him. He was not sleepy, did not want to go to the ball, and could not face the barren loneliness of his quarters. He tried to put the other alternative out of his mind. He had fought it for days now. But it was another of the chinks in his armor. It was like some insidious chemistry at work inside of him, running a certain cycle, so that he could fight it only so long and then once more had to succumb.

He took his horse to the stables behind his quarters on the square. He unsaddled the animal and left on foot, circling through dark streets to the Alameda along the river. The crumbling house stood apart from the main part of town, screened by willows and cottonwoods. Honeysuckle smothered its surrounding walls, the hot air making its scent almost sickening.

He stopped at a spindled gate, the strange excitement growing. His hands were clammy, his mouth dry. Why? She was not really beautiful. It was an illusion she created. Then why should he risk his position, his future, perhaps even his life?

He could hear her playing the *vihuela* in the patio, the air from one of Sor Juana's *villancicos*. She endowed everything she did with a harsh, metallic quality, both repellent and fascinating.

She was sitting with her back to him by the little red-roofed well. She heard the gate creak and turned to look. She rose as he walked to her and came into his arms with her eyes glittering in the moonlight, her voice breathless.

"Toribio, not so hard, you hurt, you hurt . . ."

"Veronica," he said. His body shook against hers. "Condesa."

CHAPTER FOUR

THE Barrio Analco was across the Santa Fe River from the main part of town. It was a suburb built by the original colonists for the Tlascalan slaves they had brought with them from New Spain. It was still the Indian section of town, a squalid place of crumbling adobe hovels and rotten spindle fences, beggars and outcasts and thieves. It was where Luis had gone after leaving his grandfather at the palace.

He passed the old slaves' church dedicated to the dragon-slaying San Miguel and turned down a winding alley to Nazario's *bodegón*.

The roof of the adobe tavern was typical of the country—earth, two feet thick, tamped solid onto the aspen saplings that were laid side by side in herringbone fashion across the ceiling beams. The years had dried and warped the saplings, leaving cracks through which dirt dribbled at the slightest vibration. It showered Luis as he pushed open the door. Brushing it absently from his shoulders, he glanced around the smoke-blackened taproom.

It stank of greasy chile and rancid tallow dripping on the tables from the few guttering candles. Their vague yellow bloom gave him a shadowy glimpse of the half-dozen men in the room. He saw Bigotes at a corner table, leaning against the wall, an Indian girl on his lap.

She was typical of the Analco, pocked, dirty, probably only eighteen or nineteen, looking twice her age. Bigotes was already drunk, fondling her brazenly. Eyes filmed and listless, she gave little response. Luis sprawled into the bench across from them. Luis swept his yellow hat off and threw it on the floor. The look of mingled anger and humor to his face was given savage accent. Candlelight caught a sardonic flash in his eyes and steepened the slant of his cheekbones with shadow. Bigotes tried to focus his eyes.

"Why is it, Don Luis? I can never tell whether you are laughing or ready to howl with rage."

"Because life is so stupid, Bigotes. Because it is so stupid and so funny and so ugly and so insane."

He told Bigotes what had happened. The Indian was awed.

"How could you, *patrón?* An earthquake. A natural catastrophe. Nobody so defies his parents. Even I would hesitate. Even Bigotes, who is called bastard because he has hair where no Indian should have hair."

He pawed vaguely at the scraggly mustaches for which he was named. In a fit of anger Luis struck the table.

"He cannot force me, Bigotes. He lives in the past. This is no royal family of Castile, that a son can be married off to consummate some alliance. I am tired of being a puppet. Don Bernabe pulls this string and I am supposed to jump. The governor pulls and I smile, the sheriff pulls, the council pulls, the Holy Office pulls—"

"*Patrón*, please—"

"Damn my grandfather. I spit on him. Damn the Holy Office—"

Bigotes bleated again. Sweat shimmered on his swarthy cheeks and his eyes bulged like a frog's. He was making frantic signals with his hand, looking across the room. Luis turned to see Matarife standing in the open door.

The hunchback's morion was like a tin melon sliced in half and set askew on his bony head. The narrow metal brim curved low over his eyes, almost hiding their crafty gleam. His shadow was a grotesque silhouette on the wall, humped and monstrous, wavering eerily as the wind disturbed the candle flames. At his belt was a misericord—the thin-bladed medieval dagger that had given the mercy stroke at so many executions. His fingers played with its ivory hilt for a moment. Then he sidled to the nearest table and took a seat.

Luis realized that a complete silence had fallen on the room. He tilted his head at Matarife, grinning sardonically. Bigotes let out a sigh of relief. Luis tried to relax. He got a cigar from his pocket, lighting it on the candle.

Kashana appeared in the door leading to the kitchen. She was Nazario's daughter by an Acoma squaw. Except for exotically tilted eyes, her Spanish blood robbed her of the Mongol features distinguishing so many Pueblos. The flat hips and bandy legs of the Indian were absent too. Yet, rather than try to hide that part of her heritage, she seemed to flaunt it. She wore the white cotton leg wrappings to the knees and the black mantle over one shoulder and the profusion of jewelry so typical of the Pueblo women. Her slightest motion set up a barbaric tinkle and clash among the silver bracelets on her wrist. Conspicuously absent was the usual cross hung around the neck.

Luis leaned back, the cigar tilted in his smiling lips, falling automatically into the teasing game he always played with her. "I have a new song, *chiquita*. All about a poor young man . . . loved a girl . . . Indian girl. Beautiful. She wouldn't have him . . . he took poison."

"Do you wish wine?" Kashana asked.

"Get the psaltery," he said. "I will play it and sing you my song."

"Not tonight . . . *Señor Gachupin*."

Luis frowned at her. *Gachupin* was an Aztec word. It meant Wearer-of-the-Spurs. It had originally been applied to the conquistadores and later to all Spanish aristocrats coming to the New World. Then, because such European-born Spaniards made up the ruling class, the word had taken on a broader and uglier connotation, symbolizing all that was cruel and tyrannical in the conquerors.

"Mixed metaphors, little one," Luis said. "I am a Creole . . . born in the New World . . . as you were born. . . ."

Kashana did not answer. There was something frighteningly primitive about her. It was not the face itself. In a mantilla and satin dress she could have passed for a Spaniard of the finest blood. Perhaps it was a compound—the catlike flash in her eyes, the curious arrowhead shadows beneath her cheekbones, the way she walked, animal, flat-footed, like no Spaniard ever walked. She made him think of feathered prayer sticks, of sacred meal scattered in the wind, of Earth Mother impregnated by a sunbeam.

Matarife was watching her fixedly. There was a strange expression on his face, half lust, half worship. It was a standard joke in the Analco. It had become the man's habit to show up every night at Nazario's and sit, and drink, and watch her.

Luis rose, going toward her. "*Gachupin*," he said. "Like you never said it before."

Her eyes were blank, dead, looking right through him. "It means what it has always meant."

"No, Kashana. Something more now. Up at Tesuque. Po-pe. In the *kiva*. He did not want the Spaniards to know he was there. Bigotes even tried to stop me from finding out."

She started to turn away. He caught her wrist, pulling her around. It brought her heavily against him. The sudden pressure of her breasts was like a cushiony shock. It made him forget his questioning. His bitter rebellion had been clawing for some outlet ever since he had left his grandfather. The feel of her and the perfume of her filled him with a wild recklessness.

"They say you have never kissed a Spaniard," he said.

She tried to twist free but he held her helplessly against him. Matarife pushed his chair back with a clatter and rose.

"Release her, Don Luis."

Luis was sweating. It made shining ridges of his tilted cheekbones. His smile was fixed now with the strain of holding her. She made an inarticulate sound and reached up to take the cigar from his mouth.

It freed his lips in a gesture so symbolic of the surrender he sought that it had but one meaning for him. Her head was tilted back, her eyes glazed as though with mingled acquiescence and pain. He lowered his mouth to hers.

She ground the glowing tip of the cigar into his hand.

He shouted in pain and hit her. It knocked her violently back. She struck a table, spun halfway around, and fell to the floor.

"Bastard," Matarife shouted.

He rushed at Luis. He was pulling his misericord, but before he could get it out of his belt Luis lunged into him and caught his wrist. Grappled together, they stumbled across the room. The hunchback had surprising strength. In his savage efforts to free himself he slammed Luis against the wall. Luis heaved him away. Matarife tripped on a chair and went down. He rolled over and rose to his knees. This time he got his knife out.

"*Jesucristo!*" Bigotes shouted.

Drunk as he was he managed to run in front of Luis as Matarife threw the misericord. The knife would have struck Bigotes before it reached Luis. But it missed both of them and buried itself in the wall. Bigotes turned to gape at Luis. Luis looked at the knife. He stepped forward to grasp Bigotes by the shoulders.

"Companion," he said.

Bigotes pulled self-consciously at his mustache. "Well," he said, "boils on Job . . ."

Grinning at the man's embarrassment, Luis walked to his table. He had removed his baldric and sword and had put them on the bench. He pulled the blade from its scabbard and turned back to Matarife. The man was on his feet by the overturned chair. Kashana was standing, too, watching them intently.

"My friend," Luis told Matarife, "fate and Bigotes preserved me for this. I must not disappoint them."

"No, not for this," protested Bigotes. He was sweating and he held up his hands. "You cannot be that drunk. Job's boils, *patrón*, Job's great infected boils. This is the Holy Office."

"I know who it is. Did I tell you how tired I am of them? Did I tell you how tired I am of their snooping rats' faces leering at me around corners and peering in my windows at night? Did I tell you how sick I am of their donkey ears cocked for every oath I utter and every word I let slip——"

"*Patrón*, Body of Christ——"

"I am no heretic. I am a truer Catholic than any dozen of these jackals. Is their work my Faith? Spying, informing, torturing, burning. Was this what our Lord intended? Who are the faithful? Was it not the Romans who burned the Christians? The idolators who hounded the believers till they had to hide their Faith in the catacombs? Are we any different? Cowering in our holes. Afraid to come into the light . . . express an honest opinion . . . talk openly among ourselves. Cradle to the grave . . . a file on every move we make. A slip, one mistake—the file is handed to the Tribunal. Lies, half-truths, the false-hoods of our enemies . . . we become heretics overnight." He looked at Matarife. "An honest Catholic speaks out against you and it is blasphemy. You covet his property? He is a Lutheran. An esoteric de-sign on his sword? Sorcery. He looks at the moon when he laughs. Witchcraft. Any image other than a saint in his house and he is an idolator. Forgetfulness, perjury. A book from Portugal, heresy. And at the end of it all—the rack, the flames of the *quemadero*. It is time decent men stood up and denounced this monstrosity——"

He stopped, like a clock that had run down. He swayed tipsily, sur-prised at his own drunken eloquence. The echoes of his shouting seemed to roll through the room and settle into the gaping faces turned toward him. They were stunned by his denunciation. Nazario stood in the kitchen door, hands knotted in his apron, a shocked grimace on his weazened face. Bigotes was open-mouthed, shaking his head as though recovering from a blow. He made a whimpering sound. He turned to-ward Matarife, wringing his hands like a supplicant.

"*Por favor, Señor* Sergeant," Bigotes said. "For favor, he is drunk. The young Don Luis is drunk and knows not what he says. He is simply mad at his grandfather; all this comes out, you know, it means nothing. You understand . . . he is not mad at you, he does not mean all those things, no, Mother of God, no . . ."

Matarife did not answer. He had not drawn his sword. His fingers danced a spidery gavotte against its wire-wrapped hilt. He did not seem angry or even surprised.

"Well, Don Luis," he murmured. "Well, well, well, well . . ."

His lips parted, slack and wet. The grin held neither malice nor humor. It was blank, meaningless, a little idiotic. He looked around at the men in the room, pausing at each one as if memorizing the faces. Luis knew their names would be on the witness list tomorrow. After that Matarife looked at Kashana, touched the brim of his helmet politely, and walked out. Luis lifted his sword up, shouting after the man.

"*Salud*. Go with God, you jackal."

The silence that followed seemed to mock Luis. Not a man stirred in the room. A candle guttered and spit softly. Kashana broke the spell, crossing to the kitchen and disappearing.

Luis followed her. The outburst had emptied him of his bitter frustration. He felt like a fool now and he wanted to apologize to her. He wanted to explain why it had happened, that he hadn't meant to hit her. It had simply been a reflex, a blind reaction to the pain. But he could not find her.

He returned to the taproom. The men were at the tables again, talking in low tones. They watched him covertly as he sat down with Bigotes. He tried to drink, but he did not want wine. Bigotes tried to start a discussion about horses, but it was no good. Luis felt frustrated, restless. After a while he left. He got his horse and crossed the little Rio Santa Fe, barely a muddy trickle now in the bottom of its miniature canyon.

The party was still going on at the palace, but Luis stopped at the Ribera house on the south side of the plaza. He left his horse with a servant in the stable yard and went inside. A candle burned before his patron saint, the crudely carved wooden statue of San Miguel that stood in a niche in the whitewashed adobe wall. Luis knew his mother had put the candle there. His constant questioning disturbed her. She prayed daily before every saint in the house that Luis would cease his dangerous rebellion.

How could he explain it to her when he did not clearly understand it himself? He knew most of the elders in the town condemned it as the empty revolt of a young wastrel. But if it had been no more than that he would have spent all his time with Andres and his group of rakehells, drinking and wenching and carousing. And he hardly saw Andres any more. The dissolute young men bored him. They seemed as blind as their elders to the shadow hanging over their lives.

Even when Luis went to Nazario's it was not for the drink and the

women. It was more of a search, as though in the Indian part of town
he could find something, an answer to his vague apprehensions. He did
not know exactly when it had started. His friendship with Bigotes had
brought him into close contact with the Indians, perhaps a different
kind of contact than that known to many Spaniards. It seemed he could
see so many things through Indian eyes. And it made the world look
so terribly wrong.

Luis hung his hat on a peg in the wall and dropped his serape on
the rolled mattress on the floor. As he rubbed the burn on his hand
he heard a sound at the door.

He turned to see Don Bernabe. The old man was in his shirt sleeves.
He had removed his hat, and his bald, knobby skull gleamed translu-
cently in the candlelight. He had the face of an avenging god.

Without a word he stepped back and clapped his hands. A pair of
servants came in, seizing Luis before he realized what they were doing. He struggled but they had his arms locked behind him and their
peasant strength came from a lifetime back of the plough. They
dragged him to the stable yard. They tied his hands to the snubbing
post. One of them ripped his shirt from his back. In the bright August
moonlight Luis saw Don Bernabe's manservant, Ignacio, come from
the stable with a horsewhip in his hands.

Standing at the edge of the patio, Don Bernabe said, "Ignacio . . .
you will proceed."

CHAPTER FIVE

AFTER the whipping Don Bernabe roamed disconsolately through the dim house that was beginning to whisper with the movement of waking servants. Anger was still with him. But it was not the senseless, shaking fury he had known during the early morning hours while he waited for his grandson's return.

How was it that the boy could enrage him so? Was it because he loved Luis so deeply? Because he saw in him the only one worthy of perpetuating the Ribera name? The boy had so many fine qualities. Where did this wild streak come from?

Luis's rebellion was peculiarly frustrating to Don Bernabe. He could have understood the ordinary wild oats. But the young man's actions went beyond all points of reference.

The Spanish world was petrified in a mold of traditions and customs a thousand years old. The Church, the Crown, the head of the household—they were the arbiters, their authority absolute. A man who questioned the Faith fed the flames of the *quemadero*. As a direct representative of the Crown, the governor partook of the divine right of kings. A father was as exalted in his home. His rule went unquestioned, whether benevolence or tyranny. It was common for the elders to choose marriage partners for their sons or daughters. For ninety-nine out of a hundred young men in Santa Fe, defying such a choice would have been unthinkable.

Don Bernabe wandered into the living room. One of the servants, hearing him up, had already lit tapers. There was a monastic austerity about these chambers. Candlelight gleamed against the pristine snow of the whitewashed adobe walls. From a dozen niches peered the static visages of wooden saints. In one corner a hand-carved Christ drooped on a cross under a purple canopy. The few chairs were tall, Inquisitional, their rigid backs upholstered in polychrome leather, the Peruvian serge on their seats worn and shiny. Don Bernabe took one. He had not slept all night and his bad leg ached and there was a vile taste in his mouth.

From Luis's room he could hear a faint sobbing. That would be Doña Isabel, Luis's mother. She had been awakened by the sound of the whipping. Don Bernabe cursed and rubbed his leg. A step at the door made him look up.

Luis's father entered the room. He had an elongated face, as pale and rigid as those of the wooden saints. Blue velvet knee breeches clung to his skinny shanks, and his stooped shoulders made bony points against a yellow Rouen shirt. His bloodless lips worked vaguely, assuming the indecisive shape Don Bernabe knew so well.

"Father," the man said. "Father——"

"We will not speak of it, Cristobal," Don Bernabe said. "You know how long this has been coming."

"But the lash . . . like a common slave——"

"Silence, my son."

The rough command made Luis's father stiffen. But he did not reply.

"You will remain here," Don Bernabe said. "I do not want you sniveling over your son. He knows how to take his punishment better than you."

Cristobal walked uncertainly to another chair. Don Bernabe scowled at him, thinking of all his sons now. Santos he had lost, when he was six, of the accursed smallpox. And Gregorio he had lost, the stalwart, the apple of his eye, when the boy was but twenty-two, in a battle with Apaches.

And Cristobal he had kept.

Growing nervous under the scrutiny, Cristobal stood up and went to the *trastero* where he kept his precious books. Opening a spindled door, he took out the tattered copy of Aristotle. It was one of the volumes he had brought back from Mexico City.

By the time Cristobal was twenty it had become evident that the frail youth did not have the makings of a soldier. He had begged for permission to join one of the orders, and at last Don Bernabe gave his grudging consent. Cristobal spent two years with the Jesuits at the Colegio Maximo at Mexico City, returning under a cloud of vague failure that was to taint the rest of his life. The letter from the rector made ambiguous reference to the rigors of the *Ratio Studiorum*, which had broken the health of men far more vigorous than Cristobal, but Don Bernabe never really knew whether it was his body or his mind that was unacceptable.

Cristobal now had his back turned, opening the box of cigars on the shelf. The stiff silence was like a pressure in the room, and when Don Bernabe could support it no longer he said:

"Have you not read that book enough times?"

"What?"

"I said have you not read that book enough?"

"They are good cigars."

"If you would look at me when I talk."

Cristobal was turning toward him. "I can hear all right." He saw Don Bernabe's eyes on the cigar and said, "*Con su licencia, señor.* With your license."

"Of course," Don Bernabe said. "Smoke."

Cristobal lit the cigar on one of the tapers. A servant came in with a tray of silver service and a pitcher of chocolate, beaded with fat beaten to a froth by the chocolate cook who did nothing else all day long. After pouring, the barefoot woman snuffed the candles and opened the drapes to let the first morning sunlight in. It ran in silvery flickers across the gray streaks in Cristobal's sparse hair. He held the cigar in one hand, forgotten, and was staring emptily out the narrow window.

A renewed crying from down the hall made Don Bernabe rise and stalk into the corridor, trying to hide his limp. Luis's door was ajar. In such a barren frontier even the houses of the rich boasted few bedsteads. Everyone in the Ribera household save Don Bernabe slept on mattresses that were rolled against the wall during the day and covered with Navajo blankets to serve as divans. Luis stretched face down on one, shirtless, his back striped and bloody from the whip. A barefoot servant knelt over him, washing his wounds, and the smell of ointment filled the room like rancid perfume. Kneeling beside the servant, trying vaguely to help, was Doña Isabel.

"Woman," Don Bernabe said, "we are having chocolate in the parlor."

She turned like a frightened rabbit. There was a moment of protest in her soft, self-indulgent face, dying instantly before his fierce look. The women of this land, even more than the men, were subject to the rule of their elders. With a hopeless sob she rose, passing Don Bernabe with her head bowed. Where Cristobal baffled him, Doña Isabel was

merely a matter of indifference, a pallid, waddling creature who spent
her time watering her precious *tecolotes* and listening dutifully while
Cristobal read to her from his books.

Don Bernabe had arranged the match for his son after Cristobal
had returned from the Jesuits in Mexico City. It had been a political
alliance, ultimately resulting in a seat on the town corporation for Don
Cristobal.

Don Bernabe looked at Luis again. The boy was still face down,
hands clenched, not even wincing as the servant worked over his
wounds. Don Bernabe felt a weakening, an impulse to speak to Luis,
to try to explain. Before he could move his Indian manservant scurried
in from outside.

"A runner has just arrived from Cochiti," Ignacio said. "The *pueblo*
is under siege by a Navajo war party. You are wanted at the palace
immediately."

An hour later Don Bernabe and three other *encomenderos* left
Santa Fe, accompanied by the runner from Cochiti, twenty armed retainers, and an interpreter named Pedro de Tapia. Cochiti was the
northernmost village of the Pueblos speaking the Keres dialect. It lay
ten leagues southwest of Santa Fe, and by pushing hard the Spaniards
reached it in the afternoon.

On the banks of the Rio Grande, just where it emerged from a frowning gorge, stood the huddled cluster of fire-blackened buildings. A
dozen dead bodies sprawled in the burning cornfields and empty corrals. The square swarmed with panicky Cochitenos. Near the mission
church stood some of the white-headed elders and the Indian governor,
watching sullenly as the Spaniards approached. Don Bernabe spoke to
them in Castilian.

"How long have the Navajos been gone?"

The governor's face was grimed with soot, his voice husky with exhaustion and rage. "One hour . . . two . . ."

Don Bernabe looked around the village. It was a town of over three
hundred and should have been able to summon enough fighting men
to match even a big war party. The governor sensed his thoughts and
spoke heatedly.

"How can we defend ourselves when you bleed us dry of young men?
Only last week the sheriff of the Holy Office took thirty of our strongest."

Don Bernabe glanced at Don Julian de Vega, the *encomendero* of
Cochiti, and saw his face grow red. They both knew Toribio had ex-

ceeded his authority, but they could not let the governor see how it angered them.

"I will want a dozen trackers," Don Bernabe said.

"Of what use," asked the governor. "You never catch the Navajos. This is the protection you promise us. Three raids this year . . . over twenty people killed . . . two crops ruined, our stock run off. If you cannot defend us why should we pay the tribute?"

"Enough!" Don Bernabe said angrily. By the Five Wounds, he thought, how can thirty-five *encomenderos* defend a territory a thousand miles long?

The tribute referred to by the governor was the annual tax paid each *encomendero*, every household in his allotted village contributing a cotton mantle six palms square and a bushel of corn. In return for the tribute and the labor of his Indian vassals the *encomendero* was required to give military protection. He had to reside in the capital (though he could own outlying estates) and had to provide a troop of men-at-arms ready to ride to the defense of any threatened village.

Don Bernabe had complained for a lifetime, had pled with the governor, written the viceroy, petitioned the king. But the Crown, wanting a servile colonial government, afraid to put too much power into the hands of the arrogant *encomenderos*, had kept the legal limit in New Mexico at thirty-five. And the viceroy had enough problems giving military protection in New Spain without sending more troops to the provinces. So the presidial company at Santa Fe had dwindled to less than a dozen professional soldiers. And the job of defending the province fell upon the pitiful handful of *encomenderos*.

Grudgingly Cochiti provided the trackers. One of them was a war chief who claimed he could not speak Spanish. With the Indians fanning out ahead, the column crossed the river. The monotony of creaking saddles and plodding hoofs soon lulled Don Bernabe, taking his thoughts back to Luis again, and the things he had wanted to explain.

There was the matter of politics. For a long time the *encomenderos* had been losing ground in their control of Santa Fe. The priests thought their treatment of the Indians too harsh and opposed their policies at every turn. The civilians would give them no support and constantly complained of their arrogance to the viceroy and the governor.

Could not Luis see how many of these conflicts would be resolved by his marriage? The agreeable response given by the *visitador* to the letter of proposal indicated that he expected to replace Otermin as governor and would be happy to have his daughter marry into the most powerful family in the province. Such an alliance would be priceless.

Don Bernabe struck his saddle softly. That wasn't what he really had to explain. What he wanted to talk about was marriage. He had tried several times to broach the subject, to tell Luis about himself and Doña Jacinta.

She had been dead for thirty years now. She had been the most beautiful woman in Santa Fe, and he had been infatuated. It took him weeks after the marriage to admit his mistake. It was not a mating in bed. It was a battle. A battle against fear, false modesty, ignorance, panic, frigidity. When he realized they were to have no real union as man and woman he tried to salvage what was left in some kind of companionship. But he could no more enter a woman's world than she could enter a man's.

In a few weeks they were strangers living under one roof. He found relief in town or with an Indian woman in the summer peach orchards, coming to his wife's bed only through his determination that they should have sons. . . .

Don Bernabe was lifted from his reverie by the war chief, coming back. Dust shimmered like a golden meal on the man's naked torso, and he began speaking in the Keres tongue.

"*Giss sin uzuis, gehk gi usuis. Mo shome* . . ."

Don Bernabe looked at Pedro de Tapia, the interpreter, and the man translated. "He said he went up, he went down, he looked everywhere. The enemy they are gone."

Don Bernabe scowled. "I am beginning to wonder if it is the Navajos we fight . . . or the Pueblos."

Don Julian leaned toward him, speaking in a low voice. "I do not think we should antagonize them. They are in a sullen mood."

"A public flogging would change it soon enough," Don Bernabe said.

The war chief glanced at him sharply, eyes glittering. Don Bernabe turned accusingly to the Indian.

"I thought you did not speak Spanish?"

The war chief remained silent. In Castilian, Don Bernabe said:

"I think you know our language. If you do not find these tracks you will spend a month in the dungeon at Santa Fe. Do you understand?"

For a long space he thought the man still would not respond. Finally the thick lips stirred, the voice came, flat and ugly as a snake's rattle.

"*Yes* . . . *Señor Gachupin.*"

CHAPTER SIX

WHEN Don Melchor de Cárdenas had come north as visitor to investigate the governor he had been invited to stay at the house of his brother, Don Celso. It was one of the largest and finest homes in the capital. It stood just off the plaza, between the church and the river. Delicate iron *rejas* barred its narrow windows. Slender wooden columns supported a balcony that formed a shadowy colonnade before the massive Mary-blue front door. As with most houses in New Mexico, the austere façade was merely the husk which hid the rich kernel of life within. It gave no indication of the humming activity in the kitchen, the constant passage of barefoot servants through dark-beamed rooms, the visiting and dining and entertaining in the parlors and patios behind the featureless walls. Barbara de Cárdenas, the youngest daughter of the visitor, had been given a bedroom overlooking one of the inner patios.

Lying on the bed she could look through the window and see the little tile-roofed well, the willows drooping in the twilight, the mockingbird twittering in his amole cage. She had been lying on the bed most of the day.

She hated him.

She knew she would hate him the rest of her life. It did not matter now that she had been in such chaotic excitement when she first learned the Riberas had come with a letter from Luis, one moment pleading with her father not to accept the proposal, the next moment praying to her patron saint that he would accept. Underneath the tremulous vacillation she had known what a deliverance it would be.

In New Spain few of the daughters of the aristocrats had their own choice in marriage. If the young men who sought a girl's hand did not find favor in her father's eyes she was doomed to spinsterhood or more possibly to a marriage of convenience. Until Luis's proposal, no young man had presented his letter to Don Melchor. It had been Barbara's panicky fear that she would be married off to some belching, chile-smelling old man for the sake of an alliance.

There was a tap on the door. She whirled as it was opened, fearing that it might be her father. But it was only Josefina, the Tlascalan handmaiden who had come with her from Mexico City.

"Señorita . . . the young man, he is in the patio."

Barbara turned away so the girl would not see her swollen face. "You lie."

"No, señorita. I see him in the square. He begs me for a meeting with you. Not in front of the family. He wants to see you—" the girl's voice grew breathless with excitement—"alone."

A new tantrum shook Barbara. "Get out."

"But—"

"Get out!"

Barbara snatched up a heavy silver brush from the table and flung it at the Indian. It struck the girl hard and she cried out in pain, scampering out the door. Barbara ran across the room, slamming the door, and then threw herself on the bed. She began to sob hysterically into the damp pillow. She wouldn't see him, she wouldn't. Her hate for him seemed to suffuse her, joining the hate for the whole town.

The Royal City of Saint Francis. It was ridiculous. A squalid mud hamlet. A ragged little beggar of a town crouching behind these red mountains and praying every day that it would not be obliterated by the horde of hostile Indians on every side. . . .

The thoughts grew cloudy, would no longer keep Luis from her mind. Begged, Josefina had said. Begged to arrange a clandestine meeting. Curiosity began to supplant hatred.

A man did not beg unless he was on his knees. On his knees, asking her forgiveness. She rose restlessly and crossed to the window, peeking out. She could not see him. He must be in another patio. She circled the room agitatedly, struggling with herself. She could see him. She could be cold, distant, untouchable. She could wither him with scorn. That would give her more satisfaction than not seeing him at all.

"Josefina." She clapped her hands.

There was a scurrying of feet outside, a round face peered apprehensively through the door.

"The black skirt," she said. "The red *enaguas*. Some mullen leaf for my face. I am so pale."

After a frantic fifteen minutes she was ready, her cheeks prickled with mullen leaf till they held a feverish flush, vivid red petticoats peeping from beneath the skirt, black hair held high on an ivory comb beneath a lacy mantilla.

Josefina led her through a dark passage to the patio hidden by the kitchen wing of the house. From the spindled door she heard the crackle of his pacing boots. She dismissed the maid. She opened the door a crack and saw him walking back and forth.

For a panicky moment she wanted to turn and flee. She bit her lip, gave a last despairing look at her breasts, angrily pulled her shawl across them, and stepped into the patio.

He turned instantly at the sound of the opening door. He was dressed in a buckskin jacket and knee breeches, bleached almost white by long wear, so old and worn that he might have been taken for a peasant without the expensive striped serape over one shoulder.

She faltered. She would be cool, she told herself desperately. She would wither him with scorn.

He came toward her. He still wore his spurs, and their spiked rowels dragged on the ground, jangling and clattering. He took off his yellow hat and bowed a sleek black head.

"May God give you good evening, *señorita*."

She moistened her lips. She was trembling. The remnants of her composure fled.

"*Señor*, Josefina . . . she said . . . you begged . . . I . . ."

The blurted words sounded breathless, shrill. Embarrassment flooded her, like a heat against her cheeks. She could not look at him. She looked at the ground. He spoke soberly, as though searching for words.

"The truth is, well—how does it say itself—I did not want to make a formal call . . . what I mean is, I could not . . . I could not say the things before your parents that I want to say. . . ."

She was still gripped with a painful self-consciousness. She had her shawl pulled close around her fragile shoulders, hands locked tightly beneath its folds. He continued.

"There were reasons why I acted so stupidly the other night. I mean, I wanted to make the explanation. I know I hurt you deeply and I did not intend it . . . that is to say, I did not want you to think I did it deliberately. It was just something between me and my grandfather, like an argument or something, you know. . . ."

His contrition, his boyish confusion seemed to melt her antagonism. Of course there were reasons. Why hadn't she seen it that way?

Such a strange face, she thought. Was he angry—or smiling? It was hard to tell. It frightened her a little. It excited her. Like the wooden faces carved by the village saintmaker, all odd angles and surprising hollows, the features irregular, the mouth too big or the cheeks too sharp, yet endowed by the love of the maker with an unmistakable beauty, completely individual, unforgettable.

"Are you listening, *señorita?*"

"What? Yes. Of course, yes."

He moved closer. The beating of her heart seemed to shake her whole body. Was he going to kiss her?

"What I am trying to say is, what I did had nothing to do with you personally. I did not want to hurt you. And now you can give me *la calabaza* and when we next meet we can be friends and there will be no bad feelings."

"What?" She looked at him blankly. "*La calabaza?*"

"Yes, you can give me the squash and everybody will think it was you who did not want the marriage and will think that is why I walked out of the ball the other night—"

"*I who did not want the marriage?*"

She felt the heat leave her cheeks. She knew if she touched her face now it would feel like putty, cold and clammy. It was incomprehensible to her that she had stood here, listening to him talk, listening to all those words, thinking they meant one thing while they really meant another. She drew herself up to her full height.

"*Señor*, how can you speak of humiliation? How can you think for one minute that what you did the other night meant a single thing . . . a single little thing . . ."

Something seemed to crumble inside of her. She put her hand to her mouth and turned to run. She was blind, she didn't know whether it was tears or outrage, she couldn't see. She found the door and pushed through it and stumbled down the hall. In her room she struck the bed and fell to her knees. She put her head into her arms and gave way to crying. Only tears would not come; it was simply dry, racking sobs that shook her whole body.

She thought of suicide. They would find her body here in the morning, at the foot of the Virgin's image, her pale little hand clutching the hem of the Virgin's robe, her sightless eyes turned up to heaven, and when Luis heard about it he would disappear from the town and they would think that he had followed her in his remorse, but years later somebody would find him in a monastery where he had been spending a lifetime of penance for his sin.

Then she knew that was not the way. She could not face the fires of eternal hell. She could not commit the sacrilege of taking her own life.

Still shaking and making soundless shapes with her mouth, she raised her head and looked at the table on which stood the little image of her patron saint. Santa Barbara's face was white and shining, like china, and little black lashes had been painted all around her eyes, giving them a wide, doll-like, staring look. Sometimes when Barbara had been particularly sullen with her mother, or had failed to kneel at vespers, or had committed some other transgression, she could not stand to have the eyes looking at her and she turned the saint to the wall.

Barbara crossed herself quickly, whispering, "Santa Barbara, beloved Helper in Need, grant me this one last prayer, that I may contract some dread lung disease, or a heart sickness so bad that even *dedalera* will not stimulate me back to life, or leprosy, so that he may come and watch for the many days that I waste away and then spend the rest of his life tortured by grief and remorse for what he has done to me."

CHAPTER SEVEN

LUIS stood for a moment beside his horse on the street outside the patio walls. He felt like a fool. He had thought of it as pity, had wanted somehow to make up for hurting her the other night. He had seen her as a pathetic figure, caught in the trap of a vicious custom.

Had she actually thought that he had come to declare his love? How could a woman feel that way about a man she didn't even know?

He mounted his horse and let the nervous animal break into a *paso castellano*, the sedate Castilian pace that was more than a walk and less than a trot and could rock a baby to sleep. As he entered the square a pair of riders appeared a block behind, coming from the river. He pulled rein, looking back at them.

He shrugged his shoulders to loosen their tension. It made the whip wounds on his back burn and brought the thought of his grandfather back. He had clashed with the old man all his life, but he had never felt a real hate for Don Bernabe. Now he did not think he could ever forgive the old man. A seething humiliation spread through him again.

He had no clear idea where he was going now. He only knew he could not abide Don Bernabe any longer. He only knew that he had left the house and that he would never go back. Don Bernabe had not returned from Cochiti and Luis had left without even seeing his parents. He felt guilty about it. Yet he could not face the inevitable scene, the wails and pleas of Doña Isabel, the futile sermons of Don Cristobal.

How could he feel this way? Was he different from other sons? To feel smothered by Doña Isabel's possessiveness? As though she had nothing else in the world and had to concentrate her whole being on him. To be like a stranger with his father? Whenever he came up against it like this there were the memories.

Aristotle.

Luis, at fifteen, with his embryonic interest in books. And Don Cristobal, and Aristotle. Only Cristobal did not have the talent to make the philosopher fire a young boy's imagination as the romances of Cervantes and Alemán could.

And Latin.

And mathematics. And theology. A series of failures. Until in despair the man had sent Luis to Father Pio for his formal education.

The hunting trip.

Out of everything, why should the hunting trip always come back? Seventeen. Luis at seventeen, and one of Don Cristobal's sporadic attempts at fatherhood. Cristobal had no feel for guns (Luis suspected he feared them) and when Cristobal shot the rabbit he went into the brush and vomited. . . .

Well, maybe when he was older. Maybe, Luis thought, the gap narrowed as you grew older. He would come back. In a few days, when his head was clearer and he knew what he intended, where he meant to go. He would see them then.

Ahead of him Luis could see the empty plaza. There was a magic about the town at night. The narrow streets became velvet chasms. The squalor of crumbling walls and broken spindle fences was drowned in black shadow. Moonlight gilded the walls of the towered palace. Angelic voices rose from the church, like a shaft of heavenly light, the Indian boys chanting compline.

A woodcutter who had sold all his cedar faggots crossed the square, going home. His bare feet made no sound in the thick yellow dust. His burros trotted ahead of him, twitching their enormous ears, ugly and wise as shaggy little gnomes.

And over it all, pungent, searching, was the unforgettable perfume of *enebro* smoke. It filled Luis with nostalgia. How could he identify so strongly with the town, yet feel so alien to the people?

He paced his horse down the street to the gates. The guard recognized him and passed him out. He turned south to the Royal Highway. On either flank was a scattering of hovels lying outside the town wall, pale as giant moths against the dark land. Behind the houses on his left was the feathery mass of shadow made by the willows and cottonwoods growing along Santa Fe River.

He was not far out of town when he heard running horses behind him. He turned to see half a dozen riders gallop through the gate. It was a startling rush of sound and movement. He tried to draw his sword and pull his horse off the road at the same time.

Before he could do either they were flooding around him. Moonlight glittered against armor and drawn blades. One of the men held a big rattail firelock. It was Matarife.

"You leave town, Don Luis?"

"I do," Luis said angrily.

"In the name of the Holy Office, I place you under arrest."

They were all fighting to control their excited horses. Luis still held his hand impotently against the wire-wrapped hilt of his sword. His cheeks drew in with anger. He had not thought Toribio would go through with it.

He cursed softly, finally reined his mount around. Matarife rode at his flank and the others took up the rear. For a space the sergeant still kept his firelock trained suspiciously on Luis. But it was a massive pistol, uncomfortable to hold in mid-air long, and confidence in his men made Matarife finally lower it to rest on his saddle.

An aristocrat rarely donned armor except on campaign. Yet there was too much danger to go completely unprotected. Luis wore the standard headgear, an ordinary hat reinforced with a headband of iron from which rose iron hoops to protect the skull. When he saw Matarife lower the gun he reached up as though to shove his hat back. It was a matter of timing, when they were crossing the mouth of an alley that came from between two houses to bisect the Royal Highway.

Instead of pushing the hat back he caught it by the brim and swept it down at Matarife's wrist.

The man shouted as the heavy iron hoops struck him, knocking the pistol from his hand. Luis dropped his hat and drew his sword as he spun his horse toward the alley. A guardsman spurred his animal to cross Luis's line of escape.

Their horses crashed together just as Luis got his sword free. He parried the guardsman's thrust, disengaged, twisted in the saddle for his riposte. Five Flemish spans of steel went through the guard's shoulder at the armhole of his cuirass.

The man doubled over in pain and pitched off his horse. The frightened animal galloped from in front of Luis and his way was free. He spurred his horse into a dead run, with Matarife and the other riders only a few feet behind.

The alley came to a dead end, barred by a spindle fence four feet high. He lifted his horse into a leap that cleared it and brought him down in a back yard.

He heard the first two guardsmen take the fence behind him. The leader didn't quite clear and his horse fell. The rider following went down with him in a wild screaming of horses and crash of armor.

The trail dropped down a steep bank to the river. Matted willows whipped at Luis, bruising his face, tearing his queue loose. He ran his horse into the muddy trickle of water where it would leave no prints. Going at a dead run, he was out of sight by the time he heard the guardsmen reach the river behind. They would not know which direction he took and it would give him a few precious minutes.

Riding with a high hand and the bit on the palate, he left the river bottom, urging his laboring horse across the road a quarter mile from town. Avoiding the Camino de la Canada that led northward, he headed directly into the Sangre de Cristos. He let the horse walk till the roar of its breathing abated and he could hear if he was being followed.

Now that it was over he started to tremble with delayed reaction. He could not seem to get enough air.

He entered a piñon belt. With a soft crackling the horse waded through dense crops of yellow second-season cones that littered the ground. The incense of the jaunty, twisted little trees swam around Luis like smoke. The sight of them made him smile. It always made him smile. Then he stopped the horse among them and looked around at them. He began to laugh. He threw back his head and laughed like a fool. They were his trees. This was his country, and once in it Matarife would never find him.

CHAPTER EIGHT

IT was August 8. Luis awoke at dawn in the camp he had made high in the aspens. He had slept on the ground, covered by the dank saddle blanket, and he ached in every joint. He saw the hobbled horse grazing fifty feet away. It was a roan with a black head. It had the dished face and the short Arab back, but it showed some wild blood, stocky and built low to the ground, not as finely made as the carefully bred Arabs of the aristocrats.

He walked the stiffness out of his joints and saddled and mounted and turned the horse down through the aspens. Their pale trunks were a thousand silver lances thrust into the earth. The morning breeze set up a tremulous quake and flutter in their glittering foliage. Luis was on the westward slope of the Mountains of the Blood of Christ. Far beneath lay the valley, shrouded in a mauve morning haze.

The Upper River district ran seventy miles northward from Santa Fe to Taos, a narrow valley bounded on the west by the Jemez Mountains and on the east by the Sangre de Cristos. From Luis's height that westward wall of the Jemez range looked no darker than a band of blue smoke against the horizon.

As he dropped lower the valley floor took shape in the haze. Pueblo grain fields and Spanish orchards made a bright green patchwork against the brick-red earth. To the south the Rio Grande sometimes ran near the surface of the land, banded by the shimmering emerald jewelry of summer cottonwoods and willows. To the north the river sank deep into the dark and tortured gorge it had for epochs been carving out of the rock.

Luis avoided the road and traveled toward San Juan. Nicolas Bua, the Indian governor, had long been his friend, and Luis knew he could eat and rest at the man's house. In midafternoon he reached a strip of badlands, eroded, barren of growth, and then came upon the surprise of Espanola Valley. Seeming to leap out of the waste of yellow sand hills, the valley was a vivid green mass of trees and fields stretching from mountains to river. The land was veined with the ancient irrigation system used by Indians and colonists alike. Branching off on either side of the river, wherever land was arable, were the *acequia madres*, the mother canals which in turn fed the tributary *acequias* running through every cornfield and melon patch and fruit grove.

But the ditches Luis crossed bore only a trickle of muddy water. The rows of stalks had been burned by the sun till they were curling and brown. They crackled in the wind, and it was the rustle of death. It had been another dry year. If the rains did not come soon the corn would be lost and the Pueblos would have no meal for the winter. In a corn culture, where meal was the very source of life, that meant starvation.

He saw a flock of sheep wandering dismally through the burned corn, untended. They still bore their heavy, matted winter coats, and many of them were lying in the meager shade of the stalks, glassy-eyed, too weak to rise. It surprised Luis. The Indians were better shepherds than that. The sheep should have been shorn long ago. Did they want to lose half their flocks?

Like primitive castles the houses of San Juan rose before him. It was a town of three hundred, the northernmost village speaking the Tewa tongue. It was a *visita* of San Ildefonso, the large Tewa town to the south, and had no church of its own. Only the half-sunken ceremonial chambers on the plaza, with their ladder poles leading down through hatches into the mysteries below. Before he came within sight of them Luis saw a pale mist hovering over the buildings. He heard a sound. He thought it was the booming of wind in distant timber. It was punctuated regularly by a sharp crack, like a gunshot, yet not quite like a gunshot. Puzzled, he lifted the roan to a Castilian pace.

There was a bold, earthy geometry to the shape of these towns. Everything was square, planed, cubed. Half a dozen communal buildings stood in a hollow rectangle about the plaza. Narrow alleys bisected them, and some buildings were two or three stories high. Each level was terraced back ten feet from the level below, a giant stairway that had been abruptly cut off. They were bleached and pale as old buckskin left too long in the sun. The ink stain of shadow made solid masses of their eastern sides and crawled in broken black squares onto the plaza. In those shadows and in the sunlight glaring on the rest of the square stood the people—ranked densely against the walls and along the parapets edging the roofs. They were women and children and old men. Luis could see no young men among them.

The sound was their voices, and the white mist was dust sifting up from the constant stir of their feet. On the north side of the plaza five Spanish soldiers stood in a semicircle, facing the crowd. They were in full armor. They had arqucbuses, the matches burning, the guns level at the hip so the bullets would not roll out, their muzzles covering the crowd. A few feet to their flank the horse holder stood with the reins of seven saddled Barbs. Next to him, Captain Cristobal Anaya, one of the large landholders in the San Juan jurisdiction, sat a fiddling piebald.

Behind the soldiers, built against a building, was a long *ramada*, thatched roof supported by solid cedar posts. Its deep shade was a blessed relief on hot summer days. But it was being used for something else now.

An Indian was tied to one of the cedar posts. He hung there, slack, his knees bent and his body sagging with all its weight from hands bound high to the crossbar. He was naked. They had even removed his moccasins. His back and buttocks and legs bore the bloody latticework of countless whip stripes.

At his side stood Diego Copoz. He was one of Captain Anaya's retainers. His job was a hot one, and his face dripped sweat.

"Sixty-eight, Diego," Captain Anaya said. "Are you tiring?"

Diego wiped his face with the back of a sinewy hand. He set himself and lifted the whip again. It fell with a sodden whack. The Indian jerked, more from the shock of the lash than any reaction of his sagging body. There was a centipede motion in the long phalanxes of Indians. Their husky sound of protest rose and fell. Luis pushed his horse against the mass of them, blocking the alley until they gave way sullenly and let him through. He lifted the animal to a gallop across the plaza. It made all the Spaniards look at him. Captain Anaya's face was a dark wedge of Spanish arrogance beneath the glittering circle of his morion brim.

"Stop him," Luis said angrily. "Tell Diego to stop."

Captain Anaya waited till Luis pulled the roan to a halt in front of him and then said, "It is by order of the Marqués de Gallegos. They deserted the Gallegos sheepshearing. They were hunted down and discovered in the mountains with *caciques* conducting forbidden rites."

Luis understood why there were no young men in the village. "The Marqués has no right to hold them so long," Luis said. "If you will not stop the flogging, Captain, I will."

"Martin," Anaya said, "guard this man."

One of the arquebusiers immediately swung his gun to cover Luis. Luis's face was pale with frustration. The roan fiddled in the dust. The hundreds of Pueblos had grown still, watching the two Spaniards with childish concentration.

Luis said, "At least hold off till I can see the Marqués."

"I can only do that by his order," the captain said. He lifted his voice. "Diego, are you tiring?"

Diego had been watching them. He spat, wiped sweat from his face again, drew the whip back. As the whip cracked against the Indian again Luis's body lifted in the stirrups with the outraged impulse to spur his horse through the Spaniards and run Diego down. But Martin's arquebus was pointed unwaveringly at him, and he knew one wrong move would only get him shot.

The whip cracked again. The groaning protest rose from hundreds of throats. In a bitter frustration Luis looked around the plaza. At the east end, partially hidden by the crowd, another pair of Spaniards stood guard over half a dozen Indians imprisoned in stocks.

The stocks were simply heavy split beams with leg holes hollowed out. The beams were held shut by rings and a lock at either end. There were three men to a beam, and when the top half was closed on their ankles they were forced to sit on the ground, legs extended, leaning awkwardly against a building.

One Indian was not in the stocks. He lay face down on the ground. It was hard to see where any skin remained on his naked back. It seemed to be a solid mass of raw flesh laid open in strips by the lash.

Kneeling beside him in the dust was Father Luis Morales, one of the priests from San Ildefonso who made regular visits to San Juan to hold religious services. Behind the friar was the whipped man's family. Two young boys supported an ancient, shaking crone, their young faces wooden. On the ground crouched a squaw, hands folded tightly in her lap, black eyes fixed in numb misery on her bloody husband. She bore a *kohm* strapped to her back, a cradleboard in which a fat baby gurgled and chirped.

Luis stopped by Father Morales. The flesh of the priest's face was a translucent vellum, and the bones of his emaciated hands made a skeletal silhouette beneath the papery skin. Luis did not understand how such a fragile vessel could sustain the endless labors of mission life, but Father Morales was an indefatigable worker, beloved by the Indians, and had been in the New Mexico mission field since 1664. There was something so luminous and saintly about his face that it always brought Luis one of his rare moments of respect. Despite his anger, he used the traditionally formal greeting he so often ignored.

"*Buenas tardes, le de Dios, padre,*" he said. The priest answered in a strained, trembling voice. Luis dismounted, looking sickly at the whipped man. "Is there anything I can do, Father?"

Father Morales shook his head. "Only pray with me that he does not die."

Luis knelt beside the friar and they crossed themselves and together prayed to Our Lady of Remedies. When they had finished Luis looked up.

"You know, Father, it is the first time in sixteen years that I have seen you sanction punishment for your people."

The Franciscan's lips compressed to a gray line. "It is not my wish. I have protested since morning. I pled for hours with Captain Anaya. I have prayed constantly. I cannot believe they deserve this."

The crack of the whip punctuated their words. Luis glanced back at the Spaniards, growing pale. Captain Anaya was counting.

"Eighty-seven . . . eighty-eight . . ."

The baby laughed happily and made pawing motions with his hands. Father Morales lifted a broken clay pot and fingered out some more tallow for the Indian's wounds. Luis saw that his hands trembled.

"When will our people learn?" the priest murmured. "Fray Bernal is sincere. He demands twice as much of himself as any one of his converts. But I wish he understood these people better. I wish all the bishops and doctors and prelates who pass such harsh rules governing the conduct of these children could come and live among them as we have and see what harm their stringency is doing. We cannot change an Indian's mind into that of a European in one generation—even a dozen generations. You know I am not the only priest who feels thus, Luis. We have been trying to obliterate idolatry in the New World for almost two centuries, and still it persists. Would not this indicate that perhaps some of our methods are wrong?

"There are those who see no other methods."

"What can be wrong with the ones He gave us? Gentleness. Kindness. Love. Not the lash and the stocks and the gibbet. The primitive beliefs of this people permeated every minute of their day, every breath they took. I fear the time will never come when they no longer conduct their dances or make their prayer sticks or scatter meal to the wind. All we can work for is the day when these things have lost their original significance."

"Ninety-two," Captain Anaya said. "Ninety-three."

The priest looked across the plaza, then turned his eyes away. "In outlawing their ancient rites we have robbed the *caciques* of their traditional power. They resent it bitterly. They conspire constantly against us, inciting the people, destroying all we try to build. The infection has festered for years, Luis, and I fear it is coming to a head."

"This will not help any," Luis said. He looked at the man on the ground. "Can any man survive so many lashes?"

"Three of them will not be whipped. They are the *caciques* who were pardoned by Governor Trevino in the witchcraft trials five years ago. They will be taken to Santa Fe. This time it will mean execution."

He glanced at the stocks. The crowd had obscured some of the prisoners, but now a shift in the ranks revealed the man sitting at the extreme end of the second beam. It was Po-pe.

"Ninety-nine . . . one hundred!"

The crack of the whip stopped and Father Morales looked across the plaza and rose, putting his pale hands against his knees to help himself up. "They will take him down now. I must help."

As the priest crossed the plaza, barefoot in the dust, Luis led his horse to Po-pe. The man's Navajo blanket hung from stooped shoulders and gathered in dusty folds across his lap. It was a Yei blanket. The background was the silver-gray of the holy sand used in the Navajo sand paintings, and woven into it were images of gods holding juniper twigs and other sacred symbols. Though Po-pe was still in his prime, a lifetime of esoteric disciplines had aged him prematurely. His mouth was drawn against his teeth like a flagellant scar and his cheeks were deep-sucked pits. Every line in his face seemed to be a self-inflicted wound, and the flesh had the gray tinge of ancient suffering.

"Tell me what you are accused of," Luis said.

The man did not answer. Luis knew what an intense humiliation he must be suffering, returned to the village from which he had been ostracized, forced to sit in the dirt and face the curiosity and scorn of the whole town. Yet none of it showed in his face. His eyes were half drowned in the black shadows of their deep sockets, and they stared beyond Luis, or through him, blank as wet slate, masking depths only an Indian mind could penetrate.

One of the Spanish guards approached Luis, saying, "He will not talk Spanish. It is said he has not spoken a word in our tongue since his father was hanged by Governor Trevino five years ago."

Luis changed to the Tewa dialect. "I do not mean to let you suffer this outrage. Any of you. If I obtain your pardon will you promise to speak with me and tell me your grievances and tell me what can be done to right them?"

Po-pe did not stir. He did not even seem to breathe. A fly settled on his face. He made no move to brush it off.

Luis shook his head helplessly. He mounted and rode toward the crowd. They parted before him and he trotted down an alley. As he turned the corner a man stepped from behind the building and caught his reins, halting him. It was Nicolas Bua, the Indian governor. Though he was Po-pe's son-in-law, he had been one of those instrumental in ostracizing the *cacique*. He had always been friendly to the Spaniards, and because Bigotes was his companion Luis had become his companion.

"Don Luis," he said, "where do you go?"

"To see the Marqués."

"I had hoped so. You must stop this. You must not let it happen. It would be a bad thing."

"What kind of a bad thing, Nicolas?"

"I cannot talk now." The governor glanced toward the alley. His sensitive hand tightened on the reins and there was a strained look to his ascetic face. "Po-pe must not know we have spoken. Tell the Marqués——"

He broke off, glancing up. Luis saw a pair of Indians push aside a blanket that hung in a doorway and come out onto the roof.

"Come back after nightfall," Nicolas Bua said. "I will be waiting alone in my house."

He hurried around the corner and down the alley. Luis backed the horse so he could look after the man. He could see over the heads of the crowd jamming the other end of the alley. He could see Po-pe seated against the wall with the other prisoners. More flies had gathered on his face. He was oblivious to them. He sat with his head tilted back, his eyes shadowed, dreamy. An expression of cruel repose possessed his face.

CHAPTER NINE

To the Tewas of San Juan it was *tatsapo,* the wheat-cutting moon. To the Spaniards it was August. It was the evening of August 8. At San Juan the Spaniards had done with their flogging. The punished had been carried to their houses, two of them already dead. Father Morales, after administering final sacraments and doing what doctoring he could, had left for San Ildefonso. Captain Anaya had returned to his estate, leaving a pair of guards for the three *caciques* still imprisoned. In the morning they would be taken to Santa Fe.

For a while the people remained in the plaza, gathered uncertainly around the prisoners. But there was nothing they could do and soon they drifted off to their homes. They were at dinner now, and the dusk-silvered village seemed deserted. One of the Spanish guards was dozing, and the other stood near the three *caciques.*

Sitting on the ground, his ankles chafed and aching in the stocks, Po-pe surveyed the plaza from eyes almost closed. Before he had been ostracized for witchcraft he had been *cacique* here, revered even above the war chief and the governor and the council of the elders. Such a priest was exempted from labor, his fields were tilled for him, he got his meat from communal hunts, wood was chopped and brought to his door—all so he could give his time over to prayer and meditation and communion with Those Above. When he thought about it he was filled with bitterness. But it should not be a personal bitterness. It should be for his whole people, for the contempt and abuse and pain and suppression they were suffering at the hands of the conquerors.

A scratching sound came from around the corner of the building.

The guard turned. Gripping his arquebus, he walked toward the sound. Po-pe did not move. He had known it would come. Under ordinary circumstances the Pueblos would not have dared to do anything. But these were not ordinary circumstances.

While the soldier's attention was on the sound coming from the alley, a shadowy figure loomed at the parapet above him and dropped off the building. It carried the Spaniard to the ground. Before he could recover, the figure straddled him, an Indian, tipping off his helmet and hitting him on the head with a war club.

It had not even disturbed the other Spaniard. A second Indian was already dropping off on him. The soldier's awakening shout was broken by a blow on the head. It had all been done so quickly and silently that only the prisoners were aware of it. The two Spaniards were dragged into the alley and tied.

One of the Indians reappeared. He was stripped to moccasins and breechclout. He was still breathing deeply from the long run, and sweat and dust made a gritty copper film on his body. About his waist he had the rope of palmilla fiber. There were still six knots in it and kinks where the other knots had been untied. In Tewa the man's name was Mahun—the Owl. He had gotten a key from the Spaniard and unlocked the stocks. Po-pe and the other rose, rubbing their legs and stamping softly to restore circulation. Their other rescuer appeared. He was stripped too. His name was Tsigoweno.

"You come from Pecuris?" Po-pe asked.

Mahun nodded. "Both Taos and Pecuris are with us. They have untied their knots."

Po-pe nodded in satisfaction. "Another will be untied here. You will then give the rope to a pair of runners from this village. They will carry it to Tesuque. There Catua and Omtua will take it and carry it on to the Tanos south of Santa Fe." He turned to the other *caciques.* "Get your war chiefs and the elders and your governor. Tell them the messengers have arrived. There will be a ceremony in the *kiva.* I cannot join you. I leave for Taos immediately."

The two runners crossed the square and went into the underground ceremonial chamber. One of the *caciques* went up to the governor's house. He reappeared after a while without the governor. Po-pe was not surprised.

He watched the white-headed elders come from their houses and go to the *kiva,* one by one, the two war chiefs, the medicine doctors. When they had all disappeared Po-pe crossed the square. In the fading twilight he was but a faceless shadow, and he knew he would not be recognized. He climbed the shaky cottonwood ladder to the earthen roof top and walked across its terrace to the governor's house.

A hide hung in the doorway, but candlelight from within gave it yellow edges. Po-pe pushed it aside and entered. Nicolas Bua sat on a blanket against the wall, light from a single tallow candle seeming to carve his face out of surrounding darkness. It was a deeply-lined face, thoughtful, withdrawn. The black eyes stared at the opposite wall, blank and meditative.

The dwelling was filled with a mingling of familiar food scents—the powdery smell of parched corn, the citron of candied muskmelon rind, the wine of grapes drying to raisins where they hung in bunches on the rafters. Po-pe walked from the door till his shadow fell across the other man, black and distorted beyond all human shape by the angle of light.

"Your family?" Po-pe asked.

"They are across the village."

"So you would be alone to meet someone?"

Nicolas Bua did not answer or react. Po-pe sat on another blanket, with the candle between them. He regarded his son-in-law, trying to read what lay behind the tired, thoughtful face. He was never meant to be a governor, Po-pe thought. He was never meant to rule men. He is too kind.

"You will not join them in the *kiva?*" he said.

"I talked with Father Morales today," he said. "He has again asked the superintendent that we be allowed some of our dances."

"They lie to you. To them everything we do is witchcraft. The minute we enter the *kiva* we are sorcerers. They will never permit us to go back to the old ways. They tell us Jesus and Mary will answer our prayers. Did you pray to Mary for rain this week?"

The lines grew deeper about the governor's mouth.

"The Rain Dance would bring it," Po-pe said. "But they will not permit that. They would rather let the sun burn our corn and have us starve this winter."

"Don Desidero promised help."

"When have they kept promises? While your own sheep sicken and die in the heat for want of shearers and your crops rot in the field Don Desidero brings in his harvest with men he will not pay. We can be slaves no longer, Nicolas. It is for this that Caudi and Tilini and Tleume appeared."

Nicolas Bua glanced at him sharply, then rose to pace restlessly around the room. He had been one of the governors present when Po-pe had materialized the three fiends in the *kiva* at Taos.

"When I think about those three, I wonder if the Spaniards are not right about witchcraft," Nicolas Bua said.

Po-pe's lips grew thin and cruel. This disbelief was something he had long suspected in his son-in-law. He had realized the danger of materializing Caudi and Tilini and Tleume. Claiming an alliance with supernatural demons was closer to witchcraft than the usual holy magic of a *cacique*. The Indians' definition of witchcraft was not quite the same as that of the Spaniards. But the Pueblos killed their witches.

Yet he had been convinced that it was time to give his people final proof of his powers and of the holiness of his plan. He knew their simple, superstitious minds. They needed something shocking, dramatic, mystical. And that night at Taos, with the governors of all the Indian villages gathered in the *kiva*, when Po-pe had called upon the powers of darkness and had seemingly brought the three fiends out of the ground, glowing with an unholy luminescence—that night had provided the answer. The astounding story had spread throughout the land. Already it had become a part of the people's mythology, and Caudi and Tilini and Tleume would take their seats beside the Twin War Gods and Sun Father.

"It was not witchcraft," he said. "It was a message from the gods."

Nicolas Bua stopped and looked accusingly at him. "Or was it merely three young men drugged with mescal and painted white and spirited into the *kiva* through an underground passage?"

Po-pe felt a throbbing begin at his temples. But he was careful to control his anger, because he knew he was getting his answer now, his answer to the question that had gnawed at him so long; and this man was his son-in-law and he wanted to be sure.

"Nicolas," he said. "We stood together once. Five years ago in the prison at Santa Fe. You and I and forty more, watching them hang my father and three others in the plaza. We made a vow."

Emotion made shadows in the governor's young-old face. "I believed in you then," he said. "I thought your only concern was for your people."

"How could it be otherwise?"

"When you left here two years ago and went to Taos it was because you made the new gods—Caudi, Tilini, Tleume. Was that a return to the old ways?"

"It had to be so. If I was to unite you I had to have their power."

"That is the word. Power. Something you lost when Jesus and Mary came. Something Catiti and Tupatu and all the other *caciques* lost."

The pounding was deeper in Po-pe's temple. But now that he knew, now that he was certain, he could feel no hate. He could not place this man alongside the Spaniard in his hate. He could only feel pity, a bitter reluctance.

Nicolas Bua bent toward him. "It is not too late to stop this. Sooner or later a governor will come who keeps his word, a superintendent who understands us better. They will see how impossible it is to stamp out our gods. Jesus and Mary can live side-by-side with Sun Father and Earth Mother. It can be done without bloodshed. There are some among the Spaniards who speak truth. We must trust them."

"Luis Ribera?"

Nicolas Bua could not quite hide his response, a flicker of muscle in the cheek.

"You were seen talking with him this afternoon," Po-pe said. "Was he to return this evening?"

Nicolas Bua did not speak. Po-pe was staring at the candle, thinking that he had worked too long for this. Five years, moving endlessly from town to town, talking in Tewa at San Juan and San Ildefonso, talking in Keres at Cochiti and Santo Domingo, talking to the Piros through an interpreter, to the Apaches and Yutas in sign language and with symbols painted on shields, doing something that had never been done before, uniting them all, uniting them against the hated *gachupin* invader.

"Nicolas," he said. "You misjudge me. My only thought is for my people. If I could save but one life by doing it a different way I would listen. Sit down. Tell me."

He waved at the blanket beside him where the governor had been sitting. Nicolas looked at him dubiously, then moved to sit down. He closed his eyes and pinched the bridge of his nose between thumb and forefinger.

Po-pe snuffed the candle out. In the darkness Po-pe heard the other man's quick rustling movement. But it was too late. Nicolas had been but three feet away and Po-pe rose and was on him. He found the governor's throat while Nicolas was still sitting down. His fingers sank deep into the neck muscles at the back as his thumbs clamped onto the windpipe.

CHAPTER TEN

AT eight o'clock the moon rose, flooding the land with its occult light and casting black masses of shadow beneath the timber. At eight o'clock Luis was on his way back to San Juan. His meeting with the Marqués de Gallegos had been bitterly frustrating. The Marqués adamantly refused to stop the floggings or rescind the order that would send Po-pe and the other two *caciques* to Santa Fe and their certain execution.

Luis was still a mile from San Juan when his horse began to toss its head and nicker. He took it for a warning and pulled the fretting animal into timber, dismounting and tightening the noseband so it could not whinny. In a few moments a rider appeared on the road. As he drew close Luis recognized the crotchety little pony and the potbellied figure swaying indolently in the saddle.

"Bigotes," he said.

The Pueblo checked the horse, lifting in the saddle with surprise. Then he galloped up to Luis, stepping quickly out of the saddle and grasping the young man by both arms.

"*Patrón*," he said. His voice had a husky sound, more emotion than an Indian often showed. He released Luis and stepped back, pulling self-consciously at his mustache. He looked at the ground and rolled his big head from side to side. "Well . . . I was at Tesuque . . . a wind from Santa Fe, telling what happened. I knew you would go north. At San Juan, one of the elders. He told me you took this road on up."

"I did not think Toribio would go this far," Luis said. "By arresting me he will have to reveal that he was drafting those Indians illegally."

Bigotes brightened. "I will go with you. We will go to the mountains north of Taos, where they will never find you—maybe marry a Yuta squaw. They have great ugliness and bad teeth, but I understand there are other compensations."

In Bigotes' words it sounded childishly simple, naïve. Yet Luis knew it was what he had faced in refusing to submit to arrest. No man was so completely outlawed as one wanted by the Holy Office. In the whole Spanish world there would be no haven. People who would give a murderer protection would shun a fugitive from the Inquisition.

Sarcastically he said, "My excommunication must wait, companion. I go to San Juan."

Bigotes glanced sharply at him. "Not there, *patrón*. Not back. The guardsmen of Toribio may be right behind us."

"I must see Nicolas Bua. He has something to tell me."

Bigotes moved closer. "Don Luis, you must go on north."

Luis looked thoughtfully at the Indian. "The last time you did not want me to go, it was Tesuque . . . and Po-pe was there."

A strained look touched Bigotes' face, making little ridges of muscle about his lips. Luis swung up on the roan and turned toward San Juan. He heard Bigotes follow.

"Bigotes . . . a few nights ago I had a dream. It was hot and very dusty. I was walking. A man was on a horse beside me. He kept spurring the horse. Only every time he spurred the horse it hurt me. The man looked like my grandfather. Then the man looked like you. I tried to speak, but the horse whinnied. It sounded like a church bell ringing inside my head and I could not hear what I said. You laughed. I held my head and ran. . . ."

"You think too much. If you did not think so much you would not dream."

"Dogs dream."

"Only of chasing rabbits and bitches."

"Bigotes, in our church is this image of Jesus. Love one another. Was that not it? No rich, no poor, no slaves, no masters——"

Bigotes looked away. These discussions always disturbed him. The silence came to them again, awkward, a pressure. They passed through a green flood of piñons. The scent of them was everywhere, pungent and piny. They were crouched close to the earth, most of them no higher than a man, gnarled, knuckled, twisted. Bigotes knew what they meant to Luis and commented out of old habit.

"Observe that one."

"A real *viejo*. A real twisted little old man."

"It has the skin of an old man."

Luis did not answer. They rode on. Soon Luis felt a throbbing in the night. It made the horse fight the reins and toss his head. The village appeared ahead, mystic castles under a silver moon. Bigotes brought his horse close to Luis. His splayed nostrils fluttered with his stertorous breathing.

"*Patrón*, for the last time . . . there exists danger . . ."

Luis glanced at him, then touched his sword hilt and lifted the stallion into a trot through the last cornfields. The parched husks clattered sibilantly against the horse's legs. Luis recognized the throbbing now. They were beating the drums in the *kiva*.

Luis entered the alley leading to the governor's house. He saw a line of figures silhouetted against the moon, climbing the ladder to the second story of the building. There was a rush of shadowy movement. Men seemed to appear from the earth, the buildings, from the night itself. And the beat of the drums stopped.

In the strange silence, with only the husky breathing of the crowd around him, Luis said in Spanish, "I come to see your governor."

The crowd gave way respectfully before a white-headed man. Luis recognized him as one of the elders whose Spanish name was Gregorio. He stopped by Luis, ancient face upturned.

"Nicolas Bua is not here," he said.

Luis looked at the ladder. It was empty now, but the men who had climbed it were still on the roof and he could see an edge of light around the blanket covering Nicolas Bua's door.

Luis said more sharply, "Where is Father Morales?"

"He has returned to San Ildefonso," Gregorio said.

Impatience swept Luis. "You all know me. More than once I have come across you performing the old dances. You know I have never reported it. But tonight I must see Nicolas Bua. If you keep me from it Santa Fe shall hear of the secret rites you performed in the ceremonial chamber."

A sound like the wind came up from the assembled throng. But Gregorio raised his hands, bringing a trembling silence. In a dry, bitter voice, he said:

"Very well. You shall see him."

Sullenly the men moved back. Luis dismounted, dropping his reins to the ground. Their hostility was like a pressure against him, and when one of them made an abrupt move he could barely keep from grabbing at his knife. But they let him reach the ladder, with Bigotes following, and climb to the second-story terrace. Half a dozen men were gathered on the earth roof, muttering among themselves in Tewa as they let him through. A man stood at the door, blocking their way. Gregorio had followed Luis up.

"Let them see," he said.

The guard pulled the blanket aside. On the floor inside, with a dozen lighted candles placed around him, lay Nicolas Bua. His face was painted in horizontal stripes and his body was sprinkled with corn meal, and a little pyramid of yellow pollen lay in each open palm. Bigotes and the guard and Gregorio were pressing so close to Luis that he had to keep moving inside. An aged *cacique* crouching by the wall quickly drew a strip of cloth across a bowl of water and an ear of corn on the floor in front of him. Luis stopped by the body, seeing that the feet were bare. But leg wrappings and moccasins lay nearby for his journey into the next world. The face was grotesquely contorted, the eyes open, bulging, staring. It was death in an ugly form, and it left Luis sick and shocked.

"How did he die?" he asked.

"Don Luis," Bigotes said, "death can come in many ways. Is it not enough that he is now dancing in Wayima?"

The layer of corn meal was particularly thick on the corpse's throat. But it had dribbled off the sides of the neck and Luis saw the marks there, as livid as scars. The fact that they should have taken a chance on his seeing that did not make sense.

With a swift motion he turned toward the door. Both Bigotes and Gregorio tried to block him, but he had taken them off guard. He slid sideways between their converging bodies, pushed the guard aside with a shoulder, and swept the blanket away to step out. Half a dozen men were still clustered at the parapet. Beyond them, in the plaza below, a funnel of yellow light streamed skyward from the open trap door of a *kiva*. At the edge of the plaza there was a flutter of shadows and the faint slap of running feet.

One of the men on the roof called softly, and somebody quickly closed the trap door of the sunken ceremonial chamber.

Luis heard the others come out behind him. He turned to Gregorio and said innocently, "This death must be reported to Santa Fe. You must not move the body till a priest or a doctor comes and makes sure it is not the plague."

Gregorio bowed his head. "As you say."

"Convey my sorrow to his family," Luis said. "He was a good man."

Gregorio did not answer, and Luis crossed the roof and climbed down the ladder. It was like descending into a beast's den—the stench of them, the growling and muttering as they moved reluctantly back to let him reach the ground. He mounted and passed down the alley. He rode straight out through the cornfields with Bigotes at his flank.

"Did you see those marks on his neck, Bigotes?"

"They paint their dead that way."

"Not paint. He was strangled."

"Of truth?"

"I wondered why they let me see him. A lesser of two evils. They thought they could get those men out of the *kiva* while I was looking at the body."

"What men?"

"What were they doing down there, Bigotes? They knew I would not report one of their ceremonies——"

Luis broke off, glanced at Bigotes, then touched spurs to the Barb. He saw running figures crossing through the cornfields and knew they would try to follow him and keep him under surveillance. But they had no chance against a mounted man.

The runners had left the plaza by the south side and it made him turn downriver. He didn't have time to track. Whatever he did would have to be guesswork. But they were guesses based on a lifetime of association with these people.

He found a game trail but knew they would not use such an obvious avenue if they feared being followed. They would seek land that gave them some cover yet would not impede them. He reached a fringe of badlands and knew they would not cross its tortured labyrinths; he circled to a low headland that overlooked the southward flats, stippled with the countless, twisted, cringing gnomes of the piñons and cedars. And among the trees, a quarter mile to the south, he saw the flutter of shadows.

Bigotes was just catching up to him, scrambling up onto the headland, when Luis dropped down the other side. He found an arroyo with a sandy bottom that would muffle his hoofbeats. He let his horse out in a floundering run, trying to calculate time and distance till he thought he was ahead of them, and then turned the Barb up the cutbank.

Luis had an instantaneous glimpse of them directly ahead, just crossing a rise. The silhouettes of two running men, a knotted cord dangling from the hand of one. Then, apparently without seeing him, they were gone.

Bigotes reached Luis's side at the same moment. Before Luis could spur his horse again Bigotes grabbed his arm. Luis's leg was pinned between the two horses, and Bigotes was up against him. The man was sweating heavily and his stench was almost gagging, a rancid mixture of chile and tallow and sour leather.

"You have seen them now, *patrón* . . . just runners . . . nothing more."

Luis tried to pull free. "You know something."

"Nothing. I swear it. Nicolas Bua died of natural causes and these men simply carry the message to the villages."

"By that rope?"

"It means nothing."

"I will find out what it means——" With a violent jerk Luis pulled free, twisting to get his sword out. "If I have to take them to the governor!"

Bigotes spurred his horse against Luis's left flank again and rose up in the saddle. Luis saw a knife glittering in his hand. A strange grimace contorted his face, and he was crying.

"*Patrón*," he said, crying. "*Patrón*——"

Luis rolled sideways in an attempt to escape the thrust. It left his drawn sword extending across his body, pointed upward at Bigotes. The man could not stop himself in time and impaled himself with his own lunge. Luis saw a foot of the bright blade go into the man's belly. Bigotes made a wheezing sound and his weight falling against Luis knocked the young man from the saddle. As he fell he felt the wildly flailing knife rip deep into the muscle of his shoulder.

Luis struck the ground with a stunning impact. He lay flat and unmoving, a wind of pain and helplessness roaring through his head.

Bigotes had dropped his knife. It glittered nakedly in the sand, ten feet away. Beyond it, heading northward in a panicked gallop, the yellow pony was carrying Bigotes into the trees. The man was bent forward, hugging his bloody middle, swaying so violently that Luis thought he would pitch off. But he was still aboard when he disappeared in the stunted timber.

Sick and shocked, Luis managed to gain his feet. He swayed dizzily, putting a hand to his shoulder, feeling the blood. It was a bad wound. He knew that. Why was there no pain?

He began to tremble violently. He looked around for the horse. It had run away. He could see the tracks leading eastward into the trees. He stumbled after it. He had to get to Santa Fe.

CHAPTER ELEVEN

IT was August 9. Governor Antonio de Otermin was awakened by the brazen ringing of matins from the church. His bedroom was at the west end of the palace, overlooking Santa Fe's plaza. The edge of morning light coming through drawn curtains seemed unbearably bright. He cursed and pressed fingertips against his temples. Had he drunk that much last night? These headaches were becoming too frequent.

He called for Pepe. The spidery old Catalan who had come from Spain with Otermin soon appeared, carrying the chocolate and *sopapillas* every Mexican had upon arising. Otermin sat up in bed, sipping the chocolate and languidly picking at the hollow pincushions of puff paste, fried in deep fat and drowned in hot syrup. After he finished he rose, was helped out of his nightshirt and into a pair of breeches, and sat before the baroque mirror. Patiently the manservant scraped at the heavy jowls, trying to cut close enough so that there would be no remnant of the blue shadow the governor hated so. Then he carefully shaved the backs of Otermin's hands so none of the bristly black hair would show beneath his cuffs.

Otermin sighed dismally. This was one of the two mornings a week he reserved for the Indians, listening to their petty problems, their endless complaints. Two thousand pesos a year did not begin to pay for such a job.

He was a *gachupin*, a Spaniard born in the mother country. The decay and corruption of the court at Madrid had driven him to seek opportunities in the New World. He had gone to Mexico City as a gentleman courier carrying royal orders from king to viceroy. It had not taken him long to gain an appointment. Such an impressive title—governor and captain general of all New Mexico, a province so big even the king did not know its boundaries. And then he had arrived in his capital, this squalid little mud town of eight hundred stupid peasants. . . .

His thoughts were broken by a timid knock on the door. Francisco Xavier entered. He was the Secretary of Government and War, a gray, circumspect little man who always seemed to be making scratching noises like a chicken.

"The Marqués de Gallegos is in the council chambers," he said.

"This early? Can he not wait for a regular audience?"

"He begs your indulgence. He came in late last night to answer your summons. He would like to return upriver as soon as possible. Something about trouble with his Indian shearers."

"Indian trouble, Indian trouble. It is all they talk about—and nothing ever happens." Fuming, Otermin waved a hand at Pepe, and the man fetched his coat. "Very well, who is the plaintiff?"

"Lucas Paredo, one of the elders at San Juan. He arrived yesterday and I already took the liberty of summoning him."

Testily trying to pull his coat straight across his solid rump, Otermin walked from his bedroom, through his office, his anteroom, a narrow corridor, and into the council chamber. It was a musty room with chest-high cotton hangings tacked on the adobe walls to keep the whitewash from powdering the coats of the councilmen. Sunlight streamed through the narrow windows, the motes swarming like a cloud of minuscule tadpoles in each slanting golden bar. The Marqués de Gallegos paced restlessly at the end of the room. A black velvet cloak swirled at his soft kid doublet. His Galician eyes were still puffed with sleep, but his face looked drawn and irritable.

"Well," he said, "I will hear the complaint and then I must return to my jurisdiction."

The man's arrogance infuriated Otermin. He had the usual *gachupin* contempt for colonial Spaniards. They were all Creoles here. The blood of some might go back to the finest houses in Castile, but they had been born in the New World and most of them had never even seen their mother country.

"I am not the plaintiff, my good Marqués," he said. "Let us at least wait till your accuser is present."

The Marqués turned pale, but before he could respond the Indian elder entered. Lucas Paredo's face was sunken, age-yellowed, and his toothless gums sucked his lips in till they were pleated like the mouth of a drawn purse. With him was one of the four priests who resided at the capital.

Father Juan Bautista Pio, from the City of Victoria in the province of Alaba, was a man who filled his robes with formidable stoutness. He was forever smiling and had a habit of patting his belly with both palms, as though he had just finished a good meal.

Otermin scowled at the file the secretary had placed before him. "By your petition I see that your first complaint has to do with orphans. Are you not aware of the law which protects an orphan by allowing a Spaniard to take the child into his house and see that he is educated and provided for?"

The Indian began in a low voice. "For each orphan taken there must be a permit, signed by Your Excellency. And Don Gallegos had no such permit. And he took four boys and three of them not orphaned. And they are not being educated or provided for. They are being used as carriers at the Salt Lakes."

The Marqués spoke in a spiteful voice. "I cannot make a trip down here for such minor details. I meant to request the permit when I was next in Santa Fe."

Otermin rattled the papers. "Your next complaint: Three hundred cotton mantles, woven by the women of San Juan. Is that not the annual tax owed the Marqués as your *encomendero*?"

"The tax is one mantle from each household. That would not exceed fifty mantles from our village. The Marqués ordered our women to weave the other mantles. He promised to pay us. We never got our money."

"Two hundred and fifty mantles at six *reales* apiece." Otermin looked inquiringly at Xavier.

The secretary figured quickly and said, "Twelve hundred *reales*."

"I never received the mantles," the Marqués said blandly.

"He shipped them to Mexico City along with his wool," the Indian said. "He drafted thirty men from San Juan. Each carried a load that would break the back of a mule. They walked to Mexico City. They were not paid the legal wage. They were abandoned in the capital and left to make their way back home on their own. Of the thirty, eleven died."

"This is a serious charge," Father Pio said. "You must make an investigation——"

"Are you telling me my job?" Otermin asked. "How many investigations have been made? Do we ever get witnesses?"

"Not when they are threatened with death for testifying," Paredo said.

"If this is true the Marqués has caused the death of eleven men," Fray Pio said. "He must be tried as any murderer would be tried."

The Marqués said viciously, "I will not be judged on the lies of—"

"Enough!" Otermin struck the table. The Marqués stopped, his face pale with fury. Otermin sat scowling at the desk. Without looking up he said, "I will present your complaints to the corporation, Lucas Paredo. They will give you justice. You have my word on that. You will be given justice."

The Indian glanced uncertainly at Father Pio. The friar nodded and took the man's arm, talking to him in a low tone as they left. As soon as they were out the door the Marqués came close to the table, his lips gray with outrage.

"Obviously these are lies," he said.

"How is it obvious?" Otermin asked.

The Marqués closed his hand on the hilt of his rapier. When he finally spoke his voice did not betray so much emotion. Each word was as frigid as a piece of ice falling and breaking on the table.

"The visitor has taken testimony from all the priests now, Don Antonio. I know how serious were some of those charges against you. If they are not refuted Don Melchor Cárdenas would have every cause to remove you as governor. The only thing that can give them the lie now is the support of your *encomenderos*. If you betrayed one of us do you think any of the others would remain loyal?"

Governor Otermin did not look up. "Don Desidero, I will not be threatened. The audience is at an end."

The Marqués made a spiteful sound. It was like the hiss of a cat. Holding his sword against his leg so it would not swing in its baldric and catch going through the door, he left the room. Francisco Xavier made a muffled scratching behind the governor. Otermin paid him no heed. He was seething. Arrogant Creoles. Provincial pigs.

But he knew the Marqués was right. He was in no position to antagonize his *encomenderos*. He had fought with the military faction before, as often as he had quarreled with the clergy. But now he needed them. He could not afford to estrange them all by throwing one of his captains to the dogs. If he gave the Marqués his support now the man had enough influence among the other captains to insure that they would stand solidly behind Otermin. They knew that if the visitor became governor they would not have the freedom Otermin had given them. Don Melchor Cárdenas was not the man to tolerate abuses. Otermin closed his hands till the tendons ached.

"Francisco," he said, "you will burn all these petitions from San Juan."

"But Excellency, you promised Lucas Paredo——"

"I promised nothing! All these complaints are obviously lies. These elders and *caciques* are constantly stirring up trouble against our captains——"

A commotion at the door made him break off. He heard the sharp challenge of a guard, and then the door was pushed violently open and Luis Ribera stalked in. He was disheveled, caked with dirt, his torn left sleeve coppery with dried blood.

"I must speak with you——"

"Can you not go through the proper channels?" Otermin demanded angrily. "Can you pay no one a proper respect?"

The haggard look to Luis's face accented the sharp tilt of his cheekbones. Swaying, he walked toward them. "Nicolas Bua . . . murdered. Something in the Upper River. A danger . . . a plot."

The governor stared at him, finally rose and swung a chair out from the table. "Here . . . sit down. Don Francisco, summon Dr. Roybal. Also—some wine. Now——" He turned to Luis, who had slumped weakly into the chair. He had dealt with this young man's wild-eyed accusations before and approached the matter cynically. "This Nicolas Bua . . . you saw the murderer?"

"No." Luis held a hand to his eyes. "He was going to tell me something——"

"They gave you this wound?"

Luis hesitated. "I got it somewhere else. These runners——"

"What runners?"

Luis told him about the messengers with the knotted rope. Governor Otermin became aware that Francisco Xavier had been standing at his side for some time, holding a glass of wine. Impatiently he took it and gave it to Luis.

"This knotted rope . . ."

"Their way of sending messages. Perhaps the knots indicate how many days are left before this thing happens."

"This thing . . . plot . . . a danger!" Governor Otermin threw up his hands. "Nicolas Bua was friendly to us. He had many enemies——"

Luis flung the empty wine glass from him and stood up. "Do you think I would come back . . . face arrest by the Tribunal . . . if I did not believe this? You must do something. The town must be prepared, the outlying settlers warned."

"Upset the whole province because you saw a dead man?"

Luis was pale, trembling with weakness and frustration. *"Señor,* if you do not assemble the corporation immediately I will go to the visitor. I am sure Don Melchor would like to add this to the accusations already gathered against you. A governor who is warned of danger to his people . . . and who deliberately refuses to save them."

CHAPTER TWELVE

D R. FECUNDO ROYBAL had begun his career as the viceroy's barber, and the less fortunate among his patients claimed his medical skill had never exceeded the limits of shaving soap and a trimmed goatee. But he did possess a license from the *protomedico* in Mexico City, and such was the state of medicine in the colonies that he was the only man in all New Mexico who could lay claim, however dubious, to the title of doctor.

He arrived soon after the governor's summons, a pompous, fussing, paunchy man in buckled knee breeches and a scarlet coat. Purple veins netted his jowls and he had an affliction of the eyes that kept him blinking throughout his work. Without cleansing first, he poured hot oil into the wound, then cauterized it. Luis was so weak that he passed out with the pain of the cautery.

He regained consciousness a short time later in the governor's bed. His wound was bandaged and there was a tray of chocolate and *sopapillas* beside him. The puff-paste sweets were hardly appropriate for one in his condition, but the hot chocolate helped. He had grown strong enough to sit up by the time Don Bernabe stamped in, clattering his sword and spurs like a cavalry squadron on the march. He was dusty and tired from his long ride to Cochiti, and by the sour expression on his face Luis knew he had not caught any of the Navajo raiders.

"Well, now, what is this all about?" Don Bernabe asked.

Luis stared straight ahead, cheeks sucked with strain. Governor Otermin had followed Don Bernabe. He was in control of himself now and explained briefly.

"It may be nothing," he said. "However, I thought it best to present it to the corporation."

The old man turned his fierce eyes on the governor. "And this thing with the Holy Office . . . you have not subjected Luis to any further indignity?"

"I had to report his return. My duty." Otermin paused. "My messenger, however, tells me that Toribio Quintano cannot be found."

Francisco Xavier came apologetically to the door with the information that the corporation was beginning to arrive. Luis swung his legs to the floor. Don Bernabe wheeled toward him, as though to help.

Luis did not want the man to touch him. He stood quickly, before Don Bernabe could move, and caught at the bed to steady himself. He saw Don Bernabe looking at him closely. Did the man really think the flogging could be dismissed so simply? Did he actually believe Luis had been leaving town merely to escape the Inquisition?

Luis walked unsteadily past him, through the series of rooms to the council chamber. Don Celso Cárdenas sat at the table. He was Barbara's uncle, brother of the visitor, Don Melchor. He was an aging, spidery man with commercial interests in both Santa Fe and Mexico City, habitually stooped as though from a lifetime of bending over inventories and account books.

"May God give you good morning, Excellency," he said, smiling sycophantically at Otermin. "Important matters, so early——"

Otermin cut him off with a grunt and sat down. The senior councilman appeared, Don Evora Maynez, tall, white-haired, grave. With him were the rotund, jocular Alfonso Navarro and Father Pio, smiling worriedly and patting his stomach.

The last of the councilmen to appear was Luis's father. Though the Ribera family was one of the richest in the province, Don Cristobal's satin jacket and knee breeches always looked musty and tarnished. Gray hair clung like wisps of corn tassel to his fragile skull. He was nearsighted from too much reading, and he stood blinking in the center of the room like a frightened child surrounded by his frowning elders. When he recognized Luis he started toward him, lifting a hand.

"Luis . . . what passes? All this talk about the Holy Office—your mother is frantic——"

"Later," Don Bernabe said.

Don Cristobal glanced furtively at his father. Don Bernabe ignored him, spurs clattering as he walked to the table. Luis felt an angry resentment toward the old man. But it was an old picture. Don Bernabe had arranged his son's marriage for the sake of an alliance that would give Cristobal a seat on the corporation. Since then Cristobal had been nothing more than Don Bernabe's instrument on the council.

Don Cristobal was still looking after the old man, his mouth opening and closing. It made him seem ridiculously like a fish. Luis knew a helpless need to reassure his father. He touched Don Cristobal's arm, smiling stiffly, and then went to the table.

He felt oddly subdued. How many times had he revolted against these old men, openly criticized them, sneered behind their backs? Despite his rebellious nature he had not completely escaped the stamp of this land, where disrespect to parents or an elder was close to sacrilege. A lifetime of conditioning seemed to be reasserting itself. He felt as though he were facing a jury ready to condemn him for every impertinence he had ever committed. He cleared his throat and told his story. He recounted everything but Bigotes' part. Though the man's attempt on his life was what convinced him more than anything else of the true proportions of the danger, he could not reveal it. For an Indian to make an attempt on the life of an aristocrat was one of the most heinous crimes. If Bigotes were not already dead, his execution would be mandatory. When he had finished the story there was a moment of silence. Then they all began talking at once.

"It is simply a matter of enough soldiers," Don Bernabe said. "I will march up there . . . wipe those savages off the earth——"

"This is not a war," Don Celso said. "Money talks louder than swords. What about informers . . . a bribe?"

"The treasury is too deep in the red for such frivolities," the governor snapped. "I say we arrest those runners."

"Arrest them for what?" Fray Pio asked. "What crime have they committed? If I could only talk with them they would tell me what the rope means."

"It is obvious what it means," Luis said impatiently. "They have used this method for centuries to measure time. The knots must signify the number of days left before this thing happens. Arrest the runners and we give ourselves away. The Indians will know we suspect the plot——"

Governor Otermin cut him off. "You are here to report facts, not dictate policy."

Don Evora Maynez held up a hand. It was veined like a leaf, almost transparent with age. When it was silent, the senior councilman said:

"The young man makes sense. Let him go on."

Sullenly Otermin settled back in his chair. Luis put his good hand on the table to brace himself.

"I do not know exactly how many knots remained on that rope. It looked like two or three. At least we have that much time. I do not think those runners know I saw them. If they find out we suspect something they may act immediately. It would give us no time to prepare. On the other hand, if we let them go, chances are they will retain their original plan. It would give us a few days at least to get ready. The governor can send orders to all the outlying jurisdictions. Bring all the colonists into Santa Fe with their families, quietly, discreetly, so the Indians will not suspect."

"And all they might be running from is a secret Rain Dance in one of the Indian towns," the governor said.

Luis struck the table. "More than that. Arrest those runners and you might sign the death warrant of every Spaniard outside Santa Fe.

"Forget the messengers," Don Bernabe said. "I move we take the soldiers directly to San Juan. I will get at the bottom of this if I have to raze the town."

"No, no," protested Father Pio. "Violence will not help us now. It must be up to the Church. You cannot attack a peaceful village nor arrest men who have committed no crime. Gently, gently, I will find them and talk with them."

"And give us away," Luis shouted. "What is the difference if we talk to them or arrest them or execute them? The Indians will know. The thing will happen. You must save the outlying Spaniards first."

In all the din Governor Otermin had settled back in his chair, scowling and fingering his lip like a sullen child. He waited, staring doggedly at the table, until they had shouted themselves out. Then, characteristically setting himself against the conflicting desire of every faction in the room, he looked at his Maestro de Campo and said:

"Don Bernabe, you will take a squad from the palace. You will find those two runners. You will arrest them and bring them to me."

CHAPTER THIRTEEN

LA CONDESA VERONICA DE ZUMURRAGA woke earlier that morning than was her usual custom. She possessed one of the few beds in the town, a thing of massive carved posts and velvet tester and silken coverlet that had been shipped by muleback up the Camino Real from Mexico City. The bedroom was cool and dim, with only a hint of sunlight giving a yellow edge to the shabby damask drapes. She stirred luxuriously, yawning, and then rose to one elbow and looked at Toribio Quintano, who still slept beside her.

His mouth was open, revealing the stained, crooked teeth. It deepened the hungry hollows of his cheeks, adding to the curiously ravaged look of his face. His hands lay palm up, slightly cupped, on either side of his head. It gave him the appearance of a supplicant. It made him seem pathetically vulnerable. Perhaps, she thought, it is that I know you too well. She had seen the core of him—the doubts, the wounds, the scars lying beneath his shield of cruelty and bitter ambition.

She knew what a dangerous game she played with him. This outpost, at the end of the trail, on the edge of an unknown world, was her last possible refuge. And Toribio had gotten orders from the Inquisition to investigate and arrest her as a heretic and a *morisco*, inimical to the purity of the Faith in the New World. But while he had investigated she had spun her web, baiting it with the honey of a thousand wiles learned through a lifetime of using men. . . .

That lifetime had started in Granada, the last stronghold of the Moors. For eight centuries the Spaniards had fought to drive these Mohammedan invaders back across the Mediterranean to their African homeland. In the very year that Columbus sailed for America, Ferdinand and Isabella achieved the dream and united Spain. But the Moors left their stamp on the country, the architecture of Granada, its culture, even its people. The Condesa never knew how much or how little of their blood ran in her veins. She only knew that her mother worshiped Christ in public and read the Koran behind locked doors.

The Condesa had been plain Lupe Mariscal then. When she was fourteen the Holy Office sent its Soldiers of Christ to arrest her mother. The women forced Lupe to flee to distant relatives in Seville. Not until a year later did she learn that her mother had been burned at the stake.

At such an early age Lupe had already found out about her world and the place a woman occupied in it. Among the poor an unmarried woman with no family quickly became a wife or a whore. There was no middle ground, no other road to survival.

Before she became either she got a job dancing at a *bodegón*. It was an art she had learned from her mother. The tavern was one frequented by Murillo. She heard he was looking for a model. Knowing her flaws, she contrived to be above him on a stairway when they met. It mitigated the hawkishness of her face, made it look softer, more compassionate. It was her first big step in the calculated campaign against all men that was to characterize her whole life.

Murillo was intrigued, and the height of the model's dais achieved the same illusion as the stairway. She became one of his favorite subjects. Two years later, when the Inquisition once more threatened, Murillo obtained a forged license, registered her at the House of Trade under a false name, and obtained passage for her on a boat to New Spain.

In Mexico City, as Veronica Torres, Murillo's protégée, she found entree to the circle of Echave the Younger and the other artists of the capital. One of the wealthy patrons of Echave was the aging Conde de Zumurraga. The rumor that the count had made Veronica his wife originated when she got him to put his Santa Fe property in her name. It was the house of his son, deserted since the man's death in a battle with Apaches. Veronica had heard that a new inquisitor had arrived in Mexico City with her name on his file, and she was merely looking forward to the time when the Count's powerful patronage would no longer shield her from the Holy Office. A year later, in 1679, El Conde de Zumurraga died. . . .

She rose quietly, careful not to wake Toribio, and stood gazing down at him. There were blue bruises on her breasts from his cruel fingers, and her whole body ached. Why did she let him hurt her like that? She had never allowed men to be rough before. But it went deeper than roughness, this dark mixture of pleasure and pain.

Had he been true to his promise? Had he actually reported to the inquisitor that she was not the Lupe Mariscal whose mother was burned in Granada? Or was he just leading her deeper into the trap?

With a helpless shake of her head she slipped into the next room, clapping her hands softly for Chintule, the Zapotec slave the Count had given her. The scurrying little maid soon appeared. She and Cruz were the only servants in the household and were sworn to secrecy as to Toribio's presence there. In one mahogany-colored hand she held a little tray of chocolate and *bunuelos*.

The Condesa sat at her dressing table. Sipping and nibbling, she spent an hour recreating the remarkable illusion of her beauty, the calculated compound of glitter and cosmetics and perfumes that always made her seem out of place in the primitive austerity of these rooms. She invariably dressed as though at court, a blue satin dress, a jewelled comb twinkling beneath her snowy mantilla, the jade caravel of a cabochon emerald riding the swell of her breasts.

She was just rising from her mirror when Chintule returned hurriedly, twittering that Luis Ribera was in the parlor. The Condesa glanced quickly toward the bedroom where Toribio still slept. He had never stayed the full night before. Her whole safety depended upon the complete secrecy of their relationship. Heart pounding, she hurried into the *sala*.

Luis was pacing before the cone-shaped fireplace, his boots making a brittle clatter on the polychrome tiles. The sight of him, pale, dirty, unshaven, made her stop in surprise. Then she saw the ripped sleeve and the bandage.

"*Mi corazón*," she said. "My heart, what passes?"

She went to him with hands outstretched. He took them both, dipping his black head to kiss them, his mind obviously not on the gesture. "Condesa," he said. "I had to talk to someone . . . some sane adult human being in all this cage of jabbering idiots."

She told Chintule to get some wine and led him to a chair, trying to get some sense out of him. She shook her head impatiently as she saw that the maid had already opened the drapes of the windows overlooking the patio. Luis would become suspicious if she closed them all again. But that meant Toribio could not leave by the patio without Luis seeing him. And the only other doors from either her bedroom or dressing room opened directly onto this main parlor.

Luis was leaning forward sickly in the chair now, head in his hands, telling her the whole story, the murder, the runners, the scene in the palace. And Bigotes.

"I did not tell them, Condesa. I could not. But I must tell someone. It is what convinced me more than anything. Bigotes and I were companions. Do you know what that means? All my life we were *compañeros*. A man would not try to kill his companion unless it was something terrible, would he?"

"No, Luis, no." She could see the torture in him and stroked his hair.

"A choice . . . that was it. His companion or his people. I thought I knew him—all my life I thought I knew him. And I did not know him at all. His Indian mind . . . and now he is out there . . . maybe dead . . . companion . . . from my sword——"

"You could not help it. . . . Do not blame yourself."

Chintule came with wine and the Condesa served Luis, tilting the glass to his lips as though he were a sick child. It brought a flush of color to his cheeks. She tried to keep her eyes off the bedroom door. Their voices must have aroused Toribio. Somehow she had to get rid of Luis. She could see how exhausted he was. Perhaps if he drank enough wine he would fall asleep. But every time he thought of Bigotes it seemed to revive him.

"My sword . . . up to the hilt . . . his blood, Condesa, his blood, all over my hands."

"Please, Luis, stop torturing yourself. It does no good."

He sagged back, long legs sprawled out before him, prisms of light flashing against his heavy-lidded eyes as he twirled the empty glass in his hand. She refilled it. If she could only divert him. She smiled indulgently.

"You look like something out of 'Los Borrachos.'"

For a moment she thought he would not respond. Then he shook his head loosely. "You are right. It does no good. I must stop thinking about it." He drank again. He sighed heavily, resignedly. "Well . . . take my mind off of it." He paused—then with obvious effort he said, "Well, I thought we were going to support the Mexican school."

She shook her head. "I have tried. But I suppose one must be born in this country. Echave the Elder was not really a Mexican anyway. And the Younger is nothing but a pale imitation of Rubens."

"Then we are back to Velasquez." He blinked, trying to keep his eyes open.

"You just reminded me of 'Los Borrachos.' But that is not the best of the Bodegons. The best is the 'Two Young Men Eating.' That napkin, that wonderfully crumpled napkin. When a man can excite you about a napkin you know he has greatness."

It was a fragment of former conversations, when they had talked the night out about such things. But it was strained, false. He was answering absently, automatically, his eyes staring beyond her.

"You have deserted Murillo?" he asked.

"I did not say that. Would you believe it, I posed for his first Assumption." She leaned her head back and her face grew dreamy. "Can you see me as the Virgin?"

"Easily."

"Do not lie. But then I looked the part. I swear I did. Life does things to a woman . . ."

She kept talking until his head had tilted onto his chest and he was snoring softly. The wine glass slid from his relaxing hand and broke against the floor. He stirred. She sat painfully still, afraid her slightest movement would awaken him. The sight of him, disheveled, exhausted, hurt, touched her with compassion. And with the other confused emotion she always felt.

It had started a month ago, soon after her arrival from Mexico City. A meeting in the plaza, a conversation turning to art, an invitation to see her books and paintings. The usual motives had guided her. She still had not known where she stood with Toribio. An alliance with the scion of the most powerful family in the province might prove her salvation.

Through those first visits Luis seemed content to sit and talk of art, to listen while she read Tasso or played on her *vihuela*. It had been a blow to her vanity. But her pique soon passed, because she had never possessed the simple animal interest in sex for its own sake. Men had usually failed to arouse her, and when she bedded with them it had always been more for politics than passion. Like a cat with a ball of twine she had let the curious friendship spin itself out.

She began to cherish his casual visits. Santa Fe was a lonely place for her, at best. She had never known such a hungry mind. Luis had been able to satisfy few of his intellectual tendencies in this frontier capital. Most of the population was made up of third- or fourth-generation colonists who had known little or no education. Aside from a few aristocrats who had come from Mexico City, the priests were the only educated class. And among them were not many real scholars. The tutoring Father Pio had given Luis was limited, only whetting his appetite for the culture he had finally found in the Condesa. Luther,

Calvin, Erasmus, Don Quixote, Velasquez, Gongora, Kino, whether St. Didymaus or Gestas was the penitent thief, the stigmata of St. Francis, subjects sacred and profane, prohibited and revered, there were no bounds to the world of their talk. Veronica had a retentive mind, gathering facts not so much from a love of knowledge as from an almost automatic digestion of whatever was presented to it. If he ever suspected there was anything parroted about her knowledge he did not reveal it.

What surprised her was that such a mind could be exposed to so many forbidden subjects, could explore them so avidly, and still remain unshaken in its faith. It made her think of the Jesuits, most brilliant of all, who were deliberately exposed to every criticism of their faith in order that it might only be deepened. But perhaps it was not quite that, with Luis. Perhaps it was simply the Spaniard in him, the fatalist, ruled by intuition rather than logic, the man whose passions ran too deep to be reached by the mind. Belief could be a passion, as well as love, or hate. It could give a man a core that the whole glittering world of ideas could never touch . . .

Luis was still snoring and she took a chance and rose, skirt whispering as she walked carefully to the bedroom door. Toribio stood just inside. He had to step back to let her enter. She closed the door behind her. He had on his shoes and hose and tight velvet knee breeches but was naked above the waist. His body was so lean that every rib showed, and was smooth and hairless as no Spaniard's body could be. In one hand he held his shirt, in the other his cup-hilted rapier.

"A fascinating conversation," he said. His voice was accusative, sardonic, mocking, all at once.

Her tongue wet her lips. "You can cross the patio safely now. He will not see you."

"You said he was not coming any more."

"This is the first time in weeks."

"Why?"

"To talk."

"Of what?" He let his shirt drop and grasped her by both arms, his fingers digging in. "I will go in there myself. I will put him under arrest."

Her hands grew numb. She tried to twist her arms free. "Toribio, do not be foolish. It would ruin you to be found here like this . . . ruin us both!"

"Then get him out of here!"

"*Maldito* . . . you break my arms!"

The mewing sound she made, the contorted look of her face did something to him. The savage shape left his mouth; his eyes turned strange, seemed to lose focus.

"Condesa . . . never another woman! Never! I cannot stand to think of any man here . . . his hands on you, his eyes on you——"

He mauled her, kissing her eyes, her lips, her neck. The sounds of his lust disgusted her. She was in too much pain from his savage grip on her arms to make the usual pretense of excitement. But he mistook her writhings to get free for passion.

Her head was thrown back, her eyes squinted shut. "Toribio . . . you hurt . . . you hurt too much!"

She didn't realize how loudly she was calling. Fighting with him, her body pinned to his, she heard the door open. He held her a moment longer, then released her, stepping back and wheeling. The sword was still in his hand.

Luis stood in the doorway, blinking sleepily, eyes still glazed with drink. He looked at the two of them, the rumpled bed, the shirt on the floor, and finally at Toribio.

Luis leered tipsily. "Thousand pardons," he said. "I thought this was the road to Mexico City."

CHAPTER FOURTEEN

IT was ten in the morning when Luis left the Condesa's. The walled house stood apart from the main part of town, screened in cottonwoods and willows. Heat waves shimmered along the river. Distant walls deflected the sun in blinding splashes of light. There was a parched smell to the dust that sifted like powder from beneath his boots. Far to the north pregnant black clouds moved sullenly against the mountains, as though seeking to impale themselves on the jagged spires and spill the precious cargo of rain that had been threatening the Upper Valley for days now.

Luis turned off the Alameda toward the church. He was still thinking of Toribio—in her bed. Jealousy? Foolish. He had no claims on the Condesa. He did not even know exactly how he felt toward her.

Her body. He could not deny the attraction. Then what held him back? He had often wondered. It was hard to know. Perhaps the illusion she created. The fear that one step farther would shatter it.

Or perhaps when he came to the Condesa his mind was hungrier than his body. It was a thing he had shared with no one else, man or woman, in Santa Fe. He had a sense of the precariousness of the relationship, as though he were divided in two parts, the carnal and the mental, and one could not overlap the other without destroying both. He had slept in other beds, and of each one had sooner or later grown tired. And if he slept with the Condesa and grew tired, could they go back to St. Augustine and Plato and Velasquez as though nothing had happened between them? He doubted it. Her pride would not take that. It would be like an insidious defeat to both of them, a corrosion that would soon eat away the tenuous communion they now possessed.

It all sounded logical. It sounded fine. But there was something else, some further, shadowy barrier, eluding him, disturbing him. What was he afraid of? He cursed softly. It sounded silly in broad daylight. A woman was a woman. The next time, when she bent forward like that and showed him her breasts . . .

Luis looked back at the house. Toribio had not yet appeared. It convinced Luis that the man could not afford to have it known that he visited the Condesa. If the Condesa was really under the shadow of the Holy Office, as rumor had it, Toribio could well be ruined should it become known that he had let the bed come between him and his duty. Perhaps it gave Luis a weapon. Just what kind of a price would Toribio pay for his silence?

His head began to thump under the hot sun as he crossed the square. He grew so dizzy he almost fell. He sought the deep shade of the carriage entrance to the royal quadrangle. As he leaned against the wall, sweating and weak, he saw Don Bernabe's dusty stallion among the horses inside. He asked the guard if the Maestro de Campo had brought Indians back with him.

"He just came in with them, Don Luis. He said he caught them south of Santa Fe. What passes?"

Without answering, Luis hurried into the blessed coolness of the palace. The door to the council chamber was closed but the guard passed him through. The big room was crowded, filled with the ringing clatter of accouterments and the hubbub of angry voices. Pale dust swam in the bars of yellow sunlight that slanted across the corporation. Seated at the table, the four councilmen were arguing among themselves and with Governor Otermin, who kept fiddling with a knotted rope of palmilla fiber that lay in front of him.

At his flank stood two Pueblos from Tesuque, Catua and Omtua. They were stripped to the waist, guarded by three soldiers. Near them, talking with Fray Pio, was Don Bernabe. Dust made a gray spider web of the wrinkles in the flexible tops of his boots, pulled hip-high to sag in stiff creases against his thighs.

There were other Indians in the room, standing at the opposite end of the long table with another soldier. Luis saw Pedro de Tapia, the Tano interpreter. He was short, thick as a powder keg, bowlegged. He had an Oriental face with slyly pouting lips and a flat nose, its nostrils splayed and flaring like an excited stallion's. He wore more jewelry than a Pueblo squaw.

With him were the Indian governors of San Cristobal, San Marcos, and La Cienega, and the war captain of Pecos. He was named Juan Ye. He had the gaunt, hollow-cheeked look that branded so many of these men whose lives were dedicated to ordeals of the body and the spirit. His broad body was draped in a turkey-feather cloak hung with little copper bells from Mexico that tinkled with his slightest movement. Luis could make no sense from the angry counterpoint of loud voices, and he approached Father Pio. The friar answered his question in an agitated voice.

"Pedro de Tapia came in with these Tano chiefs about half an hour before your grandfather arrived with Catua and Omtua. It is impossible to believe, Luis. Impossible!"

Governor Otermin pounded the table to quiet the arguing men. He glared at Catua and Omtua. "I am not going to waste further time questioning you. If you will not tell me of your own accord I might as well let you know that Juan Ye has already told us what you are up to. I want him to repeat what he said just before you arrived."

Juan Ye glowered around the room—finally began. "Ever since Governor Trevino hanged Po-pe's father and the three other *caciques* five years ago, Po-pe has been going among the tribes. He has been preaching and telling them that they can bear this slavery no longer. Now some of the tribes have agreed to revolt. It is even said that some of the Apaches and Yutas will join."

"Why have you remained loyal?" Otermin demanded.

"We do not trust Po-pe," Juan Ye said. "We believe he seeks power for himself rather than the good of the people. We also do not think the Pueblos are strong enough to win."

Otermin scowled at the runners from Tesuque. "You have heard. Now I will give you two promises. The first is that if you continue refusing to speak you will be hanged. The second is that if you tell me the truth I will spare your lives."

The two Tewas stirred. The scar tissue of old whip stripes made a livid gridiron on Omtua's dusty back. Luis remembered that two years before Don Bernabe had found the youth with five others conducting a forbidden Deer Dance in the mountains. He was looking stubbornly at the floor and his fists were clenched. But now that he had been betrayed, there was not much use in remaining silent. Glaring balefully at the Pecos war chief, he said:

"Juan Ye speaks truth. The Pueblos of each village are to kill the *gachupines* in their district. No Spaniard will be spared . . . no woman, no child, not even the priests. When all the outlying estates are wiped out, all tribes will come to Santa Fe. You are all to be killed. There will not be a *gachupin* left in all New Mexico."

His voice rose as he spoke, becoming bitter, fanatical. When he was finished his head was raised and he was staring defiantly at the governor. The room broke into an uproar again.

In all the noise Governor Otermin's voice sounded curiously calm. "And the ropes?" he asked Omtua.

"They tell the time. For each day remaining there is a knot."

Automatically every eye in the room turned to the rope. Four knots.

"Well," Don Evora said, "it appears that Luis was right. And now, when their messengers do not appear, they will know we have discovered the plot. And we have lost four days in which to prepare."

Otermin shoved back his chair and rose. "You exaggerate this like a bunch of old hens." He paced across the room, waving a hand at Omtua. "This man would have us believe the whole Pueblo world is up in arms. Obviously that is not true. The Tanos have already shown their loyalty. With the messengers captured, how will the Keres south of Santa Fe know what is happening? That only leaves the Tewas. Of them San Ildefonso and San Juan cannot be involved. The Marqués de Gallegos was here this morning and would have informed me had he noticed any unrest. What does that leave us? Tesuque is too small to do harm. Taos and Pecuris. Do you think they will have the courage to act alone? I will send a warning. The *alcalde* can arrest this Po-pe and the war chiefs and the other leaders and hold them till things quiet down."

The man's eternal complacency infuriated Luis. He started toward the table. "You must do more than that . . . order the settlers in, send soldiers to protect them."

The governor's face looked apoplectic. He shouted at the guards. "Take him out. I will not put up with him any longer. Get him out."

The guards hesitated to put their hands on one of the Fine People. But the governor shouted again and they obeyed. Luis was too weak to struggle much. When they had him in the corridor they released him, apologizing effusively. He sagged against the wall, his head spinning. He saw that Father Pio had followed him out, closing the door.

This man had been Luis's father-confessor. He had taught Luis Latin. They had studied Herodotus and Torquemada together, had read Aristotle and St. Augustine. Though the Franciscan was disturbed now, the twinkle was not quite extinguished in his eyes.

"My son, you must not be so upset. You have always been one of the few Spaniards who truly knew these Pueblos. You should be the last to believe this wild fiction."

"Father, I do not want to believe. But there are those things . . . Nicolas Bua . . ."

"A tragic thing, Luis. But I am inclined to agree with the governor. A personal grudge."

"But Juan Ye——"

"They are afraid. They are holding a secret Rain Dance at one of the villages and do not want us to find out. They take this method of misleading us. I will go to Tesuque and talk with my children."

"Father, you cannot. They will know we have found out now, they will be waiting——"

The man smiled calmly. "Tesuque is my *visita*, Luis. They are my children. If there are some who have sinned I will confess them and absolve them. It has happened before. I know my children."

"But you cannot go—alone, unprotected——"

"Our Faith protects us, Luis. And I will not be alone." He looked at one of the soldiers. "Pedro Hidalgo has promised to accompany me."

Seeing that Father Pio could not be dissuaded, Luis said, "Then I will go also."

"You are in no condition, my son. You have great weakness from the wound; I can see it."

Luis stepped away from the support of the wall. The corridor seemed to tilt. He saw the priest hold out a hand, heard him say something. He knew he was falling. It was the last sensation he had.

CHAPTER FIFTEEN

I T was August 10. It was the day of Saint Lawrence. It was 7 A.M.
Governor Otermin went to attend early Mass at the church. He was
crossing the plaza when he saw Pedro Hidalgo gallop into the square.
He was surprised to see him so soon because Hidalgo and Father Pio
had left for Tesuque about three that morning. The man pulled his
lathered horse up before Otermin. He was covered with dust and
blood, gasping his story.

"Excellency . . . Tesuque. Dawn—the church empty. In the village
—nobody. Father Pio insisted on hunting. A quarter-mile north. Ravine! El Obi, many others—war paint, bows, lances. Father Pio: 'What
is this, my children, are you mad? I will help you . . . die a thousand
deaths for you.' They would not listen. A dozen arrows in his body.
El Obi shot first. I could do nothing for him. Nothing! I barely saved
my own neck——"

Governor Otermin returned to the palace with the man. He ordered the church bell rung and sent messengers to the houses outside
the quadrangle and the Analco across the river. The bell was soon ringing. The town shivered with its insistent clangor. As the brazen warning
went on and on the streets began to fill with people. The plaza became
jammed with horsemen and carts and servants and women on foot all
hurrying to the safety of the walled quadrangle. There were over eight
hundred people in the town, and the carriage entrance was choked
with the streaming crowd for an hour. When they were all inside the
heavy gate was closed and Governor Otermin emerged from the palace
with the corporation and three priests and some of the officers. A cart

had been drawn up at the edge of the large patio and the governor mounted it.

He was a man more at home barking commands at his troops than making formal speeches. Waiting for the crowd to grow quiet, he pulled nervously at his collar. He glanced at the Reverend Father Francisco de la Cadena, who stood with him in the cart, and then at Father Farfan, standing below by one of the wheels. At last the mob was quiet enough for him to begin.

"*Señores y señoras*—" He hesitated, moistening his lips. A girl giggled nervously. "In the name of the Two Majesties, our Almighty God and our beloved king, I, Antonio de Otermin, the duly appointed governor and captain general of this royal province of New Mexico, have thought it expedient—that is to say—for a measure of security . . ." He trailed off. He pulled at his collar again and angrily discarded the pretentious phrases. "What I mean is, you have been brought here for your safety. There has been uncovered a plot . . . a rumor of something among the Indians. So far the only real trouble has been Father Pio, killed at Tesuque—"

Father Cadena raised his hands. "We should not be grieved for Father Pio but should rejoice in his martyrdom. How many of us wished to die for Our Lord Jesus Christ in like ministry and have not been granted their wish?"

Otermin had waited with ill-concealed impatience till he could speak again. "The point is, there is no cause for alarm. You faced the same threat five years ago, under Governor Trevino, and nothing came of it. We know the Tanos are still loyal. Their chiefs came to warn us of the plot. I have sent notice to Upper River jurisdictions. When the Indians find us prepared they will stay peacefully in their villages. We will find the murderers of Father Pio and hang them in the plaza—"

"No," Father Cadena said. "This innocent blood must not be like that of Abel, which cried aloud for vengeance, but shall be a fountain of supplication for the repentance of those apostates who have forsaken the Cross!"

Otermin shook his head, lips compressing in stubborn anger. "We cannot permit them to go free. They must be made an example. It will nip this plot in the bud. I promise that with the bodies of the murderers hanging in the plaza tomorrow you can return to your homes in safety. I give you my word: There is no cause for alarm."

Taos lay twenty-five leagues north of Santa Fe, in a mountain valley seven thousand feet high. It was the northernmost of the *pueblos*, one of the largest, a town of two thousand people. In the most secret of its sixteen *kivas* sat Po-pe.

In the Stygian darkness of the underground chamber, he sat before Shipapu, the symbolic hole in the floor through which mankind had originally emerged from the Underworld. It was the dawn of August 10. He had been here for a night and a day, ever since returning from San Juan, fasting and meditating and communing with Those Above. He knew he would fast for three more days, until the date set for the revolt, but already visions had come to him.

A light fell on him and he stirred, blinking painfully. He saw that the hatch above him had been opened. From outside a drum throbbed. Jaca spoke from the hatch. He was a war chief of Taos, one of Po-pe's closest conspirators.

"I would not profane your fast, but from San Juan there are words of smoke. Catua and Omtua have been captured. The Spaniards know. The people of Tesuque have already fought."

Po-pe stared at the darkness in front of him. In a strained voice he said, "Then we must act now. Send the signals. Pass the words with smoke to every village. Today is the day."

He heard Jaca climbing down outside. He tried to rise but his legs were numb from sitting so long and would not do his bidding. He grasped the ledge running around the wall and finally managed to gain his feet. He groped for the ladder. The fast had left him dizzy. He must not let the others see his weakness. It was a good weakness. It came from the gods and gave a man strange powers. He climbed slowly into the daylight, blinking to adjust his eyes. In the sky to the south he could see a ragged trace of smoke and knew it to be a remnant of the signals from San Juan. On the ridge just east of Taos fresh signals were being made. The words would be read at Pecuris, six miles away, and would be transferred to the villages farther south. In a short time every Indian town along the river would be aroused.

As Po-pe climbed into the open he saw that the roof tops were swarming with women and children. The warriors were coming from other *kivas* where they had been feasting and dancing in preparation for the coming battle. Those who were not prepared were daubing themselves with paint and arming themselves with shields and lances. The *caciques* moved among them with prayer sticks and sprinkled them with sacred corn meal. Po-pe walked to the edge of the half-sunken chamber. He held up his arms. When they were silent he spoke.

"There will be no time for the scalp dances. No time for prayers or holy acts by the priests. Let my vision consecrate you. I was visited by Nan Kwijo herself. She took me to the Blue Stone Mountain and showed me all the world. It was once again our world. The tongue of the *gachupin* was heard no more. Jesus and Mary were slain by the Warrior Gods. They died. They did not live. Our ancestors once more revealed themselves in black thunderheads over the mountains. Rain fell upon dead Spaniards and upon living Indians. The drum was once more heard in the *kivas* and the dances were seen on sacred days. The corn grew and the melons grew and Kapika once more smiled upon the hunt. Walls were built from earth to heaven on all three roads. They kept the Spaniards out. If the Spaniards assumed the form of a coyote or a wolf and got in some other way I was given powers. I surrounded them with darkness and took their arms. I slew them. They died. They did not live."

Po-pe joined the braves and led them by the hundreds southward through the valley. As Po-pe ran he heard one of the warriors he had brought from San Juan begin the Tewa scalp dance song.

"Wembo o ipi na-a ri
Pu nan kang ngi wagi
itshu hwa ko ho-o . . ."

Angrily he told the man to be silent, they must not be heard. But as he ran on he could not forget the words. Every beat of his running feet seemed to send them pounding through his head.

". . . But yourselves you have to blame
Thighs earth-covered and streaked.
You die stretched-out lying now,
Mouth earth-covered and streaked . . ."

When the twin towers of the church were visible ahead the warriors took to cover, advancing on the mission through stunted cedars and thickets of brush and the dry irrigation ditches. They reached the buildings and climbed over the walls of patio and cloister. The bell ringer was just climbing into the belfry to ring matins. He was a sixteen-year-old boy whose loyalty to the priests was so strong that he had not been taken into the confidence of the Indians. He tried to yell a warning, but they pulled him from the ladder and killed him.

They ran through the church, shouting. They tore down the images of San Geronimo and Our Lady of Health and hacked them to pieces with their *macanas*. They set fire to the altar and clothing in the vestry.

Father Pedrosa ran into the church. He stopped, coughing in the thick smoke. Jaca ran toward him with a club. The priest raised his hands.

"Jaca, my son, it is not I you kill, but Our Lord. Would you take your place beside Iscariot?"

Jaca slowed down, hesitating. He had been baptized by this priest, had confessed to him, had spent all the mornings of his life at Mass in this church.

With a contemptuous shout, Po-pe crossed in front of Jaca. He drove his spear into Father Pedrosa's chest. The priest fell on his face on the floor with the spear protruding out of his back.

Mouth earth-covered and streaked.

The sun in his eyes awoke the Marqués de Gallegos in the bedroom of his house two leagues south of San Juan. He was still stiff with the long ride from Santa Fe yesterday. He had gotten home late at night. His son had told him that Captain Anaya had been there with a report of Po-pe's escape. The Marqués had dispatched a messenger immediately to Captain Anaya with orders to hunt Po-pe down and kill him. He half suspected that Father Morales had let Po-pe go. The priest was too indulgent. It was time to get rid of him . . . a transfer . . . the Marqués would write his brother in Mexico City.

Don Desidero yawned and looked at his wife, the corpulent Marquesa, just beginning to stir at his side. He rose and called for his manservant. Diego did not come. The Marqués dressed impatiently and went through the house, calling again. The noise aroused his sons and their families. The Marqués went into the patio.

It was empty. Even under ordinary circumstances there were always guards. They were nowhere in sight. The stableboy lay crumpled and bloody by the carriage house. Diego's dead body sprawled in the open gate.

It was hard for the Marqués to accept in the first shock. But the meaning could not be avoided. The Indians, slave and servant, had killed all the Spanish retainers who would remain loyal to the Gallegos', and then had deserted.

The Marqués hurried to the carriage entrance. But he was too late. A mass of warriors from San Juan approached through the cornfields. He tried to get the heavy gate shut, but they reached it and he knew he could not hold it against them.

He turned and ran for the house, shouting for his sons to arm themselves. He got his daughter, Antonia, and took her to his bedroom. His wife stood by the window in her nightdress. Alberto and Juan joined him with their wives and children. The Marqués had only a single pistol loaded when he heard the Pueblos come into the house. He knew how futile it would be to shoot one Indian in all that mob. He gave his pistol to his wife.

"When they enter the room, my beloved," he said.

The Marquesa took the pistol. "Antonia?" she asked.

"I will care for Antonia," he said. "Now, do you know the method?"

"The muzzle in my mouth?"

He nodded. He embraced her and made the Cross on her white face with his kisses. Then he placed Antonia against the wall and stood before her, a sword in his hands for the Indians, a knife for his daughter.

Juan and Alberto went down in the first rush. The Marqués placed the point of his knife against Antonia's heart.

"Forgive me, little one," he said.

She stared at him with enormous eyes. Before he could thrust, an Indian slashed him with a *macana* and knocked him away. The Marqués put his sword into the man and tried to swing back to Antonia. But a second Indian clubbed him to his knees. Another grabbed Antonia and ripped her dress off. Before he was struck again the Marqués saw his wife take the muzzle of the pistol from her own mouth and shoot Antonia in the face.

San Ildefonso lay six leagues north of Santa Fe, a village of eight hundred Indians and two resident priests. The habit of a lifetime caused Father Luis Morales to awake shortly after dawn. He waited for matins. But there was no sound of the bell. He sighed and thought indulgently of the young bellringer who had overslept. He would have to scold him again.

He rose and shook out his rough blue cassock. He was getting old. Sleep no longer refreshed him, and his joints ached from the hard bed. He had pains in his stomach, too, and Dr. Roybal had suggested that a handful of parched corn was not enough to carry a man through the day.

But the day stretched before him, like so many others, seven days a week, during the sixteen years that he had been here. The first thing after matins was always Mass. This morning it would celebrate the day of San Lorenzo. Leading the men in a song, Father Morales would march with them to their work in the fields. It was the end of sheep-shearing, and every available man was needed for the mission flocks. After blessing them and getting them started he would return to the mission.

For Father Morales the morning meant school. Class was held in the halls adjoining the dormitories back of the church. There were two dozen children under eight who must be taught to speak Latin. That would enable them to make the proper response at Mass and vespers. And another class of older children learning Castilian. From these he had chosen seven of the brightest and was teaching them to read.

At ten o'clock he would hold choir practice. He was teaching them the Nolasco *villancicos*, with words by Sor Juana.

Near noon would come a visit to the infirmary. There were always a dozen or more Indians waiting with some complaint or other. Juanito's broken arm. And the woman to be buried. He must remind the sacristan to lay out his black cope.

It would make him late to the workroom. There was a whole class of young women to be started in weaving and dyeing. He should inspect the convent wall the men were repairing. Probably have to lay a course of bricks himself to inspire them. And then, if he had time, he would return to the sheepshearing. The men would be exhausted by then and he could take someone's place in the pens.

After vespers, final prayers, and catechism, the Indians would retire to their homes and the friars to their cells. Here Father Morales would spend a precious hour reading St. Augustine or St. Thomas, until weariness blurred the words before his eyes. Then he would snuff out the candle and kneel to pray.

"Grant that I may not so much seek to be consoled as to console; to be understood as to understand; to be loved as to love; for it is in giving that we receive; it is in pardoning that we are pardoned; and it is in dying that we are born to eternal life."

Father Morales left his cell and found his companion priest, Father Antonio Sanchez de Pro, crossing the cloister. Father Antonio said he had looked into the village and there was no sign of people. Father Morales asked him to ring the bell. Surely it would summon them.

As the friar went to the belfry Father Morales hurried through the nave. The sacristan was nowhere in sight. He would have to don his vestments without help. The shuddering clang of the bell began to make the thick mud walls tremble. In the sacristy Father Morales put on his white amice and kissed the small cross in the middle and touched it to the top of his head. He put on the alb and tied the cincture around his waist. He pinned the maniple below his elbow and placed the stole around his neck and crossed it over his breast. He had donned the chasuble when he heard the Indians enter the church.

He went out of the sacristy and saw Father Antonio backing toward the altar. The Indians filling the doorway were all men. They were naked and painted and carried arms. Father Morales called them his children and told them they could not celebrate the Holy Mass in such fashion. The sacristan was among them, and he would not look at the priest when he spoke. He called him Father and said they had not come to celebrate Mass.

Father Luis understood. He took his cross in his hands and knelt to pray for them as they came toward him.

At Jemez, eighteen leagues due west of Santa Fe, Father Jesus Morador was awakened by a shouting outside his cell. Before he could rise the door was thrown open and a dozen Indians rushed in. They pulled him up and stripped him of his sleeping garment. They dragged him outside and they struck at him with clubs and fists. In the cloister three young men held a big struggling hog with rawhide ropes. The others tied Father Jesus naked on the hog and turned the hog loose.

Jemez was made up of five villages and had a population of thousands. The hog ran squealing through crowds of warriors who struck at the priest with knives and lances. From the roof tops women spat on him and screamed epithets. The children threw stones and drove the hog back and forth through the town till it was exhausted and fell to the ground. They untied the dazed and bleeding priest.

One of the warriors had gotten a pair of big Spanish spurs, and he forced the priest to rise to his hands and knees and then mounted him like a horse and spurred him and made him crawl on all fours across the plaza. Again the warriors struck at him with clubs and thrust their knives and lances into him till he fell dead beneath his spurred rider.

CHAPTER SIXTEEN

AT five in the afternoon of August 10 Ensign Lucero and Antonio Gómez arrived in Santa Fe. They had come from Taos. The *alcalde* of that jurisdiction had on August 9 received a rumor of impending trouble and had dispatched the two messengers previous to the uprising. The first sign Lucero and Gómez saw of the revolt was on the morning of the tenth when they reached the jurisdiction of La Canada, north of Santa Fe. They found the *alcalde*, Luis Quintana, besieged in his home with the other Spaniards of the district. Unable to break through and give aid, the two messengers had ridden on. They saw more evidence of the revolt from a distance, burning houses and several dead bodies. But the threat of Pueblo war parties made them fear to stop for further investigation.

Their report caused Governor Otermin to order his Maestro de Campo north with a squad to reconnoiter and ascertain the true condition of the Upper River.

Through that night and the next Luis Ribera tossed deliriously in one of the rooms of the royal houses. On the afternoon of the twelfth Don Bernabe returned from his scout to the north. The officers and corporation were assembled to hear his report. Fifteen minutes later Don Cristobal left the council room, sickened and shaken by what he had heard.

Outside the door he had to stop and lean against the wall. He thought he was going to vomit, as he had that time when he and Luis had gone hunting and he had shot the rabbit. It was strange that such a memory should come now. Why did violence always horrify him so?

A pair of soldiers passed, staring at him curiously. Quickly he turned and crossed the courtyard, avoiding other people, turning his eyes aside. He wanted to get away, escape, a small, dark room somewhere, away from the world's overwhelming cruelty. No, not dark, because he could not read. And he must read, he had to read, it was the only refuge that he had left.

He saw a group of women approaching and veered away, going quickly into the royal houses where the Cárdenas family had been staying. He shut the door and stood against it, his face clammy.

He blinked his eyes, and things seemed to swim into shape. His wife, fat, double-chinned, nodding, asleep in the chair. His son, on a mattress at her feet, on the floor.

How had he gotten here? He hadn't meant to come here. He didn't want to talk with Isabel now. She would question, those eternal questions, and he could not answer, he knew he could not tell her, he had to get away—

As Cristobal pulled the door open again the noise woke Doña Isabel. "What?" she asked. She sat up with a start, looking around blankly. Even before she saw her husband she reached up automatically to touch her gray, straggling hair. Hurriedly she tried to pat it back in place. She was breathing heavily, as though winded. "You have bad news, Cristobal. I can see it in your face."

"No. Nothing." He knew he had to divert her. "Why do you not go in the other room and get some sleep? You have been up all night. I will sit with Luis."

She looked uncertainly at her sleeping son. Satin hissed, stays creaked, and she was on her knees beside Luis. She pulled the blanket tenderly up to his chin. She made a motion of caressing his tangled black hair, though her plump hand did not touch his head.

"Little one, my baby," she whispered, "it is all right, my boy, my own little child, you will get well, just wait and see; your mother is here and you are safe—"

Cristobal leaned against the door, watching her. Strong emotion was like a sweet sickness in his mouth. He had wanted to be a priest. It had been the one great desire in his life. Then he would have been wed to the Church and all the people would have been his children. Would he have failed them as miserably as he had Doña Isabel and Luis?

Where was the flaw? Not his body. Its frailty was a poor excuse. Father Morales was more fragile. Yet who had worked harder, who had more courage? If only he had been able to give Isabel the love she needed. They had been joined by Don Bernabe's whim. They had been strangers before the wedding.

And that night, that first terrible night, when he had stayed on and on in the parlor, suffering the torture of the sly joking from the wedding guests, getting drunk for the first time in his life because he was afraid to go into the bedroom where Isabel waited. And Don Bernabe had finally dragged him to the door, like some balking animal, some whining cur, before all of them, and had pushed him inside. . . .

He heard his wife rise from beside Luis. She turned toward Cristobal. He saw her fat underlip trembling. He started to lift his hand toward her. Then he dropped it. She pressed both hands against her soft cheeks and turned away. He watched her move into the other room. He wondered how he had ever found the courage to get in bed with her that first night. He felt toward her as he would a sister. Would it have been the same with any woman?

He sat in the chair. He heard Isabel praying in the next room, heard her lie down. In a short time she was breathing heavily. Luis stirred and opened his eyes. He regarded his father blankly. It disturbed Cristobal.

"Well," he said, "you do not look so feverish."

Luis moistened his lips. His voice sounded feeble. "Dr. Roybal said the worst is over."

There was an awkward silence. Why did he always feel so balked before his son? The sense of latent violence in young men always made Cristobal apprehensive in their presence. Was not Luis getting more like Don Bernabe every day? Or could he see something of himself emerging in the boy? What about the restless mind, the search for knowledge, the love of ideas, books. Why could they never talk of books? Why could they not sit into the small hours of the night, as Luis did with the Condesa, just talking?

"Has Don Bernabe come back yet?" Luis asked.

Don Cristobal turned away. He almost got up from the chair. He could feel something slipping, something giving way inside, the way it had when the pressures of the *Ratio Studiorum* had grown too much for him at the Jesuit college in Mexico City. He gripped the back of the chair. He was being stupid. He was being very stupid. He could not hide from the horror by simply not speaking about it. He could not spend the rest of his life with his head in the ground. He felt ashamed before his son. Without turning around, he began to speak.

"Your grandfather has returned from his ride to the Upper River. They counted thirty Spanish bodies, scalped and mutilated, along the

road between Santa Fe and Santa Clara. In a ravine south of San Ildefonso they found the two dead messengers Governor Otermin sent
north on the ninth. That means the Marqués de Gallegos and the other
alcaldes of the Upper River never received warnings of the revolt. San
Ildefonso was deserted, the church a smoldering ruin. Inside they
found the murdered body of Father Morales, still clutching his cross,
and Father Antonio. The Indians were fortified at Santa Clara, and
Don Bernabe decided it was too great a risk to go any farther. Apparently every Spaniard in the Upper River has been wiped out, every priest killed, the churches sacked, desecrated, the homes burned,
everything destroyed."

After Don Cristobal had finished the recital of horror he stared emptily at the wall, his face gray and drained. Luis did not speak. Cristobal
could not look at the young man. He knew what would be in his face.
At last, in a voice that Cristobal did not recognize, Luis said:

"Surely the governor has ordered all the remaining Spaniards to
Santa Fe now."

Don Cristobal shook his head. "Otermin sent a courier south to the
lieutenant governor, requesting García to come to our aid. But Otermin
has not yet ordered Quintana to leave La Canada and come in. He
has not even ordered the people in Galisteo Valley to come in."

"Mother of God," Luis said. "Holy Mother of God."

That evening a messenger came from Cerillos, eighteen miles south
of Santa Fe. He said that the Spaniards there had gathered in the
home of Sergeant Vernabe Marquez. They were being besieged by
warriors from San Marcos and other villages. The fact that these Tanos
were involved meant that Juan Ye and his village had gone over to
the Indians. It was a bitter blow to the Spaniards. They had counted
heavily on the loyalty of the Tanos chiefs.

A detachment of soldiers was sent to Cerillos and managed to get
the refugees back to the safety of Santa Fe. The story they told piled
horror on horror. Apparently the whole of Galisteo Valley south of
Santa Fe was devastated. No word had been received from Fray Bernal,
the superintendent at Galisteo, and it was assumed that he and all
the Spaniards with him had perished. Otermin was finally moved
on the morning of the thirteenth to send couriers ordering the remaining Spaniards into the capital. The only one left to answer the summons was Quintana and his people at La Canada, who managed to
fight their way to safety.

On the fourteenth another refugee staggered into town. It was the

Marqués de Gallegos. There was a bandage on his head, veritably glued to his skull by a mat of dried blood and flesh. He was more dead than alive. He said that everyone in his jurisdiction had been massacred. During the battle in his home he had been struck on the head. Lying among the bodies of his household and the half-dozen Tewas that had been slain, he was apparently taken for dead. The Indians had stripped him and scalped him and had left him in the burning building. The pain of the flames had revived him and he had crawled into the fields. Hiding from the roving war parties, delirious much of the time, he had made his way to the capital.

That night a patrol captured two Tewas who told the Spaniards that the Pueblos had completed their devastation of the province outside Santa Fe and were now converging on the capital.

CHAPTER SEVENTEEN

ON the morning of August 15 Luis could no longer bear to remain in bed. Over the protests of his father and mother he got up and dressed. He was dizzy and weak, but he insisted on going outside.

It was a strange scene. Like cattle the people had been herded into the royal quadrangle, over a thousand of them now in a square of buildings and patios no bigger than two city blocks. Those who had not been able to get quarters inside had bedded down in the open, rolling their mattresses against the walls to sit on during the day. It was like the plaza on market day, densely crowded, dusty, smelly, the babble of voices never still. The men moved restlessly through the crowd, smoking, talking in subdued voices, their faces drawn and strained. Women sat on mattresses or benches, gossiping nervously, trying to sew, or simply waiting.

There was only one source of water for the whole fortress, a ditch that ran from the river and came in under the wall. A heavy guard was posted both outside and inside the wall, rationing water to the long line of servants who filled their buckets at the muddy trickle.

Luis's first thought was for the Condesa. He knew she would not be in the royal houses, and he went past the barracks toward the stables where the bulk of the servants and the poor were quartered. The kitchens of the palace were not adequate to feed all the people, and cook-fires had been built in this rear area. The odor of chile stew and simmering beans filled the air. But Don Cristobal had told Luis that they were already running low on food and it was being rationed too. Luis saw Nazario turning a quarter of beef on its spit. He looked for Kashana, the man's half-breed daughter, but she was nowhere in sight. He wondered if she had escaped to the Indians.

The colonists had brought their stock into the quadrangle with them. Hundreds of cattle were jammed into the corrals, bawling with thirst. But there were not enough pens for all the animals. Dusty ranks of horses stood at rope lines, pigs rooted in the dust, cackling chickens scratched and scurried underfoot. The ground was littered with droppings, and a haze of dust hung constantly over the milling herds. Luis moved unsteadily through the filth and the crowds until he saw the Condesa sitting on a mattress against a stable wall. Her *zambo* coachman crouched at her side like a watchdog. The little Zapotec maid was keeping the flies off with a big turkey-feather fan. The Condesa kept a smaller fan opened across her face. As crowded as the compound was, no one was near her. The shadow of the Inquisition was like some dread disease, instilling a greater fear in the rabble than anywhere else. The maid saw Luis and said something. The Condesa looked over the top of her fan, then rose quickly, a pathetic eagerness in her voice.

"Companion——" As he stopped before her she reached out and touched pale fingers gently to his bandaged arm. "Your wound . . . they would not let me see you."

"I am all right. How about you?"

"I have managed."

"Is there anything I can bring you? Are you getting enough food?"

"We will not starve."

There was a distinct pause. He had rarely felt awkward with the Condesa before. Was she thinking of the other day—her house—Toribio? Dust settled on them and he caught a hint of her perfume in the barnyard stench. She had not lowered the fan. He knew what this sun and heat and dust would do to her face. In a low voice she said:

"Out here we get so many wild rumors. How bad is it . . . really?"

"I will not lie to you. Santa Fe is cut off."

"How many Indians?"

He thought a moment. He had seen the official figures. Excluding the towns of the lower Rio Grande and those of the western Hopis, there were twenty-nine *pueblos*. "There are about thirty thousand Indians," he said. "If they have all joined in this, that would mean between three and four thousand warriors."

"And the Spanish?"

He hesitated. With another woman, with his mother, he might have tried to spare her by evasion or a lie. But there was something about the Condesa that demanded complete honesty. There were about three thousand Spaniards in the whole colony, he knew. Most of them had settled in little groups at the estates and ranches that hugged the Rio Grande along the hundred and twenty miles between Taos, north of Santa Fe, and Isleta, far to the south. The only settlement outside of Santa Fe large enough to be called a town was at Isleta, where Lieutenant Governor García was in command of the Lower River district. But Luis knew that none of those outside the walls could be counted on now.

"There are about a thousand people here now," he said. "Otermin has taken an official muster. Capable of bearing arms . . . one hundred and fifty-five men."

He saw her fingers tighten against the fan. It was the only reaction she gave. Finally she touched his arm again.

"You must not make it too long the first day. Thousand thanks for coming."

"If you need anything . . . anything at all . . ."

"Thousand thanks. I will send Chintule."

He was feeling weak and there was a buzzing in his ears, but he could not yet face the hot confinement of his quarters. He went to the chapel of Our Lady in the eastern tower of the palace. He had prayed for Father Pio since hearing of his death. But he had wanted to do it here, in the officers' chapel, where he had knelt in so many confessions to the priest, where he had confided in the friar more than in any other man—the hopes, the plans, the grandiloquent dreams, petty spites, desires, fears, mistakes, lusts, questions, doubts, all the secret corners of him that had remained hidden from the rest of the world. He knelt on the prayer stool and said ten Our Fathers and five Hail Marys. He prayed.

After he finished he went outside. He asked the sentry who was on duty in the tower room. The man told him Emilio and Torres held the watch from the hours of tierce to sext. Laboriously Luis climbed the narrow stairway. Halfway up he could hear the two men in their habitual argument.

"Croak on, old crow," Emilio said. "Damascus is the only steel."

"Heretic!" Torres said. "How can you twist a few strips of old tin together and have a blade? What do you know of steel? Of Toledo, sperm of fire, womb of the river?"

Luis reached the upper doorway and saw Emilio Valdez standing at one of the ports. The slant of morning sunlight glittered against the morion tilted back on his sweating head. The big brass ring dangling from one ear and the red kerchief on his head beneath his helmet gave him a wild, gypsy look. He was one of the pathetic handful of regulars attached to the *presidio*. The Santa Hermanedad had arrested him for highway robbery near Acapulco seven years ago. As was customary, he was given his choice of execution or conviction to a lifetime of military service on one of the frontiers.

"I will take a stronger blade," Torres said. He sat on the floor against one wall and he had his sword out. "Gift of the Tagus . . . its white sand and clear water." He clanked his sword against his armor. "Born only on darkest nights, when the red-hot steel shows its temper true or false."

"Blessed be the hour," Luis said.

Torres looked up in surprise. Then he grinned and said, "Blessed be the hour in which Christ was born." He made a thrusting motion with the sword and Luis could almost hear hot steel hiss in the water. "Holy Mary, who bore him." Torres thrust again—the master smith immersing his blade in a bucket drawn from the river Tagus. "The tempering will be good."

"If God wills," Luis said, finishing the ritual.

Torres cackled, made a big job of rising, and came to greet him. When Luis was fifteen Don Bernabe had turned him over to this old soldier for his military training. What Bigotes had taught Luis in the ways of a horse and a woman, Torres had taught him in the ways of a sword. The man occupied a unique position in the capital, being the only other salaried official beside the governor. As royal armorer he received three hundred and fifty pesos a year. At sixty-three he was little more than a skeleton held together by sinews and a few stringy muscles. His face was yellow and seamed and furred like a peach that had dried for years in the sun. He had only five teeth left, and he was always testing them with sucking noises. He spent half the day holding mescal in his mouth, hoping it would cure his diseased gums. He preserved the dignity of his office with royal pride, wearing full armor in the hottest weather.

"If you want to toss for it I will relieve one of you," Luis said.

"With that arm?" Emilio asked. "*Por Dios!* For God, if you do not get back to bed in a minute we will have to carry you back. Your face bears the color of a winding sheet."

Torres nodded sourly. "And when you are stronger we must get back to work. If a man is getting through your guard that high your riposte is slowing down."

"Companions," Emilio said.

They both looked at him. The convict was staring intently through the embrasure. Tension made the coppery flesh shimmer across his hard cheekbones. They joined him.

Height gave Luis a curious view of the town. Before him lay the plaza, twice as long as wide, a pale sheet of dust stretched among scattered buildings. Directly across from the palace, on the south side of the square, was the two-story Ribera house, colonnaded across its front by the slender posts supporting the balcony. Beyond it the other houses led the eye toward the river. Their flat roof tops made a haphazard patchwork of earth-colored squares and rectangles. Their mud surfaces had a blinding glare in the brilliant sunlight. At ceiling height the *vigas* appeared, the rafter ends that protruded from every wall at two-foot intervals and cast slanting spears of shadow blackly against the adobe.

Beyond all the buildings was the Rio Santa Fe, a vivid band of green cottonwoods and willows that hid the trickle of water beneath their massed foliage. And south of the river was the thinner scattering of buildings, interspersed with the green squares of cornfields and melon patches, the Analco. It was in this Indian suburb that Luis saw the motion, furtive as clouds passing the sun. The movement assumed shape, men, some naked, others wearing cuirasses and morions, some with bows or the Pueblo *macanas*, others carrying halberds and Spanish swords.

"They are painted," Emilio said.

"Torres," Luis said. "Sound the alarm. Get the governor."

By the time the governor arrived the Indians filled the cornfields of the Analco, and the clank and rattle of their arms came from the distance like the tinkle of a thousand bit chains. Otermin stomped up the stairs, followed by a retinue of officers. He glanced at Luis and then looked out the window.

The Indians were beginning to cross the river, choking the bridges and wading to the knees in the muddy water. A few of them had horses. One rode a handsome *overo* with a silver-mounted saddle. About his waist he wore a red taffeta ribbon, and he carried a pair of swords, a halberd, and had holstered on his saddle a pair of firelocks.

"That is the war chief of Pecos," Otermin said. "Captain Madrid— you will go to him, offer him safe conduct to the palace, in my name."

After the captain left, Luis followed Otermin and his staff into the main patio. It was jammed with people, and the governor ordered a squad of soldiers to form a cordon and move the crowd back to leave an open space around the gate. Then he sent for Pedro de Tapia, the Tano interpreter, who had remained loyal to them.

The man came scurrying from the stables. The copper bracelets encircling his arms to the elbows tinkled slyly. The immense turquoise earrings twisted and turned against his swarthy cheeks. The silver rings covering his thick fingers glittered in the strong light. He stopped before Otermin, posturing and sweating.

"This Juan Ye speaks Spanish," Otermin said. "But if there is any difficulty with certain words I will need your aid."

"I am at your disposal, Excellency," Tapia said. The insides of his flaring nostrils were pink as those of an albino horse.

Captain Madrid came through the shadowy tunnel of the carriage entrance, flanked by the Pecos chief. Juan Ye's face was a gruesome mask of sweat and glaucous war paint, and he let his eyes move arrogantly over the crowd. Dispensing with formalities, Governor Otermin said:

"John, why have you done this crazy thing, an Indian who speaks our tongue . . . who is so intelligent . . . living all your life among us, where I placed so much confidence in you?"

"They have made me war captain," Juan answered.

"And what is that red ribbon about your waist?"

"It is from the missal at Galisteo," Juan said. A woman cried sharply, and a sullen mutter swelled from the ranks of the soldiers. Juan Ye sat up in his Moorish saddle, his face turning savage. "Yes, you might as well know, we have killed all the priests and the *gachupines* at Galisteo and many other villages. And if you do not surrender to our demands you will die too."

An outraged shouting rose from the assembled people, and Captain Madrid cursed sharply and started to draw his sword.

"Captain," Otermin bawled. "It is with my word." It checked the hot-blooded officer, and Otermin turned back to Juan Ye, waiting till the tumult died. "You speak of demands."

"This white cross means peace. The red one means war. Choose the white one and there will be no war, but you must all leave the country. Choose the red one and you must all die, for we are many and you are few and having killed so many Spaniards and priests already we can kill all the rest."

Luis saw Otermin's hands strain into fists. He scowled at Juan Ye a long time before speaking.

"Then you are betraying us . . . when only six days ago you warned us of the runners from Tesuque and said you regarded us as friends."

"That was when you appeared strong. Now you appear weak, and we have decided to join the others."

"John . . . you and your people are all Catholic Christians. How can you live without your padres? You have perpetrated all these crimes already, but there can still be the pardon if you will return to obedience. Go back and tell your people in my name what I have said. Tell them that if they accept it and go home quietly I will promise them amnesty and pardon for all they have done."

The Indian regarded the governor insolently. "How can they believe you, when you have betrayed them so many times before?"

"By the Two Majesties I swear it. By God and His Most Catholic Majesty Carlos the Second."

"There is only one Spaniard here I would believe."

"Who is that?"

"Luis Ribera."

There was a restless mutter from the crowd. Governor Otermin looked behind him till he found Luis, who moved from among the men. He had been on his feet a long time and was feeling dizzy and unsteady. But he tried to meet Otermin's eyes levelly.

"Tell him I speak the truth," Otermin said.

Luis did not speak. An utter silence had settled over the crowd. Otermin was pale with the humiliation of being forced to turn to Luis for aid. But he touched the cross hanging around his neck.

"By the Holy Virgin, I swear it."

Luis was thinking of the whippings, the executions, the briberies, the lies. Holy Mother, he prayed, help me. But he could not speak. It was too late, and he could not speak.

Otermin's eyes grew bloodshot with fury. Juan Ye smirked, lifted the two painted crosses in a mocking salute, and wheeled the horse to ride back outside. As soon as he was gone Otermin shouted at a soldier:

"Sergeant Tellez—arrest this traitor, throw him in the jail!"

Don Bernabe stepped in front of Luis. "The lad is in no shape for that dungeon. Do you forget that he risked his life to bring us the first warning?"

Otermin was shaking. "Then confine him to his quarters. Get him out of my sight——"

The tumult of the patio drowned him out. Many of the women had dropped to their knees and had begun praying and calling on the saints. The captains and civil officials crowded around their governor, all talking at once.

"The white cross, the white cross," Don Celso Cárdenas cried excitedly. "We cannot fight so many—massacre—think of Galisteo, Father Bernal, Father Morales——"

"They have already shown their treachery," Don Juliano said. "Accept the white cross and what is to prevent them falling on us as soon as we reach open country?"

"The red cross!"

"The white cross . . ."

Luis felt sick. His body began to shake, and he turned and stumbled alone through the crowd to his room.

CHAPTER EIGHTEEN

LYING in his room, Luis could look out the door and see the preparations for war. He saw the horse handlers bringing the war horses of the *encomenderos* from the stables. He saw Ignacio bring Argel, his grandfather's stallion with the single white foot. He saw Don Bernabe appear, buckling on his cuirass, and help Ignacio load the two firelocks holstered at his saddle. He saw the long line of officers and men forming at the door of the chapel where Father Farfan and Father Cadena were holding confessional.

The line still extended from the officers' chapel when a sentry raised a shout and announced that Juan Ye was returning. Otermin received him as before. The Indian asked that all classes of Indians were to be given up by the Spaniards, that all Apache slaves and prisoners be released, as the Apache allies among the Pueblos were asking for them. Don Bernabe was standing at Luis's doorway and Luis heard him mutter savagely.

"They are playing for time. They are waiting for the rest of the allies to come from Taos and Pecuris and the Tewa villages."

"John," the governor said. "You know there are no Apaches among us. Go back and tell your people that unless they cease their outrages about San Miguel and leave the Analco there will be war."

Juan Ye left again. The Spaniards stood beside their horses, testing cinches, tightening armor, waiting in the hot afternoon sun. A sentry told Otermin that the Pecos chief had reached the Indians. Soon a strange wailing sound rose from beyond the river, a howl of rage coming from hundreds of throats. The Indians then blew trumpets and rang

the bell of Saint Michael's and began to move toward the palace. Otermin mounted his nervous stallion and turned toward his men.

"I will give you the advice Hernando Cortez gave his conquistadores
when they first touched the shores of New Spain. Charge with short-
ened lances held high, and always thrust for the face or the throat. A
lance through the body is harder to disengage, and your enemy can take
the shaft in his hands and pull you out of the saddle. Heed this word
and more of you will remain alive at the end of the day." He drew his
sword and held it before him like a cross. "Now: In the name of God
and the King."

"*Santiago!*"

A hundred Spaniards echoed the ancient battle cry of Saint James.
They swung into their saddles, and Otermin led them out the gate.
Two by two they passed Luis's door. At the Castilian pace they rode.
A *la gineta* they rode. With the short Moorish stirrup they rode to give
them greater leverage in the lance thrust. The helmets and the cuirasses
and the bronze stirrup plates and the lance tips gave off a jeweled glitter
in the blinding sun.

When they were gone the dust settled back into the patio and there
was silence. Luis stirred restlessly on his bed. He was glad he was too
weak to go, and he felt like a traitor. Where did he belong? He would
have to take his stand sooner or later, he knew that.

He stiffened at the first crash of gunfire. The people were crowded
along the walls and at the gate, watching. The sounds of battle came
to him for an interminable time after that, the rattle of arquebuses,
the shouts, the clank of armor, the scream of horses.

A dying sun stained the Sangre de Cristos with the crimson mantle
that had gained their name. A report came in that Otermin had driven
the Tanos to the edge of the Analco and with one more sortie would
have them in the open where he could cut them down and force them
to flee. Then the sentries in the tower at the northeast corner of the
royal quadrangle reported more Indians on the slope above the town.
They swarmed down through the trees and began firing at the walls.
A messenger was sent to Otermin. The Pueblos from the north had
arrived. With victory in his grasp, Otermin had to quit and return to
protect the palace.

There was sporadic fighting during the night. The next day the Spaniards had a true measure of their peril. Hordes of Indians were camped
on every side of the beleagured fortress. On the slopes of the mountains
overlooking the quadrangle were the tribes from Taos and Pecuris and

the Tewa villages of Nambe, San Ildefonso, Santa Clara, San Juan, and Tesuque. The Tanos investing the Analco had been joined during the night by powerful Keres tribes from Cochiti and Sia and Santo Domingo.

The colonists waited in dread for the first mass attack. What could one hundred and fifty-five Spaniards do against three thousand warriors?

But the Indians were apparently waiting for more reinforcements. It was rumored that warriors were still to come from the Keres village of Acoma, far to the west. It would be a formidable addition. Acoma was one of the largest towns, with fifteen hundred people.

War parties moved unmolested along the river and through the outlying parts of Santa Fe. They sacked the houses and barricaded themselves in some of the buildings south of the plaza.

Luis's fever was subsiding now, and his arm was not so swollen. He was up and down most of the day, trying to regain his strength for the battle he knew was to come. His grandfather spent the time storming at the servants and quarreling with the other officers. The old man was in a black mood. Ignacio, his personal servant for thirty years, had been lost in the battle the day before. The man was a full-blooded Tewa from Tesuque, and Luis harbored the suspicion that he had deserted to the Indians but did not want to deepen Don Bernabe's loss by mentioning it.

The next day the first mass attack came. Twenty-five hundred warriors hurled themselves against the royal houses. Luis was still not strong enough to fight and had to content himself with helping to load for an arquebusier in the chapel tower. Outside the main gate the Spaniards had constructed a ravelin—a half-moon fortification of trenches and earthen breastworks. Here were placed the two brass culverins, the same cannons Onate had brought north with him in the first colonization. Their devastating fire broke the attacks on the east side of the quadrangle. But they could not prevent the Indians from cutting the ditch that brought water to the royal houses, nor stop them from storming the front of the palace. They soon set fire to the east tower, and the whole Spanish garrison had to go outside to save the chapel.

They fought all afternoon and by nightfall almost every Spaniard was wounded. They had driven the Indians out of the plaza, and they barricaded themselves once more within the walls. But they had been unable to regain the ditch, or mend it. A thousand people huddled miserably inside the quadrangle without water.

Despite his burning thirst, Luis slept the night through, exhausted by his work in the tower. For breakfast he had a bowl of thin *atole* and half a piece of bread. His father said it would have to last him all day. There was not a grain of wheat or corn left in the garrison. The Indians attacked again during the day and were beaten off. Near evening Luis was assigned to guard duty with Emilio. Their post was the hole in the wall through which the ditch had brought water from the river. The ditch was dry now, save for a trickle of mud in the bottom, and a heavy chest of drawers had been dragged into the hole to block it.

Emilio sat against the wall, chin on his chest, eyes glazed with exhaustion. He had fought for ten hours yesterday and had stood watch half the night, and it was all he could do to keep awake. Beside him lay his morning star. Armament had not changed much in the century and a half since Cortez came to the New World, and though Emilio's archaic mace dated back to medieval times it was his favorite weapon. The morning star was the spiked iron ball, as big as two fists, attached to a hickory handle by a short length of iron chain. It was a lethal weapon and could crush a head like an eggshell.

Emilio looked disgustedly at the chest blocking the hole in the wall. "We might as well seal it with adobe and know we are safe. They will never get water through there again."

"It is our only hope," Luis said. "They tell me some of the animals have already died."

Across the compound Luis saw Toribio. Captain of the guard from vespers till compline, he was making his first rounds. He stopped to pass a word with the sentries at the main gate and moved on. Matarife followed at his heels. It did not alter the strange aura of loneliness that hovered over Toribio wherever he went. He could stand in a crowd and still seem alone.

"That Matarife—always with him," Luis said. "What passes, Emilio? Were they in Mexico City when you were?"

"Aye. Toribio was only a familiar of the Holy Office then. But Matarife was always there—a dog at his heels. I do not know, Don Luis. It has been a mystery."

The sheriff passed a line of women huddled against the wall. They drew their shawls over their faces or looked away. He seemed oblivious to them. Exhaustion lent accent to the ravaged look of his sunken, pocked cheeks. There was a long red scar on his face, puckered and healing badly, and his cuirass was dented in a dozen places from the fighting. As he approached the post Luis gave him the all's well.

Toribio halted by the ditch. "Have you seen Pedro de Tapia?"

"The interpreter? Not today."

"The governor wants him. He is not to be found."

"His loyalty always did seem false to me," Luis said. "He was one of their war chiefs. Perhaps he has slipped out and gone back to them."

Toribio did not answer. A sardonic glow had been in his eyes while they talked, a watchful, calculating look. Luis knew what was on his mind. It was their first meeting since Luis had seen the man at the Condesa's. Lowering his voice so Emilio could not hear, Toribio said: "By indications—you have not spoken of what you saw the other day."

Luis smiled bleakly. "I thought it might be more valuable to me if I kept silent."

"Do you think silence will buy your freedom?"

"That lies with you."

Toribio did not answer. He seemed too exhausted to feel anger. His face had a brooding, melancholy look. Matarife stirred behind him, fingering his misericord and peering at Luis like a bright-eyed monkey. Toribio turned and walked away. His spurs tinkled and clanked. He always wore them, even when it was unnecessary.

Luis watched the two men go. If he had received a reprieve, he realized it was a dubious one. Perhaps Toribio would not be content simply to buy his silence. As long as he remained alive Luis's knowledge would threaten the sheriff. There were too many ways of stopping a man's mouth, and Toribio knew them all.

Luis saw that Emilio had fallen asleep against the wall. He shook the man. Emilio looked up, startled. He licked cracked lips.

"I cannot help it, Don Luis. My eyes they will not remain open."

"If they see you sleeping on guard you will be shot. Crawl behind those barrels. I will warn you when Toribio comes again."

Emilio crawled among the barrels that had once been filled with water. They hid him from the courtyard. Luis paced, trying to get his mind off his intense thirst. It was dusk now and he looked northward. Thunder growled among distant peaks; he could see the faint flash of lightning. Somewhere up there the long threatening storm had broken. It might not move down to Santa Fe but it would put water in the Rio Grande. The irony of it struck him. The Indians would certainly take it as a sign. Jesus and Mary had failed them, but as soon as they had replaced their old gods they had been given water.

He thought of Bigotes up there somewhere, in the storm, with the wound in him, the pain. Or maybe he did not feel pain now.

Luis closed his eyes.

"Bigotes . . ."

When he opened his eyes a woman stood before him.

She looked so Indian that he reached for the hilt of his sword. Then he saw that it was Nazario's daughter. It was Kashana.

"I thought you had run off to the Indians," he said.

She showed him a clay pot. "I came for water."

"You know there is none. You are not even supposed to be here."

How could there be any shape to her body beneath all that clumsy clothing? How could he be so conscious of it? Over her white cotton dress she wore the traditional black mantle. It was wrapped around her body, over her right shoulder and under her left arm, held in place by a Navajo belt of immense silver bosses. And he realized why he had not heard her approach. Though she wore the heavy white leggings, she was barefooted.

"At the *bodegón*," he said, "at the tavern of your father, that night I got drunk—you knew about the revolt."

"No."

"You must have known. *Señor Gachupin*, you said."

"It was just a feeling," she said. "All the Indians had it. Many of them did not understand exactly what, they only knew . . . something."

A change had come to her face, the sullen withdrawal that always turned her eyes so blank. So Indian. It made him think of all the times they had clashed, the nasty little game that had developed between them, making him goad her and mock her in an attempt to break through her impassive shell. It seemed stupid now, childish.

"Kashana," he said. "You and I—there is no use fighting any more."

He had stepped toward her and it caused her to back up. She looked like a startled deer. There were no deep shadows to outline the exotic shape of her face, the oblique hollows, the Oriental cheekbones. It made her seem softer, innocent.

He followed her back. "I mean it. I was drunk most of the time. I came to the tavern when I had fought with my grandfather or the governor or somebody else. I had anger at the world and I had to strike back at something. It should not be this way between us."

She continued to back up. But they had angled across one of the royal houses and a few more paces backward would take her into a blind corner. He held out his hand.

"Kashana. You never told me what it meant."

Watching him warily, questioningly, she said, "In Keres, Kashana means White Corn."

She backed into the wall. She looked around, as though surprised. He expected anger, an attempt at flight. But when she turned her face back to him her eyes were lowered and she did not move.

He did not want to offend her again. He had never seen her like this and did not want to break the mood. But there was a growing throb at his temples. There was that consciousness of her body. Exhaustion and thirst and fever made him giddy, filled him with a drunken recklessness.

"Kashana," he said.

She fought him. Her hands clawed frantically, raking his face. He kissed her. Her body arched, trying to drive him back. She struck wildly at him. She made frantic whimpering sounds and clung to him. Her nails ripped his face, and then she took the bleeding cheeks in both hands and kissed him open-mouthed. Her body was heavy and soft against him and he felt her shudder. She bit his cheeks, his lips, his neck. Her hands tore at his clothes, trying to push him away, trying to pull him closer.

There was a sound somewhere behind him, like a shout. He took his lips from hers, tried to turn and look. She fought to twist free. She struggled to hold him. There were more shouts now, a gunshot, a piercing yell. She had led him behind an angle of the royal houses so that he could not see the south section of the quadrangle. He had to run from behind the wall.

All he could see in the growing darkness was a rush of movement across the compound. A fight had begun at the gate—a struggling knot of shadows, Spanish curses, the flash of gunfire. Nearer, where the ditch came through the wall, was another fight. Emilio!

Drawing his sword, Luis ran toward the spot. As he drew near, the figures gained definition. The body of a half-naked Indian lay in a heap at Emilio's feet. Another was circling him with a lance.

Before Luis could reach them the Pueblo lunged. Emilio dodged and swung his mace. The spiked morning star struck the Indian's head with a sharp crunch. The man went down without a sound.

Luis saw that the heavy chest no longer blocked the hole in the wall. It completed the picture for him. The Indians had crawled in by the ditch and pushed the chest away from outside. They had not seen Emilio behind the barrels, and all but two of their party had gotten inside and started across the compound before Emilio woke. Now the Indians had overwhelmed the guards at the *zaguán* and were opening the main gate and setting it to the torch. They rushed through the tunnel-like entrance to attack the rear of the ravelin outside.

At the same time a horde of Indians burst upon the front of the ravelin, coming from the timbered hills and the outlying buildings of the smoldering town. The Spanish guards and gunners in the ravelin, completely unprepared for the attack on their rear, were caught in the jaws of a nutcracker.

The shouts and first gunshots had already aroused the palace. A shadowy mob of infantry ran from the barracks, armor clanking, sergeants shouting orders and questions. A dozen doors in the royal houses were flung open and the yellow shafts of light from within made fluttering silhouettes of the officers as they plunged into the courtyard.

"Stay here," Luis told Emilio. "Get that chest back in the hole."

He ran for the gate. Governor Otermin plunged from the palace in his shirtsleeves, wiping chile juice from his mouth with the back of one hairy hand, holding his sword in the other.

"The gate," Luis yelled. "They already have the cannons. They will be inside next."

Otermin joined him, running toward the gate. The Pueblos had already overwhelmed the gunners in the ravelin and were turning the cannons around. A few Spaniards had managed to fight their way free and were making a stand in the *zaguán*. The flames of the burning gate flickered redly against dented cuirasses, plucked painted faces from the outer night like contorted Halloween masks.

Otermin pointed his sword at a mounted figure. "Captain Madrid, you can do nothing alone. Mount a squadron of lancers. We will need them to save the guns!"

Then they were in the tunnel of the *zaguán*, and Luis was one of the shouting band of Spaniards struggling to stem the Pueblo tide.

Fighting beside Luis, the governor was struck in the face by an arrow. He dropped his sword and went to his knees. Luis jumped in front of him, hacking at an Indian who tried to finish off the wounded man. Otermin retrieved his sword, caught Luis's belt, used it to pull himself up. Wiping blood from his face, he plunged once more into the battle.

Spanish infantry filled the tunnel now, a wall of armor and swords that drove the naked Pueblos back into the half-moon ravelin outside the walls.

Beyond the red circle of firelight Luis had but a dim sense of the mass of Indians swarming on the earthen parapets of the ravelin. All along the outside of the royal houses a howling mob of them had thrown scaling ladders against the walls and were trying to reach their tops.

Then Luis was stunned by a blow against his morion.

He fell to his hands and knees. In the smoke the man who had struck him loomed above Luis, distorted and unrecognizable. All he could see was the quilted leather *esquipile* the man wore and the upraised arms holding the halberd to strike again.

A Spaniard stepped across Luis, hacking head-high with his sword. The man in the leather tunic staggered back, clapping both hands to his slashed face. The Spaniard who had saved Luis was his grandfather.

"On your feet, man," shouted Don Bernabe.

Luis recovered his sword and rose beside the old man. He saw that they were only a short distance from the cannons. A dozen Indians were working frantically to haul the pieces from their embrasures and turn them on the Spaniards.

"*Santiago*," bawled Don Bernabe. "Trust God and hammer on."

Roaring the ancient battle cries of Castile, he and Luis ran into the thick of the Indians around the nearer gun. Otermin joined them, and their savage rush carried them to the cannon. From the parapet twenty feet to their flank an Indian discharged his arquebus. Otermin took the ball in the chest, staggering and falling.

"Back to back," Don Bernabe shouted. "Let their bile out with Ribera steel."

The backplate of Luis's cuirass clashed against that of his grandfather. Knife in one hand, sword in the other, the two men hacked and slashed at every painted face that came within reach.

Surrounded by the howling savages, the two Spaniards seemed to bear charmed lives. It was more than armor and a yard of steel protecting them. A fierce exultation swept Luis, a brand of excitement he had never known before. He began to shout with Don Bernabe, cursing like a wild man, screaming the Santiago every time his blade found a new mark.

Then the moment was gone. They were surrounded by their own again, and the Indians were driven from the embrasure and the perimeter of battle spread away. In the momentary respite the old man turned to his grandson. His bony cheeks were caked with powder smoke, wet with blood, and he was gasping mightily for air. But a fierce pride blazed in his eyes. He pounded Luis on the shoulder.

"*Muy hombre!*" he panted. "Very man!"

Luis grinned recklessly. He could not help it. He realized that it was the first time he had smiled at Don Bernabe in months. But how could you hold any hate for a man who had stood back to back with you in such a battle?

A pair of soldiers were trying to carry Otermin back within the fort. He struggled to his feet, shaking them off. The bullet had torn his pectoral badly and his shirt was soaked with blood, but he would not leave the field of battle.

"We cannot hold them here," he said. "Save the guns—get them inside!"

A score of arquebusiers had gained the breastworks of the ravelin now and were pouring a withering fire into the storming ranks of Pueblos. It enabled the Spaniards to hold the redoubt till Captain Madrid could bring horsemen to the cannon. They put rawhide ropes on the guns and dragged them through the gate.

Wave after wave of the crazed enemy was thrown against the Spaniards crouched in the ravelin. Knowing it was but a matter of minutes before they were overwhelmed, they retreated after the cannons. There was another savage battle inside the entryway, with the Pueblos hurling suicidal charges against the narrow passage.

Then word came that the cannons were set up again across the courtyard. The Spaniards retreated into the compound, leaving a field of fire for the guns.

The first wild rush of the Pueblos through the *zaguán* was met by a blast from both guns. The Indians were massed a dozen deep in the narrow tunnel, and the heavy cannonballs cut a terrible swathe through their bodies. The bloody carnage checked the Indians a moment. Those who had not been hit drew back to the outside in fear and horror.

Despite his wounds, Otermin moved swiftly among his men, issuing orders that drew the arquebusiers up in ranks on either side of the cannons. He was none too soon. The Indians made their second rush before the royal artillery was reloaded. This time it was the arquebusiers who stopped them, pouring a galling fire into the running mass. Again the narrow bottleneck made them helpless targets.

Standing near one of the cannons, Luis was sickened by the sight of the mangled bodies writhing in the smoke-filled passage. He turned away, muttering under his breath, "For God, do not let them come again."

Apparently the Pueblos realized the futility of trying to gain the palace through the narrow gate. They did not charge a third time. Smoke from the burning gates cast a merciful curtain over the dead and dying in the *zaguán*. The Spaniards did not dare give them aid for fear they would be shot down from outside.

The exhausted soldiers stood in their ranks, leaning on halberds and swords, or sat beside their arquebuses, grimy faces turned tensely toward the wall. Herded like cattle into the stableyard or crowded into the cramped rooms of the royal houses, the women and children and servants waited anxiously. A constant sound flowed from them, hardly human, like the wail of sick animals.

Luis felt utterly drained, sick and trembling in reaction to the violence. When a soldier came to tell him the governor wished to see him, Luis shambled listlessly through the ranks toward the palace. A chair had been placed before the main door to the palace. Governor Otermin sat in it, surrounded by his officers.

Dr. Roybal had already cauterized two arrow wounds in his face and was working on the deeper wound in his chest. Luis halted before them. Otermin swore as Roybal burned him.

"Enough, butcher! You are not branding sheep." The governor looked angrily at Luis. "You were the officer at the ditch?"

Luis nodded dully. "Yes."

"Can you never address me properly?"

"Yes, *Excellency*."

Otermin scowled at him. "Well . . . how did this happen?"

Luis hesitated. How could he explain it? Toying with a wench while he was supposed to be on guard. But it had not started out as toying. How *had* it started? There had been too much excitement up till now to look back, to see the implications. Had she lured him away? But how had she known the Indians would be coming? Then he remembered the disappearance of Pedro de Tapia.

The plan had not come from the Indians then. It had come from Kashana.

"Well?" Otermin said.

Yet how could he be sure? It all had not been an act. That surprising burst of passion he had drawn from her had been no pretense. It could not be! Then how much was real and how much false? Or was any of it false? If he told them the truth they would execute her. He might be condemning an innocent girl.

"Who was the guard with you?" Otermin said impatiently. "If you will not speak, perhaps he will."

There was a stir among the soldiers and Emilio stepped forward. "The blame is mine, Excellency. I was asleep."

"No, no," Luis protested. "He is only trying to cover up for me. It was my blunder." He realized now that he had to lie to protect both of them. He could not betray Kashana without being sure of her guilt. And a guard who slept at his post would be executed. He said, "There was a sound by the royal houses. I sent Emilio to investigate. I was so exhausted that I did not hear them pushing the chest out of the hole. They were upon me. While I fought two of them, the others ran for the gate."

The governor was only half convinced. He closed his eyes and pressed the ends of his fingers tightly against his temples.

"You cannot be human," he said. "One single human being could not possibly cause me so much trouble."

"So the boy made a mistake," Don Bernabe said. "Has he not redeemed himself? Could we have gotten the guns back without him?"

Otermin opened his eyes. But he did not answer. All about him the soldiers were looking toward the east. A crimson glow was seeping into the sky behind the walls. There was a sound like someone crumpling stiff paper. A shadowy scarf drifted across the rising moon, gradually blotting out its light. The smell of smoke reached Luis, pungent and acrid. Its black cloud drifted over the royal houses like a funeral pall.

"The town," Dr. Roybal said. "They have fired the whole town."

CHAPTER NINETEEN

THROUGHOUT the night the burning town reddened the sky above the royal houses. Throughout the night the Spaniards huddled in the main patio behind their cannons, fighting off attack after attack. The Indians marched around the quadrangle outside, chanting victory songs and mocking the Spaniards with the Latin liturgy. The barbaric sound was joined from within the walls by the crazed bawling of cattle and the whinnying of horses that had been for two days without water. The men were as frantic as the animals. One soldier lay on his face all night in the bottom of the irrigation ditch, licking pitifully at the mud. Others in desperation reopened wounds and sucked their own blood.

Luis was so sick and weak from the battle that he finally had to go to his quarters and lie down. He managed to sleep but he woke before dawn. His dreams had been full of strange laments. He could still hear them from the patio outside. There was a painful pressure behind his eyes. His throat was dry and burning and his tongue so swollen that he could hardly swallow. Unable to lie still, he rose and went outside.

He saw that it was the women wailing. Three Spaniards had been killed in the battle for the cannons. Each lay in a newly-made pine coffin, a candle at the foot and the head. Their families were gathered around the coffins for the *velorio*, chanting in unison the prayers and hymns of devotion to the patron saints. Over it all, like the piercing ululation of animals in pain, came the laments of the women.

The candles cast a weird light against their chalky faces, their glazed eyes, their slack mouths. Sometimes it was the wives, rocking back and forth and screaming or sobbing their grief. When they grew exhausted a mother took up the chant, or a daughter. Other women held the weaping ones and comforted them.

Luis wanted to escape the chilling sound. He crossed the courtyard toward the stables. Kashana was on his mind. He had to find her. To get the truth out of her somehow. To know if she had really lured him away from his post yesterday, if he was protecting a traitor. Yet—half Indian—traitor to whom?

He saw Toribio making his rounds of the sentry posts. Behind him walked the inevitable Matarife. The quilting on the sergeant's leather tunic had been cut in several places, and the cotton stuffing was coming out. His simian face was rendered even more macabre by an ugly wound, a deep slice that ran from his ear to the point of his jaw.

It stopped Luis—remembering the unrecognizable figure that had loomed above him in the smoke of battle yesterday, the upraised halberd, the leather *esquipile*, Don Bernabe hacking the man across the face. Luis had taken it for granted that it was a Pueblo. He watched until Toribio and Matarife disappeared among the ranks of soldiers.

It was a long time before Luis moved again. He turned a corner of the royal houses and saw a figure huddled on a bench before a door, crying pitifully. It was a girl. She raised her head as he approached. Her voice shook with suppressed hysteria.

"Father, is there not anything left? Not even a drop of wine, sacramental wine, anything? I cannot stand it any longer—anything—burning up, just anything——"

He saw that it was Barbara de Cárdenas, and said softly, "I am not your father, and I have nothing to drink."

She peered closer, recognizing him. "Oh," she said.

She bowed her head, knotting her hands in her shawl. He saw that she was trembling and biting her lip. He remembered how he had thought of her. Seventeen. That mysterious, sad, exciting, tearful age between girlhood and womanhood, a silly goose, giggling one moment, blushing the next, lace and perfume and cascara and white lead, a pathetic attempt to give bloom to a weed, daydreams of knights, white horses, maidens in the tower.

It was a picture that had irritated and disgusted him. But now he could only feel sorry for her. He knew the abysmal terror these last days must have held for her. He sat beside her.

"I know you still must hate me——"

"I do not hate you," she said. Her voice trembled. "It is a matter of indifference to me."

"Of course. I only wanted to say—to tell you—this cannot last forever. We will probably make another sally at dawn and get the water back. Then when the Indians see that we are impregnable within the walls they will offer us some terms of peace."

She moistened her lips, looking up at him. "Are you sure?"

He was lying. He knew he was lying. But the feeble hope in her voice made him go on. "Of truth. Do I not know these people? They are unable to sustain a long campaign. They will go away. Then you will learn the beauty of this country."

She said bitterly, "How can you feel that way, after this . . . ?"

"Have you ever taken a close look at the piñons?" he asked.

"Ugly, twisted little things."

"And the smoke of the *enebro*. Surely you have smelled the cedar smoke. Once you do, you can never forget it."

"I will be glad to forget it."

He looked toward the Mountains of the Blood of Christ. "Up there are places. Places where you run when you are hurt. Places you go when you just want to be alone. You can sit all day long and just look. It is the feeling you get when you pray."

"Cruel," she said. "Cruel."

"There is beauty in cruelty too——"

She rose, her voice high, shrill. "My father says that everything outside Santa Fe has been destroyed. That means all the missions. That means over twenty priests killed. That means hundreds of colonists murdered. How can you sit here . . . how can you sit here and talk about beauty?"

She knotted her shawl fiercely in her hands. Her face looked twisted, wild. She turned and ran toward one of the royal houses where her family was staying. She pushed blindly through the door, and before it was closed behind her he could hear her break into a hysterical sobbing.

CHAPTER TWENTY

Don BERNABE had tried to sleep behind the barricades in the patio during the night. But he was too thirsty and his bad leg ached too much and the noise never seemed to stop. Outside the Indians made the night hideous with their orgies. And inside, for endless hours, the women had been lamenting.

A movement by the royal houses distracted his attention. It was Luis crossing the courtyard. Don Bernabe felt a flush of affectionate pride. *Muy hombre,* Luis. How magnificent the boy had been. They were together now. It had been in Luis's eyes after the fight. Don Bernabe had seen it happen to other men in battle, the sudden forging of a bond that nothing else could have created. It was ironic, in a way. All his life he had sought to bridge the gap between them. And in the end it had not been love or understanding that achieved it, but blood and death. Well, perhaps that was Spanish too.

A messenger came from the governor. All the officers were to meet in the palace. A decision must be made. Don Bernabe's bad leg was completely numb. He rose with the help of the barricade and rubbed his thigh, cursing the pain that came with renewed circulation.

In the palace it was unanimously agreed that they must make a last attempt to drive the Indians from the town and regain their water supply. The long lines of soldiers once more formed in front of the chapel. Don Bernabe was one of the first to confess to Father Cadena. The lines moved forward slowly and some of the men coming back out were telling their beads in penance and the gray morning light made their faces look waxen and staring.

A servant had saddled Argel and was bringing the stocking-footed horse to Don Bernabe. The man was Pedro, one of the Spanish retainers of the Ribera household. Don Bernabe missed Ignacio. He missed the old Pueblo's affectionate grumbling as he helped load the big eighteen-inch firelocks or buckled the armor on his master. He could not believe Ignacio had gone over to the Indians. The man had been with the Riberas for over forty years. Don Bernabe had taken him in as a youth, when he was orphaned. He had educated him, trained him, made him a personal body servant. They had been on a hundred campaigns together, saved each other's life a dozen times. It was inconceivable that Ignacio could betray such a trust. He had been lost in battle, that was all. He had been lost in battle.

The soldiers gathered around their officers by the barricades, and the patio was slowly filled with the muffled clank of their armor and the murmur of their voices. It was the only sound. The candles had burned out at the coffins and the women were silent. They had spent their grief and were huddled near the long pine boxes like statues in a crumpled vigil.

Don Bernabe saw Luis emerge from the chapel and cross to his quarters. He reappeared in a short time, buckling on his cuirass. Doña Isabel followed him out the door.

Luis kissed his mother and left her by the doorway. Don Bernabe saw another figure appear at the door and halt there indecisively. It was Don Cristobal. He stared at the soldiers as though with the impulse to join them. But when Otermin had ordered the captains to pick a hundred men for this last sally no one had even considered Don Cristobal. It seemed quite natural, even in such an extremity, that no one expected him to fight.

Luis joined the troops and stood beside his horse. Don Bernabe wanted to tell him how proud he was and how he hoped they would be able to fight back to back again, just once more, somewhere out there.

"Well," Luis said. "I hope we get the water. I have a big thirst right now."

"Yes," Don Bernabe said. "I have a big thirst too."

Andres Rodrigo led a fretting stallion through the lines. The young man looked uncomfortable in his armor. The battered morion formed a curiously Spartan contrast to his puffy cheeks and licentious lips. The bottom of the cuirass dug into his soft belly and he kept tugging irritably at it. When he saw Luis watching him he made a show of nonchalance.

"Well," he said, "Father always wanted me to be a soldier."

Neither Ribera answered. Andres pouted disconcertedly and moved on. Governor Otermin was up on his black stallion now, and he moved out in front of the men.

"*Señores*, your officers have their orders. The sentries in the towers report that the Indians are massing near the church for an assault. It will be our first objective. Remember that your blood is of Castile and your steel of Toledo, and they have conquered half a world."

Don Bernabe mounted, unsheathing his sword. His dozen armed retainers formed behind him, hefting their lances. The arquebusiers were ranked back of the cavalry, bullets in their mouths, guns loaded. Governor Otermin lifted his sword in signal and the cannons fired through the entrance, blasting away whatever life lay beyond.

"*Santiago!*"

The hoarse cry coming from a hundred throats carried Don Bernabe through the gate. Ahead of him he could see the ruins of the town. The blackened houses still smoldered. The streets were heaped with rubble. Half the walls of church and convent were fallen and smoke still rose from the roofless nave.

There were hundreds of Indians at the east end of the plaza, gathered before the church. They had already started to scatter before the charge.

But there was no organization to them and scores were still in the path of the armored horsemen when they struck. There was a shock to that first impact which jarred a man in his saddle. Don Bernabe felt it break the back of the Indian mob.

An Indian struck him from behind with a *macana*. It broke the joints of his cuirass and knocked him out of the saddle. Dazedly he rolled over, drawing his knife and trying to pull the plates of his broken cuirass together. He looked up and saw an Indian standing above him with a Spanish sword. It was his manservant.

"Ignacio," he said.

Andres Rodrigo galloped out of the smoke. His horse was charging directly at Ignacio. Andres could have run the man down before Ignacio thrust at Don Bernabe. But an Indian by the wall drew his bow, aiming the arrow at Andres. With a broken sound Andres wheeled his horse, dropping his sword as he threw himself forward in the saddle. The arrow flew high above his head. Ignacio plunged the sword into Don Bernabe's unprotected chest.

The battle carried Toribio Quintano to the far corner of the convent before the first clash ended. The fighting was spread out across the square and down the narrow streets now. Toribio fought to hold his snorting stallion. The smell of blood excited the sheriff and the killing excited him and now he was like the horse; he did not want to quit. In the disorganized mob of struggling men he saw Matarife and a pair of the Inquisitional guard.

"In the convent," Toribio shouted. "A bunch of them went in the convent."

He led Matarife and the men around to the rear gate. On the way they saw the *visitador*, Don Melchor Cárdenas, lying face down by the wall. One of his retainers was crouched beside him, and he told Toribio that Don Melchor was dead.

The cloister was still filled with smoke from the smoldering interior of the kitchen and workshops. Shadowy figures ran back and forth across the open court. The Spaniards rode them down, lancing them. Toribio saw a man crouched under the arches of the gallery. It was Andres Rodrigo, cowering on his knees in the shelter of the broken wall.

"Andres," Toribio shouted. "Get up. Find your horse." The young man gaped up at him, eyes blank. Toribio swung off his horse, holding the reins with one hand. With the other he grabbed Andres by the shoulder and shook him. "There is more fighting to do, more pigs to stick."

"More pigs to stick," Andres said. He began to laugh. His whole frame began to shake and he put his hands over his face. "More pigs to stick," he said hysterically. "More pigs to stick. Body of Christ."

Toribio's lips grew thin with contempt. He put his foot against Andres and shoved and the man fell flat in the rubble, still shaking. Disgustedly Toribio said:

"*Maricón.*"

The Indians were gone from the east end of the plaza. The charge had broken them and scattered them into the streets leading to the river.

In the shelter of the church wall, Otermin held council with his officers. He pointed out the squads of infantry already penetrating the streets that radiated from the plaza, their arquebuses crashing in sporadic volleys. Most of the buildings had been destroyed and offered little cover to the Indians. But Torres told Otermin that part of the Ribera house was still intact and a body of them were fortified there. The open square offered no cover for an attacking force, and the arque-

busiers had been unable to take the house. It occupied a key position
on the plaza and they could not afford to bypass it.

The house was a shambles. The posts of the portal extending the
width of its front had burned away, allowing the balcony to collapse
in a heap of blackened timbers that blocked the front door and windows. Most of the roof and east wall had fallen, and gray tendrils of
smoke still drifted from the smoldering wreckage. But the west wing
and the walls of the courtyard were still standing, and infested with
Indians.

Otermin explained that he could not afford to risk all his cavalry
in a direct charge as long as there was no way to get into the Ribera
courtyard, where the mass of Indians was barricaded. The gate had
to be opened first, and that could only be done from inside. He asked
for a volunteer to lead a troop in the first assault and attempt an entrance.

Luis Ribera requested the job. Otermin glanced searchingly at his
grim face, remembering the insolence, the clashes, the insults. But he
had to admit that Luis had proved himself in battle. Otermin finally
nodded.

Luis gathered his men. There were nine of them now. Some had
been household servants, some sheepherders or *vaqueros* on the Ribera
ranch east of Tesuque—but all had ridden with Don Bernabe on a dozen
Indian campaigns, acting as men-at-arms when he was called upon to
fulfill his obligations as *encomendero*. Each had a pair of firelocks beside his sword and lance. Luis told them not to use the pistols till
they were inside and received the order from him.

Governor Otermin deployed a squad of royal arquebusiers to positions in the ruins flanking the Ribera house. As soon as Luis left the
cover of the church they opened fire. The first volley kept the Indians
down.

The armored charge carried the rest to the house. Watching from
the church, Otermin saw that Luis was the first to spur his excited
stallion through the gaping hole in the east wall.

Luis could hear his men crashing into the room behind him. Like
mythic gnomes in some forgotten cave the shadowy forms flitted
through the wreckage of the smoking room and flung themselves
screaming at the Spaniards. For five minutes it was a bloody nightmare.

But it was a lesson the Indians had to learn over and over again, from Cortez's first campaign onward—the superiority of horse over foot, of armor over naked bodies, of discipline over fanaticism.

When it was over and the broken remnants of the Indians were fleeing back through other rooms toward the courtyard, Luis recalled his men with shouted commands. They gathered at the door leading to the bedrooms, and he saw that there were but six of them left in the saddle. They could not get their horses through the narrow doors and reluctantly they dismounted. With Torres at his elbow Luis led them toward the rear. They fought their way down a hall and into Don Bernabe's bedroom.

Luis crossed to a window. Outside he could see the familiar patios, in ruins now. Indians were running back and forth across the courtyard, taking positions behind barricades or at holes they had knocked in the walls. Others lay on top of the stables and outbuildings, firing at the Spaniards outside.

"Your pistols now," Luis said. "Three load and three fire."

"Two can load," Torres said.

Luis looked at him. Then, unsmiling, he clapped the armorer on the shoulder. Together they crawled out the window.

There were half a dozen Indians near the gate. The first fusillade from the Spaniards at the windows dropped three of them and the others scattered. Another bunch charged from the stables. Luis and Torres discharged their pistols, hitting two men and driving the others back to cover.

A figure rose from behind the wall, spear poised. As he lunged at Luis, Torres jumped between them and flung an empty pistol at the Indian. It hit the Pueblo in the face and he fell backward. But the spear had already been thrown. It struck Torres instead of Luis. It went through his throat, and he dropped his other firelock and raised both hands to the long shaft and fell against the wall.

Luis checked his headlong run. The Indian lay on his back, stunned by the thrown gun, hands held to his face. It was Po-pe.

Luis stared at him in surprise and indecision, then wheeled toward Torres. The old armorer was crouched against the wall, both hands holding the spear in his neck. He waved feebly at the Indians dropping off the roof tops or crossing to intercept Luis. When he spoke blood bubbled from his mouth.

"You cannot stop now . . . only a second . . . another second . . ."

Luis knew he was right. Cursing helplessly he pivoted and ran for the gate. With arrows glancing off his morion and cuirass he reached the *zaguán*. He dropped both empty pistols so he could grasp the heavy bar and lift it from the sockets on the gate. He put his shoulder to the heavy portal and heaved it open.

He heard a hoarse cheer from the plaza. Spanish cavalry poured into the narrow street. The clash of armor and thunder of hoofs was deafening.

Luis wheeled, sword and knife out, back against the wall. The Spaniards in the house were keeping up a steady fire, but two of the Pueblos had gotten through. The first one came against Luis with his *macana* swinging. Luis thrust under the blow. The war club missed him and his sword went to its hilt in the man. The Indian's charge carried him heavily against Luis, limp as a sack of sand.

The first Spanish horseman charged through the gate.

It was Otermin and he rode the Indian down. Then the patio was filled with Spaniards. Luis fought his way through the melee to the well. Po-pe was gone. Torres had quit trying to get the spear out. He looked up at Luis, trying to speak.

"Blessed be the hour, Luis."

The words ended on a choked rattle. The eyes turned blank and staring. Kneeling beside him, Luis gently closed the lids.

"The tempering will be good . . . Torres."

For the rest of the morning the fight surged back and forth between plaza and river. The narrow streets were filled with bitter hand-to-hand combat. Wherever there was a wall left standing it became a fortress for the Indians. The Spaniards had to clear these nests out one by one, sometimes taking the ruin by assault, sometimes burning it about the defenders. At last the Spaniards gained the wall along the Alameda and drove the Indians across the river into the Analco. Then they set to work repairing the ditch and running water back into the royal houses. When the first muddy trickle appeared within the walls a pathetic wail of triumph rose from the palace courtyard.

The Indians had withdrawn from the town, leaving more than three hundred dead behind them. The exhausted Spaniards rested inside the quadrangle once more. Don Bernabe, Don Melchor Cárdenas, Torres, and two other Spaniards had been killed. A Requiem Mass was held and they were buried in the courtyard. Luis Ribera remained alone at his grandfather's grave long after the others had left. Luis was kneeling and his head was bare and bowed and he had both hands on the simple wooden cross, gripping it tightly.

Forty-seven prisoners had been captured and through the dusty afternoon Otermin sat in his chair in the courtyard, interrogating them.

They said that the country was laid waste from Taos to Isleta, that Lieutenant Governor García would not come to the aid of Santa Fe because he had fled southward with what few colonists had escaped the atrocities along the Lower River. The information was officially noted by Francisco Xavier, and then the forty-seven Indians were executed.

But it would only be a matter of time before the Indians cut off the water again. Dozens of animals had already died of thirst and starvation. The people themselves could not hold out much longer. There was nothing to eat and they were suffering miserably. Many of the soldiers were too badly wounded to fight, and the others were so exhausted that it was doubtful if they could sustain another battle. Otermin held council with the corporation, the captains, and the clergy, and it was decided that their only remaining chance was to try to cut their way through the besiegers and join García below Isleta. That night the Spaniards tried to sleep, expecting to die fighting in the morning.

CHAPTER TWENTY-ONE

ON the morning of August 21, 1680, a thousand and twenty colonists marched from the royal houses. There were scarcely a hundred men capable of bearing arms. The people had no food to take with them, not a crust of bread nor a grain of corn. There were a few sheep and goats, four hundred horses and cattle, and only two carts. The best horses were used to mount the soldiers. The remaining animals and the two carts carried the sick and wounded. The rest of the people, priest and old man, woman and child, had to walk.

In a straggling column they moved from the gates and through the devastated town. Behind them they left the cannon, spiked and useless. The cavalry fanned out of the flanks, picking their way through rubbled streets in constant expectancy of attack. Ripples in a vast pool, the sound spread outward from the host, an indivisible compound of scratching feet; of mutedly clanking armor; of children's cries quickly stifled by a mother's hand; of animals bleating and whimpering.

They were just outside the town walls when dawn came. A streak of silver in the gray eastern sky, broadening, turning pink, rose-colored, touching the mountain peaks with flame, obliterating them with a blinding burst of light.

As one the people turned toward the mountains, waiting for the howling horde of savages to descend upon them. But nothing came. The mountains and foothills massed blackly against the eastern sky. And on the ridges they could see the silhouettes and the smoke of signal fires beginning to filter upward. All morning long the column crawled through the flat tableland, sandy, grassless, conical hills breaking the horizon, stippled with the ubiquitous cedar.

Before noon the first one fell, an old woman near the end of the column. Her husband knelt beside her, pushing at her and talking to her, until someone sent for the priest. Father Farfan came and looked at the woman. He knelt quickly and began the final sacraments. After the softly murmured Commendation of the Soul he crossed himself and rose, touching the woman's husband.

"We cannot stop to bury her here, my son. Tonight, when we halt, we will hold the Requiem."

They put her body in a cart and moved on. All afternoon the people moved southward, choking in the dust that hazed their line of march, stumbling in their growing weakness and exhaustion. All day long the signal fires spiraled heavenward and the Indians were visible on the flanks of the column.

Luis had been assigned to the rear guard. The ordeal of the last days had aged him. His face had the gray tinge of long sickness. Without water to shave he had let the blue shadow of a week's beard stubble the gaunt hollows of his cheeks. His eyes, feverish and red-rimmed, were sunk deep in their sockets, and his lips were as dry and cracked as the edges of an old wound. He could feel his empty belly sucking at his spine, and he had trouble with his vision. Twice in the forenoon dizziness had almost made him fall from the saddle. His arm was swollen again, and he could feel a steady throbbing from wrist to shoulder.

Captain Roque Madrid commanded the detachment. He was no longer the dashing cavalier. His plume was ragged and drooping, and his handsome uniform was torn and blackened by powder smoke. He kept watching the Indians silhouetted on the eastern foothills, anxiety stretching his classic features taut.

"Why do they not attack? I am more suited to fighting than this eternal waiting."

Luis was almost too exhausted to talk. "Maybe they have had enough."

"For God, they could wipe us out."

"And they know what it would cost them. The prisoners told Otermin they lost over three hundred men in that last battle."

"I suppose you are right. Why throw away their men when the land will get us anyway?"

"That does not sound like you, Captain."

"Face facts. Not enough food left for another meal. Over five hundred miles of open desert. They are dropping like flies now. What will happen at the Journey of the Dead Man?"

Luis was too drained to argue. He saw a woman near the end of the column fall. As he drew near he realized it was the Condesa, a pitiful heap of tattered silks and satins, with the black-faced Zapotec bent over her. The little maid tried to pull her up again but was too weak to do it. The rest of the column stumbled by, either unaware of her in their misery or looking down at the women like drugged people.

"What passes, you *bribóns*," Luis called. "Help her."

The women of the Cárdenas family shuffled by. Doña Piedad, the visitor's wife, walked with her fragile chin held high, her eyes closed, her lips tightly compressed in an ashen face, like a martyr marching to the cross. She had been sick for days and was apparently in too much pain to be aware of what happened around her. Her whole being seemed squeezed down to the bitter concentration of putting one foot in front of the other.

Barbara stumbled at her side, whimpering and clinging to her hand. When Luis called the girl looked at him and then down at the Condesa. Her lips pursed as though she would spit.

"That *puta?*" she said.

She moved on, scuffling up dust that settled grayly on the Condesa. In a bleak anger Luis spurred his flagging horse to the fallen woman and swung off. Weakness made him drop to his knees as soon as his feet touched ground.

"Where is her coachman?" he asked. "Where is that *zambo?*"

"Cruz was wounded yesterday," the maid told him. "He rides in a wagon."

He grasped the woman's shoulder, shaking her. "Condesa, you must get up. Veronica——"

Her voice came feebly, muffled. "Cannot, Luis, cannot—so tired—pity of God——"

"You can ride my horse."

"No . . . must not. You know the governor's orders—not enough horses for the soldiers anyway."

"Damn the governor's orders."

With Chintule's help, he finally got the woman on her feet. She sagged against him for a moment, keeping her face turned away, hidden by her *rebozo*. It was a shawl that must have cost two hundred pesos in Mexico City, its brilliant stripes threaded with gold, soaked in olive oil before weaving to insure lasting softness. It seemed like a pathetic vanity, in all this suffering and death. He finally got her aboard the horse. For a moment, in the course of mounting, the shawl dropped from her face. There were no more cosmetics, carefully lighted rooms, dim coaches. There was only fatigue, the ravages of hunger, and the pitiless light of the sun. The impeccable illusion was shattered. Her face looked pursed and seamed, repellent as a bird of prey.

She saw him looking at her, and in a gesture of ineffable defeat she pulled the shawl back across her face. Her voice was a whisper, barely audible.

"Thousand thanks . . . companion."

There was a Requiem Mass that night for three, and Father Cadena wore what white vestments he could obtain because two of the dead were babies. Some of the cattle and sheep were butchered and spitted over the campfires for food. Long before the meat was done the lines began to form, and the pleas became so insistent that the cooks had to hand out rations still raw.

Luis obtained portions for his father and mother, who were too feeble to stand in the long lines. There were no plates, and he had to carry the meat in his helmet. The sick and wounded were everywhere, and their moaning never stopped. He picked his way through the sprawled bodies till he came to his parents, seated against the wheel of a cart. His mother was wrapped to the eyes in a tattered Navajo blanket, shivering in the bitter chill of the desert night. His father held a cross in his lap. Luis saw with surprise that it was the white one Juan Ye had offered the Spaniards before the battle. Don Cristobal smiled strangely at Luis.

"Shall I confess thee, my son?"

"Confess?"

"*Ad mayorem Dei Gloriam*," Don Cristobal said. He nodded his head. "To the greater praise and glory of the Lord."

Luis looked helplessly at his mother. Her round face was pale, strained, and her lips trembled. She caught Luis by the hand and pulled him close, speaking in a feeble, breathless voice.

"I have the great fear, Luis. Your father, he found that cross, going out of town. Something has happened . . . his mind. All that time without water, without food, the terrible things, the killing, all the killing . . ."

Luis looked at his father's eyes, glazed and childish and staring into another world.

Doña Isabel began to shudder. He gripped her hands tightly, afraid she would break, grow hysterical.

"Why do we find out so many things too late, Luis? I wanted to love you and I only drove you away——"

"No, mother, please——"

"Can you know how it was? Can you know that I was once beautiful, the parties, the young men, the music, the laughter? Then that house—like a tomb. And I drove you from me. My possessiveness. What else did I have? Not your father. Not Don Bernabe. In a tomb, with only you, once in a while, moving farther and farther away, not knowing what I was doing, knowing, unable to help myself."

Her hands were icy, and he held them against his body to warm them. "It is not too late," he said. "This has done things. I understand things better now. Perhaps we have all learned something. It is not too late."

"Is that the church bell ringing?" Don Cristobal asked. "I must go into the vestry and prepare for Mass."

On August 24 they reached the Rio Grande. The cottonwoods and willows were a jade necklace strung on the swollen brown snake of the great river that shimmered and glittered as it uncoiled in the sun. The storm in the mountains had filled it over its banks, and it was flooding the broad bottoms. The heat sucked moisture from the water and from the glaucous mud and turned the air to a white fog that swam thickly over yellow sand bars and through the trees. On every side the land stretched away from the river, a vast buckskin hide crumpled and wrinkled by some giant hand. Browning salt grass unfolded its tawny carpet eastward to the mountains. Checkerboarding it like patches of snow were bare stretches of ground where the rain had fallen months before and had formed an ooze that filmed and dried under the sun till it cracked like the glazed shards of alabaster pottery.

In the heat and haze and dust the column moved downriver.

Governor Otermin reprimanded Luis for letting the Condesa ride his horse. Without the cavalry the colonists would be at the mercy of the Indians who still hung on their flanks. The horses must be saved for the soldiers. But soon he had to rescind the order. The carts were full, and the pack animals were carrying all the wounded they could manage. The old and the sick were still falling, and the soldiers began picking them up and riding double.

They reached Santo Domingo. It had been the sacerdotal seat of all the missions in New Mexico, headquarters for the superintendent and his staff. The Indian village was deserted, the church locked. When they opened it they found the sacred vessels in the sacristy—six silver chalices, a hand basin, a salver, seven cruets, a thurible—all inexplicably left untouched. The irony was deepened when they found the signs of a violent battle outside and the common grave containing the bodies of Fathers Lorenzana, Talaban, and Montesdoca, and five lay Spaniards.

The column moved downriver.

The Marqués de Gallegos had recovered enough to ride with the cavalry. He wore a bandage on his head to cover the grisly sight of his healing scalp but could not bear the weight of a helmet. He joined Captain Madrid's detachment on the twenty-fifth.

That was the day they began to pass the Spanish estates between the *pueblos* of San Felipe and Sandia. There were seventeen of them in one stretch of eight miles. Otermin detached Madrid and his squad to scout the great fortresslike houses that lay off the main road. They found the house of Pedro de Cuellar sacked and burned. They found the house of Captain Augustin de Carbajal burned and the bodies of the captain and his wife within its blackened walls. They found bodies farther on along the road. They found Cristobal Anaya, his wife, six sons, and four others, lying nude in ditches beneath the trees.

The riders halted by the corpses. Luis stared at them sickly. He had seen too many of them. He was numb with the horror.

The Marqués de Gallegos joined them by the ditch. He wore the long Spanish boots yellowed by the brine of his horse, their flexible tops folded down carelessly below the knee. Governor Otermin had given him a handsome cloak, but it was torn and soiled now and half the silver bullion embroidery had been ripped off. His sword, lifting the cloak out into a tattered tail behind, gave him the look of a shabby rooster. He was branded with the terror he had known. Beneath the bloody bandage on his scalped head his eyes were sunk deep in a chalky face. They glowed with a weird zombie stare. When he spoke the little muscles jumped in his neck, gray strings jerked taut by spastic convulsions.

"Look well, Don Luis," he said bitterly. He pointed a finger at the scalped, mutilated bodies. "Your innocents did this. Your oppressed, downtrodden, abused, misunderstood children. Do you understand them now? Would you dine with them in their hovels? Love their babies. Laugh at their jokes. Are they still high enough on the scale of humanity to comprehend the Faith? To be treated any better than the beast you hunt down in the forest?"

"You are right, Don Desidero," Luis said. His voice was shaken and savage. "They are beasts."

On the twenty-sixth they reached the Pueblo village of Sandia. The dust was everywhere, powdering the road like cornstarch, graying the ragged cottonwoods, making a yellow lake of the plaza. The town seemed deserted. Nothing stirred on the roof tops, in the narrow alleys. Willows drooped in ragged pennants over empty corrals and dry irrigation ditches. Luis remembered Santo Domingo, deserted like this, dead, and the sacred vessels that had been found in its church. The same thing must have been in Governor Otermin's mind. He dispatched scouts toward the town. From his position on the flank of the main column Luis watched them go.

The riders fanned out, walking the horses toward the town slowly at first, apprehensively. Sunlight splashed blindingly against adobe walls. Like a mirage the terraced buildings rose from the silver shimmer of heat haze.

Nothing happened and the riders gained confidence, closing up, moving into a trot as they crossed the last cornfields. In the dusty hush Luis could hear the distant clatter of shriveled stalks against the horses' legs.

It was drowned in a rattle of gunfire.

From the church, from the doorways of the houses, from the deep *acequia madre*, the Indians appeared. It was unreal from a distance.

One of the scouts pitched from his saddle and the others closed with the Indians. Governor Otermin led out another squad to give support. A lancer rode down the column telling the remaining soldiers to hold their positions.

Luis saw someone walking across the fields. Everyone had been intent on the battle, and the single man leaving the line of march had gone unnoticed. He was already halfway to the Indians. He held a white cross before him.

"Father," Luis called. "Come back. We are to remain here."

Don Cristobal did not seem to hear. Fear closed Luis's throat. He spurred his horse after the man.

The shock of Otermin's charge had broken the Indians, scattering them through the fields. A dozen of them ran for the safety of the buildings, and Don Cristobal was directly in their path. Luis shouted again. Don Cristobal lifted the cross, calling to the Indians.

"Repent, my children, give up thine apostasy, this madness that has seized thee . . ."

He broke off as an arrow struck him in the body. He went to his knees. He disappeared in the swarm of their bodies. Luis saw them kicking at him, stabbing him. His voice rose in a quavering cry.

"I will confess thee and give thee penance, thou will be absolved in the eyes of the Father . . . the Son . . ."

The words were drowned in their fanatical shouts. Luis charged into them, knocking a pair from their feet with his horse, cutting at them with his sword. Other Spaniards were coming, and the Indians broke away. Luis swung off his horse and dropped to a knee beside his father.

Don Cristobal was already dead. His face looked strange. It became the face of Torres . . . Don Bernabe . . . Father Pio. The blood covering his body seemed to fill Luis's vision. He began to shake and the sweat broke out on his face and when he tried to make a sound his throat convulsed.

He got up and saw a pair of Indians running toward the church. He made a sound more animal than human and went after them. They dodged behind the adobe wall of the churchyard and he saw one of them pound on the door till it opened and then run into the church. Luis followed him.

The nave was thick with smoke. A heap of charred and smoldering wood barred his way. Straw had been piled in the nave and set afire. The only thing it had damaged, however, was the choir loft above the door. The heavy *vigas* supporting the loft had burned away, and part of the structure had collapsed. It had pulled down a section of the wall, and the only thing that kept a greater mass of the crumbling adobe from caving in was one of the charred beams still slanted against it.

Coughing in the smoke, half blinded, Luis had a glimpse of movement back in the charred wreckage of the choir. He danced through the hot embers and saw a shadowy form huddled beneath the slanted beam.

The Indian dodged, and Luis's rush carried him heavily against the wall. Before he could turn, a war club struck his morion. Like the shuddering reverberations of a great bell the stunning clang seemed to shake his whole body. It drove him to his knees. He saw the man lift the club again. He wanted to react, but his head roared and his body was numb.

At the same time a Spaniard galloped through the door, almost lying across his horse's neck to avoid being swept off. Luis had a glimpse of Matarife's scarred face.

The Indian wheeled around as Matarife drove the horse at him, lance held high. The Indian was an easy target. He was too surprised to dodge. But somehow Matarife missed.

A thousand pounds of horseflesh crashed into the slanted beam. The wild squeal of the horse and the groaning crack of the burned beam were one ear-piercing sound. Luis saw the horse wheel free and tried to follow it to safety. He was too late. The shattered beam gave way. There was a deafening roar. The wall fell in on him.

CHAPTER TWENTY-TWO

THE Spaniards had named it the Rio Grande y Bravo. From the beginning the life blood of the colony had flowed through this River Great and Fierce. It was the single artery of all Spanish New Mexico, spreading out the meager veins of its tributaries that enabled some of the more daring colonists to venture a few miles east or west. Its source lay far northward in the mythical red mountains known only to the Indians.

At Cochiti was the last gorge. Southward the river found the desert. It was still high desert, almost a mile above the sea. But it had already dropped two thousand feet from Santa Fe.

The plateau was left behind. The trough widened in the descending plain until it lost shape and identity. To the east the Sandias and the Manzanos still made a jagged wall, but the westward mountains were often invisible in distance. The river lost its rush and grew muddy and phlegmatic and flowed through a desert seemingly without limit until it reached El Paso del Norte.

It was three hundred and fifty miles from Santa Fe to the nearest Spanish colony at the Pass of the North. And the colonists had gone little better than a seventh of that distance. On August 27, just below Sandia, they were only fifty miles south of Santa Fe.

The altitude and cooling breezes of the capital were gone. The Spaniards were entering the heat of the desert. They had been making twelve or thirteen miles a day. After Sandia the average dropped to nine. It was a mark of their growing exhaustion.

The Inquisitional guard was one of the detachments forming a cavalry screen on the right flank of the column. There were only five of them left, led by Toribio Quintano.

They spent most of the day in the flooded bottom lands. Their horses slopped through the braided channels of silty water or labored across yellow sand bars that steamed in the sun. They wandered among the majestic trunks of great cottonwoods that stood like the silver columns of a ruined temple. The trees towered a hundred feet into the air. Their curling lemon-colored leaves were a million miniature papyrus scrolls. Nuthatches and bluebirds peeked from abandoned woodpecker holes in the trunks, and last spring's oriole nests hung from high branches and twirled in the slightest breeze. Buzzards flocked along the lower branches, stretching their ugly red necks and making death rattles with their wings. Every time one of the colonists dropped along the road a chorus of raucous croaks came from the birds, and they soared from the trees to circle over the fallen Spaniard.

Toribio's eyes ached from constantly staring across the brazen surface of the swollen river for some sign of the Indians. He closed them and pressed them with his hands. He turned to glance listlessly at the Spaniards.

It was like watching people move through a nightmare. They were gray with dust. Their coats and dresses hung from them in gray cerements. Their mouths gaped with exhaustion in their gray faces, and their eyes were so sunken that they became empty sockets in a gray skull. They stumbled, shambled, shuffled, dragged themselves along, one step after the other. They fell. They rose again. They staggered on. Now and then one did not rise, and the priest moved wearily back along the column and performed the final sacraments and tried to find some place in the carts for the body until the inevitable Requiem could be held over the burial that evening.

This was their seventh day on the road. They had not eaten in two days. The few sheep and cattle had long ago been killed. They could not butcher another animal. All the remaining cattle and the horses were loaded to the limit with the sick and the wounded. To kill one would be tantamount to killing the people on its back.

Hundreds of them were barefooted. Every time they stepped they left dark stains that were quickly blotted out by the following feet or the dust that constantly stirred and settled over the colonists. The sound never stopped. The wail of babies, the pitiable crying of children, the miserable lament of women, the groans of the sick, the shouts and crazy laughter of the delirious.

Toribio looked over their heads, back toward Sandia. Matarife followed his glance. Nothing was in sight but the stumbling column and the barren Sandia Mountains against the sky and the smoke signals rising from the mountains.

"What did I tell you?" Matarife muttered. "He is not coming. He will not come."

"You are sure?" Toribio wondered how often he had asked it. "You saw the wall fall in?"

"An ant could not crawl out." Matarife leered. "The Indian was before me. A baby could have stuck him. I missed. My horse hit the beam and the wall fell in. Who could say it was not a mistake?"

Toribio did not respond. He was thinking about yesterday. He had told Matarife that Luis must be put out of the way. He could not afford to have the young man reach Mexico City with his knowledge of Toribio and the Condesa. Toribio had never hoped the chance would come so naturally.

Nobody had seen it. After Otermin defeated the Indians at Sandia everyone had been afraid that the other Pueblos following the column would join in a general attack. Otermin was unwilling to invite such disaster by staying in the village longer than was absolutely necessary. Ramon Escudero, the brother-in-law of Barbara Cárdenas, had reported that he saw Luis near the church. A hurried search by a pair of soldiers brought the report that the fire set earlier by the Indians had caused the choir loft to burn and collapse, pulling down part of the wall, but the church was empty. The Spaniards were compelled to march on without further search. . . .

A turn in the road brought the stumbling colonists near Toribio. He saw that a woman had fallen near the end of the column. She had long ago worn the bottoms out of her shoes, and the red satin tops clung pitifully about her ankles. The soles of her feet were nothing but raw and bleeding flesh. A wizened little monkey of a maidservant bent over her, trying to lift her. Toribio was directly beside them now and saw that it was Chintule and the Condesa.

Her face turned up and her eyes fluttered as she saw Toribio, towering above her on his horse. She whimpered and made shapes with her mouth. Her hand lifted in feeble supplication.

"Toribio," she said.

He glanced quickly aside to see if she had been overheard. The people stumbled by like sleepwalkers, unheeding, uncaring. He did not stop his horse. He let it walk on by her. With his face turned away he said in a vicious mutter.

"Do not speak to me, ever!"

He paralleled the column till the road veered away from the bottoms again and he was once more among the trees with his men. He was trembling. He grew dizzy and sick and had to grip his saddle to keep from falling off.

Why did her face look like that? Why did it look like his mother's face when he had hit her so long ago?

In Tlascala.

He tried to drive away the memory. But it would not go. Tlascala had once been the capital of the Indian tribe living in the mountains between Mexico City and the gulf. Though the Spaniards had built their church and their great houses on the surrounding estates it was still very much an Indian town when Toribio was born there in 1650.

He remembered the single stone room to house a dozen people. He remembered the Indian he had thought to be his mother, Zicuetzin, almost blind from a lifetime of cooking over open fires. He remembered the enormous quantities of *pulque* drunk by Cacama, her Tlascalan husband.

Toribio soon showed his Spanish blood. There was a Castilian haughtiness to his narrow face, his thin lips, his hooded eyes. It caused little comment. *Mestizos* made up a great part of the population now. Zicuetzin had been a handmaiden at the Sobremonte house, and old Don Nicolas Sobremonte's lechery was well known.

Toribio remembered *encomienda*. The Indians in the Tizatlan quarter were vassals to the Sobremonte family. The Sobremontes had maguey lands as well as corn and cattle, and it doubled their labor needs.

Every January the usual quota of able-bodied men was demanded by the *encomendero*. They were taken out to the maguey fields and herded into a compound at night and guarded. Each morning they went into the fields and tapped the big maguey plants. They cut a natural bowl into the heart where the milk would drain from the fat green leaves. In the evening they collected the sweet musky fluid and carried it to the vats. Fermented it became *pulque*. Sold in the capital it made a fortune for the Sobremontes.

The plants would run for months before they bled to death. Too often it left the Indians no time for their own fields. Toribio was six. That year all the men in his family were in the maguey fields. The rains came early. The Indians said they had to tend their own fields. The Sobremontes would not release them. Irrigation ditches had to be repaired. After that the ploughing was upon them and the planting.

Zicuetzin tried to repair the ditches and do the ploughing in the family field. She was carrying a baby and she lost it. She could not finish the work, and by the time the rest of the Indians returned it was too late for the corn. Toribio remembered the babies crying in the night that winter (an Indian baby rarely cried) and how he finally crawled out into the dry field and ate dirt to fill his belly and drive away the ache of hunger.

Toribio remembered *repartimiento*. Hardly a year went by without someone in his family being conscripted. When Toribio was fifteen the sheriff from Mexico City drafted fifty Tlascalans and took them into the northward mountains. A famous miner had been denounced to the Inquisition as a Judaizer, and his impounded ore had to be transported to the capital. The loads were far too heavy. Toribio saw one of his brothers slip on the steep mountain trail. His pack carried him off, and he plunged a thousand feet to his death.

In Mexico City they were released. They were not paid. They had to make their own way home. For each district there was a *corregidor de los Indios* appointed by the crown to protect the Indians and see that they received just treatment. Toribio and some others filed a complaint with the *corregidor* of Tlascala. They cited the abuses they had suffered on the trip, the punishment and the overloading and the ones who had died and the refusal to pay. They cited the laws forbidding the Holy Office to conscript Indian labor.

The complaint was not acted upon. Either the *corregidor* was afraid of the Holy Office or a bribe had closed his mouth. A few days later some men caught Toribio in an alley and beat him senseless. The same thing happened to all the others who had complained. They did not complain again.

The next year Toribio and his father and forty others were drafted by a local Spanish merchant. The Indians were marched to Vera Cruz. They were loaded with a hundred pounds of cocoa apiece and started back to the capital. Many of the mountain Indians, unused to the steaming lowlands, died of the *matlazahuatl*. Toribio crouched on the trail beside his father and watched him vomit his life away.

"Can this be all?" the boy asked. "Is there nothing we can do?"

Cacama's laugh was a death rattle. "Do not let your Spanish blood delude you. Just drink plenty of *pulque*. You will learn about that. If you drink enough *pulque* nothing matters."

Next year in Tlascala the *chiahuiztli* killed the wheat. It made corn doubly precious. Royal agents confiscated all the corn for the crown and stored it in public granaries. Officials began the inevitable speculation, and Spaniards were the only ones with the price. Toribio remembered the bloated bellies and the sorrowful eyes of the dying children huddled against the ancient stone walls. Zicuetzin was dying when she called him to her side.

"Something you must know. Sobremonte blood in you . . . the truth. But not mine. I did not bed with Don Nicolas. I am not your mother."

His eyes were blank, uncomprehending.

"Doña Ana Sobremonte," Zicuetzin said. "She is your mother. Cacama is your father. When he was *mayordomo* of their estate. . . ."

"How?" he said helplessly. "How could it be . . . ?"

"Don Nicolas was in the capital when you came. Only Doña Ana and the midwife knew. Your Indian blood. They gave you to Cacama . . . threatened . . . death if we told. To Don Nicolas and the world you had died. . . ."

The Indians ate maguey worms. They ate rats trapped in the houses. They killed all the dogs in the town and ate them. There came a time when Toribio knew he could take no more. He had watched Zicuetzin die and his sisters die and now only he and his younger brother, Ixtlil, were left. It was not till years later that the boy became known as Matarife, which meant Slaughterman in Spanish.

They sat together in the cold stone room like emaciated yellow skeletons, and Toribio was looking back through his life. He was trying to recall a time when he had not ached with hunger or with cold or with labor or with beatings.

"I am going to the Sobremonte house," he said.

Ixtlil gaped at him. "Are you crazy? They will not give you food."

"I do not want food."

It had been on Toribio's mind ever since Zicuetzin told him she was not his mother. Like everyone else he had taken it for granted that his Spanish blood came from Don Nicolas. If Don Nicolas had not died when Toribio was five the idea might have occurred to him sooner. But Zicuetzin's confession put a new aspect on the matter. It revived the possibilities, the overwhelming possibilities.

With the name of Sobremonte he could take advantage of the Castilian law that allowed any subject above the rank of peasant to acquire the privileges of nobility. The bankrupt crown was selling many things beside titles and offices. With enough cash for a *gracias a sacar* a man already granted nobility might even buy dispensation from the quality of *mestizo*. He would be Don Toribio Sobremonte then and once away from Tlascala who would know him as half-breed?

Ixtlil pled with him to forget such madness. He argued with Toribio all the way to the Sobremonte house. It was almost dark and they mingled unnoticed with the faceless shadows of the other servants coming and going about the house. Ana Sobremonte's habits were well known. She was a widow now and always observed vespers alone in the chapel near the gate. Toribio slipped in by a side door.

Doña Ana rose from the prayer stool. She was tall and white-headed, her face shrouded in a black shawl. She did not seem surprised or frightened. Toribio made his bitter demand. There was a distinct white fur on the woman's aging lips. She peered closely at Toribio and then made a rattling sound in her throat.

"If I legitimized all the spawn of my dead husband half the *mestizos* in Tlascala would be clamoring for his name."

"Don Nicolas was not my father," he said. "Cacama was my father."

Something happened to her face. It went as dead and waxy as the crucified Christ behind the altar. Toribio felt hot and sweat broke out on him. A chill seized him and he began to shiver.

Doña Ana bent toward him and her voice shook. "Do you want to get yourself killed?"

"Who will know?" He spoke in a breathless rush. "Simply give me the official thing, the paper—whatever makes it legal. I will go away. If there are questions I am the son of Don Nicolas, that is all."

A weird light filled her eyes. He had the feeling she was looking through him, beyond him, into time. "Do you know what it is?" she said. Her voice was hushed, filled with whispered hatred. "Do you know what it is to be a slave . . . a Turk in a harem? One house, another. What is the difference? Walls . . . a prisoner. In your father's house. Watched, guarded. Never without a duenna. Never speak without asking permission. Talk to the ones they allow, dance with the ones they permit, marry the ones they choose. In your husband's house . . . do you know how much older Don Nicolas was than I? That first night— so drunk he could not do anything. A week later I took the coach to town without asking. A beating. And how many days after that . . . how many? I saw him in our bed with an Indian girl. . . ."

There was a flush to her cheeks, a macabre grimace on her furred lips, as though she were again relishing that night of wild rebellion against her masters. But the look faded. Her eyes lost their distant focus and fixed on him again, black and piercing.

"Your father was warned. Think you I would publicly announce my shame?"

"You are not the only one who could announce it."

Her lips began to tremble. "If you breathe one word of this I will have you killed."

He looked into her furred, haughty face. But for this woman's vagrant lust . . . if she had bedded with her husband instead of Cacama . . .

"I would have been a Spaniard," he said. "I would be the son of Don Nicolas Sobremonte." He caught her arm cruelly. "I will not go back. You will give me my name."

She opened her mouth to cry out. He struck her across the mouth.

"*Puta!* You did this. I would not be here. Indian, bastard, son of a whore—could you do no worse? Could you not spawn a dog? Make me a monster? Two heads, blind, an idiot, something fit for a whore, worse than a whore—at least they are paid!"

She was up against the wall and could not back away. He was giving vent to a frenzy that had been accumulating for a lifetime. He clawed her and beat her until she sank to the floor. He was aware of somebody pulling at him. Ixtlil. He saw servants rushing through the front entrance, and he turned blindly and plunged out the way he had come.

In the fields they outdistanced the household servants. But there was one, a rider, coming out of the night with a machete. He pulled his horse up to swing. The flat of the blade struck Ixtlil across the head.

Before the man could wheel the horse Toribio pulled him out of the saddle. The man struck hard and lay stunned. Toribio caught the excited horse and brought him back to Ixtlil. Toribio put him over the horse, head and feet dangling. He mounted behind and kicked the animal into a dead run. . . .

They were fugitives now. For attacking one of the fine people an Indian could be put to death. In the mountains, moving toward Mexico City, Toribio nursed Ixtlil back to some semblance of health. The boy's neck had been broken so that his shoulders were humped, the right twisted high above the left. Toribio would never lose his sense of guilt, of responsibility.

They reached Mexico City and joined the starving hordes of beggars in the Zocalo. Toribio would never tell, not even in the confessional, the things he and Ixtlil had done to stay alive during those first years in the capital. . . .

A tanager made a red-and-yellow flash, spiraling skyward from the trees. It jarred Toribio from his brooding memories. The last golden bars of the afternoon sun slanted through the trees, glancing brazenly off the glittering scrolls of the leaves. The air swam with the rancid smell of wet bottom-land grasses, the odor of mud, ancient and rotten, the parched smell of baked dust.

Toribio saw that the column was halting at a *paraje*—one of the permanent camp sites established every ten or fifteen miles along the whole length of the Royal Highway. Toribio waved his men into camp and remained alone at the edge of the trees. Apathetically he watched the last of the column join the crowd in the clearing. A few stragglers kept stumbling in. One of the last was the Condesa, hobbling painfully, helped along by her wizened, black-faced maid. She reached one of the carts and fell to the ground, groaning in pain.

Toribio had a single blanket rolled behind his cantle. He untied it and unrolled it across his saddle and unsheathed his knife. He hacked a long strip out of the blanket, three inches wide, and then cut it in two. He got off his horse and led it into the camp. He had meant merely to drop the strips of blanket as he walked by. But when he neared the cart he saw that the Condesa lay huddled against its big solid wheel, hidden from the rest of the camp. He dropped to a knee beside her and put the strips of wool on the ground. He took her hand and placed it on the wool and closed it with his own hand.

"Take this. Wrap it around your feet tomorrow. When it is gone I will give you more."

He rose quickly and walked on.

CHAPTER TWENTY-THREE

ALL the way downriver the colonists had been kept going by two thoughts: The hope that the Indians had lied to them and that they would find Lieutenant Governor García still at Isleta; and the even more desperate hope that sooner or later they would meet the mission caravan that came north every three years with supplies for the missions and the colony. It was known that the father quartermaster, Fray Ayeta, had left Mexico City on September 30, 1679, with twenty-eight loaded wagons and a herd of animals. The trip usually took six months, and the train was long overdue. Even the most outrageous delays en route could not have kept Fray Ayeta from reaching New Mexico before this. He must be somewhere near. Hourly the colonists watched the trail ahead. The food in the wagons would save their lives.

On September 3 the Spaniards reached Isleta. They found it deserted, as the Indians had told them, with no sign of García. Governor Otermin sent four couriers ahead in the dim hope that they might catch the lieutenant governor, with orders that he halt his band and report back to Otermin.

On September 6, thirteen leagues south of Isleta, the colonists were met by the lieutenant governor at the deserted Valencia estate. García and his refugees had been at the Fray Cristobal camp site when the couriers caught him. He had left his people there and answered Otermin's summons.

His report shattered what feeble hope remained in the Spaniards. His own band was in sorrier condition than the colonists from Santa

Fe, sick, starving, exhausted, without any food or ammunition. And he had seen no sign of the mission supply train.

The next day the colonists passed Socorro, a *pueblo* of six hundred. These were Piros who had not joined the northern Pueblos in the revolt. They gave the Spaniards a small supply of corn, and many of them joined the column.

Barbara de Cárdenas was riding in one of the wagons. She had been there for two days now, since fainting on the road. She was jammed in with her sick maid, Josefina, and a score of wounded soldiers and women too ill to walk, and dying children. She was dizzy with hunger and ached all over from the constant jolting of the wagon. She had long since stopped trying to hold herself rigid against the side, away from contact with the sweating bodies, and was sprawled heavily against a delirious lancer who had been wounded at Sandia.

A man stumbled past. Barbara saw that it was Nazario Aguilar, the one-eyed innkeeper from the Analco. He was asking the same question he had been asking ever since they left Sandia.

"Have you seen my daughter? Has anyone seen Kashana?"

"We have not seen," a soldier said wearily. "She was part Indian, truth? Perhaps she ran off."

"She would not. These Piros are not her people. She is Keres, from Acoma. She is my daughter. Has anyone seen her?"

Barbara's mother walked beside the wagon. She held on to its side and lurched and stumbled as though she would fall with each new step. Her eyes were closed. She walked blindly and held herself up by the wagon. Her face looked waxen like the faces of the corpses they had been burying every night. Her bloodless lips moved all the time in soundless prayers. Barbara thought it was the strength of the prayers alone that kept Doña Piedad going.

Late in the afternoon a dust cloud was seen on the horizon. Riders emerged, the sun glancing off Spanish helmets. Thinking it was the long-waited supply train, the ragged soldiers fired their arquebuses and a few colonists raised a feeble cheer.

But the new arrivals proved to be only twenty-seven soldiers under Captain Pedro de Leiva. They were the advance guard of the supply train. The mission caravan was still far south of El Paso, fifty leagues away. Leiva's men had been able to carry with them only a small quantity of corn, biscuits, flour, chocolate, and sugar.

On September 13 Otermin's column joined García's Lower River refugees in their dismal camp at the Fray Cristobal *paraje*. The corporation recorded under oath that the combined columns now numbered

2520 people. That night the colonists finished the emergency rations brought by Captain Leiva. The next morning the sun rose on the horror ahead.

The camp site stood at the northern end of the Fray Cristobals, a jagged chain of mountains that rose at the very edge of the Rio Grande. Their broken spines and tumbled gorges turned the country on either side of the river in to a virtually impassable badlands. It forced the trail to turn east till the mountains lay between the travelers and the river. Then the route ran for thirty leagues through the graveyard of the Royal Road, the ninety miles of waterless desert that had long ago earned its name of Jornada del Muerto.

Governor Otermin, the Marqués de Gallegos, and eleven other soldiers left the column to ride ahead in an attempt to reach the supply train and hurry it along. The rest of the colonists broke camp and began their march into the Journey of the Dead Man.

They were moving into a trough thirty miles wide, walled to the west by the Fray Cristobals and the Caballos, the east by the San Andreas Mountains.

The San Andreas were high and startling on the left flank, blue-black with cedar brake and piñon, except for the single gilded tower of the granite Salinas Peak. On the right flank, in the first brilliant flood of sunlight, the eastward slopes of the Fray Cristobals took on cruel shape. Unsoftened by grass or timber, their ridges glittered like the edges of upturned knives.

The heat grew steadily through the morning. The wounded in the wagon began turning from side to side in a futile effort to escape the sun. Barbara had no covering for her head except her shawl. There was a burning sensation at the base of her skull, and when she opened her eyes she thought she was blind. It was hard to get her breath. She felt suffocated. She was drenched in perspiration.

Finally she realized that her mother was not in her usual place at the side of the wagon. Dully Barbara looked through the stumbling ranks. She saw someone lying down. Another figure was bent over her. It was the Condesa, on her knees, trying to rouse Doña Piedad. The others shuffled past, too drunk with exhaustion to see or simply looking at the fallen women as though they were some curiosity in the road.

"Stop the cart," the Condesa called.

She had to call again several times before the driver would put his weight on the yoke and drag the oxen to a halt. He stood leaning feebly against one of the animals, not even looking back. The Condesa tried to rise. She failed. She crawled on hands and knees to the cart.

"It is Doña Piedad," she said. "She still has life. You must make room."

One of the wounded soldiers groaned. "What room? *Virgen Santísima*, I am crushed now."

The Condesa looked at Barbara. "It is your mother. You must give her your place."

Barbara tried to rise. She sank back. "I cannot walk."

"I will help."

"I cannot . . . I will fall down . . . die."

The Condesa began to breathe stertorously. Spittle formed at the corners of her mouth. "Listen . . . what kind of a creature are you? You live because of her. She suffered to bear you. They had to cut you from her. You are the blood of her body. The tears from her eyes. What kind of a creature are you?"

Barbara buried her face in her hands and began to cry softly. A sound of contempt came from the Condesa, halfway between a groan and a sob.

"No wonder Luis could not love you."

The words had a strange effect on Barbara. She stopped crying. She tried to remember the look on his face that night in the garden.

"I thought so," the Condesa said.

"I hate him," Barbara said.

"You love him."

"He is dead."

"What if he is alive? What if he hears about this? How Barbara de Cárdenas let her mother die in the road . . ."

"What passes?" shouted the driver. "We cannot stop here."

The colonists were straggling around the cart, beating up a haze of dust with their shuffling feet. The Condesa leaned so close her face almost touched Barbara's.

"He will hear. If Luis has life he will hear about this, and then you will never have a chance, never again will you be able to go to him, to look him in the face, never again, never again, never never never again. . . ."

She couldn't seem to stop. She kept saying it over and over. Barbara began to cry again. She lifted her hand. It was an immense weight. The fingers kept slipping off the side of the wagon. Still crying she tried to move herself along the floor. The Condesa caught her tattered dress and tried to help. At last her feet were on the ground. She swayed heavily against the woman, almost knocking her over.

"Good," panted the Condesa. "With me now—we will get her."

Somehow they got Doña Piedad into the wagon. Barbara stumbled behind, supported on one side by the Condesa and on the other by her Zapotec maid. In the afternoon they reached the lava flow around the Las Tusas *paraje*. For the rest of the day, like a bed of nails, it cut and slashed at the feet of the Spaniards.

The thin soles of Barbara's suede shoes were soon worn through. She tore her petticoat into strips and tied it about her feet. In a short time it was cut to ribbons. The Condesa unwound some of the bloody strips of blanket from her own feet and gave them to Barbara. When that was ripped to shreds Barbara began using pieces of the single sleeping blanket she carried. By the end of the day she had used it all.

In the evening they reached Alto de las Tusas. Scattered across the barren flats on either side of the road were the charred remains of fires built by former travelers. Barbara sank to the ground near the wagon. She examined her bloody feet.

"I do not have the pain," she said. "Why is that? I cannot feel the pain."

The Condesa groaned. "It is the mercy of God. After a while one becomes numb."

A feeble shudder ran through Barbara's body. "I had such a fear of death. I think now I could embrace it like a lover."

"You are growing up. If you live through this you will be a woman."

From the kegs in the wagons the soldiers began rationing the water. Barbara saw Don Celso let his wife drink his share. The priests passed among the sick and wounded with smaller containers. Barbara's mother had a *tus*—an Apache jar of woven squawbrush, coated with piñon gum to make it watertight. The priest poured in Doña Piedad's ration and then helped lift the *tus* to her lips.

They broke camp at dawn of the fifteenth. They left ten new gravestones behind in the little graveyard beside the road. From somewhere the Condesa had gotten more blanket strips to bind her feet. She gave half of them to Barbara.

They left the cutting lava behind. A wasteland of glaring sand stretched in every direction. With so many wounded to transport they had not been able to carry as much water as they should. The last of it was passed out in camp that night.

The next day a wind came up. It blew sand steadily into the faces of the colonists until the flesh was raw and bleeding like their feet. It filled the nostrils of the animals, clogging them so that they could not breathe. A horse began bucking and pitching, and stampeded others. A dozen of them ran into the desert, throwing their burdens of sick and wounded. The cavalry tired to catch them but their own mounts were too exhausted, and one man killed his horse running it in the heat.

That night they reached the camp called Cross of Anaya. Doña Piedad asked to be lifted out of the wagon and laid on the ground apart from the others. Then she called Barbara to her. She put a hand on Barbara's arm and pulled her close. Doña Piedad's ashen lips trembled spasmodically, and for a long time she tried to speak without making any noise. Then the words came.

"In my clothes . . . the *tus*. Pretended to drink, so they would not know . . . saved it for you . . . all there . . ."

Barbara felt the woven water jar, muffled by yards of wool skirt. "Mother, it is yours—you must drink."

"It would be a waste. Heed me now. One can go without water five or six days they say. Save this. When you think you cannot stand it, pray. When you know you will die, pray. Keep praying until the *paraje* at Perillo. Then and only then will you take your first drink. Just a little at a time. It is the only way you will get through alive. And do not let anybody know. Some of those *ladrónes* from the Analco would kill you for it."

The effort of so many words had exhausted Doña Piedad. Her hand dropped to the ground. Helplessly Barbara looked at the gray face. It came to her that she had never really known her mother. Doña Piedad had simply been someone to sew with in the parlor, to walk with in the plaza, to be indifferent toward, to resist learning from (cooking, proverbs, prayers, how a proper lady talked, walked, sat down, got up) to gossip with when there was nothing else to do, to pout at, to resent, to listen grudgingly to, to be bored with.

Barbara bowed her head. "Mother," she said. "Mother."

They marched from the Cross of Anaya at dawn. Behind they left thirteen new graves. Large rocks scattered beside the trail had been used as headstones. One Cárdenas retainer had carved the legend: Doña Piedad Maria Cárdenas, Anno Domini 1680, *Ruegue por su alma.*

Pray for her soul.

Barbara seemed to have used up her grief during the night. Now it was like a luxury denied her, buried beneath her general misery. She held the *tus* against her body, hidden beneath her skirt. Just feeling it there, feeling the water slosh inside, made her thirst a thousand times worse.

A woman from the Analco stumbled against her. Barbara jerked away, glaring at her. *Ladrónes.* That was what Doña Piedad had called them. Thieves. Trying to get it from me. Willing to kill me for it. Why is that old man looking at me?

She stumbled and fell. She was on the ground, coughing in the dust and there were hands pulling at her.

"Leave me alone," she said. "Stay away, murderers, filth from the Analco, it is mine, do not touch me——"

"Barbara," the Condesa said. "It is I. Veronica. You do not understand. You must not lose your head now."

"I understand. I do not need your help. Do not touch me."

She got to her feet and began to walk again. She did not know how long it was. The sun seemed to be directly overhead and she could not see. She was dizzy and she began to laugh. It was funny really. She was the only one who would live and they had thought she would be the first to die and they had taken her out of the cart deliberately so that she could die and they could have the water and now she had fooled them. She laughed until she was so weak she could not laugh any more. Ahead the sun glittered on the towers of Mexico City, and she could hear the bells ringing.

"*Caracoles,*" she said. "A new viceroy must have arrived."

She heard someone groaning and she looked about her. She was huddled on the ground and it was almost dark. Two figures crouched beside her.

"Where are we?" she asked.

"La Paraje de la Laguna del Muerto," the Condesa said.

"How can that be? We just left the Madrid camp."

"It has been a day. We have traveled over two leagues."

Barbara remembered the water jar and hunted it frantically beneath her skirts. She found it and turned so the Condesa would not see and held it to her like a baby and rocked back and forth, murmuring and whimpering. The Condesa moved as though to help. Barbara pulled away.

"Let me alone. Take care of yourself."

The Condesa sank back. She had been burned by the sun till her face was scabby with blisters and cracked flesh.

Andres Rodrigo rode past, stopping by one of the soldiers. "I have such a thirst," he said. "I do not think we can go any longer without water."

The soldier did not answer. He rode away. Everyone knew how Andres Rodrigo had let Don Bernabe die back at Santa Fe. They showed him no contempt. They just seemed embarrassed in his presence. He turned to Barbara. He still had his boots on and two blankets rolled behind his saddle.

"Tell the officers we cannot go any longer without any water," he said. "If everybody agrees we could turn back to the river now."

She did not answer either. She bowed her head. She wanted him to go away. She did not want to think about the water. The water. She could not think about the water. If she thought about the water she could not stand it. She could not stand thinking about the water. She would drink the water and then when she needed the water most the water would be gone and she would die without the water. She would not think about the water. She would think about something else.

Proverbs.

She would think about all the proverbs her mother had taught her. The one about Santa Cruz. In Santa Cruz it is said that the toll of the bell is not for the dead but to remind us that we too may die tomorrow. He who ties well unties well. Short men and fools are recognized from afar. He who runs with wolves learns to howl. He who ties well ties well, in Santa Cruz a short man rings the toll of the bell, he who runs with fools learns from afar, a short wolf learns to die . . .

There were more dead that night than at any previous camp and the people had to work in shifts to dig the shallow graves and they were so weak that it took them most of the night to inter the bodies. They left the Lagoon of the Dead on the dawn of August 17. They had been four days without food of any kind and two days without water. All day long the people died.

Near noon a woman went out of her head and ran raving into the desert. Her husband tottered after her and fell on his face a hundred yards from the road. The colonists marched on, gazing at him apathetically. A mounted man stopped by him and inspected him and said he was dead. Later a man announced that he was Governor Otermin and would lead them to water. A score of colonists followed him into the Fray Cristobals. García sent some soldiers to bring them back, and in the struggle the man who thought he was Otermin was killed.

Barbara stumbled past the body of a man who had fallen and saw that it was her uncle, Don Celso. Somebody told her he was dead. They told the Condesa that her *zambo* coachman had died in the wagon. Barbara saw some soldiers lifting the dead body of Luis Ribera's mother into a cart. She saw the priest administer final sacraments to Luis's maternal grandfather, Don Evora Maynez. A soldier estimated that for every league they advanced through the Jornada fifteen people were dying. That meant five people to the mile. If they had buried them where they fell it would make a new grave every thousand feet.

The only ones left of the Cárdenas family now were Don Celso's wife who was Barbara's aunt, and Engracia, Barbara's married sister. Engracia had been stumbling along behind the second wagon with her baby in her arms. Sometime near noon Barbara saw the baby fall to the earth. Engracia went to her knees over the child.

"Will someone not help? My arms will no longer support him."

An old man stopped above her, swaying visibly. "*Señora* . . . the child has been dead since yesterday."

Nazario stumbled past, tugging feebly at people and asking, "Have you seen my daughter? Have you seen Kashana?"

All through the day Barbara clutched the water jar to her. Just two more days. She felt so weak. Just two more days to Perillo and then she could drink. How could anyone feel so weak? She knew she could not stand it that long. But she would die if she did not wait. She knew she would have to drink before she got to Perillo. She heard the water slosh. She whimpered and hugged it to her. Two days was too long.

Someone had fallen beside her. Barbara stared blankly. After a long time she realized it was the Condesa, with the Zapotec maid crouched beside her.

"Water," Chintule said. "If she could only have water. She is dying for it. A drop would save her. Just a drop."

Barbara sank to her knees. Chintule shook the Condesa and pled with her to rise, but the Condesa did not respond. Barbara hugged the *tus* to her and rocked back and forth. She whimpered. She began to shudder.

"Condesa," the Zapotec maid said. She shook her mistress, pleading. "*Patróna——*"

The Condesa moaned softly. She did not open her eyes. Barbara began to cry. There was not enough moisture in her body for tears, but she was crying. She took the water container from beneath her skirts. She was so weak it took her a long time to get the top off. Chintule stared uncomprehendingly at the jar. With her fingers Barbara parted the Condesa's lips and let the water trickle between them. The mouth filled and the water spilled across the woman's face. At the sight of it Barbara groaned. The Condesa choked, and the movement of her head spilled more water from the jar.

"Hold her head up," Barbara said. She was still crying. "We must not choke her to death. I think it must be done with extreme slowness."

Chintule lifted the woman's head. Again Barbara tilted the container to her lips. Once more the Condesa choked, her whole body going into a feeble convulsion, and more water spilled. Barbara cried and worked to get some water down the woman's throat.

At last the Condesa revived. She opened her eyes and saw the jar. She caught it with both hands. She drank weakly at first. Then she became more greedy. Barbara tried to hold her back but the Condesa fought her off. As much water streamed off her chin as into her mouth. Barbara looked at the precious water sinking into the sand.

"Mother of God," she said.

She fought the Condesa for the *tus*. Infected by their struggle the maid gave way to her own thirst. All three fought over the water, cursing each other. They rolled in the sand. They made snarling sounds and rolled back and forth in the sand and clawed at each other and struggled for the container.

Barbara finally tore it from the Condesa's hands. Fending the maid off, she put it to her lips. Nothing came out. She bent over backward and tilted the woven jar against her mouth. Still there was nothing. She emitted a broken cry and took it in both hands, shaking it. She put it down and bent over it and began to cry again.

Spent by her effort, the Condesa lay back. She stared at Barbara and then at the jar. Her eyes were no longer glazed.

"Why did you let me do it?" she asked. "Why?"

"You would have died," the maid said.

Barbara stopped crying. She began to laugh. She shrieked with laughter. "No importance," she said. She could not stop laughing. "He who ties well unties well."

That night it was hot. The earth remained hot, and the heat was like a pressure in the air. A hot wind came up and blew hot sand steadily against them, and the people huddled against each other or lay on the ground with their heads covered and panted feebly for air.

Barbara saw Toribio Quintano sitting by the horse lines. He was regarding his mutilated feet. Two days ago his horse had become so loaded down with sick and dying children that he had been forced to walk and lead the animal. The rocky land had soon shredded the thin soles of his fine boots.

Barbara wondered why he did not cut up strips of his blanket and wrap them about his feet as the Condesa and others had been doing.

She remembered him sleeping in a blanket before Sandia. But he did not seem to have a blanket now.

It made her look at the ragged length of blanket in the Condesa's lap. Every night the woman got a new strip of wool like that. Barbara never saw where it came from. She had been too exhausted to care. She looked back at Toribio.

If she had not been so weak she would have laughed at her own foolishness. Not him. Not the sheriff of the Holy Office. He would not even go two steps out of his way to keep his own mother from dying.

When Barbara woke the next morning her tongue was so swollen that she could hardly breathe. She had no desire to go on. She listened to the people dragging themselves to their feet all about her. She listened to the babies crying and the men groaning and the women coughing weakly and whispering prayers to their saints. She did not want to go with them. She did not even feel any fear at the thought of being left behind. She just wanted to go back to sleep.

"Get up," the Condesa said. "You must get up."

"You go on. I will stay here."

"No. You must get up, Barbara. You must . . ."

Finally the Condesa got her to her knees. Barbara was so weak she could not rise any farther. She was dizzy and she fell on her face again. She wanted to cry but she was too weak to cry. She wanted to tell the Condesa to leave her alone but she was too weak to talk. The Condesa asked for help, and a pair of soldiers lifted Barbara erect. With the Condesa and Chintule holding her up she tried to walk.

"I am so weak," she said. "My head buzzes."

"You will feel better. Simply keep walking."

She began to feel pain in her feet. Soon she could not bear it. She sank to her knees.

"My feet . . . I cannot stand it."

The Condesa took the strips of blanket from her own feet and wound them about Barbara's feet.

"These are the last," she said. "We will have to make them do as long as possible."

The Condesa had to get the soldiers to lift Barbara up again. They were in rocky country. The wool was cut to shreds before noon. Again Barbara could not bear it. She sank to her knees, and she was so weak that she did not even try to tell the Condesa about the pain. The Condesa took off her expensive *rebozo* and began tearing it up.

"You cannot," Barbara said. Her voice sounded far away. "The sun . . . your head . . ."

The Condesa wound the strips of her shawl around Barbara's feet till they made a thick padding. She and Chintule helped Barbara up again. The three of them walked together, holding each other erect.

That was the fourth day the colonists had gone without water. No hour passed without someone dropping by the road, either dead or unable to go on. Many could not bear the pain of their feet any longer and were crawling on all fours.

With her head uncovered it was not long before the Condesa began to suffer from the heat. She complained of dizziness. She had hallucinations.

"Over there by the lake . . . the Count of Zumurraga. Such an old man . . . cannot perform the function. But I really never cared, is that not curious? Maybe it is why we got along so well, I never really cared, and we talked of so many things. . . ."

She fell and pulled the other two with her. Barbara crouched over her and fanned her and massaged her till she regained consciousness. They got her on her feet and started again. Later that afternoon Barbara said:

"It is so windy. Is the wind going to blow the sand up again?"

"There is no wind."

"What is that roar?"

"Barbara!"

The Condesa was pulled to her knees when Barbara fell. She looked dully at the girl, who lay face down on the sand. She shook her. It did no good. She remembered how Barbara had revived her, and she massaged the girl and fanned her. She worked until she was too weak to do anything more. Two of the soldiers who brought up the rear halted their horses by the woman.

"Is she dead?" one of them asked the Condesa.

"I cannot tell."

"You must not stay here. You will die."

"I will stay here. She may be alive."

The soldiers were carrying children and there was no more room on their horses. Reluctantly they reined around and followed the last stumbling figures of the column. A man crawled past the Condesa on his hands and knees. She saw that it was one of the convict soldiers named Emilio. When he was gone Chintule tugged at the Condesa.

"Save yourself," the Condesa said. She put a hand on Barbara's neck and felt the feeble pulse that she had been unable to feel before. "There is still a flicker. Go on. When it is cooler she will revive."

The maid whimpered and did not move. The Condesa lay across Barbara's body and put her arms over her head. They spent the night without moving from the spot. The next day Barbara was still unconscious. In the afternoon a wind came up. The sand blew for hours. It filled their noses and eyes and mouths. It covered Barbara, and the Condesa had to keep digging it away. When she grew too weak to dig she lay across Barbara, reduced to small motions with one hand around the girl's mouth that kept her from smothering. By nightfall she thought she was going to die. She made her Act of Perfect Contrition.

"O my God, I am sorry and beg pardon for all my sins, not so much because these sins bring suffering and Hell to me, but because they have crucified my loving Saviour Jesus Christ and offended Thy Infinite Goodness, I firmly resolve with the help of Thy Grace to confess my sins, to do penance, and to amend my life. Amen."

She awoke to a bright pain in her eyes. It was the light of the rising sun. She opened her eyes. She could see nothing at first. Then mirages took shape. She saw mounted men. She tried to call out to them. No sound would come. She tried to rise and could not. She crawled toward them on her stomach. Her throat convulsed a long time before any sound would come. Crawling toward them she finally managed a cry. She cried out again, more strongly, and then collapsed. In a little while she heard horses stamping about her and looked up again.

"Of truth?" she said.

One of the riders dismounted and knelt by her. "We are from the supply train. It met your people at the Alivio *paraje*. There is food and water for all. We were sent back to find those who had fallen by the way."

"Over there." The Condesa waved behind her. "She still has life, she must still have life."

A man rode over to the heap of sand covering Barbara. He swore and said, "Good luck that you were here, *señora*. We never would have found this one."

CHAPTER TWENTY-FOUR

HE had memories. He had vague memories of faces and bodies and pain. Of walking, talking, crawling, of a strange country with snow-topped mountains rimming the world like whitecaps on a dark sea, of a small place full of smoke that made him cough and a woman sitting beside him and singing in a strange tongue.

Luis Ribera opened his eyes. He was lying on a bed of boughs that rustled with his slightest movement. About him were the crumbling walls of a small roofless chamber. In one corner he saw the ashes of a recent fire and the small bones of rabbits and birds scattered on the floor.

He became aware of himself. The Rouen shirt and velvet jacket were in tatters. Through countless rips in his ruined breeches his legs looked frighteningly scrawny. He could not move his left arm without a throbbing flood of pain, and he saw that it was covered from shoulder to elbow with a crude buckskin bandage.

He tried to remember where he was, how he had gotten here. Thinking was an effort that made him dizzy. He was rolling over on his right side when he heard the scratch and rattle of someone approaching. A figure was silhouetted in the entrance to the chamber. An Indian. A woman.

"Kashana," he said.

She looked like something from the Stone Age. Her hair had come unbraided and hung lank and matted on either side of her haggard face. Grime stained her buckskin dress, and her black mantle, draped diagonally over one shoulder, was in tatters. Her cotton leg wrappings had come loose and collapsed in a thick heap about her ankles, dirty ends trailing. At a makeshift buckskin belt were hung Luis's powder flask and bullet pouch. In one hand she held his ball-butted firelock, and in the other, by its ears, she held a dead rabbit.

"You . . ." he said helplessly. "You . . . this place."

"Yapashi," she said. Her eyes were almost accusing.

The name was familiar. It was one of the towns sacred to the Pueblos, half myth, half reality, claimed as a point of origin by many villages. Kashana put the dead rabbit and the heavy pistol by the fire and sat down. She began tugging at her leg wrappings, as though just becoming aware of their sorry state, self-conscious as a daughter of the fine people whose hair was out of place. It was a glimpse of femininity she had never shown him before.

He said brokenly, "The last I remember . . . Sandia . . . the wall falling on me."

At first he thought she would not answer. She pulled at the leg wrappings, her face turned down so that all he could see was the top of her head. In a muffled voice she said:

"My father kept guard on me. He the man did not let me run away. At Sandia he got in the fight. Therefore I ran away. I ran by the church and an Indian ran out and told me how you were dead inside. I waited until he was gone and then I went in and pulled the adobe away. You were asleep. You were not awake. The beam——" With her hand she showed him how it had been jammed against the wall in a slanting position so that he was protected and not crushed. "Therefore you could breathe and were not dead."

"But this place . . . we must be fifty miles from there," he said.

Again he saw her reluctance to talk. Finally, "I got you awake. You were crazy and you talked about things I did not understand but you could walk. We went by night. You could go no farther than this."

"How long have we been here?"

"I have lost count."

"The people . . . the Spaniards?"

She shook her head from side to side. He studied her face. The slant of afternoon sunlight turned it coppery, the oblique cheekbones, the tilted eyes, an Oriental idol. He wondered how it could appear so fragile and still emanate the sullen strength of a primitive race. He wondered why she had done this, a woman who had showed him nothing but hatred before. Or had she?

"That time at Sante Fe," he said. "When the Indians took the cannons at the gate." He saw that her hands had grown still, the slender fingers strained tight against the dirty strips of cotton leg wrapping. He said, "You were supposed to distract my attention, truth? So I would not see them attacking." She kept her head bowed. Her hands did not move. Insistently he went on. "The kiss. Just to distract my attention. Nothing else."

He remembered the biting, the clawing, the passion. She was not that good an actress.

"But something happened," he said.

She did not speak.

"Something you hadn't planned on."

"Nothing!" she said. "Nothing happened."

"Then why did you do this?"

She did not answer. She pulled his knife from her belt and began skinning the rabbit. When she was finished she lit a fire with flint and steel and spitted the rabbit. When they had gnawed the last shred of meat off the last bone she changed the dressing on his wound. She removed the buckskin bandage, and his first whiff of the putrefying flesh gagged him. He turned his head away while she washed the swollen arm with hot water. Half a dozen prickly-pear paddles were heaped in one corner. She chopped one up and chewed the pieces and mixed the pulp with gunpowder and with some precious fat that had dripped from the rabbit into a broken pottery bowl. She caked the poultice deeply on his wound and wrapped it again in the buckskin heated over the fire. Whenever he woke that night he could feel it drawing, insistently, painfully, like a hand squeezing the putrescence from the wound.

Through the following days his fever rose and fell, and when it was high he tossed and sweated in the crumbling little room for hours he could not measure. Sometimes he lapsed back into delirium, and those days were lost to him. But he began to see improvement. His arm did not seem so swollen, the poultice was slowly sucking the infection out of his body, the fever was burning itself out.

Each morning Kashana left and each evening she returned with their food. But the hunting was bad and soon she had used up their ammunition. They were reduced to eating field mice trapped in the ruined city or piñon nuts that were not yet ripe. She hunted the roots of the wild onion and the lily and brought him rotten berries of the ground tomato and milkweed that they had to eat raw, and sometimes she made him tea from the flowers of the coyote plant.

He had too much time to think when he was alone. Bigotes. Don Bernabe. Don Cristobal. Father Pio. The shock had not yet worn off. He thought of the Pueblos. He sat once more beside the Marqués de

Gallegos on the road above Sandia and looked at the mutilated bodies of his people and was swept again with the bitterness of final and complete disillusionment, the unbelievable hatred for a people who could do such a thing. He called them beasts.

There came a day when he could crawl around the room, another day when he could stand. Soon afterward while Kashana was off hunting roots he explored the ruins. There were countless chambers, stone-walled, roofless, all connected, larger than any community dwelling of the Pueblos he had ever seen. The silence of centuries hung over the buildings. He wondered how many ages ago the brown people had lived here, turned silent by the appalling solitude, as Kashana was turned silent, hunting as she hunted, dressed in their furred robes, firing the pottery that still left its shards scattered through the rooms. Why had they left? War? Pestilence? Drought? Or had the gods spoken?

He came to a last crumbled wall and crawled through a breach in the big tufa blocks. There was scrubby timber near at hand, the knuckled junipers he loved. He was already dizzy and weak from the unaccustomed exertion. He left the buildings and toiled to a high point. The timber broke away and he stopped suddenly, the breath sucked from him by the view.

On every side the world swept away into awesome depths. He was on top of a towering mesa. Once it had been part of a vast tableland. Some upheaval of nature had cracked the surface, creating countless parallel canyons thousands of feet deep that ran from east to west. The ridges of volcanic rock remaining between the cracks were in some places only a few hundred yards wide, in others several miles from edge to edge.

He knew where he was now. He was somewhere far west of Santa Fe, west of the Rio Grande. He was in a part of the province few Spaniards had ever seen. He was in the *potrero* country.

Luis grew stronger as the days passed. Something was coming to a head during that time, a pressure in Luis, a restlessness. There came a night when he could not sit idly by the fire, relaxed, warmed, his belly full at last. He rose and paced restlessly around the camp. Kashana sat against a wall, looking into the fire. She paid him no heed.

It struck him how much of the time they had spent together without talking. It made him remember the ocean of words that had flowed between himself and the Condesa. She had made all other women seem shallow to him, stupid, hopelessly inarticulate.

Yet silence seemed as natural to Kashana as talk to the Condesa.

Something would have been spoiled by too many words. Like a couple of animals, he thought, in their cave.

She had made a bone comb and had washed her hair at the creek and combed it for the first time in weeks. She had done it up in braids, and they lay in enamel-black plaits against the bowed line of her neck. Firelight danced on the arrowhead points of her cheekbones. She sat with one leg beneath her. The thigh strained in a sleek curve against the buckskin. It seemed hard for him to breathe.

Without looking up, she said, "Do not tire yourself."

"I am stronger," he said. "You would be surprised."

He stopped by her. She looked up at him. The position made the line of her neck look strained. It pulled her lips away from her teeth in a curiously penitent expression. The firelight flashed in her eyes. She made a quick motion to rise and get away.

He caught her shoulders. She was on her knees against his legs, and she fought to get free while he tried to pull her up to him. Her wild lunging forced him backward, and he tripped and fell and pulled her with him.

He rolled over on the ground, and it brought him sprawling across her body. He caught her hair in both hands and held her head rigid while he kissed her.

She fought savagely to get away, and he fought to hold her. It was all done in a sort of wordless fury. The only sound they made was their harsh breathing and the scuffle of their straining bodies on the ground.

She jerked her head from side to side to avoid his lips. She caught his head with both hands and kissed him with an open mouth. She writhed in her efforts to escape. She arched against him with a frantic moaning sound. Her hands clawed and sought to push him away. Her hands pulled him to her.

CHAPTER TWENTY-FIVE

NOVEMBER at Yapashi. Purple mountains against a turquoise sky. The nights bitterly cold and the rains beating the piñon harvest to a sodden mass beneath the twisted trees and the ice forming a jeweled crust on every stream. Snow would be next and all the animals gone.

The hunting had grown steadily worse, and both Luis and Kashana knew they could not last through the winter on the mesa. They were already near starvation. Kashana said the only place they could survive was with her mother's people. The village was a hundred and ten miles southwest of Santa Fe, fifty miles west of the Rio Grande itself. The people had not taken part in the battle at Santa Fe or the killing along the Rio Grande. They were too distant to suffer the oppression as had the Indians closer along the river. They had a priest but no *encomendero*. Most of them did not know what it was to work for a Spaniard. Kashana told him she was a member of the Antelope clan, from which the rulers of the village were chosen. Many older members of the clan had not been in sympathy with the rebellion, and she was sure they would spare Luis's life if she asked them to.

He knew he was not strong enough to reach his own people. They were too far to the south. Hundreds of miles of winter desert and hostile Indians lay between. He had to go with Kashana. It was his only chance of survival.

They climbed down out of the *potreros* onto the floor of the high desert west of the Rio Grande. Luis had never been so impressed with the immensity of this country. Everything was on a scale almost too vast to comprehend. Like motes they crawled across the endless miles of the tableland, now winter gray, now buckskin, now red with iron. Then one day the two people reached a barrier cliff that banded the horizon, enormous slabs of brick-red rock, broken, cracked, towering for hundreds of feet above the flats. They had come to mesa land.

They toiled past the southern tip of the first barrier and saw beyond it more mesas, smaller, more clearly defined, some almost cubelike, flat-topped, all four sides rising sheer from the plain.

Frozen, exhausted, they labored on. The mesas closed in about them, forming gorges, canyons, a gigantic labyrinth to be threaded. Then one sunset the labyrinth opened out again. They were on the floor of a valley that ran westward for five miles, ending in a wall of beetling crags. In the center of the valley, halfway between them and the westward wall, was another mesa.

It was the most fantastic Luis had yet seen. Its perpendicular walls hundreds of feet high, overhanging in some places, made it a dizzy island in the air. Erosion had turned its sheer escarpments into a wonderland of light and shadow, the black mouths of mysterious bays, the engineering of giant buttresses, the Oriental glitter of slender minarets. An enormous rock balanced on the edge of an abyss. A natural bridge arched sublimely across a plunging crevice. Huge water-carved columns stood separate from the cliffs like the broken idols of a vanished race. It was all stained crimson by the sun, hazy, crumbling, a Babylonian ruin. After staring at it a long time Kashana said:

"It is Acoma."

CHAPTER TWENTY-SIX

WHEN Hernando Cortez and his Spaniards first saw Mexico City in 1519 it was an Indian capital. It was called Tenochtitlán and built on a lake almost a mile and a half above the sea. It lay in the fabled Valley of Anahuac, a basin thirty miles wide and fifty miles long, walled on every side by some of the highest mountains in the New World. The stone pyramids and pink palaces of the Aztecs rose from islands in the lake, and the islands were separated by canals and connected by bridges and causeways.

One hundred and sixty-two years afterward, in 1681, Mexico City was a Spanish capital. The Aztec buildings were gone, torn down to fill the lake, but there was still enough water to leave many of the bridges and canals. There were four hundred thousand people in the eight square miles of the walled capital—and the Zocalo was its heart.

This Plaza Mayor was a microcosm of the city, a place of fantastic contrasts. Every morning the filth-laden waters of the Canal de las Canoas were covered with Indian canoes sunk to the gunwales with vegetables or half buried beneath the exotic flowers grown at the floating gardens of Xochimilco to be sold at the Portal de las Flores on the Zocalo. The portal was only one of the dozens of public markets that edged the square. Under their palm-thatched roofs were silver heaps of onions and scarlet strings of chile; merchants haggled over silks from Cathay and linen from the Netherlands; butchers killed hogs and quartered sheep, oblivious to the swarming flies and hysterical yapping of scavenging dogs. The smell of incense so characteristic of the city

could not compete with the odors of fresh blood and garbage and decay
that hung over the Zocalo.

Over it all was the endless clanging of bells that regimented the
life of the city—the tinkling between formal hours to regulate the de-
votions of the nuns and monks in the convents, the melancholy tone
of the Ave Maria calling the devout to first Masses, the languid pealing
of the great Doña Ana in the cathedral tower to announce the noon
hour.

Spokes from the hub, the streets spread outward from the Zocalo,
few of them cobbled, most of them mere dirt alleyways that were
turned to shadowed canyons by the houses standing wall to wall on
both sides. Most of these houses were of stone quarried nearby, the
tezontle of the Aztecs, a peculiar traprock so porous and pitted that
its surface took on the look of a tangled and petrified beard. The house
at Number Five Calle de las Plateros was made of such hairstone,
darker than the pink Aztec palaces, almost maroon, roofed with red
Puebla tile and trimmed and corniced with the somber gray *chiluca*.
It was a big house, three stories tall, with delicate wrought-iron *rejas*
barring its windows.

At one end of the house, overlooking the street, was the round tower
room. If one of the shutters in this room was opened a crack a person
standing there could look down the Street of the Silversmiths and see
a portion of the plaza.

Barbara de Cárdenas stood there.

She stood indifferently, looking but not seeing. May 25, 1681, a
typical spring day for the capital. Crisp, clear, with a wind shepherding
fleecy clouds across the achingly blue sky and banking them against the
white tower of Popocatapetl far to the southeast.

The Condesa Veronica de Zumurraga sat across the spacious room,
tuning her *vihuela*. Her husky voice joined the discordant twang of
strings. "Of what do you think, little one?"

"I think I am bored," Barbara said.

"Simply that I am a prisoner should not allow you to become one,"
the Condesa said. "You must get out, a party, young men."

Barbara stirred restlessly. "Is that the answer, Veronica? I have a
feeling . . . I cannot explain . . . when we were in Santa Fe, coming
down the river, at El Paso, I thought all I wanted to do was get back
here . . . I thought I would be happy the rest of my life in this
place . . ."

"There will be adjustments, little one. A new life to make. It will
take time."

"Life," Barbara said. "I felt closer to it out there on the Jornada, when we were dying. I could see things so clearly. It has withdrawn again, behind a veil."

The Condesa laughed softly. "Perhaps you learned too much then, *chica*. Too fast. It will take time for you to understand it all."

Barbara glanced at the Condesa. In the shadowed corner the woman looked stunning. A tiara of pearls sparkled in her black hair. Her brows were thin arched stencils above the belladonna brightness of her eyes. She wore an expensive brocade dress from the household wardrobe, let out to fit her, the skirt held out by half a dozen petticoats, the bodice gored and tightly fitted and edged with lawn. Barbara thought it made too much of the breasts, but she had not spoken. At least she could not argue with the whole effect. One would never know how recently they had left the harrowing ordeal of the Jornada.

The colonists had arrived at El Paso on September 13 of the previous year. An official count had placed them at 1947. At Fray Cristobal, at the northern edge of the Journey of the Dead, the count had been 2520. It still sickened Barbara to remember. Over five hundred of them, in that one stretch thirty leagues across, dying in the carts, wandering into the desert, sinking to the road unable to go on, the headstones left behind at every camp site. . . .

At the La Toma *paraje*, twelve leagues above El Paso, the colonists had settled down for the winter, sustained by grain and meat from the Guadalupe missions. Bitter weather was upon them, and the priests and women and even Governor Otermin worked side by side to erect shelters.

Barbara was the only one remaining of the large Cárdenas family. But the Gallegos' had been friends of her father in Mexico City and the Marqués offered her his protection. A party of colonists was going on to the capital and they joined it. Over the protests of the Marqués de Gallegos, Barbara insisted that the Condesa accompany her.

The Marqués's reluctance was only based on hearsay. He knew nothing firsthand of the Condesa's career in Mexico City, and her relationship with the Inquisition was still only rumor. Barbara was the only one who knew some of the substance behind that rumor. The ordeal in the Jornada had created a deep bond between the two women, and the Condesa had admitted to Barbara that she was on file with the Holy Office. Barbara knew what a risk she would incur by giving such a woman her friendship. Yet without the Condesa she would not be alive.

In Mexico City they had contrived to make it appear that the Condesa left the wagon train in the plaza and engaged passage on a coach to Acapulco. But that night Barbara had met her at the cathedral and had taken her to the tower room of the Cárdenas house. Chintule and Josefina were the only two servants who knew the Condesa's identity. None of the others had seen her come in, and they were forbidden to enter the tower room. Barbara had told them that the Condesa was one of her cousins from Santa Fe who was near death from the Jornada and must not be disturbed. . . .

The clop of shod hooves in the street below broke into her thoughts. She saw a man on a miserable horse. His velvet breeches were tawdry, his cloak patched, his yellow vicuña hat shabby and faded with age. But his stirrups were coupled short, *a la gineta*, and he sat his battered Moorish saddle with all the pride of a nobleman. He held himself haughtily oblivious to the street life flowing about him, the barefoot slaves and the sedan chairs that were forced to circle him and the half-naked Indians who squatted in shadowed doorways. A beggar clutched at his knee, and he jabbed the man away with his spur. In the crowded street he had a look of unique loneliness. In front of the Cárdenas house he halted his horse and looked up at the windows. The face was surprisingly familiar, ravaged, sardonic.

Barbara said, "It looks like Toribio Quintano."

The *vihuela* made a discordant twang behind her. She heard the rustle of the Condesa's skirt, and the woman was at her side. The Condesa took one look into the street and then snapped the shutter closed. Her face looked white, strained.

"It cannot be," she said. "We left him at La Toma, he is still there, he must be——"

Barbara grasped her arm. "Do not have the fright. If he came back they must have removed him from his post. He looked so shabby. He could not be sheriff and look that shabby. He does not have the power to arrest you."

"I was not thinking of that."

"Of what, then?"

"Nothing. Maybe I was. I do not know." The Condesa sent Barbara a strange glance and then turned away, locking her hands together. "Barbara, I can stay here no longer——"

"Where would you go?"

"But I cannot let you take the risk any longer."

"It cannot be as great a risk as you think."

"How would you know? Your *limpieza de sangre*—your purity of blood. How would you know what it is to be a woman alone? To be watched day and night, followed everywhere you go, the informers putting down everything you say, the familiars twisting whatever you do? Have you ever seen an Act of Faith?"

"The last one here was years before I was born."

"Then you do not even know what that *quemadero* is for at the east end of the Alameda. You have never seen them tied there, with the faggots piled around their feet. You have never heard them praying and smelled their burning flesh——"

"Condesa!"

"And when you pass the palace of the Inquisition what do you think? Have you seen the dungeons?"

"No—of course not."

"Have you ever seen them carry someone from the rack? Broken and twisted like some doll they had stepped on!"

The Condesa made a small sound and pressed her long fingers to her cheeks. Then she reached behind her neck. A comb appeared in her hand. It had been hidden in the mass of her hair. She did something, and a thin blade slid from the comb.

"They will not do those things to me," she said.

Barbara gazed at the blade, deeply shaken. This was not the first time they had talked of the Inquisition, but the Condesa had kept the depths of her emotion hidden before. The Holy Office was as much a part of their lives as the cathedral on the square, the bells that never stopped ringing, the beggars around the public fountains. Barbara had not realized how much they took it for granted. She had never been so close to someone under its threat.

The Condesa made the blade disappear and hid the comb once more in the abundance of her hair. She closed her eyes. "Forgive me. One should not dramatize it. One should learn to live with it, like a weak heart or a headache or leprosy."

"It is so unjust. You are a better Catholic than most of us."

"My mother was a *morisco*. It is inconceivable to them that I do not bear the taint."

There was a knock on the door. Chintule had been crouching near the Condesa's chair on a mattress rolled against the wall. The little Zapotec maid rose and scurried to the door on silent bare feet. She admitted Josefina, who announced Don Gómez Gallegos and his brother, the Marqués.

"Keep them in the patio; I will receive them there," Barbara told her maid. As the girl left, Barbara crossed to kneel before the Condesa and take her hands. She said, "They have come to take me out to the estate. I will be back as soon as possible. In the meantime—do not worry. You will stay here forever if you like. You will never have cause to use that comb."

CHAPTER TWENTY-SEVEN

THE black lacquered coach clattered across the Cárdenas patio and into the tunnel of the *zaguán* that pierced one wing of the house and opened on the Street of the Silversmiths. Once in the street the coach turned toward the plaza. Barbara sat inside. She wore a cloak of blue satin with an immense upturned collar that made her face look small and big-eyed and very grave as she faced the two Gallegos brothers.

Don Gómez Gallegos was forty-five. He had a meticulously preserved look. His olive cheeks were smooth and shiny, and his narrow chin was pointed by a precise goatee. There was a sumptuous announcement of estate in his Dutch linen shirt with collars to the shoulders, his knee-length vest edged in gold.

He came from a family of rich landholders and was one of the finest legal minds in the colonies. The archbishop had recently recommended him to fill the vacancy left in the *audiencia* by the death of Barbara's father. The twelve judges of the audience had a twofold function, acting as an advisory board to the viceroy and also sitting as the highest criminal and civil tribunal in the colony.

Don Desidero, the Marqués de Gallegos, sat beside him. He was dressed as sumptuously as his brother, with the powdered wig that he always wore now to cover his scalped baldness. The look of the genteel Mephisto was gone from his face. It was marked by the horror he had suffered. The flesh of his cheeks had the yellow, papery look of old parchment. His eyes were sunken, and when he turned them on anyone they became fixed and staring.

"My brother tells me you have decided not to go to Spain," he said.

Barbara stiffened against the seat as the coach lurched. "I was born here, Don Desidero."

"There are still some relatives," Don Gómez said. He spoke a precise, lisping Castilian. "Your aunt Ramona in Peru, Cousin Nuno in Madrid. Your father was a rich man, Barbara. They will be like bees to the honey."

"You said the will was unbreakable."

Don Gómez tilted his head quizzically and smoothed his hair with a lean forefinger. It was jet-black hair, varnished with a pomade that perfumed the coach. He had been a close friend to Barbara's father, and when Don Melchor had taken his family to Santa Fe he had made Don Gómez executor of the estate till the family should return.

"As your father's only direct survivor," Don Gómez said, "the will should protect you. But there are always unforeseen contingencies. Litigations could be instituted that would drain away most of your estate even if you won. For your own good perhaps it would be better to go to Madrid."

She shook her head stubbornly. "I have made my choice."

Don Gómez smiled. "You have changed, little one. You could never make a decision before. As much as picking a skirt for a party left you in a state of shock for days."

They passed through the Zocalo and went eastward out of the city. They crossed the broad valley, flowering with the first showers of the wet season, and reached the Cárdenas land in the afternoon. The Indians were like ants on the hillsides, planting corn with pointed sticks in the ancient way. Stone walls and masonry aqueducts green with moss paralleled the road. Ahead Barbara saw the familiar *cuezcomate*—the great clay urn of the granary in which shelled corn was stored.

A pair of Indians sat against the adobe wall of a shed, their legs stretched out, their feet in stocks. Nearby stood half a dozen barefoot Indians in ragged white *tilmas,* and three mounted men.

"Are those my people?" Barbara asked.

"Some of them," Don Gómez said. "The one on the bay horse is your *mayordomo,* Fecundo Rascon."

"Will you stop the coach?" Barbara said. "I want to know what is going on."

The Marqués started to protest, but Don Gómez sent him a warning glance, then called to the coachman. The driver swung the team around and brought them to a halt by the granary. Fecundo Rascon walked his horse to them and was introduced to Barbara through the window. The overseer was a dark man, thick-lipped and sullen, wearing greasy rawhide clothes. He had a pair of firelocks holstered at his saddle, beside a heavy machete. The other two riders had arquebuses in rawhide scabbards slung from the saddle.

"Who are the ones in the stocks?" Barbara asked.

Rascon scratched his beard with broken, tobacco-stained fingernails. "Indians from the village. They deserted the ploughing."

"Why?"

"Their wife was having a baby, their great-grandmother was sick, they had to plant corn—the usual reasons."

The men in the stocks were naked to the waist, and as one shifted uncomfortably she saw that there were raw whip stripes on his back. It made Barbara think of Luis Ribera. Why should it make her think of Luis Ribera?

Don Gómez gave an order, and the driver swung the coach back onto the road. With Fecundo Rascon following they climbed the slope to the house. Here at last were trees, an avenue half a mile long of the giant, rutted *ahuehuetes* that dated back to the Aztec times. The gate at the end of the trees was guarded by crumbling stone towers, and a massive stone wall surrounded the compound. The house was a long one-story building fronted by a portal—a dozen arches of pink hairstone roofed with crumbling red Puebla tiles. The aged housekeeper and a pair of retainers waited under the arches. Barbara had not been here in two years, and they greeted her with tears in their eyes.

In the parlor they were served chocolate and *buñuelos* and *queso de tuna*. Rascon brought out the books and Don Gómez attempted to explain them to Barbara. But she was still thinking of the Indians in the stocks.

She excused herself, pretending that she wanted to inspect the kitchen. The housekeeper was rattling about among her pots and pans. After a few words with her Barbara stepped out back. She saw one of the Indians at the corner of the house, an old man with a face furrowed and colored exactly like a prune. She went to him.

"I do not remember you," she said.

"I am Jacobo—from the free village."

These free villagers were for the most part pure Indian, Aztec, direct descendants of the Nahuatl tribes that had occupied the Valley of Anahuac before the conquest. They did not belong with the indentured retainers who maintained the estate all year and lived in the little compound near the main house. Their villages were far back in the mountains, and they came to work only during the rush seasons of planting and harvest. Barbara looked toward the clay granary where the Indians sat in the stocks.

"Don Melchor was my father, Jacobo. I want to treat you as he treated you. There is something wrong here—something I do not remember. Pepe Leon was overseer when we left. What happened to him?"

Jacobo moistened his lips, looking at the ground. "Don Gómez wanted him to hire us without pay. Pepe would not do it. Pepe said your father had always paid the legal wage—a *real* a day. If some did not want to work they were not whipped. There were plenty to take their place. Don Gómez got rid of Pepe and brought this Fecundo Rascon from the city with those other men who carry guns."

"And you are not paid?"

"Now they come after us in the mountains and bring us down at gun point." Jacobo waved his hat toward the men in the stocks. "Pablo he had worked for two months, four weeks over the legal limit. His own field needed planting and they had not paid him."

He looked past her suddenly, and his eyes widened like a little child staring into a dark room. She turned and saw that the Marqués de Gallegos stood in the door.

"It is time to go, Barbara," he said.

In the coach, on the road going back to Mexico City, Barbara sat facing the two Gallegos brothers. She was thinking of Luis Ribera again. She remembered how he had been denounced to the Holy Office for protecting the Indians of his *encomienda* against illegal impressment. How could a person believe in anything that much? To defy the Holy Office.

And on the Jornada the Condesa had said Luis would not love her. Luis would not love her if she did not give up her place in the wagon to her mother who was dying. Would he not love her now for being a coward?

She looked out the window. She was being silly. Thinking that way about a man who was dead.

"What was Jacobo talking about?" the Marqués asked.

Barbara glanced at the man's mordant face. She remembered what a classic picture of nobility he had been in Santa Fe—the epitome of Spain, the don, grave, arrogant, in icy command of himself at all times. Now he seemed extremely nervous. He drummed his bony fingers on the window sill. His lips pursed, thinned, flattened against his teeth. He pulled self-consciously at his wig, waiting for her answer.

Barbara said, "As a judge my father could not hold his estate in *encomienda*, could he?"

"Of course not." The Marqués gripped his knees tightly. "No royal official can."

She looked at Don Gómez. "Then you must get the labor of these Indians under *repartimiento*."

Before his brother could answer, the Marqués made a waspish sound. "Call it *encomienda*, *repartimiento*—call it anything you like. It all boils down to the same thing. The labor is necessary. If we cannot get it one way we will get it another."

"By whipping and threats and armed guards?"

"You exaggerate," Don Gómez said. He smiled indulgently at Barbara. "Your father's books have been showing a loss for a long time. For years I have tried to get him to cut costs. The measures I have taken are not so unusual. Every landowner in New Spain comes to it sooner or later."

"Then you are breaking the law in my name."

Don Gómez sighed. "My dear, this question of the juridical status of the Indians has been one upon which the theologians and legal theorists have clashed since the conquest. The Crown is always issuing new codes, the Laws of Burgos, the New Laws, all trying to protect the Indian. The Church has tried many times to have *encomienda* abolished. The first time it happened Spain almost lost the colonies. Without labor how could the land be worked? Agriculture ceased. Trade stopped. Colonists began returning to Spain in droves. The decrees had to be revoked."

The Marqués nodded, saying spitefully, "And the second time a bloody civil war broke out in Peru. The viceroy was killed. *Encomienda* had to be restored again. With such a history, should it not be obvious that a labor draft of some sort is vital to the life of the country? It will never be abolished. There is too much at stake, too many men would be ruined."

"And the Gallegos' among them?" Barbara asked.

They both glanced sharply at her. The Marqués had suffered severe burns in the fire at his home during the revolt, and the scars made a mottled white flecking against the angry flush of his cheeks. A tremor ran through Barbara. What had possessed her? A child, a little girl, to argue with these men who knew so much more than she. These rich, powerful men, who ruled a whole colony, who had seen everything and knew everything, who had looked into the king's eyes without flinching. She suddenly knew what the Condesa meant about a woman alone. She squirmed down into the seat, locking her small hands tightly in her lap and staring miserably at them. She had never felt so little or frightened.

Don Gómez did not seem to be as angry as his brother. He had a habit when amused, of tilting his head and brushing at his lacquered hair with a forefinger. He smiled ironically.

"Is this acute political consciousness not rather sudden? A year ago you hardly knew who our viceroy was."

She was surprised herself. For some reason it made her think of the Jornada. How could the anger of these men compare with the things she had known there? Don Gómez had not seen everything. He had not seen the Journey of the Dead Man.

Barbara said, "My father always thought of the Indians who worked for him as his people. I want to treat them like human beings. Under this system of *repartimiento* what are my duties?"

Don Gómez adjusted his knee-length vest. Then, with a deprecating lift of his shoulders he said, "You must present a petition to the *corregidor* stating your needs. You will be allowed ten per cent of the able-bodied men in the free village to help you during the rush season of planting and harvesting. Each period must not last more than four weeks, and you must pay each man a *real* a day."

"That sounds simple enough."

"Barbara, you do not understand the realities of this thing. These laws were made up by some creaking clerk in the Council of the Indies who never got outside Seville. How can you make such an arbitrary ruling as ten per cent of a village, when one village might have fifteen hundred men and another twenty, when one planter might have a hundred acres to harvest and another a hundred thousand? This amount will never meet your labor needs. Four weeks is much too short a period."

"Then we will hire extra labor."

"Your wealth is tied up in land. You do not have the cash."

"Can I not get a loan?"

"I suppose so . . . a mortgage on the land. But the risk——"

"Can I not pay it off after the harvest?"

"Yes . . . but if it stormed, flooded you out . . . what if you got rust on the wheat? A hundred things could happen."

"Do I not run that risk anyway?"

"But at least you are not mortgaged. The land would still be there——"

"Don Gómez, I do not want to sustain myself on the misery of a whole village. I saw what happened at Santa Fe and I am just beginning to understand it. I want you to fire that Rascon. Get me a new overseer—one from the Indian village."

"You ask the impossible," the Marqués said savagely. "You are one of us, Barbara, the aristocracy, the fine people. In doing these things you are undermining the very foundations of your own class."

A little rope of muscle twitched in his neck, and once more Barbara felt herself shrinking from his wrath. How could it be this way? How could she feel like an adult one moment and a little girl the next? Her palms were clammy. Her mouth was so dry she could hardly speak.

"You must remember, Don Gómez, you were only executor until the return of the family. As much as I appreciate your help, you told me yourself that by the terms of the contract and the will the estate is now in my hands."

"*Cuerpo de Cristo!*" the Marqués said.

Don Gómez held up a hand to restrain him. He tilted his narrow head quizzically at Barbara. Then he bowed it in defeat.

"As you wish, Barbara."

"Not that way, not as though you were indulging a child."

Don Gómez regarded her gravely. "I do not make that mistake, Barbara. Somewhere, sometime in this past year, you have become a woman."

CHAPTER TWENTY-EIGHT

THE Condesa spent a miserable afternoon after Barbara left. A hundred times she walked to the shutter, opening it a crack. Perhaps she had been mistaken. The shadows of the street were deceptive. Perhaps it had not been Toribio.

It could not be. She did not want it to be. She had left that behind her, at La Toma. Coming to the capital with Barbara had seemed her only possible escape. Her position at La Toma was much more precarious than it had been in New Mexico. In the chaos of the uprooted provincial government Toribio was not sure enough of his own status to give her the protection he had at Santa Fe.

She had admitted to Barbara that she was suspected by the Holy Office. But she had kept her relationship with Toribio secret.

She circled the room restlessly. She wanted to pray. She felt a suffocating need to kneel with a priest and pray. She did not find it strange that she had turned to the Church. Her mother had taught her both faiths, so that she could kneel to the Cross in public and pray to Allah alone. But since leaving Granada at fourteen she had lived in a Christian world.

Despite her parroted knowledge of so many things she was basically a creature of emotion. She could quote the heresies of Luther or Calvin, but they did not move her. In her loneliness she needed something stronger than philosophies or even the furtive recital of a Creed whose God must always remain secret. The visible Church was something to cling to, the confessional a refuge, the priest a tangible link with God.

And always she had fought to see this Faith and the Holy Office of the Inquisition as two different things.

The history of the Inquisition was not unknown to her. Before its final emergence in Spain it had existed in several forms in France and Italy, an instrument designed by the church to correct all immorality and disbelief. But in 1480 Ferdinand and Isabella had been trying to join their separate kingdoms of Castile and Aragon and drive the last of the Moors from the peninsula. To unify their people religiously and to draw the rabble to their banners they used the spark of religious fanaticism. They invoked the Holy Office of the Inquisition against the *conversos* and *moriscos*, the Jews and Moors who publicly professed conversion to Christianity and who worshiped their own gods behind locked doors. On such tinder the fires of the Inquisition blazed higher than ever before. The mob answered the call, the foreign invaders were swept from the peninsula, the Faith was purified, and Spain united.

But it linked the Holy Office irrevocably to the Crown. The Inquisition became as much a thing of state as of Church, a Spanish institution, local, political, fanatic. It grew wealthy off confiscations from the rich heretics—and the inevitable corruption of power set in.

Now the Holy Office had such a grip on the minds of men that even the Popes and traditional Catholics who deplored its excesses could not take any action against it for fear it would tear the whole Spanish world away from Rome. . . .

The Condesa went again to the window and looked out. She could not deny it any longer. She wanted to see Toribio. In Santa Fe she had seen him as a means to an end, had used him in self-defense, as she had used so many other men, playing upon his vanity, his pride, his lust. But something had been changing, even up there, something had been happening. How could that be? A man who hurt her. Why should he be the only one who had ever given her true passion?

She heard a tap at the door. Thinking it was Barbara, the Condesa told Chintule to unlock it. Josefina stood outside. A man stepped past her. He stopped within the door, a shabby shadow in the candle-lit room. The Condesa put a hand to her throat. There was a pressure behind her eyes, making them ache with each pound of her temples.

"Do not worry," Toribio said. "Josefina got me in without the other servants seeing." He motioned toward Chintule with one sinewy hand. "Get out."

He closed the door and locked it after the maid had left. He stood with his back against its deep and intricate carving, and the candlelight glittered against his eyes. Strain made little ridges of the muscles about his mouth.

He let his cloak drop off as he came to her. He pulled her to him so fiercely that she felt the points of her pelvis grind against his. His teeth bruised her lips.

"Toribio . . . not so rough . . . it hurts."

"You want it that way."

"No! *Que animal!* Please, please, please."

He tore her dress, getting it off. The bed sagged beneath them. She began to cry. She would not let him hear her, but the tears were squeezed from her tightly closed eyes and fell like silver beads across her contorted cheeks. The bells in the cathedral began ringing for *la oracions.*

The bells had not yet stopped when he lay back against the bed. She could hear his heavy breathing subside slowly. She did not open her eyes. She could taste the salt of tears, and her arms and shoulders throbbed where he had gripped them.

"Vespers is still ringing," she said. "They are all kneeling in the plaza. We should have prayed."

"Must we pretend even when we are alone?"

"You have a sickness, Toribio."

"I am perfectly healthy."

"You have a disease inside you. It is that you do not believe in anything. It will eat away at you from the inside until there is only a shell left and then that will crumble. A man should believe in something."

He rose to one elbow and she opened her eyes to see him looking down at her, a suspicious frown making a deep crease between his heavy black brows. She knew she was making a mistake. This was not the way you talked with a man. You must never let him see beyond the mask, must maneuver him, flatter him, delight him, the perfect courtesan. Mother of God!

She smiled, a glittering, metallic smile, and pulled herself against him. She kissed his neck and his shoulders and pressed her face against his chest.

"*Que barbaridad*—what barbarity. How can you love like that and have the strength left to move?"

She felt him relax a little and looked up to see the frown gone from his face. He ran his hands hungrily over her body, the firm breasts, the lavish hips.

"When one looks at that," he said, "one can forget the face."

She felt the skin go tight across her cheeks. Was his cruelty deliberate? There were things she could say too. Sweat shimmered on his lean body. She knew how he hated its hairless, coppery smoothness, so evocative of his Indian blood. She knew how long he had tried to cultivate a beard and what a few miserable scraggly hairs had grown.

He pushed her away, a petulant look coming to his face. "Well, Condesa," he said. He always liked to call her that. Anything to belong (royalty, the fine people), even an illusion. "Well, do you not wish to know what has happened?"

She lay back, smiling apologetically. The smell of him was strong, almost goaty. She murmured, "Pardon, *querido*. I was only lost in the pleasure of being so near you again."

He looked beyond her, eyes beginning to smolder. "I am no longer sheriff of the Holy Office in New Mexico."

"Toribio, no!" She tried to sound deeply concerned. "It cannot be. How could they replace you?"

He stirred restlessly, sat on the edge of the bed. "Everybody is being toppled. This mess, Otermin, investigations, complaints——" He made a vicious gesture with one hand. "No importance. I still have patronage. I am working for Don Gallegos again. He promises to make me a Soldier of Christ, a familiar of the Holy Office here in the capital."

"A marvel." She paused. "You did not find out where I was from . . . the Holy Office?"

"I did it on my own. I talked with some of the Spaniards who came down with you. They said you had taken a coach to Acapulco. I checked there. No passport had been issued, and I knew you had no connections on the coast. I suspected it was a ruse. I have been watching this house. Yesterday I saw Chintule in the carriage entrance." He stood, oblivious to his nakedness, and paced to the window. He opened the shutter a little. It was growing dark outside now. He said, "The Tribunal might add two and two also."

"They do not know me like you."

"They are not stupid. You are still on file, Condesa. If another investigation starts I am not now in a position to turn it aside. You cannot stay here. Sooner or later somebody will find out."

"Where can I go?"

"There is the Indian quarter—the Romita."

She lay back. She closed her eyes. She felt the small comb secreted in her hair. It pressed against the back of her neck. She began to shiver.

"Is it cold?" she said. "Please shut the window."

CHAPTER TWENTY-NINE

IT was November now in New Mexico. November 1681, by Luis Ribera's calculations. He had been at Acoma almost a year. They had told him that it was thirty-six leagues southwest of Santa Fe. They had told him that it was a rock, three hundred and fifty-seven feet high, almost a mile long, seventy square acres on top. Near the northwest end, on top, were the community dwellings. There were three main blocks of buildings, each a thousand feet long, North Row, Middle Row, Last Row, separated by streets.

The long buildings vaulted skyward in three great steps, each story terraced back the width of the room below. The walls were made of adobe or of flinty sandstone blocks. The ceiling beams were cedar or pine hauled from the mountains thirty miles distant, thatched over with peeled sticks, then hay, then covered with a layer of earth.

One of the rooms on the third level of North Row was Luis's cell. He spent the days sitting in the doorway or at the edge of the roof, watching the strange life of the Sky City pass by. He sat in the doorway this morning, shivering despite his buffalo robes. His legs were shackled with leg irons some Acoma had brought from Santa Fe.

It had drizzled during the night and then frost had come before dawn. Black cloud castles still tiered the horizon. The dirty milk of congealed puddles shimmered on the roof tops.

Beyond the buildings, beyond the edge of the mesa, three hundred and fifty-seven feet below, lay the plain. Limited only by the edge of the world, its iron-reddened earth stippled with gray cedars, it ran on every side to a horizon barricaded with the jagged walls of distant mountains. In the middle distance northward rose Katzimo. A dark tower of rock, a mesa even taller than Acoma, it dominated the misty plain. In legend the Indians had lived on its top before coming to Acoma. But now they said it was inaccessible.

Closer, just beyond the edge of the roof, Luis could see the bare rock of the street, stained black by rain and frost. Tubby squaws tended beehive ovens at the edge of the plaza. The blue smoke was shredded by the wind as soon as it escaped the chimneys, leaving only a hint of its damp and piny odor on the air. The wind always blew up here. It came in unbalancing gusts, a giant clapping his hands, it boomed, it thundered, it whined, it sighed, it always blew.

A few people were abroad, huddled in their blankets. Arabic silhouettes in their robelike mantles, three girls returned from the reservoir, balancing five-gallon jars of water on their heads. A pair of old men met in the plaza. They spoke for a moment. Before parting each took the other's hand and breathed on it. They went their separate ways.

This was how it began. The morning. The first fragment of the pattern he had come to know.

Yactye was the hour just before dawn, when light first showed in the east. They awoke. Each had his duty. A child went outside to make prayer. He sprinkled pollen to the coming sun.

The *cacique* prayed too. He went to look at East Point. He prayed for the whole village.

The girls took their jars to one of the rock sinks. They brought them back full of water.

The women were never idle. Every morning they swept the floor. They made the fires. They cooked the meals. They were the potters, the weavers, the bearers of children, the grinders of corn, even the builders. As the earth was reborn in the spring, so was the village. While the men were in the fields the women replastered. They plastered the walls outside with a fresh coat of adobe. It covered the spider web of cracks that winter had brought to the walls. They whitewashed the inside with gypsum.

In autumn evenings they ground corn. At *kobonote*, the hour of sunset, they brought their *metates* and bags of corn to appointed houses. They joined the men. The women ground corn into blue meal. The men made shoes. They sang the corn-grinding song.

Ioho, waitilanni
Ioho, waitilanni.

Tzi washo iyanii
He-yo-ye . . .

The men worked. In March the dry stalks and pink brush choking
the irrigation ditches were cleaned out. Under the waxing moon of
April all the men took their *wahatees* to the fields. Such hand planters
were branches with a crook near one end. The man put his foot on the
crook and drove the stick into the ground, and broke the ground. He
planted corn and melon seeds in the broken ground. After planting
they played the stick game. It was an appeal for rain. It was played
with sticks like the bows of the Hero Twins. The two war captains
played it, and the winning stick was placed in the corn fields.

The men danced. All year round they danced. The hunting dances
in the winter, the Buffalo Dance and the Deer Dance, the Eagle Dance
in the spring, the Acequia Dance, the Corn Dance, the Rainbow Dance
in summer.

The men hunted. They went in big groups when they hunted rabbits.
They went in little groups when they hunted deer. Four men went
hunting for deer. They sang a song as they went.

> "From Acoma I am going,
> I, the man, am going.
> I put sewed-up moccasins on my feet,
> I, the man, put on moccasins.
>
> I paint my body with yellow,
> With red,
> With blue,
> With white clay color.
>
> I go sometimes with a song . . ."

This was their life. This ritual, this harmony, this cycle, keeping its
measured pace with all the cycles of the earth. To be a part of it was
a subtle narcotic. After a year it was hard for Luis to resurrect the
abysmal outrage he had known during the revolt. It was hard to connect
these people with the people who had committed the atrocities on the
day of San Lorenzo. He had come prepared to hate. But even though
he was their prisoner he could find nothing in them to hate. . . .

Kashana made a soft rustle in the room behind him. He turned to
see her spraying water on the floor with her mouth and sweeping the
dampened adobe clean with Apache plume. Her hair was unbraided,
hiding her tilted face like a coarse veil, so black it would reflect no

light. It took him back almost a year, to the first time he had seen her in the room like that. They had been at Acoma but two weeks and had been given their living quarters on North Row. One morning he saw her talking intently with her mother at the edge of the roof. Later she came into the room and sat down and unbraided her hair and loosened her clothing. There was something so ceremonial about it that it had caused him to question her.

"It is so the child may learn to enter the world easily," she said, "without stricture and without pain."

She said it placidly, looking at him from serene eyes—the earth accepting the seed. He was puzzled by his own response. He did not seem as surprised as he should be, as confused. All he felt was a strange humility. It seemed like a new emotion to him.

It made his obligation stand before him in simple terms. It had been implicit in that first violent union at Yapashi, in every night they had loved since.

But it was more than obligation. He wanted this woman. He was surprised at how simply and with what strength he wanted her. And the child. He wanted it to be his child, in every sense of the word.

He said, "Will your people permit me . . . a husband?"

A flush touched her face. Her eyes shone and then she looked quickly down at her hands.

After a while she asked, "Can you accept our gods?"

He did not answer. He knew no regrets in giving up the Spanish world. He had rejected so much there. But his faith was a different matter.

He had often discussed it with the Condesa. How could a man question so much in his life and still remain unshaken in his faith? She had reminded him of the Jesuits, the great teachers, who were presented with every possible criticism of the Church so that their faith might only be strengthened.

Perhaps Kashana had lived long enough with Spaniards to know what she dealt with. She said:

"I will not ask it of you. But the child must be brought up in our ways."

Again he could not answer. To raise his child without the Church? He could not conceive of it.

Yet was it something that could be answered now? What hope did they have of ever seeing a Catholic priest again? It seemed impossible to him that the Spaniards would retake New Mexico. The defeat had been too devastating. The Crown had become increasingly indifferent to the province. It had proven a barren, unprofitable appendage to empire, and Spain would probably be glad to relinquish it. Kashana had been watching his face carefully. She stood up. She said:

"The child will be raised in our ways or there will be no marriage."

The next day the *cacique* came. He was an ancient. He was named Tyame—the Eagle. He wore a Navajo blanket like a poncho, black symbols against a white field, gathered in deep folds about his emaciated body. His hair was white, coarse as horse-mane, hanging far below his shoulders and held by a blue *banda* about his head. He had the luminous, distantly focused eyes of the ascetic. One of his chief duties was to act as penitent for the sins of his whole tribe, and he was an intimate with the sweat house, the scourge, the ecstasies to be found alone and fasting and naked in the wilderness communing with Those Above.

He sat beside Luis against the wall. Luis knew that Tyame was one of those who had kept him alive. When Luis and Kashana had first arrived, Kashana told the Acomas that the Spaniards had meant to kill her at Sandia. She said Luis had risked his life to save her and had been wounded in the act. Kashana was Tyame's niece and a member of the Antelope clan. From this clan came the rulers of the village, and it held much power among the Acomas. That Luis had saved the life of Kashana meant much to the Antelope people, and they had defended him in the long house. The war chiefs and younger men had wanted to kill him. But Tyame had said how they would lose their honor by killing him after he had saved Kashana. The gods would frown and people would suffer.

Though the Indians refused to speak the hated language of Castile any more Tyame knew that Luis had not yet mastered Keres, and when the old man finally spoke it was in Spanish.

"Among your people a *mestizo*, a half-breed is held in contempt."

"My people have great faults," Luis said.

"Here it is not so. Here your child will receive equal affection from all. Love was given us by the gods and therefore we have no right to divide it or question it or say how it shall be parceled out."

"I want to share in the giving."

"And raise the child to worship our gods?"

Luis did not answer. Tyame turned to look at the ruins of the church on the southeast edge of the mesa. Luis knew the old man was thinking about Father Maldonado, the Catholic priest who had been at Acoma at the time of the revolt. The young warriors had thrown him over the side of the cliff.

"We are far from Santa Fe here," Tyame said. "We did not suffer under the Spaniards the way the other Pueblos did. The feeling is not as fierce as when the young men killed Father Maldonado. People are willing to give you time. Perhaps if you live among us long enough you will learn to accept our gods. But with the child it is different. The child will be raised in our ways whether you consent or not. Would it not be better to give him a father?"

Luis stared emptily at the horizon. He had slept little last night, trying to find the answer. He realized Tyame was right. As far as the child went, he was helpless. Then where was his duty? Right now it lay in being a husband and a father.

"Tell Kashana she will have her wish," he said.

The ceremony was brief and simple. He was introduced to Kashana's uncle, Pesana, and to his wife, Seeka. As near as he could interpret it they corresponded to the best man and best woman, standing by while the *cacique* gave his blessing to the match, then taking Luis and Kashana to their quarters.

"Among our people it is thus," Pesana said. "The man upon marrying enters the clan of his wife. The house and the things in it belong to her. They do not belong to him. If you leave, the only possessions you may take are your weapons, your farm tools, and your clothes. If you come home some day and find these things outside the door you know you must depart." He removed the handsome buffalo robe he wore and gave it to Luis. "This is my gift."

Seeka gave Kashana womanly advice and presented her with a gift of fine turquoise jewelry, then the two people left, and Luis looked across at his bride who stood with her eyes downcast and her freshly washed hair loose and still damp enough to shine in the candlelight.

"You must not fight me any more," he said. "It is no longer necessary. We are together now." She moved her head. It might have been a nod. He said, "I have always wondered if you did not fight yourself, as well as me."

She continued to look at the ground.

"Stop looking so damn meek," he said.

She raised her head. Her lips parted and her teeth showed, small and pointed and savage, in one of her rare moments of humor. They both laughed. They stopped self-consciously.

He picked up the candle and snuffed it out against the wall. In the darkness he knelt before her and unwound the cotton leg wrappings and removed her moccasins. He could feel her tremble. He rose and untied her sash and took off her mantle. He took off her dress. Her body was slender, sleek, ivory cool.

He caressed her and she leaned against him, heavy in acquiescence. He thought he had won.

Then she trembled again. She moaned. She made a broken sound and her hands began to tear at him in their wild contradiction, pushing him away, pulling him to her.

Sitting before the door now, watching her sweep the room, it was hard to reconcile the sedate picture with the savage he found in the night. This year among her people had changed her outwardly. Most Pueblo women married young and aged soon. At fourteen or fifteen many were mothers. They had left their girlhood behind and had become placid matrons. The heavy folds of the mantle and the bulky cotton leg wrappings gave Kashana the same appearance. She kept her head lowered much of the time. A deerlike shyness had entered her way of speaking.

The baby, tightly bundled into his cradleboard, was hung from one of the rafters. Kashana had named him Migenna, because he had been conceived upon the red earth of Yapashi. The baby stirred, and Kashana stopped sweeping and reached up to take the cradleboard down.

Only the baby's face was visible above the wrappings. It was a round face, tawny, creviced with eyes and mouth. The crevices assumed strange shapes. The tiny hands pawed air. Kashana sat on a rolled mattress against the wall and bared her breast. Her face, tilted above the cherubic lips and busy hands, was soft and shining with motherhood.

She raised her eyes and saw how fondly Luis was looking at the baby. He met her glance and they smiled together. It was a rare moment. There were so many other times when she seemed withdrawn from him. As though she sensed his thought her smile faded. He wanted to save the moment. He held his arms out quickly.

"Now," he said. "He has had enough. I do not want a pig for a son."

She covered her breast and brought Migenna to Luis. He propped the cradle board against the wall beside him.

Migenna's head lolled. The pudgy lips were slack and the eyes looked crossed, trying to focus on Luis's face.

"Now, my son," Luis said. "I wish to have a talk with you about life, man to man."

"Is he not a little young?"

"That is the trouble with today's youth, they do not face reality

soon enough," Luis said. He waggled a finger at the baby. "First off,
you must not listen to these old grandmothers. The truth. They tell
you that yelling into a big pottery jar will shorten your life. It is not
so. It simply makes a hollow sound."

"Luis!" Kashana said.

"And if you wish you can whistle all you want at night time."

"No. He will blow his life away."

"And if you see a crow at night do not worry."

"It is the worst of luck. If you tell him these Spanish lies I will take
him back."

She realized he was teasing her and stamped her foot. Luis laughed.
She seemed about to join in. But her eyes went to something beyond
him and it stopped her. He saw a man coming up the ladder and over
the parapet at the edge of the roof.

He was one of the war chiefs. His name was Tsiki. In all the coun-
cils he had been the most ardent advocate of Luis's death.

He wore a robe of rabbit fur laced together with yucca fiber. He
wore a pair of hip-length war moccasins. Their uppers were folded
down to knee height. They flapped sibilantly against his calves. He had
a narrow face as hard and shiny as varnished mahogany. Strange scars
made a chalky latticework against the dark flesh. Luis had always wondered whether they were from a war club or from flagellation.

Tsiki stopped a foot from Luis, towering over him. He folded his
arms across his chest, beneath the robe. The pallid light made glittering
prisms of his eyes.

"Cashtira," he said. It was the Keres word for Spaniard. The word
had a different sound than when Tyame said it. Like the sound when a
man said maricón in Spanish, or padrote. "Spaniard, there is a man
here. He has known you."

Puzzled, wary, Luis said, "I will see him."

"We held council with him in the long house. He told us many things
about you. He spoke the truth." Tsiki looked at Kashana. "The truth.
This cashtira did not save your life."

"It is a lie," Kashana said.

"Is it?" Tsiki's smile was enigmatic. "The vote within the long house
grows more divided. Soon there will be more for the death of this
cashtira than against it."

Luis saw someone else climbing over the edge of the parapet. He
rose into silhouette slowly, one movement following the other with
painstaking care, moving as a very old man would, conserving his
strength.

Luis rose and hopped awkwardly across the roof, almost tripping on his shackles. He grasped the man by both arms, shocked at how skinny they were.

"*Compañero*," he said. His voice shook. "Companion . . ."

Bigotes looked at him and Luis saw the shadow in his eyes. Bigotes looked down and Luis allowed his hands to drop away.

"Yes," Bigotes said. "Well, *patrón*, I am happy to see that you are alive. Job's boils! You do not know how happy I am that you are alive."

"Myself as well. I am happy that you are alive, Bigotes."

There was an awkward silence. Tsiki watched them insolently, arms still folded beneath the blanket. Luis touched Bigotes' arm.

"Inside—why not inside?"

The Tewa shuffled past Kashana, giving her an embarrassed smile. Luis remembered him as he had been—a sly bear, full of life's juices, vital as the earth. Now he was emaciated and aged. His face had a peculiar yellow color, and Luis thought that if he touched the flesh it would feel dry, papery, like cornstalks shriveled by the sun.

Stooped, holding an arm across his belly, Bigotes shambled to one of the blankets rolled against the wall. When he sat down he squinted his eyes shut and made a wheezing sound.

"That thing." Luis looked at his stomach. "It has been like this all the time?"

Bigotes did not answer.

"You knew I was here?" Luis said.

Bigotes nodded, not looking up. "I was at Tesuque. A hunter brought word. He had heard it from somebody else. A Spaniard they were keeping alive here. I wondered . . . I had to see."

Luis tried to smile. "It is not so bad. I am married now. Did you ever think I would be married?"

Bigotes got out a pouch, some corn husks, and rolled a pair of *cigarrillos*. He got out his flint and steel and *eslabón* and lit the cigarettes. He handed one to Luis. The young man closed his eyes and drew deep.

"Well, I suppose you would like to know." Bigotes said, "They talked to me in the long house. They asked me a lot of questions about you. If you really saved Kashana's life. I guessed that was why they kept you alive. I said yes."

"Thousand thanks," Luis said.

There was another silence, and then Bigotes said:

"Governor Otermin. He tried to make a reconquest this month. He came north with about two hundred and fifty soldiers. A battle at

Isleta. Four hundred Indians. He beat them and he burned Alameda and Paruai and Sandia."

Luis knew a surge of hope. "Santa Fe . . ."

Bigotes shook his head. "He could not get there. The weather became bad. The horses of Otermin gave out. He did not have enough men. He had to go back to El Paso."

After a while Luis said, "Can you tell me about my mother? The Condesa? Any of them?"

"I do not know. I heard nothing about them. This Po-pe. You should know about him. He lives in Santa Fe now. No longer like a *cacique*. Changed. Worse than a Spanish governor. Killing those who oppose him . . ."

Luis knew what was on his mind. He said, "Po-pe made a tour of the country while I was still at Yapashi. He had already visited Acoma before I got here."

"Which does not mean he won't come again," Bigotes said. "He must have heard the rumors about a Spaniard living here. He would probably come to see if he was not having so much trouble."

"Trouble?"

"There is a lot of quarreling. Some of the villages have deserted him. They do not like the way he rules. Taos and Pecuris want to make Tupatu ruler instead of Po-pe. Po-pe is afraid to leave Santa Fe. Tupatu might take over. But it will not always be so. If Po-pe gets things under control . . . if he hears definite word that you are here. . . . You must do something."

"What? They guard me like a roomful of gold."

"You sound like you do not want to escape," Bigotes said.

Luis looked at the floor. He dragged in smoke and then watched it stream from his nostrils. Bigotes pulled at his scraggly mustache. It made Luis think of the yellow horse.

"Whatever happened to the little yellow horse with the whiskers?" he asked.

"I still have him," Bigotes said.

"Remember when we got him drunk on mescal and he knocked Governor Otermin down in the plaza and sat on him and we could not get him off the governor?"

"That was very funny," Bigotes said.

"Yes, that was very funny," Luis said.

They were silent. Outside Luis could hear the children shouting at their stick games in the street. Bigotes ground the butt of his cigarette against the floor.

"Well . . . I guess I had better go."

"You will come back?"

Bigotes glanced up. Their eyes met. Bigotes looked away. He put one hand carefully against the floor and held his other arm across his belly and got up. His face was squeezed and shriveled-looking. Luis rose, arms dangling at his sides. Stooped over, Bigotes shuffled to the door.

"Bigotes," Luis said.

Bigotes paused, waiting. Finally he said, "Well, I had better go."

He walked to the ladder and climbed down, making heavy work of it. Kashana came from the doorway of her aunt's house, the cradleboard on her back. She watched Bigotes go down the street. The children stopped their stick game to stare at him, shambling past them, stooped and humpbacked as a dwarf.

"My sword," Luis said. "And now he is like that all the time."

"Is it his real pain?" she asked.

"It does not have to be that way," he said. "I tried to tell him. Companion. Did I not call him companion? It is not a matter of forgiving. Just something that happened, and I have forgotten. Why could I not tell him? I wanted to."

"Because you knew it would not do any good. How could it ever be the same again? He will hurt like that till he dies. It will always remind him, whenever you meet. What he tried to do to you."

Luis went back inside. He sat down and closed his eyes and leaned his head against the wall. He heard the children begin their stick game again in the street.

CHAPTER THIRTY

Four was sacred.

Everything was four.

There were the four stages of man. There was babyhood, childhood, manhood, old age. There were four directions, each with its god. There were four priesthoods, the Ya-yas, the medicine doctors, the warriors, the hunters.

There were four seasons.

Winter passed, with ice milky on the rivers of New Mexico and dried golden leaves clinging to the cottonwoods. Spring passed, with peach trees brightening their pink blossoms. Summer passed, with thunder shaking the mountains. Autumn passed.

Man's measurements gave way to those of nature so that it seemed impertinent to try to remember whether it was January or February, Anno Domini 1683 or 1684. It was simply another morning when Luis came from his house and took his seat by the door, wrapping his blanket about him and staring moodily into the vastness of a gray plain under a sunless sky. The mountains at the edge of the plain were edged in white, and the streets of the village below were black and glistening with ice. Luis shivered in the bitter cold.

His shackles clanked as he crossed his legs. He contemplated them bitterly. He was sick of them. Bowels of Judas, he was sick of them. He had thought he could be patient. He had thought he could prove his willingness to earn their trust and live among them. But there was an end to a man's patience. How long had it been now? How many years had his bones ached? How many more months did he have to sit before this door rubbing tallow into the running sores around his ankles? Almost every night now he woke to find himself tearing at the shackles in a smothering panic to get free.

Luis saw Tyame come from his doorway and cross the roof tops toward him. The aged *cacique's* hair was a snowy nimbus shining about the wrinkled ruin of his face. Age had stiffened his joints noticeably since Luis had come, and he walked with rheumatic care. Luis greeted him.

"*Qoua tzino, Tyame. Tek atomatse wei-not.*"

Tyame returned the greeting and agreed that it truly would not be warm today. They were speaking Keres. Luis used the language with skill now. He knew how to make its smothered sounds, its surprising explosions, its noises like the chirping of crickets or the puff of expelled air. Tyame lowered himself against the wall, rubbing his knees and then wrapping his blanket carefully about them.

After a while Tyame said, "It has been two winters since the man Bigotes came. In the long house that time Bigotes told us many things about you. He said how you were our friend."

Luis said, "It was when I thought you were like children, persecuted, innocent——"

"Like your saints?"

Luis was surprised at the thought. "In a way."

Tyame looked thoughtfully into the vast distance. Finally he said, "My grandfather told me many stories. He said how there was this coyote. When the coyote was very young he had weak eyes. They were not strong. In the shadows all appeared black. In the sunlight all was very white. This coyote's mother warned him to stay close till his eyes grew stronger. But he went into the shadows of a thicket hunting for berries. A bee stung him. Therefore this coyote ran out of the shadows. He stayed in the sunlight. He would not get hurt where everything was very white. He hunted for berries around a rock in the sunlight. The rock was a wolf and it ate this coyote."

"That is a very good story," Luis said.

"My grandfather said how there was this bear cub. He waited till his eyes were strong. The shadows were not as black as they had first seemed. This bear cub could see beehives in some places. But in other places he could gather berries without getting stung."

"What about the wolves?"

"There were too many of them. Therefore this bear cub could not drive them all away. But he could see that all the sunlight was not white. He could tell the difference between rocks and wolves. He lived a long time."

"Were you like the coyote when you were young?" Luis asked.

"Most of us were. A few of us learn to tell the rocks from the wolves. Even among those it is a man with great luck who can kill one of the wolves during his life," Tyame said. The wind boomed hollowly down the narrow streets. The wind thumped the walls like a great drum. Tyame shivered and pulled his blanket tighter. He said, "I will tell you about Po-pe. He the man was a good priest in the beginning. He the man wanted to help his people. But his promises he has not kept. The Great Wall he put up did not hold back the Spaniards. Governor Otermin came that winter, killing and burning. The rain Po-pe called has not come. The crops fail. He the man has not given us as much protection as the Spaniards did. The Apache and Navajo war on us constantly. Some villages are destroyed all. The hunting is bad."

"It is not good," Luis said.

"And now," Tyame said, "Po-pe is a worse tyrant than any Spanish governor. He and his lieutenants take whatever women they please. The tribute they exact is higher than any paid to the Spaniard. Many have come to hate his rule. Tupatu of Pecuris and Juan Ye of Pecos have turned against him."

"Can they not overthrow him?"

"He is still too powerful. But warring among ourselves has divided us again. If the Spaniards returned now they could defeat us. But there must be a leader among them this time honest enough to keep his promises and strong enough to make his people keep them. And then there must be one among the Spaniards to speak for us. One to say how we did not want the war and how we opposed what Po-pe preached and how we are willing to accept Jesus and Mary again if we are permitted to keep Earth Mother and Sky Father also."

Their ulterior motives in sparing Luis almost made him smile. He knew it did not really reflect on Tyame's humanity. But the wily old man had been looking ahead. If the Spaniards returned it would certainly assuage their wrath to see one of their own people spared, acting as spokesman for Acoma. Luis thought about it. He said:

"I will speak for you."

Tyame's eyes kindled. "*Kaua-al, cashtira,*" he said. "Thank you, Spaniard."

He placed something on the ground beside Luis. He rose, gathering his blanket carefully about him, and walked away. Luis looked at what Tyame had put down. It was the key to his shackles.

CHAPTER THIRTY-ONE

SPRING came slowly to Acoma. There was precious little seed corn to plant, and the men did not have the strength to clear any more of the irrigation ditches than was absolutely necessary. Many had died that winter, and the bellies of the children were bloated with emptiness and air. The first rabbit hunts were discouraging, and what few rabbits they caught were nothing but skin and bones from their long winter fast. It was one of these spring mornings. Majestically moving cloud galleons cast dramatic shadows across the mesa. Migenna brought Luis a broken bow.

They sat cross-legged before the door, facing each other, solemn as a pair of braves, while Luis mended the bow with strips of rawhide and glue made from piñon gum. Migenna was almost five summers now. His face was already thick-lipped, broad through the cheekbones, Indian. But he had the Iberian hollows at his temples, Luis's strange trick of looking angry or humorous at the same time.

"When the bow is fixed," Luis told his son, "you must be careful where you shoot the arrows. You know that lightning was born when the War Twins shot an arrow into the sky——"

He stopped, crossing himself automatically. Was he beginning to think like an Indian? Talking of pagan gods as he would talk of the saints?"

"How did the arrow make lightning?" Migenna asked.

"I do not know."

"The father of Shiwana tells him stories."

"I will give you a prayer to say against lightning," Luis said. "Saint

Barbara, holy maid, save us, Lady, in thunder and lightning afraid."

Migenna looked at him uncertainly. Luis smiled and held out the bow. The boy took it and rose, frowning down at his bare feet. He curled his brown toes. He made a mark on the roof with his foot.

"What do you wish to ask?" Luis said.

"Well . . . what is a *cashtira?*"

"A *cashtira* is a Spaniard. They lived in a village far to the east by the river great and fierce."

"Are you a *cashtira?*"

There was a pause. Finally Luis said, "Yes, I am a *cashtira.*"

Migenna scowled at his feet. He put one on top of the other, teetering. He wheeled and ran across the roof, shouting at another boy who appeared in a doorway.

Luis heard a rustling movement behind him and turned to see Kashana standing in the doorway. In one hand she held one of the jars he had made while he was shackled. He had built it up from ropes of clay, coil on coil, so that the surface had a ribbed texture. He had glazed it with piñon gum and syrup of yucca root and fired it with cannel coal. He had painted it black.

"From the beginning," Kashana said, "I have thought you made a Spanish promise."

He knew she had overheard him tell the boy the prayer to Santa Barbara, and said, "I did not mean it. It slips out once in a while —"

"You wait," she said. "You hope that someday a priest will come and you can make Migenna a Spaniard."

He stood up. "Are the boys not being raised in your ways? Have I not kept my bargain?"

She turned back into the room. Her left hand was coated with thick *yeso*. She put her hand into the jar for more of the whitewash and began smearing it on a section of the wall. Above her Hoshken hung from the rafter in his cradleboard. He was really their third child. The second had died at birth. Hoshken pawed vaguely and made chirping noises. Luis put his fingers up, and Hoshken wrapped his tiny brown cherub's hand around it. Luis swung the cradleboard back and forth and Hoshken gurgled and made pleased faces.

Kashana continued to plaster the wall. She had removed her mantle. When she reached high it pulled her cotton underdress against her taut hips. They were fine hips, a strong round shape of muscle and flesh. Luis moved behind her.

"Kashana."

"I must finish this."

"Last night——"

"I had been baking all day."

With her back still turned she moved away. In a fit of anger he went to the door and yanked down the buckskin hanging, plunging the room into gray dusk. She whirled around but he was already halfway to her. In a motion of defense she lifted the jar. He pulled it aside, tearing it from her grasp and splattering the gypsum over the blankets and utensils on the floor. The jar broke against the wall. She tried to lunge past him.

He caught her around the waist and flung her back. She was spread-eagled against the wall. She looked like a little child cornered for a whipping. Her hair was down over her face, all her black hair, and through it he could see the coppery color of her cheeks. He was breathing hoarsely from the struggle. But the desire was gone from him, even the anger.

"Kashana," he said, "what is it? There were times . . . you and me . . . good times."

She turned her face aside. Her eyes were closed. He had never seen her cry. He wondered how close she was to it now. He started toward her again, holding out his hand. She moved her head from side to side, a motion of miserable negation. It stopped him once more. He put his hand vaguely to his face. He looked at the floor. Above him Hoshken made the cradleboard swing and laughed delightedly.

"Well," Luis said, "I guess I will go for a walk."

He went outside and wandered aimlessly across the roof top. He saw men emerging from the Ladder Trail that led up the sheer face of the mesa from the fields far below. He saw Hanai and Chotika meet in the street. They were old men. They were members of the medicine society. When they had finished talking Hanai breathed on Chotika's hand and Chotika breathed on Hanai's hand. They parted.

Luis had known them for years now. He thought of them as he had thought of Torres. After the first barriers were down they had climbed shaky ladders to sit beside him where he was shackled. They had talked with him. They had smoked with him. They were his friends.

Did he really know them?

Would he ever really know any of the people here? Would he ever know Kashana?

What had happened? How had it seemed so simple at first? Kashana seemed to move farther away from him every day. Had they ever actually been close? Every day she seemed to become more Indian.

Was she the only one changing? Luis thought of what Tyame had said. The coyote and the bear. Luis knew how the allegory applied to him. The fires of the rebellion had burned a lot of adolescent illusions out of him. Luis no longer looked upon the world in terms of complete whiteness or complete blackness. The Indians were neither the innocent children they had been to him before the revolt nor the beasts they had been during the terror.

Then what were they?

It amused him to remember how he had thought he understood these people before the revolt. How could youth be so arrogant? Now he had probably seen more of their ways than any Spaniard. Yet he still had not penetrated beyond the surface. He had observed enough to know what a vast portion would always remain hidden from the Spaniard.

Their whole life was a ritual, a constant supplication for favor from the beings that watched over them. The ceremonies that the Spaniards called dances were the major rituals. Each was a sacred rite, a prayer for rain, for the cure of sickness, for success on the hunt. The Indian did not smoke or eat or run foot races or sing songs or play games or even mate for pleasure alone. Each had its underlying religious significance. Each was in its own way an invocation.

Luis wondered if this was the essential difference between the two races. The Pueblo conceived himself not to be a master of creation, born to rule and conquer. He believed that a single underlying principle imbued all things, in which he shared equally with the birds, the beasts, all the things of the earth.

Luis could see the peace and harmony of their lives. It was more than he had ever found in Santa Fe. But there was something still just beyond his grasp. All he had wanted was to be freed of his shackles. All he had wanted was to walk among them and belong.

Sweet Virgin! This city in the sky a thousand years old, unknown to the rest of the world. These laughing brown people living out their ceremonious lives in an exotic dream.

CHAPTER THIRTY-TWO

IT was the fourth year of drought. The whole tableland of New Mexico was drying up. The cracked mouths of a thousand canyons gaped wide in their mute plea for water. In late spring the melting snows of the mountains far to the north had caused some rise in the rivers. But that soon passed, and the water settled back into the thirsty land or flowed on to the sea and the rivers were once more muddy trickles in the seared bottomlands.

At Acoma the meager crop of corn was dying. The *cacique* announced a prayer for rain.

The men retired to the *kivas*. They purified themselves. They painted masks. They prayed. The women cooked.

Kashana cooked *mutzenee*. A fire was built in the corner fireplace of the room. Three rocks held a flat stone above the flames. Despite starvation some precious blue cornmeal had been hoarded for the ceremony. With it went salt, water, and tallow, to make the thin batter. Kashana rubbed the batter onto the hot greased stone with her fingers, starting in the center and working toward the edges. Almost immediately the blue bread was done. It loosened from the rock and came off in paper-thin sheets. She folded the sheets in squares and piled them in a stack.

The sight of it gave her hunger pains in her empty stomach. She could taste it. Without putting it in her mouth she could taste it, and the smell of it was exquisite torture. She got up and went outside so she would not weaken and eat the sacred bread. She tried to stop thinking about it. She looked out over roof tops. The Sky City. The place to which she belonged.

She had not been born here. Nazario had been a trader in earlier years and had met her mother at Acoma on one of his trips to the westward *pueblos*. The Catholic priest at Acoma married them, and Nazario took his woman back to his tavern at Santa Fe. It was where Kashana had grown up. It was where she had learned what it meant to be a *mestiza*.

The half-breeds were classed with Indians in the contempt and abuse they received. Yet they were denied most of the privileges granted the Indians by royal decree. The Pueblos escaped the jurisdiction of the Holy Office. The breeds came under its fearsome rule. The Pueblos were given enough land to support their villages. The breed received no such grant. Laws fixed Indian wages and limited the time they could work. The breed was lucky to find any job. Most of the beggars in any town were *mestizos*.

In the Analco the degradation was completed. There were few girls beyond the age of twelve or thirteen who had not prostituted themselves. Kashana had run away many times, only to be caught by Nazario or some soldiers from the palace. Though Pueblo morality saw no sin in pre-marital sex, Kashana could not stand the idea of selling herself to the Spaniards she hated. Luis had been one of those Spaniards, symbol of the conquering race that had spawned her but would not accept her.

Yet, counterpart to her hate there had always been something else. She had seen the difference between Luis and the other young noblemen who came to the Analco for their debauches. He did not seem to come for drinking or wenching. It was more like a search. As though he were seeking something among the Indians and outcasts of the Analco that he could not find in his own people. And he made none of the arrogant attempts to seduce her that came from Andres Rodrigo and the others. It was true that he wanted her. He was too honest to pretend differently. But it had been more of a game between them, a teasing game.

And when he had put his hands on her and she had torn them off, the feel of them had remained on her body like a burn for hours afterward.

Was that all they had then? Was it the needs of her body she could not deny? Was it herself she really fought, her hands tearing at him, trying to hurt, trying to push him away, and all the time pulling him to her? Was it herself she hated, for wanting him, when she should loath him?

What about the other feelings? What about her pride when the people came to watch him weave or admire his pottery? What about her tenderness when she saw him sitting like a brave with Migenna and explaining everything so carefully?

Miserably Kashana pushed her hair away from her flushed face. She had to finish the baking. She went back inside again.

When she had used up all the batter Kashana placed the stacks of thin blue bread on a mat and carried it across the roof. Already the people were gathered along the parapet and in the streets. She saw Luis near the ladder. He turned and smiled at her. She bowed her head and climbed down the ladder and took the bread to a place near the *kiva* of the Winter People. She then joined her aunt and uncle in the crowd on the south side of the plaza. She did not want to be with Luis today. The ceremonies always made her want to be Indian.

The sky was empty of clouds and vividly blue. Even with the wind blowing the sun was hot. Sweat made a coppery shine on the dense ranks of solemn faces. Kashana was jammed against a wall by the suffocating press of the crowd. Sometimes she thought she could not breathe. They waited patiently through the forenoon for the ceremonies to begin. Then a breathless hush settled over the crowd and Kashana knew it was time.

The *kurena* were first to appear, boiling from the hatch of the *kiva* like a gang of schoolboys. They were the spirits of dead ancestors. They were revered shades who protected the living through their mediation with the gods. They swarmed down into the plaza. Their bodies were painted. On their bare bodies was black and white paint.

Striped.

On their faces was white paint. Gray clay matted their hair. In their hair were tied corn husks. Corn husks that rustled weirdly. Rolls of dry rabbit skin girdled their waists. Rabbit skin circled their ankles. They danced.

There was a conference among the *kurena*. Runners were sent out. To the four directions they were sent out. They returned. Whooping and shouting they came back. They brought news of raiding Apaches. The *kurena* grew excited. They whooped some more. They formed lines to protect the crops from Apaches. They conferred. They summoned the dancers.

It caused everybody to look eastward. They looked at the *kiva* of the Summer People. They looked at the great wand. It rose ten feet from the *kiva* top. At its top were green macaw feathers. Beneath the macaw feathers were parrot feathers and woodpecker feathers and colored beads and ocean shells.

As the people watched the wand was taken down. It was the signal for the dancers to appear.

The dance was an invocation to the gods that gave the corn, that brought it to maturity, and that now were implored to protect it from enemies.

Tombes began to throb. The chorus started to chant. Fifty voices, male, husky, reverent. The stamp of their feet and the pound of the drum in muffled counterpoint.

The rain priest came first. He came with the sacred wand. He came down the steps of the *kiva* and into *kakati*. The dancers followed into the plaza, a man and a woman alternating, bells tinkling, a man and a woman, shells rattling, a man and a woman, all the colors of the sun and the growing things streaming from the ten-foot wand.

Soon sweat gleamed on their faces. About their churning legs swirled the kirtles. Embroidered with symbolic designs, the kirtles flapped against their legs. Also the white rain belt and the fox skin hanging at the back. Green parrot feathers fluttered in their loose hair. The girdle of shells over their right shoulders rattled. The turtle shells at their knees rattled.

The women danced more demurely. They wore the ceremonial skirt, short and black. They wore the red embroidered belt and all the jewelry they possessed. On each head was the *tablita*. It was a thin board. It was painted sky color and cut at the top into mesa shapes. Into cloud shapes. The women were barefooted.

Dust was a silver film through which the dancers appeared as tapestried figures, massing, turning, changing formation, a solid square, a circle, a line, all the changes as slow and majestic as the wheel of stars in the sky. Two hundred arms rising and falling in unison, two hundred legs, two hundred feet, woven, interwoven. It was like the gigantic basketry of the gods forming before Kashana. Or she could close her eyes and let the drums be thunder, the voices wind, the rattle of shells the seeds falling into the earth.

It was all a feeling too mystical to articulate. She only knew that when she sat in church and heard the choir sing and listened to the priest chant his litany she could not believe; and that when she watched the Green Corn Dance bring rain out of a cloudless sky or saw a hunter talk to the god in the cougar or watched the *cacique* face

East Point and lift his arms in prayer while Payatyama flooded the world with light and life—she believed.

There was a stir in the crowd and a murmur of voices behind Kashana. It was not part of the regular chant and it caused her to turn around. She could see through the thin gathering of bodies behind her. A group of men had appeared at the far end of the street between Middle Row and Last Row.

One of them was Po-pe.

It was almost as though he had come from below, from Shipapu, the Underworld. Kashana knew all the trails were always guarded. Po-pe could not have gained the mesa unseen. The war captains had permitted this. She knew it. Tsiki's warriors had let Po-pe pass without warning the people.

Kashana was startled at the change in the man. She remembered the gaunt ascetic in Santa Fe—the tortured mask of his face, the sunken eyes glowing with strange visions. They were no longer sunken. They were puffy slits in cheeks tumescent with self-indulgence.

And Po-pe who had forbidden them the use of the Spanish tongue wore a Spanish cloak on his shoulders trimmed lavishly in bullion. And he who had bade them wash off all traces of Spanish baptism with amole roots and river water wore a Spanish sword with a jeweled hilt and Spanish rings of gold and jade.

He was surrounded by a score of Tano warriors. Kashana recognized three of Po-pe's closest conspirators in the revolt. There was the half-breed from Santo Domingo named Catiti, glittering and arrogant in his Spanish helmet and cuirass. Jaca, from Taos, displayed long Spanish boots drawn to the hip and a pair of walnut-butted firelocks in his belt. Francisco wore a slashed doublet and carried a halberd with a broken blade. She saw the jeweled interpreter, Pedro de Tapia, with his flat face and pink, flaring nostrils.

Coming up the southernmost street, Po-pe was hidden behind the buildings of Middle Row. Luis stood on the first level of North Row and would not see the Tano leader until he reached the plaza. Kashana began to push against the crowd, trying to get through and warn Luis. But the mass of Indians would not yield.

The Summer People had returned to their *kiva*. Only the *kurena* were left in the square. They chased children. They made burlesque advances to girls. They mocked people who had committed social transgressions during the year.

They postured before an old man. They pantomimed. Eating. Great rage. Everybody laughed. They knew the old man had given way to anger at mealtime. It was considered bad form.

A surging change in the mob pushed Kashana back. She saw that Po-pe was halfway down the street. More people had become aware of him. There was a growing murmur. He was looking arrogantly through the crowd. His eyes touched a girl and stopped. His eyes flashed in the sun like the jewels on his fingers. Po-pe looked at Tsiki's wife. He smiled.

"You will let me pass," Kashana said. "I ask that. You will let me pass."

But the crowd in front of her was packed tight. She could not get through.

The *kurena* darted about the plaza. They pulled out a young man of the Badger clan. They got a girl of the Badger clan. They made postures of copulation before the couple. Everybody laughed. But the laughter was bad. It was not good. It was wrong for those of the same clan to mate.

The *kurena* capered to their next victim. In their antics was retribution. In their clowning was denunciation. They were the conscience of the people.

Kashana heard another gust of laughter rise from the crowd. But she could not look. Po-pe's eyes had found her.

He smiled again. He moistened his lips. The sweat made little silver beads on his face. She could not stop looking at him. She put her hands on the people. She pawed at them, trying to get through the crowd, as though feeling her way through a dark room.

The ceremonial wand was removed from the *kiva* of the Winter People. The rain priest emerged carrying the ten foot wand, and the men and women of the Winter People followed him into the plaza and formed lines for the dance.

The crowd swayed against Kashana to give the dancers room. It caused a break in the ranks. She fought her way through at last. She circled the dancers, darting across the open plaza.

The buildings of Middle Row no longer hid Kashana from Luis. She saw him standing on the roof of North Row. But two of the war chiefs stood near him. Tsiki and Kaitneh were only a few feet away, edging closer.

The drums stopped.

Kashana checked herself against the wall, looking back for an instant. Po-pe had entered the plaza. Oblivious to the dancers he stood in the open square, staring at Luis. Kashana realized that in her attempt to warn Luis she had unwittingly betrayed him.

Po-pe spoke in a booming voice. "It was told me that a Christian lived among you. Did I not say how the gods would punish those who disobeyed my commands?"

Tyame appeared on the roof of the winter *kiva*. The dancers had stopped now, a static tapestry of green feathers and white shells and black skirts and copper flesh. The wind was the only sound. It moaned dismally through the broken columns buttressing the face of the cliff.

Tyame spoke. "The gods do not listen to you. The rain you promised has not come."

"And that is why?" Po-pe answered, pointing a jeweled finger at Luis. "Do you think your prayers will be heard as long as a Christian remains among you?"

Kashana saw Luis make a move. Tsiki and Kaitneh grabbed his arms. Po-pe gave a signal to his Tano warriors.

"Get the *gachupin*."

CHAPTER THIRTY-THREE

THE *kivas* of Acoma were not separate from the buildings, as were the round half-sunken ceremonial chambers of the other villages. They were integral with the long communal houses. They were square, one story high, the roof top hatch reached by characteristic double ladders from the street. They were the womb of the Indian world, sacred, esoteric, belonging to the dawn of man. Luis had never thought he would see inside one.

The *daut koritz kiva* was in Middle Row. Luis lay on the floor. His hands were tied with rawhide and his feet were tied. Po-pe had wanted to kill him immediately. Tyame and the elders had objected. They were still arguing in the long house.

The only light in the *kiva* came from coals smoldering in the fire pit. Two Tewa guards sat on the stone bench built around the walls. Behind them were painted plumed snakes and tiered clouds with eyes and noses and mouths, shedding rain and lightning. In the weird glow the man seemed to join the stylized figures.

Beside Luis stood a third man. He was Pedro de Tapia, the Tano who had acted as interpreter for Governor Otermin before the revolt. He wore thin bracelets, wrist to elbow, that shimmered like the wire wrappings on a sword hilt. He wore Spanish boots pulled to the hip and a belt hung with dozens of silver pendants. He had just climbed down the ladder that led to the hatch in the roof and he was still wheezing heavily.

"A great discourse in the long house," he said in Spanish. "I was surprised how many wanted you alive. I think they would have fought to save you, if they were not outnumbered."

Luis did not answer. Tapia smiled slyly. His thick lips peeled like fruit rind from his stained teeth.

"Po-pe's appearance has caused more Acoma warriors to join Tsiki, however," Tapia said. "Every minute of the argument means another man who wants you killed."

Luis did not doubt it. He knew what a shock Po-pe's appearance had caused in the Sky City. It had been years since Acoma had seen him, and the people had tended to forget the power of his personality.

"But Po-pe will take no chances," Tapia said. "If it does not seem that he can sway the Acomas by discourse he will send someone to kill you. He might even come himself. He might leave Jaca or Francisco to hold them in talk, and come. Or Tsiki might send someone. Someone will come."

Luis wondered if Tapia was the man. The Tano was naked above the waist, bellied like a Buddha. Greasy sweat leaked from the deep creases in his paunch. He smelled like spoiled mutton.

"Those who fawn on Po-pe grow fat," Luis said.

"But many are not fat. People starve in the villages."

Such an admission surprised Luis. He could not help glancing at the guards. Was that why Tapia spoke Spanish? Some of the Indians had never learned the language well. Six years without speaking it—much could be forgotten. Luis looked up at the fat, sweating face. What was Tapia getting at? Was he hinting at their dissatisfaction?

Tapia said, "If the Spaniards come back surely they would execute Po-pe for what he did in the revolt. They would execute Tupatu also, and Juan Ye of Pecos." Tapia paused. His grin was pawky. "Then there would have to be new Indian governors. There would have to be a governor of Pecos."

Luis felt his scalp prickle. A bargain? Was Tapia hinting that he would help Luis escape in return for some kind of deal? "Who among you would want to be governor?" Luis asked.

Tapia twirled an emerald ring on his puffy finger. His piggish eyes were tinged yellow at the corners. They slid toward the guards, then back to Luis. They made him look like a cat toying with a mouse. Luis felt his excitement fade.

"How could the Spaniards make a bargain with traitors?" he asked suspiciously.

Tapia's face twisted like a child in a tantrum. He kicked Luis in the ribs. Luis gasped in pain. He thought Tapia would kick him again, but a noise from above made Tapia turn and look up.

The hatch had been slid aside, and a funnel of light shot in. A figure was silhouetted in the opening. The ladder shook as the man began climbing down. Luis saw that it was Chotika, an aged *cheani*. Following him came Hanai, a medicine doctor in the same society. They were two of the old men who had befriended Luis. The third man was Pesana, Kashana's uncle. He shut the hatch.

"You are not from Po-pe," Tapia said.

"We are from Tsiki," Pesana said. "We come to prepare the Christian."

"Prepare?"

From a niche above the bench that held religious paraphernalia Hanai got some pottery bowls. He got some malachite ore and white bean meal and water and mixed it together to make a paste of turquoise blue. In another bowl he mixed iron-stained sandstone and water for red. The smell of wet and ancient earth filled the room.

Hanai squatted beside Luis and dipped his fingers into the sandstone and painted red stripes on Luis's face. The medicine doctor was immeasurably old. Skinny legs protruded from the folds of his blanket, stringy with muscle. Every fragile blue bone was visible in his hands, and the papery flesh was yellow and covered with brown spots.

Across from him squatted Chotika. His ancient face was dehydrated and furred and brittle as old parchment. Streaming white hair obscured his eyes and most of his mouth. He cut Luis's clothes off with a knife and left him naked. He cut little holes in each garment to let the life of the garment out. He cut Luis's black hair. Eyebrow length across the front. Chin length at the sides.

"So Iatik wears her hair," he said.

"Mother of all people," Hanai said.

The Tewa guards had stood and had drawn near. They were behind the sweating Pedro de Tapia and Pesana, watching intently. Chotika took off Luis's moccasins and placed them beside his bare feet for dancing in the next world. Then they pulled Luis around so his head pointed north. Luis had the vivid memory of Nicolas Bua's dead body at San Juan, his face striped with earth colors, his hands holding little heaps of sacred meal, the moccasins by his bare feet.

He could not believe it. He looked up at Pesana. Kashana's uncle. The man who had stood with Luis at the wedding. The man who had told him how to be a husband. The man who had shared the food of his household with Luis and Kashana because Luis was not allowed off the mesa.

Pesana turned his eyes away.

There was a rumbling sound. It could have come from a great distance or it could have been in the room with them. The chamber seemed to vibrate. They all looked at the closed hatch. The sound came again and the hatch rattled.

"*Kwa tan hoo re taa,*" one of the Tewa guards said in an awed voice. "Thunder now rumbles."

From the niche above the bench Hanai took a rawhide thong two feet long. He gave it to Pesana. The man crouched beside Luis and wrapped the thong around his neck. There was something ceremonious about it. He drew it tight and knotted it. He put a billet of wood through the knot. A twist on the billet would strangle Luis. The medicine doctors stood up. Pesana would not meet Luis's eyes. He watched Hanai expectantly. It seemed that the men had stopped breathing in the room. It seemed that there was no sound. Luis could see sweat rolling down Tapia's fat belly and gathering in his navel. He could feel sweat on his own naked painted body. He closed his eyes. He began to make a silent Perfect Contrition. He wanted a priest. He did not think he had ever wanted a priest so badly. If a priest were there he would not be afraid. He knew that. He would not be afraid. Father Pio, he thought. Father Pio.

The thunder came again.

"It is time," Hanai said. "The gods have spoken."

Pesana twisted the billet violently. Luis felt his eyes bulge and his tongue come up into his mouth, swollen and gagging. He began to thrash in a panic he could not control. He could feel the cord biting into his throat and all the muscles of his neck contracting to make sound and no sound coming out.

He went blind. His eyes were wide and staring but he could not see. Then a white light flashed somewhere. In his crazed struggles he twisted against Pesana. The man seemed to pull him. It took him into the glowing coals.

He was burned, and again he felt his neck swell with the futile impulse to shout.

There was a pounding in his head. He thought it would burst. The frantic threshing of his bound body scattered coals over the room.

Suddenly the cord was loosened.

He gasped and fought to suck air past his swollen tongue. His throat convulsed and he gagged and started to cough. A sweating hand was pressed against his mouth.

He surged up, fighting, but the hand pressed him back. He could breathe through his nose, and he fought against the smothering panic that made him want to gag and struggle for air. It was completely black before his eyes. The white flashing was gone and he could see nothing.

He lay against the hot ashes of the fire pit, fighting to control his breathing. He was nauseated and shaking. He was bathed with sweat and rigid in reaction to pain. He finally understood the darkness. His wild thrashing had scattered the coals and they had gone out and now there was no light. The silence was weird after the wild sounds of their struggle. Pedro de Tapia said:

"A candle. Somebody make light."

Quickly Pesana rolled Luis over on his belly. Luis could feel the raw burns all over his back. The rawhide had cut into the flesh of his neck and he was bleeding. There was the flash of flint and steel, then somebody held a burning candle. It did not give much light. Pesana's hand was on Luis's back, a warning pressure. It made him lie still. He did not understand yet, but it made him lie still.

"His spirit dances in Weyima," Chotika said.

"He has gone back to Shipapu," Hanai said.

"The place from whence people emerged."

They were talking as though he were dead. Could they actually believe it? Pesana knew he was not dead. That hand on his back, like a signal. The man who had told him how to be a husband. It made him understand. These men had not come from Tsiki. They had come from Tyame.

He realized why Pesana had rolled him into the fire pit, scattering the coals and putting out the light. He knew the role he had to play.

The guard was bringing the candle across the chamber. Luis thought of holding his breath. But he could not hold it that long. They must not see him breathing. They must not see his ribs move.

He would breathe very shallowly. He would concentrate on it. He would think of nothing else. He would not think how close they were or how long it would last because suspense would make him breathless.

The candle gave poor light, even closer. Pesana had left the thong around his neck. It was still tight enough to dig into the bloody flesh, though Luis could breathe. His throat was raw and aching. It was a battle not to gag, cough, retch.

He had to prepare himself. He had to be ready for whatever they might do. If they kicked him or probed or tested he could not respond. He had to be perfectly slack. Dead.

Pedro de Tapia came over and dug a toe into his ribs. His body moved heavily, inertly to the pressure.

"He has gone back to Shipapu," Chotika said.

"He died quickly," Tapia said.

Was he suspicious? Or was it an idle comment. Why should he be suspicious? It was all very logical. Men did not question the expected. They had expected someone to come from Po-pe or Tsiki to kill him. They were strangers. They had no way of knowing that Pesana and the medicine doctors were from the *cacique* and not the war chief.

"Is it not strange," Pedro said, "how small a man looks when he is dead?"

Like spiders, hands settled on Luis. He remained loose. He had to remain loose. It was Hanai and Chotika. They turned him on his side, careful to keep his face turned from the Tewas and Pedro. They doubled him up, tying his knees against his chest. They began wrapping a mat about him.

A new crash of thunder seemed to make the room tremble. There was a rushing sound on the roof.

"*Kwa po hoore yemu,*" the Tewa guard said. "Rain water now is falling."

Kashana had seen it happen often in her lifetime. The sky clear and burning and blue all day long and the earth whitening and drying up. Then the dark heads of the gods appearing behind the mountains, the black thunderclouds that moved ceremoniously across the sky and darkened the land with their grotesque shadows as they came. The roar of thunder and the jagged spears of lightning and the downpour.

There was awe in it and mystery, but there was no surprise. It was known to their lives like breathing or eating or dying. They danced and the gods answered.

It was a typical summer storm. Rain was a slanting wall of water that shimmered in the last daylight and washed long pale streaks against the dark mud walls of the buildings and danced a crystal dance on the black rock streets.

The storm had driven all the villagers indoors. But Kashana did not go inside. She stood at the corner of the plaza and Middle Row. Her black hair streamed down her face, and her dress was plastered against her body. She kept wiping the rush of water from her eyes and watching the *daut koritz kiva* westward down the street.

Standing by the double ladder of the *kiva* were the half-breed Catiti and five of the warriors Po-pe had brought. They were huddled against the wall, looking at the roof top above them, as though uncertain whether to seek shelter or not.

Kashana saw men appear at the hatch of *daut koritz*, awkwardly lifting a large object with them. It was the body. Wrapped in a cotton blanket and yucca matting. A woman's sash tied about the matting. Symbol of the cord which had first joined him to his mother. Hands folded across the chest. Knees drawn up. Composed in the fetal crouch. Returning to the womb of Earth Mother.

Fear made her sick. Need of Luis flooded her like heat. Did they have to kill him to make her realize how much she wanted him?

But he was not dead. He could not be dead. Pesana had explained that. Pesana had come from Tyame to tell her what she must do and what the other women must do.

The men climbed down the ladder. Pesana and Chotika were carrying the body. Hanai followed. He carried Luis's clothes with the holes cut in them. He carried a little bowl of water and a little bowl of cooked food so that Luis's spirit could feed on its aroma. All the appurtenances of death. All the details of ritual and form to make the Tewas believe.

The procession moved down the street. Catiti and Pedro de Tapia and the Tewa warriors followed in a long line. The rain smashed against them with solid weight. She could see their shoulders bow beneath it and could see that they would rather be out of it, warm and dry in some shelter. Thunder roared again. The Sky City trembled.

Seeka was first to appear. Kashana's aunt came out of the alley bisecting the first and second blocks of North Row. She paused a moment, looking at the solemn procession, and then turned to climb a ladder. Her wet robe clung revealingly to the feminine shape of her buttocks. She climbed slowly, looking back over her shoulder. Catiti stopped. He looked up after Seeka. Po-pe's cohort had become notorious for that. Wherever they traveled with him they took what women they wanted. They had become worse than Spaniards. It was what Tyame had counted on. Kashana was near enough to hear their voices.

"Catiti," Pedro de Tapia said irritably.

Catiti wiped the pouring rain from his eyes. "I have had enough of this. Is it not finished? I am not going to drown just to see them put a dead man in the ground."

Seeka had disappeared over the parapet. Catiti climbed the ladder after her. The Tewa warriors filed past, slowing down, watching their leader disappear. Tapia trailed them uncertainly. As the procession neared the plaza Kashana stepped back of a beehive oven where she would be hidden. They turned the corner into the square. The Tewas had dropped behind the men bearing the body. They looked sullen and miserable in the pounding rain.

A girl appeared across the plaza. She was very young, obviously a virgin. Kashana had seen Pedro de Tapia watching her when he first arrived.

He hesitated. The rain streamed over his bulging belly in silver channels. He looked at the girl. He wiped a hand across his slack mouth. The girl turned behind a building. Tapia cast a last glance after the men and then followed the girl.

Deserted by the leaders, the Tewas had nothing left to hold them. Sick of the rain, seeing no reason to follow the bearers any farther, they gave in to the temptation that had been prodding them since their first arrival on the rock. One by one the women appeared and one by one the Tewas followed them. The somber procession dwindled until only the pair carrying the body and the other medicine doctor was left.

They moved like shadows through the growing darkness. Kashana had held back for this. There was one more danger. Her uncle had warned her of it. He said it was her job.

By the time the last Tewa had disappeared the bearers passed the long house and reached the cemetery. The adobe walls of the grave-yard extended northward from the mission of Saint Stephen. Some of the mission buildings had been burned and partially destroyed during the revolt, but most of the church still stood. It had been built over fifty years ago by the Indians under the direction of a Catholic priest. Every handful of adobe in its ten-foot-thick walls had been carried from the plain below in blankets or buckskin sacks. The two square towers with their open belfries were stamped against the sky in dramatic silhouette by each new flash of lightning.

As the men bearing Luis reached the cemetery a man emerged from the long house. The driving rain whipped at his Spanish cloak. He was tall for a Pueblo. Taller than any of the other warriors who had come with him.

Kashana waited for others to follow. But no more men appeared. It was what Tyame had feared. He had considered that Po-pe might send someone to kill Luis. He had also considered that Po-pe might become impatient and go to give the order himself, slipping out while Jaca or Tsiki held the others inside the long house with oratory. It was why Kashana had waited. It was why she had been chosen. Many had seen

the way Po-pe had looked at her earlier in the day, and they knew it
was her job.

Po-pe had to lean against the force of the rain as he started toward
the village. The motion of the bearers carrying Luis into the walled
graveyard caught Po-pe's attention. They were distant shadows, unrecognizable in the streaming rain. But curiosity made him turn and walk
toward the graveyard.

Kashana was at the corner of the church. She moved away from the
wall. There was another bright flash of lightning. In a glow brighter
than any sun the man and woman were illuminated. She saw his face
gaping at her. It bore the same expression she had seen in the plaza
earlier.

She turned and moved hurriedly down the wall of the convent. He
wiped rain from his eyes and followed. She came to a breach in the
crumbling wall and stepped inside. In the black corridor she stopped.
She stood against the wall and said a prayer to Oyesis and Hayasi. She
gave proper thought to her mother, her babies, and finally to Luis. She
gave most of her thought to him.

Pesana had promised that none of the women would suffer. There
would be men watching each one. As soon as the bearers had carried
Luis into the walled graveyard the men would break in on the women
and stop the Tewas.

But Kashana was too far from the village. She was not even sure that
the men knew where she was now. She had a knife in her sash. She
pulled it out and held it at her side. She heard Po-pe halt beyond the
breach, breathing like an animal.

"*Opina,*" she said to herself. "Come in."

CHAPTER THIRTY-FOUR

THROUGH those years the miserable handful of colonists had clung to the edge of New Mexico, watching and waiting as the forlorn hope of returning burned down to a last dying flicker. Technically the province still existed. The capital had simply been moved from Santa Fe to El Paso. But in actuality a territory whose vague boundaries made it as big as Spain had been torn from Spanish hands, and for seven years a dreary succession of governors had failed to win it back.

An indifferent Crown would not allow enough troops or supplies for the monumental task of reconquest. The few campaigns up the Rio Grande had been little more than gestures, quickly defeated by bitter weather, inadequate forces, or overwhelming Pueblo armies. In 1681 a new revolt occurred among the Mansos and the Sumas around El Paso, and the Spaniards spent the next three years subduing them. The savage warfare and the severe drought that came at its end left the colonists at the Pass of the North more impoverished than ever.

In 1687 a man named Pedro Reneros de Posada was governor at El Paso. In that same year New Spain was ruled by a viceroy known as Brazo de la Plata because of his false arm. His reign was a gaudy one, studded by a succession of balls and parties and public functions. In mid-September Don Gómez Gallegos gave a party in the viceroy's honor. Barbara de Cárdenas was one of the guests.

She did not get home till near dawn. She slept till the afternoon rain woke her, pattering on the roof of her tower room. She called Josefina and had breakfast in bed. Then the Tlascalan maid opened the drapes and Barbara put on a chemise and satin mules and sat before her mother's mirror while the little maid brushed her long hair, telling off the customary hundred strokes by tens because she could count no higher.

The glass of the mirror was tarnished with the coppery patina of great age. It reflected the image of a woman.

Barbara still caught herself being surprised at what had come with the years. The face was no longer the fragile, shapeless oval of pallid flesh and frightened eyes. The brows were heavy and arched. Her eyes were as big, as vividly black. But they did not have the perpetually surprised look and did not fill with tears at the slightest inconvenience.

She had on only her chemise. Beneath it her body swelled and receded, the light playing a satiny game on its curves and hollows. She remembered how frantic she had been about her breasts. At seventeen her flat chest and her lack of suitors had been the biggest problems of her life.

Now . . . well, perhaps they would never be as big as the Condesa's. But then the Condesa, even six years ago, had been worrying about becoming a cow.

Six years ago . . .

It saddened her to realize it had been that long. She had tried many times to locate the Condesa but had found no trace of her. She knew the woman had wanted it that way for Barbara's sake as much as her own. It was safer for a person to know nothing about someone wanted by the Holy Office.

"No comb or mantilla today," Barbara told Josefina. "Just braid it And then the petticoats, four—the red, the yellow, the blue—"

"And the silk dress with the low neck, and the knit stockings, apple-green, and the French slippers—"

"Basta, basta—do you want me to look like a courtesan?"

The maid giggled. "It is simply that Don Diego is with the others downstairs."

Don Diego, Don Diego. Barbara made a face at herself in the mirror. Then she rose and walked impatiently across the room, the maid half running behind her in a frantic attempt to keep braiding her hair. Barbara wondered if it was the thought of going downstairs that disturbed her, or the news she had to send her manager at the estate. She was low on cash again and soon would be unable to pay the Indians. A core of them were loyal and would remain on the promise of being paid after harvest. But too many others would quit as soon as there were no wages.

It had happened before. Those first years had been hard. She had found that running an estate of such size was an almost overwhelming task for a young, inexperienced girl. She discovered the deception of wealth that lay in land and properties rather than in actual cash. The only time she saw any real amount of money was when the crops were sold in January. But that was soon gone. Her establishment in town was expensive to maintain, and the rest was drained off by taxes, tithes, and the costs of litigation that had been going on ever since the will had been read.

Finding a good *mayordomo* for the estate had been another frustrating problem. Through a series of bad managers she had lost crops by inefficiency or sheer stupidity. One man had stolen half a harvest from her and had sold it through the smugglers and thieves at the *baratillo*.

Don Gómez was always asking her to let him help, to let him put in a manager of his own and get her out of trouble. But she knew the abuses that implied and had stubbornly refused to surrender.

She shook her head hopelessly. Josefina had finished helping her dress now. She took a last look in the mirror and crossed to the door that led into the sitting room comprising the other section of the tower. This opened onto a narrow stone stairway that led down to the broad hall on the second floor.

When she reached the corridor the door of a bedroom farther down opened and her cousin Nuno Alcazar came out. As Don Gómez Gallegos had prophesied, Don Melchor's will had been contested, and litigation had been instituted in Madrid by a dozen aspiring heirs. Some of them had even come to Mexico City to present their claims or propositions. Nuno Alcazar claimed to be the son of Barbara's grandfather, born out of wedlock in Vera Cruz. He had papers legitimizing him and granting him equal privileges and inheritance with the other sons. He had put in a claim against a large part of the estate, including the Santa Fe property of Barbara's uncle, Don Celso Cárdenas, who had died on the Journey of the Dead Man. Don Gómez Gallegos, as Barbara's legal counsel, claimed a forgery. Such papers were usually issued in triplicate; but there was no certification in Mexico City, and the only way to get validation was to send to Spain. It was an interminable process. The case had been before the court for years, and Barbara had spent a small fortune on lawyers in Madrid.

Balanced on skinny legs, Nuno's pear-shaped torso, with the big end settled into paunch and rump, gave him the grotesque look of a top-heavy humpty dumpty. He had spent two years at Versailles and could never forget it. He affected the great powdered wig, curled and scented, made popular at the French court by Louis XIV. The silver-plated heels on his white kid slippers clicked like castanets against the stone floor of the hallway.

"Ah, good cousin——" He waved his silk handkerchief at her and she smelled its perfume while he was still ten feet away. "I have just heard the latest, naughtiest tidbit from the palace. In the little silver box the viceroy guards so carefully, you know, the one everybody thought was snuff . . . what do you think? Cantharides."

She knew he thought her hopelessly naïve and was always mocking her with allusions he did not think she understood.

"The tailor presented me with a bill this morning," she said. "What did he do, cut the coat out of gold?"

He waved a soft white hand, glittering with rings. "You know it is only until I get my allowance from Seville——"

"Your debts are always bigger than the allowance, Nuno. You have not been off my books from the day you got here. I have told the tailor you are to get no more credit in my name."

His mouth popped. "Cousin—you cannot, what will I do? The vice-regal ball—I cannot go naked."

"No," she said, looking him up and down, "spare us that."

She turned and went downstairs. She could hear the shrill laughter and incessant prattle from the parlor. She felt as though she were stepping into a cage of twittering birds. She walked into the big room with its paneled ceiling, its jasper floors, its cathedral windows. The velvet draperies were drawn against the day, and a hundred candles cast their winking light over the gathering.

Near the brazier sat her aunt, Doña Ramona, busily engaged in embroidering a *tápalo de matrimonio*. She always reminded Barbara of a stuffed, sugar-powdered *sopapilla*. Flesh covered her body in soft billows, overflowing her corsets and the tightly laced bodice of her purple taffeta dress. She was an aunt by marriage, wife of the late Don Pedro Cárdenas, elder brother of Barbara's father and a judge in the Lima *audiencia*. When she heard that Barbara was the only survivor of Don Melchor's immediate family the widowed Doña Ramona had hurried from Peru to console and advise her.

"*Buenas días*, Barbara," she said brightly. "It is time you came out of that dismal tower room."

Behind one of the intricate chairs stood Don Diego de Vargas Zapate Lujan Ponce de León. Josefina had told Barbara he was here, yet she could not help hesitating at the door. It was something that had happened to Barbara before, something Vargas did to a room, without moving, without announcing his presence in any way, like the glow of the sanctuary light giving life to a dark nave.

Perhaps it was some quality of strangeness in his face. The cheeks had a hard, chiseled surface and were touched with a curious sallowness. It made Barbara think of malarial coasts, of gloomy castle corridors that never saw the sun. He had the habit of holding his chin lifted slightly, giving the effect of remoteness, a man who held his own counsel and could not share much of himself. Yet his eyes were not remote. Brilliant and black, they had a jeweled impact. Barbara remembered the awe she had felt for the Marqués de Gallegos because he had looked into the eyes of a king.

"God give you good days, Señorita Barbara," Vargas said. His hair was not queued. It was parted in the center and hung loose to the shoulders, and his bow made it swing straight and black as horse mane against his sallow jaws. "We were just discussing the viceregal ball."

Barbara lifted her skirts and took the chair Vargas had offered her. He was from one of the most illustrious houses of Spain and had come to the New World fifteen years before as *capitán del pliego del aviso*, carrying royal orders from the king to the viceroy. Among them was the confirmation for Barbara's father as a judge of the *audiencia*. Vargas's friendship for the Cárdenas family had begun then.

Soon after his arrival in Mexico City he had been appointed *justicia mayor* of Tlalpujagua, a mining camp in Michoacan, and later administrator for the royal quicksilver. He maintained residence in Mexico City, but his duties kept him out of the capital much of the time.

"Did you come all this way just for the viceroy's ball, Don Diego?" Barbara asked.

"That and politics," he said. "They are seeking another governor for New Mexico. I thought the Crown was going to give the province up, but this memorial the Marqués de Gallegos is presenting to the king has caused quite a stir."

Barbara knew that the Marqués had already left for Spain. His brother, Don Gómez, had told Barbara about the memorial. She had thought of it as simply another futile attempt to gain the Crown's interest in the reconquest of New Mexico. That Diego de Vargas should give it such credence surprised her.

Thoughtfully she asked, "Do not the claims in the Marqués's memorial seem fantastic? That he was the first to discover this Sierra Azul? The mines were known of before he was born."

"He does have a map—and that is more than anyone else has produced."

The emphatic tone of his voice made her look at Vargas. He had a taste for fine things. A doublet of royal lion skin made a tawny sheath for his lean torso, the short sleeves puffed and slashed at the shoulders to reveal a crimson silk lining. His breeches were of yellow Castilian satin, gartered at the knees with bullion, and his cordovan shoes had diamond buckles. But the way he stood and moved and spoke imparted a sense of Spartan austerity that made the gaudiest clothes seem grave.

Barbara could not help wondering—had Cortez looked that way? What was it about a Spaniard? Vargas was a man of the world. He had won renown fighting for his king in Italy, had spent years in the cynical corruption of court politics, possessed more titles and estates than almost anyone else in the New World. Yet without hesitation he was willing to consider sacrificing it all, to risk his life and reputation in an unknown world, all over the fantastic claims of a perfect stranger.

How could these dreams of mythical riches still haunt men after a hundred and fifty years of disillusionment?

After Cortez discovered the fabulous treasures of Montezuma, and Pizarro captured a Peruvian emperor who ransomed himself with a roomful of gold, men would believe anything. The first explorers had been drawn into New Mexico by the fantastic legends of Cibola—but instead of the golden cities Coronado had found only the mud towns of the Pueblos.

Still the myths would not die. As early as 1581 reports had reached Mexico City of Sierra Azul, a range of mountains in the Moqui country containing more silver than all of San Luis Potosi and enough quicksilver to supply all the Spanish world. But the Moqui country was enemy land, too distant from Santa Fe to colonize, too threatened by Apaches and Navajos to yield its true secrets. So the few men who wandered into the area kept bringing back their unsubstantiated reports, and Sierra Azul slept on for a century in the realm of fantasy. . . .

Nuno wandered in, still pouting. He pulled the skirts of his silver encrusted vest carefully aside as he sat down. He sprawled in the chair, sullenly picking among the sweets on a table. Doña Ramona held up the *tapalo*.

"See what I have embroidered, Barbara. Aurora riding her chariot. Perhaps I will get the silver fringe on in time to present it to you and Bernardo."

Barbara flushed. Bernardo Rico merely smiled dreamily to himself.

He stood near the window, hardly seeming aware of them. He moved with studied grace, making a pretended pass with an imaginary cape. He was a bullfighter.

Doña Ramona was always maneuvering to attach Barbara to one young man or another. Sooner or later it came out that they had some connection with Barbara's aunt. Only last night Bernardo had let slip that he came from Lima.

A servant ushered Jaime Pulgar into the room. He was a Creole— one of the pure-blooded Spaniards native to the New World who were little better than parasites in the capital, fawning upon the *gachupines* for favors, meaningless titles, minor political posts, or any other crumbs that might sift through the grasping fingers of the Spaniards from the mother country. Jaime attended Nuno like a sycophant, even mimicking his languid gestures. Barbara could never quite decide whether he was courting her or Nuno.

After an elaborate greeting the Creole turned breathlessly to Barbara's cousin. "Nuno, I have a new, wonderful, naughty little *palabreja oscuro* that is said to come directly from the viceroy's own bedchamber."

Barbara looked at them distastefully as Jaime began the ambiguous little riddle that sounded so obscene and had such an innocent answer. After Nuno guessed the answer the conversation descended into the cesspool of palace gossip and local scandal that made up so much of their world. Barbara stirred restlessly. She felt suffocated. The smell of perfume and pomade and powder gagged her. When she could bear it no longer she excused herself and went downstairs.

The house was built around the patio. On all four sides of the enclosure great stone arches supported the building above and formed shadowed galleries. It cast a massive medieval spell over the patio. The walls and arches and center fountain were checkerboarded with a green and yellow wainscoting of glazed Puebla tiles. Exotic palms cast welcome spears of shade across the masonry floor, and a parakeet preened and chattered in an amole cage. Barbara sat on the edge of the fountain and trailed her fingers in the cool water.

The disgust for Nuno and Jaime was still with her. It made her think of the others in their corrupt circle. It made her think of all the young men she had come to know in the capital, the letters from their families, the proposals at the masked balls. She was twenty-four. Already passing the marriageable age in the Spanish world. And not without the normal fears. Sometimes in the night she woke and lay sick and trembling at the thought of growing old alone.

Who, then? Bernardo Rico? The arrogance, the vanity. Jaime Pulgar? Unthinkable. Francisco Estrada. Spoiled and dissolute.

What made her see such things in so many of them? What was it that seemed to taint the young men of the capital—like the smell of rotten fruit? Or was it simply something inside her, a restlessness, a dissatisfaction that made her magnify their flaws. It seemed related to the whole pattern of her life. She felt an emptiness, an insidious lack. The management of her estate and household occupied much of her time, but there was no fulfillment in the routine. The social life of the capital no longer excited her. She thought of New Mexico. Of the Journey of the Dead Man. She remembered what she had told the Condesa. She had felt closer to life on the Jornada than ever before or since.

She heard someone enter the patio and looked up to see Don Diego de Vargas. He had put on his stiff taffeta baldric, in which was slung his Toledo rapier. A huge emerald glowed in its hilt, and the sword held his yellow silk cloak out behind like the tail of a vivid cock.

"I could bear it no longer," he said. "Why do you put up with those leeches?"

She sighed. "Mother always told me that our family ties were stronger than we realized. I did not understand her then. There is loneliness. This is such a big house. It would be so empty without someone—even them. Aunt Ramona is not so bad. I think her little schemes to get me connected with her branch of the family are rather amusing. And her presence gives the aura of respectability to my household. A man . . . you could not realize how necessary that is. . . ."

"I do realize," he said. "I know our world too well." He paused. "And Nuno?"

"Not so amusing, I will grant you. But Don Gómez thinks it safer to have him at hand until the estate is settled. Sooner or later Nuno's miserable little plots become evident, and I can forestall them. He would be much more dangerous working against us where we could not see him."

"An ironic situation," he said. "And all on the advice of Don Gómez Gallegos."

"One of my father's oldest friends."

"You must know how he feels about the way you manage your estate."

"Of course. All the *encomenderos* are horrified. They think I am undermining their whole way of life. I admit Don Gómez has put pressure on to have me go back to conscript labor. On the other hand he has done all he can to help me. I trust him, Don Diego."

Vargas did not answer. He glanced at her strangely and then turned to look into the fountain.

He made Barbara think of a statue—chill and grave and precisely carved. She wondered if he was as aloof from the passions of ordinary men as he seemed. She doubted it. Sometimes she thought she felt the heat of a fire that burned deep within him.

Once, at the viceregal ball, when he had danced with her . . .

Yet what had it been—really? Just a look, a pressure of his hand. He had a wife and child in Spain, and it was whispered that he kept a mistress in Mexico City and had two or three illegitimate children. Would that kind of man be content forever with such a role, the family friend, the very proper escort to Mass or an occasional public function? It was a puzzle that sometimes made her uneasy in his presence.

Despite their disparity in ages she could not deny the attraction he held. There was a masculine force to him that she missed in so many of the others. There was the faint scent of tobacco and fine red cordovan to him. It stirred her. She could not deny it. She looked at his sinewy hands and thought of them on her body. She blushed with a mingling of excitement and embarrassment. She looked quickly back at her own hands locked in her lap, as though afraid he would see her thoughts.

Nuno was right. She was naïve and she was a virgin and it infuriated her.

CHAPTER THIRTY-FIVE

MEXICO CITY was a Spanish capital. Yet of its 400,000 people only 70,000 were Spaniards. The rest were Indians and *mestizos* of every mixture. They occupied six of the capital's nine *barrios*, wards that had their own governors, priests, and churches. One of these wards in the northwest part of the city was the Romita.

It was a suburb of narrow streets, crumbling stone buildings, thatched huts. It was a notorious meeting place of thieves and cut-throats and smugglers who dressed in the costumes of witches or sorcerers to frighten the ignorant Indians so they could pass their merchandise without being molested.

The capital was miserably policed. The twenty halberdiers stationed at the palace had their hands full guarding the viceroy. The few city constables could do little more than keep the night watch and patrol the streets near the Zocalo. Even the agents of the Inquisition avoided the Romita, for the Indians did not come under their jurisdiction. It was where the Condesa had gone.

She had been there since she had left Barbara. She had a cramped room in a long building at the edge of a canal. She called herself Ynez and did not mix with the other people in the building and came out rarely, mostly at night. Toribio paid her rent and gave her money for food. But there were times when it ran out, or he had to leave the capital on business for the Inquisition. She knew that if she took another man Toribio would find out sooner or later. But she could not starve. So she danced.

She knew how dangerous it was and did it only when she was desperate. But she had lived in another world as the glamorous Condesa de Zumurraga. She doubted that any of the outcasts in this place had seen her at the viceregal balls or in the glittering soirées of Echave and his fellow artists.

In the summer of 1689 Toribio was sent to Vera Cruz to investigate a denunciation made by the local commissioner. Within a week the Condesa had spent her last *tostón* for food. She waited two more days and then knew she would have to go to El Renegado.

It was a miserable tavern a few blocks from where she lived. The rafters supporting its low ceiling were blackened with smoke. The raw smell of *pulque* mingled with the greasy odor of chile and the reek of the rotting straw on the floor. In one corner were two kegs, one of *pulque* and one of *tepache chiche*, a drink of corn, honey, and water. The *zambo* named Escandon sat on a stool by the barrels, a dipper for serving drinks in one fist, a machete for rapping over-eager knuckles with the other. The Condesa had danced here before and did not even bother to cross the smoky room to ask Escandon's permission. He would be glad for a little entertainment to draw in some customers. When he saw her coming down the rear hall he called to Ochorios, a soldier who had been blinded in service on the frontier. He started with a strong chord on his guitar and then let his fingers wander over the strings in a haunting, barely audible melody.

The Condesa let her cloak slide off into the hands of her maid. She glanced quickly around the room, recognizing none of the sweating faces at the tables. She moved out onto the floor.

She wore one of the dresses Barbara had given her, silk, silver-blue, a full skirt, and a bodice laced down the back. It was sleazy and worn and patched but probably the richest garment the tavern had ever seen. She had carried on a grim contest with time. Cosmetics and care and hours before the mirror still effected the illusion of beauty with her face. But she had grown heavier. She could not understand that. There were so many of these times when she and Chintule went for days without food. Even when they ate she nibbled like a bird and exercised and had the little Zapotec maid pound and massage, and still the added pounds had come. She knew that most women of her age would have surrendered long ago. But she could not give up. She fought bitterly every new ounce, every added day.

Back arched, bare shoulders lifted arrogantly, hips a swaying provocation, she crossed the floor in the opening *paseo de gracia*. There were none of the tentative *palmadas* and murmurs of approval so traditional in gypsy camps. There was merely a shouting roar from a dozen of the drunken breeds seated at the tables.

"*Viva*," they yelled. "*Viva gitana . . .*"

Gypsy, she thought contemptuously, *what do you know about gypsy?*

As with all her accomplishments she imparted a sense of brilliant metallic surface to her dancing, an effect of painstakingly polished technique unwarmed by any fires of true passion. But for the crude gathering it was enough. She arched, she wheeled, she snapped the castanets softly beside shimmering hips.

She pirouetted. She stamped. Her arms rose, fell, undulated, tipped with the aphrodisiac of clattering castanets. But still with her head down, eyes half closed, curiously demure, refusing to look at them. The guitar picked up its tempo.

"*Andale! Gitana! Zarabanda, zarabanda——*"

She gave way to their shouted demands. In a motion of pure arrogance she flung up her head, staring boldly into their faces. It was a signal for their shouting to grow wilder.

Frantic pirouettes carried the skirt high about the white columns of her thighs. Her breasts strained against the bodice. Her hips swung, beckoning. Her rapacious fingers fluttered incessantly with the ceaseless crackle of the castanets.

She whirled in a last abandonment and stopped abruptly, stamping once. She lifted her arms and flung the castanets down in a final *brazeo*. She dropped to one knee, head bowed. Her hair had come loose and hung in a thick black mass before her face, touching the floor.

After the wildness of the dance it evoked the picture of a woman spent, subdued, completely subjected. They shouted and stamped and she heard the ring of a few coins on the floor. When the noise died she lifted her head and began to sweep the handful of *reales* and *tomines* into her skirt. And saw the face in the crowd.

It was like a physical shock.

A long face, so gaunt and starved it looked almost wolfish. A bearded face, the beard so long that the constant rubbing of its ragged edge had left a stain on the chest of the rawhide jacket. The hair was so matted and dirty that it was like coal, dead and black and refusing to reflect the light. It was not queued but was tied with a strip of rawhide into a thick club at the nape of the neck.

But what shocked her was the dished Iberian temples that she could never forget, leaving little hollows of shadow just back of the eyes, and the way all the angles of the face seemed to tilt so that when he smiled he looked like a dreaming satyr and one never knew whether he was amused or angry.

"Holy Mother of God," she whispered.

She became aware that her stunned look and her attention had made several others in the crowd glance at the man. She picked up her skirt, weighted with the money, and hurried into the shadowed hall.

Hidden from the crowd, she watched the man rise and leave. He was wide through the shoulders, but it was a bony wideness, and the rest of him was so narrow that he reminded her even more of a starved animal. A ragged serape hung from one shoulder. His rawhide jacket and breeches were stained almost black with grease and dirt. Nevertheless they bore the chalky patches of age and use across the knees and seat. He had no sword but there was a long stiletto stuck naked through the garter at one knee.

The Condesa hurried down the hall, going past Chintule. She let herself into the dark alley and started toward the street. She was halfway there when his tall figure appeared at the end of the alley. She stopped.

"Luis?"

"Condesa?"

She made a smothered sound; she dropped her skirt, heedless of the coins that scattered on the ground, and ran to him. He held her tight, laughing and saying her name over and over.

She pulled back and took his face in her hands for a moment, holding it tight, pressing her hands against the hard jaws. "A beard," she said breathlessly. "Such a beard. Oh, Luis, Luis . . . I thought . . . name of God . . . I did not know . . . all these years . . ."

Still smiling he took both her hands in his. "It cannot be many years, companion. You have not changed a bit."

It made her feel like the Condesa again. With Toribio she felt like a courtesan or just a plain whore. But with Luis she always felt like the Condesa.

"How did you find me?" she asked. "Such an accident."

"No accident. I have been hunting. You told me once that someone wanted by the Holy Office was safer in one of these *barrios* than some outlying town."

"Of truth," she said. "Look how conspicuous I was at Santa Fe. Here I am the proverbial needle." Her first excitement was gone and caution returned. "We cannot stay here. My room . . ."

He stooped to help her pick up the dropped coins. Chintule came hesitantly from the shadows to help the Condesa into her shabby cloak.

The woman looked at the handful of coins, then pressed them into the Zapotec's bony hand.

"*Tamales* . . . from the square. Bargain your best. Don Luis looks as hungry as we," the Condesa said. She watched the maid disappear down the alley like a shriveled, black-faced gnome. She sighed. "Chintule has been my salvation," she said.

She gathered up the skirts of her cloak and led him through back alleys and across a bridge to the long, one-story adobe building that fronted on a canal. The women drew their water from the canal and did their washing in it and threw their garbage and offal into it. Its black surface was choked with debris, and the pestiferous stench could not even be locked out by closed doors. In her room the Condesa lit a candle. The light washed against bare walls, spiderwebbed with cracks, scrofulous with crumbling adobe.

She seated herself on the rolled mattress against the wall. He dropped his serape on the table and sprawled tiredly in the single chair. She still thought of Luis as one of the fine people and expected him to show some reaction to the miserable quarters. But he seemed indifferent to the surroundings.

"Well," she said, "what does one say . . . so many years . . . how to begin? It is wonderful, indescribable . . . but still so hard to believe. Luis . . . for favor, you must tell me——"

He studied his sinewy hands thoughtfully. He began by telling how Kashana had saved him and had taken him to Acoma. He told her briefly of his life at the Sky City. He told of his escape—how Pesana had pretended to kill him in the darkness of the *kiva*, how the women had lured the Tewa guards away as he was carried to the cemetery. Hidden from the village by the walls, they had let Luis out of the matting and he had escaped down the dangerous Dead Man's Trail.

The storm had been his ally, wiping out whatever tracks he left. They had given him only a knife and a bag of parched corn and cured meat. On foot he traveled southward, forced to detour and backtrack constantly to avoid the Indians. He ran out of food and lost his bearings. He did not say how long he remained in the desert. She got the impression it was months, perhaps the better part of a year. He passed over it quickly, but in the grim desolation that touched his eyes she saw what a harrowing experience it had been.

Finally he found his way into New Spain. He heard that Posada was then governor of the New Mexican colony at El Paso and his first impulse was to present himself there. But caution made him investigate first. Under an assumed name he talked with a priest at one of the outlying settlements who had worked with Governor Otermin. He learned that the Condesa had gone south to Mexico City. Luis learned also that he had been listed as dead on the official muster roles taken by Otermin in 1681. But the priest had seen nothing in the reports from Mexico City to indicate that Luis had been reconciled or burned in effigy. That meant his case was still on the books, and he would subject himself to arrest by the Inquisition if he revealed who he was. It turned him down the long Camino Real to the capital. For months he had lived as one of the outcasts in the Indian wards, hunting for some trace of the Condesa.

"I guess I had no plan then," he said. "Even hunting you, I really had no plan. But I have learned something here, Condesa. I have learned that I cannot spend the rest of my life that way, hiding, hunted, living worse than an animal, waiting for the day they find me."

She almost rose. "You do not mean—give yourself up."

He smiled ironically. "No. I am not ready to gamble on burning at the stake."

"Then . . . what?"

"I want to go back to Santa Fe."

He said it simply, without emphasis, yet she could see the hunger in his eyes. She wondered if this was the core of what had happened to him, the source of the deep change she had sensed. He looked at her broodingly, then glanced around the room.

"No books, no *vihuela,* no Velasquez. Do you not miss it?"

"Bitterly," she said.

He leaned his head back, closing his eyes. "Was I hunting something, companion?"

"Like nobody else ever hunted. In all those talks, those books, those words, those thousands of words—"

"We can have it again?"

"Can we? They seemed so wonderful—Plato, Aquinas, Aristotle, all those shining abstractions, those wonderful ideas. Now . . . like going in a circle. Juggling shadows. There is an emptiness. I do not think I could go back."

"You have been out in the world."

"More than that."

"You have a fine mind."

"But not that kind of a mind. Not an intellectual. I have more of Don Bernabe in me than Don Cristobal. I cannot be a scholar. I was just pretending . . . some kind of a game. Why are the young so arrogant?"

He rose, as though unable to remain still. He crossed the room and stopped, staring at San Miguel. "Was I a rebel?"

"Luis, when we are young—"

"Was I a seeker? So much smarter than the old men, so much deeper than the fathers, putting all the fine words together, the fine ideas, solving all the puzzles of the universe?"

"It was not as ridiculous as you make it seem."

He stopped, smiling sadly. "It must have been. A bull in a china shop. All that shouting, all that noise. Did it change one thing? Just one thing? Bowels of Judas!" He sat in the chair again, staring blankly before him. "What happens, Condesa?"

"I think we get tired," she said. "As we get older, we just get tired."

He was silent. He scratched his heavy, matted, black beard. At last he said:

"At Acoma . . . this *cacique*. Tyame. I think he had some great kind of wisdom. Not a thing you get from books, or lofty philosophical discussions, or anything with the mind. He went into the wilderness. He fasted. He starved himself."

"We have our great mystics."

"It was not just Tyame. It was all of those people, Condesa. I saw how they believed. Not knowing it with the mind. Simply feeling it with—with their whole being—and their questions, all their questions answered with this feeling—"

"Is that not true among us?"

"Not quite," he said. "We have the feelings and then we devise words . . . we devise words to explain it . . . and pretty soon the words become more important than the feeling . . . we lose something, I do not know—"

"Maybe many of us, Luis. But you—I think maybe it is why all the ideas will not satisfy you. You are that other way. Underneath you are a man of feeling and it is too strong."

"For a while I thought so," he said. "I wanted to think so. Among the Indians—this feeling—it is their whole way of life. Everything they do is a part of it somehow. It gives them something—a peace, a harmony, a communion—beyond our conception. I only had a hint of it before the revolt. I thought I knew it all then, remember?"

"Yes."

"But at Acoma—after I got over the revolt, when I could think of the Pueblos as human beings again, when I knew they were not monsters and knew they were not saints too—I saw more. Just a little more. No white man will ever really see all. Or even much. But I thought it was enough. I had rejected my own people. I thought what they had there at Acoma, the whole thing, was better. A thousand days up on that roof top, watching them, seeing what it was. A thousand nights alone, sitting there, thinking, feeling, trying to feel, to belong—sometimes closer to the source of things than I ever had been before. But—how many years? Five, six. If a man is going to do it he can do it in that time, truth? Tell me, Condesa. Truth?"

"And you could not do it."

His head was bowed. He sat that way a long time, not answering. Then he straightened and looked at her.

"So what is left?" he asked. "When it is all stripped away, one layer after another, pride, arrogance, affectations, the pseudo intellectual, the rebel, the Don Quixote, one illusion after another, all the things you cannot be, the things you are not—what is left? The thing that you are. Is that not so? The thing that you really are."

"So you are a Spaniard," she said. "And you have come back to your people."

He was staring blankly at the floor. He was silent for so long that she thought he did not mean to answer. Finally he said, "Santa Fe is where I belong. I have learned that much. But just returning is not enough. Something else will have to be achieved. Something between the Pueblos and the Spaniards, something new, some new trust, some faith that did not exist before."

"Can it be done?"

"I cannot do it alone. I know that. But if I could help . . . I think Tyame gave me the key. There must be one among us they can trust. He must be the one in supreme authority and his word must be the law to both the Pueblos and the Spaniards. If Otermin had been that man things might have been different."

She made a disgusted sound. "Where is such a man? In all New Spain. These governors, Ramirez, Posada, Cruzate—and now the Marqués de Gallegos is petitioning."

"If he is appointed our last chance will be destroyed. But there is talk of resistance against him in the Church . . . this other man, Diego de Vargas."

She nodded. "I knew him. He was a friend of the Count's. He has greatness, Luis. But even so, even if he were appointed, how could you . . . ?"

"The whole point. If he was convinced that I could help him enough he might intercede. He is powerful, highly placed, of a noble house. A pardon might be obtained."

She smiled bitterly. "From the Holy Office?"

He closed his eyes and pinched the bridge of his nose. "Well . . . what else is left?"

She folded her hands tightly in her lap, studying them miserably. She could not take this last hope from him.

"Have you seen Vargas?" she asked.

"Not yet. Part of my safety lies in the fact that the Holy Office thinks me dead. If I go to Vargas myself and he refuses me, he will surely inform them. I need someone to sound him out first——"

She thought a minute. "He is a friend of Barbara de Cárdenas."

He smiled sadly. "After the way I treated her?"

"That does not matter. She has changed too, Luis, grown up." The Condesa looked at him obliquely, wondering how far she should go, if she should tell him how Barbara really felt about him. Or did she know how Barbara felt? Was it any more than a suspicion? After all, what had Barbara actually ever said? The Condesa stirred restlessly. "I have not been in touch with Barbara for years. I did not want her to know where I was—for her own sake. But I could send Chintule—arrange something."

"I would be grateful."

There was a furtive knock on the door. Luis rose quickly, and she saw that he had pulled the stiletto from his garter at his knee. She held up a hand to caution him. She knew Chintule's knock. She admitted the little Zapotec. The maid had half a dozen tamales in her shawl, still steaming and fat with meat and cheese. The Condesa got a plate, and the three of them gathered around the rickety table to eat.

"Where are you staying?" the Condesa asked Luis.

He wiped juice from his lips, smiling sardonically. "A fine gutter with a southern exposure."

"I wish I could ask you to stay here. It would be too dangerous. Toribio Quintano——"

"You still see him?"

"Are you jealous?"

He matched her mood, tilting his head quizzically. "Should I not be?"

The teasing look left her face. She was gazing into his eyes. The roof of her mouth went dry. She remembered how these moments had come before, at Santa Fe, when the veil of words suddenly shredded, and it was as though they could see each other clearly; and she wondered what it was that made him hesitate, that made them companions instead of a man and a woman. The moment grew awkward. Self-consciously she broke the silence.

"Do you still dream?"

She thought he would not answer for a moment. Then he smiled, a little wryly, and looked down.

"I do not dream about women as much. I thought I would never stop dreaming about women but now it is not so much."

They had finished eating and Luis broke the mood abruptly, rising and reaching for his serape. With the gesture that was so Spanish and could not help looking so arrogant he tossed it over one shoulder. She rose and followed him to the door.

"If you see Toribio I should not come here too often," he said. "Every evening at compline I will be at the bridge on the other side of the canal. If there is news you can send Chintule." He took both her hands, smiling at her. "Thousand thanks, companion."

She watched him walk into the night until she could no longer see him, and then she closed the door and stood with her hands pressed against it and her eyes closed. She heard Chintule stir behind her and opened her eyes and turned. The shriveled little Indian was looking at her almost accusingly.

"He would not beat you," Chintule said.

"Little burro," the Condesa said affectionately. She picked their only candle off the table and placed it before the Virgin of Guadalupe, standing in a wall niche. She said, "Now you will kneel with me, Chintule, and we will pray for Luis Ribera."

CHAPTER THIRTY-SIX

DURING the following days Luis waited impatiently for some word from the Condesa. He had long ago become an indistingishable part of the listless pattern of life in the Romita. At night he slept rolled in his serape under one of the crumbling bridges. During the day, if there was no work, he mingled with the crowds in the plaza or squatted with the beggars against the church wall, his straw sombrero pulled low to hide his face from the sun and the passer-by.

Sometimes he wondered ironically what his grandfather would have thought of him now. He honestly believed Don Bernabe would have starved to death rather than degrade himself with work and begging and scavenging as Luis had. It was a part of the Spanish pride Luis had rebelled against. He wondered if he had ever possessed it. Or had it been burned from him by the fires of the revolt, the animal depths to which he had descended in the desert simply to survive? He had learned now to beg without shame. He had learned to dig in the garbage and filth of the gutters for something that might keep him alive another day. It was a sort of flagellation, a spiritual discipline, as though in degradation he could find the humility that would guard him from the arrogance and intolerance that had been so hateful to him in his own people.

But during these last months of 1689 things had been better. Louis XIV had begun his long anticipated campaign to annex the Palatinate. Mannheim and Heidelberg had fallen, and the French armies were besieging Philippsburg, the gateway to the Rhine. As a member of the League of Augsburg, committed with Sweden and Austria to stand against French aggressions, Spain was drawn into the conflict. Her colonies soon felt the effects. As was usual in time of war, commerce with the mother country dropped to its lowest ebb. Since the colonies were forbidden to trade with any other nation local industry had to supply the demand normally met by Spain.

Cigar and cotton factories in the Romita that had long been idle were once more in operation. Luis's skill with clay, gained through the years when he had sat shackled before his door at Acoma, got him a job with the local potter. The pay was miserable, barely enough to buy his food, but it was far better than what he had been doing to stay alive.

Every night at compline he went to the bridge near the Condesa's as he had promised. It was over a week before Chintule came to him with word that arrangements had been made. Luis was to meet Diego de Vargas at the Cárdenas house on an evening when the rest of Barbara's family was attending a ball at the palace.

At the appointed time Chintule took him southward to Number 5 Calle de los Plateros. In darkness they waited among the beggars across the street till they saw the little door in the large gate of the carriageway open a crack. Luis crossed alone and was admitted. He stepped through the door into the blackness of the *zaguán* that ran like a tunnel under one wing of the house. A shadowy figure led him from the tunnel to a roofed gallery whose great stone arches opened onto a patio. At the end of the gallery stood a huge door studded with brass. Inside was another hall where a candle burned in a star-pointed wall sconce of heavy tin, mottled and yellowed with the patina of time. By its feeble light he saw that the woman leading him was Josefina, the Tlascalan who had been Barbara's handmaiden in Santa Fe.

She led him up a broad staircase. Luis knew that most of these houses near the Zocalo had been built by the conquerors who came with Cortez. The floors were of polished jasper, the great slabs of stone laid by Aztec masons whose art was a heritage of those mysterious builders of the Pyramid of the Moon at Teotihuacán. The huge ceiling beams and massive doors and intricately carved wainscoting were of the giant *ahuehuete* trees uprooted from Montezuma's own gardens on the hill of Chapultepec.

They went up the narrow stone stairway to the door of the tower room. Josefina knocked softly. The door was opened. Luis stepped in.

He had remembered a child. It was the only picture he had of her. He had remembered a child, fragile, sexless, with panicky hands, and a white face, and eyes that would never meet his. It had been impossible for him to imagine the woman that stood before him.

She was not tall, yet her lifted chin and her quiet poise gave the illusion of tallness. Her dress was taffeta, black with a heavy skirt that flared wide from a slender waist. Her glossy hair was braided into a tall tortoise-shell comb from which hung a mantilla. It was triangular and woven of black silk net so fine that the flowers embroidered on it seemed suspended invisibly in mid-air. Her Spanish shawl was the color of cream, a fringed crepe de chine that would rustle with her slightest movement.

Once he would have been ashamed that a woman should leave him at a loss for words.

"I would like to pay you a compliment," he said. "I would like to pay you a very flowery compliment."

She smiled. "You were good at that, Don Luis."

She wore none of the cascara or *albayalde de Mexico* that calcimined the faces of so many women with a weird lavender cast. Her cheeks had the faint olive color that was so Spanish, and her black eyes held such a bright luster that they seemed touched with tears.

"It is so strange," he said. "I thought we would never meet again."

"Yes . . . I thought we would never meet again also."

"Well, you have a fine house here."

Unexpectedly she laughed. "We are being so stuffy. But I feel . . . after so long, it should be something special . . . but whatever one says seems so awkward. I thought you were dead, you know. We all did. When I first heard . . . you cannot imagine . . . but you know that, and we have stood here long enough. Perhaps food will help. I thought you would be hungry."

"Before that . . . I want to make it clear. If there is any danger, I mean the Holy Office . . . I would not want to cause you——"

"Would I have arranged it? I was quite willing to take the risk with the Condesa—keep her here——" She broke off, the clasping of her pale hands expressing concern. "How is she, Don Luis? When Chintule came . . . the first I had heard in years since the Condesa left. I tried to find her so often——"

"She did not want you to . . . for your own sake," he said. "She is as safe and well as can be expected."

Josefina had brought in an immense silver tray burdened with napkin-covered dishes. She set it on a table, and Luis took a chair across from Barbara. Josefina retired. For a moment Barbara was occupied with serving. Luis saw that her only jewelry was a big gautchupourri brooch that must have been her mother's, dark and glittering against the swell of her breasts.

She would never be as full as the Condesa. But there was a sense of rich, yielding womanliness to the body beneath that dress.

She looked up. She saw how intently he was looking at her, and a hint of color touched her cheeks. She had uncovered a pair of partridges.

"Stuffed and pickled, from Chalco," she said. "This *clarea* is from my own estate. I think it is as good as Malaga."

He tasted the white wine, sweetened with sugar and cinnamon. When he glanced up he surprised a strange, searching look in her eyes. She looked quickly down at her own food.

"Well," she said, "naturally I have a great curiosity . . . your story, all those years up there, those lost years. Chintule could not tell me much . . . something about living with the Indians."

Before he could respond there was a knock on the door. Barbara rose to answer it. He saw that she unlocked the door before opening it. Luis stood as the man stepped in.

"Don Diego," Barbara said. "Don Luis."

Don Diego de Vargas dipped his head in a grave bow. The man had a lean face, so sallow that it looked almost jaundiced through the narrow cheeks. The eyes were deep-set, vividly black, disturbing in their fixed and glittering attention. Luis read austerity into the hard jaws, worldliness in the ironic mouth, perhaps even cynicism.

The silence continued so long, with both men studying each other, assessing, appraising, that it was Barbara who finally grew uncomfortable.

"We have some food, Don Diego," she said. "The *clarea* you like."

The men accepted it as a signal. Luis seated himself and Vargas took a chair at the table. Barbara poured more wine.

"Now, if you will excuse me——"

Vargas held up a hand, sinewy and corded from the sword and the rein. "Do not leave. We prefer your presence."

She smiled, showing her pleasure frankly, and took a chair. Vargas tasted the wine. He looked at Luis. He made no random movements. He was perfectly still. Only his eyes seemed alive, like vivid black jewels.

"For favor, Don Luis, I have been told your situation by Señorita Cárdenas. Were it a matter of true heresy I should have refused to consider it."

"There are a dozen royal decrees against the Holy Office employing *repartimiento*," Luis said. "How can it be heresy to uphold them?"

"Just so. And you think I can help."

"I do not ask something for nothing. I have heard that you offered your services for the reconquest of New Mexico."

"Of truth."

"Why?"

The bluntness of it made a little muscle flicker in Vargas's lean cheek. Then he smiled gravely.

"At least no one could accuse you of sycophancy, Don Luis. Why should any loyal Spaniard wish a reconquest? Why did Queen Isabella fight the Moors? What Spaniard can bear to let this humiliation remain?"

"And you would avenge the Mother Church?"

"How could I, Don Luis, when she would not seek vengeance herself? Does she not forgive repentant sinners?"

"And those who did not repent?"

"If they had crimes on their heads, such as the murder of our colonists, they should be executed."

"To the Pueblos it was a war. Since when do Spaniards execute enemy soldiers?" Luis asked.

"They must see that we look upon it as murder, that in our eyes they were not enemy soldiers but our own people, vassals to the king, children of the Church. If a Spaniard turned apostate and committed the atrocities that they did he would surely be executed."

Luis could not help being impressed. The man did not evidence the rabid need of revenge Luis had seen in Otermin and Gallegos and Cruzate, yet he did not try to cloak his real intentions in ambiguities.

"You are highly placed," Luis said. "The ear of the viceroy, the king, even the *Suprema*. If they are so interested in the reconquest and can be convinced that what I know might swing the balance from failure to success, a pardon might be obtained for me."

Vargas put the glass down and rose, holding his baldric so the rapier would not catch in the chair. He moved to the brazier. His walk was deliberate and measured, a military stride. He held his hands over the coals. Tendons made a ripple of light and shadow across their sallow backs. He said:

"You put great value on yourself. How can I assess it?"

Luis began by telling Vargas about Tyame, the old *cacique* at Acoma. He told how many of the Indians at the Sky City had been against the revolt. How all the Pueblos were being decimated by Apache raids.

"The Indians are suffering now more than they ever did under our rule. They are beginning to realize how much our protection meant.

They see that famine and flood come with their gods as well as ours. I am convinced that if Po-pe could be deposed half the Pueblos would join us immediately."

"Who are the men we can trust?"

"Tyame at Acoma. Luis Tupatu at Pecuris. He is probably the strongest. And Juan Ye of Pecos——"

"Otermin said he was the worst rebel of all."

"But an honest man in his way. And the leader of one of the biggest Tano towns. If we could win him over——"

"Aside from that, what do théy want? Is there something . . . a key . . . ?"

"Three things, I think. First, there must be no more *encomienda*. The *encomenderos* would start abusing their privileges again and the whole cycle would repeat itself."

Vargas had dropped his hands to his sides and stood with his narrow Spanish back turned to Luis, listening.

"Secondly, the Church must be more lenient. There were plenty of priests who knew that."

"Otermin favored this Father Francisco de la Cadena——"

"A bad choice. He was stationed mostly at Santa Fe and dealt more with Spaniards than Indians. There is another man—Fray Salvador de San Antonio."

"Just so. That is two things. You said three."

"You must keep faith. It is the most important thing of all. If you ever break a promise, if you are ever caught in a lie, if you ever start betraying them—it will be the end."

"This is of great interest," Vargas mused. "I have talked with a hundred men who had been there, who were supposed to be authorities on the subject—and not one mention of keeping faith."

"Why should they consider it now when they did not before?"

Vargas had his head bowed, as though deep in thought. It was remarkable to Luis how immobile the man could remain and still express so much vital force. At last Vargas said:

"This Tyame, at Acoma—why should he keep you alive?"

"Hé wanted a go-between. A spokesman. Someone to convince the Spaniards of how many at Acoma were against the revolt. He knew you would believe a Spaniard far quicker than an Indian. But he also wanted someone to speak for the Spaniards. He would not surrender his people to another Otermin. He knows peace can be kept only by a man of honor, strong enough to enforce his promises. I think Tyame trusted me. He knew that if I said the Spanish leader was such a man it would be true."

"Hm." Vargas touched his minute goatee. "And the other leaders—this Juan Ye of Pecos——"

"*Por favor*," Barbara said. It made them both look at her. "For favor, Don Diego, I was in the palace when Juan Ye came to talk with Otermin before the battle. He would not take the governor's word. He said there was only one Spaniard he would believe. He asked for Luis."

Vargas turned completely around. Glow from the coals cast a red haze over the shiny ridges of his hard cheeks. He studied Luis with black, unblinking eyes.

"Do you know the Moqui country?" he asked. When Luis nodded, Vargas said, "Did the Moquis talk of . . . did you ever find any evidence of this Sierra Azul?"

Luis sank heavily against the back of the chair. A silvery blankness came to the surface of his eyes.

"I have heard the fairy tales," Luis said.

"Not fairy tales. Facts. Over a hundred years ago Fray Augustin Rodriguez found eleven mines in New Mexico. Ore from one was found to be half silver. His report is still in the archives. So is the diary of Captain Farfan. Onate sent Farfan to the Moqui country in 1598, shortly after New Mexico was colonized. Thirty leagues west of Moqui the veins were found—brown, black, water-colored, blue, green. One assay showed eleven ounces of silver per quintal."

Vargas circled the brazier as he talked. Luis found it hard to reconcile the man's restlessness with the godlike composure of a moment before.

"And now this memorial that the Marqués de Gallegos has laid before the king," Vargas continued. "If his reports about the mercury in Sierra Azul are correct, there is enough for the whole New World. You know how vital quicksilver is in the process of extracting the silver from the ore. Up to now we've had to depend on Spain and Austria for the mercury. This war has virtually cut us off from our source of supply. Last year at Tlalpujagua we had to go back to smelting. One can only extract high-grade ores that way. Our production was cut in half. Another year like that and the managers will be bankrupt. Sierra Azul would save us——"

"I was on two campaigns into the Moqui country and never heard a word of Sierra Azul from the Indians," Luis said. "My grandfather knew the Moqui country better than any Spaniard, and he did not believe in the mines. To my certain knowledge the Marqués de Gallegos was never in the Moqui country."

Vargas gave no reaction. His eyes remained fixed on Luis, brooding, shadowed. The silence seemed to gain weight. Barbara stirred apprehensively. Luis heard the crepe de chine rustle against her shoulders. Vargas pulled his coat shut in a decisive gesture.

"An interesting talk, Don Luis. I will give it all my most careful thought."

He bowed to Luis, bowed lower to Barbara. She rose and accompanied him to the door, and Luis heard the man murmur a formal parting. As Barbara shut the door Luis rose and paced restlessly to the window. The heavy wine drapes were parted six inches and he stared through them at the dark night. Barbara walked back to her chair and sat down, watching him silently.

"What is it in us?" he said. "This Spanish addiction. Gold and salvation. And more gold, I think, than salvation."

"Is it only Spanish?"

"What kind of a reconquest would that be?" he said. "We might as well send Otermin back, Penalosa, worse."

She was angry now and she did not bother to hide it. "I have known this man for some time. You will find none better in New Spain. He is interested in the mines. Find me a man who is not."

"And who will work the mines? The Indians. It will be the same thing all over again, the same abuses, eighteen hours a day down in those holes, until they drop dead——"

"No, no. I know what he has done at Tlalpujagua. The Ordinances of San Lorenzo, the Recopilaciones, all the royal decrees protecting the Indians—they are followed to the last article. Did not the miners themselves choose him as *justicia mayor*? Perhaps he has the Spanish flaws, Don Luis. But there is more. Some greatness. Were you not touched by it? Are you so saintly? Why do you wish to go back?"

"Because it is where I belong. Because everything else has been burned out of me, and I know a man cannot move the world; he will be very lucky if he has the strength to achieve one little thing, just one thing, and I want to go back and make it so the Spaniards and the Indians can live together."

"And then you will be happy."

"Yes, I will be happy."

"So when you boil it down it is your own happiness you seek. Is that so unselfish? Are you so much better?"

She was breathing heavily, and it made her body seem riper, more womanly, within the dark dress. The gautchupourri brooch rose and fell with the movement of the swelling white flesh above the neck of her bodice. He did not want to be conscious of it. He did not want to look at the white flesh.

"*Señorita*, I am sorry. I did not think this would happen to me again. I thought I had met every possible disillusionment and nothing that happened would matter this much again. I am grateful for everything you have done."

"How can you tell at one meeting?" she said. "Give him a chance. See what he does. Talk with him again. I will try to arrange it." She hesitated. The anger was gone from her now. There was the strange dark look to her eyes. Confusion. A plea? It disturbed him. It disturbed him as much as the sight of her flesh. She said, "Now . . . you did not finish eating."

He sat down and picked at the partridges. But it was no good. The scene had created a tension between them, and they could not break it down. He did not want to leave. He was angry with himself and with Vargas, but he wanted to stay and look at her and smell her perfume and hear her voice. It was no good.

"Well," he said, "I had better go."

"You have not finished your food."

"It was delicious. *Toque de la queda* is at ten. I cannot risk being out after curfew."

She led him downstairs and through the silent house. They did not speak again till they were at the little door set in the big gate of the *zaguán*. It was so dark in the tunnel that he could not see her.

"You must give Vargas a chance," she said. "How will I keep in touch?"

"Through the Condesa. She will send Chintule to you."

"Luis——"

She stopped abruptly. After a moment he said, "Yes?"

She did not answer immediately. Finally, "Good night, Don Luis. God keep you."

He stepped through the door into the dark street. He started northward toward the Romita. He had gone many steps before he heard the gate shut behind him.

A strange thought was in his head. I did not tell her of Kashana, he thought. Why did it bother him so? Why should he feel guilty because he had not told her about Kashana?

CHAPTER THIRTY-SEVEN

THROUGH the spring Luis waited in the Romita. Despite his first disappointment with Vargas he knew that the man was his last chance to return to New Mexico. Chintule kept contact with Barbara and passed on what news she could. There was little to report. Barbara had met with Vargas several times. The man was doing what he could. But the Holy Office guarded its secrets jealously.

Toribio was making his regular visits to the Condesa, and both she and Luis knew it was too risky to see each other often. Luis kept up his contact through Chintule. Every night after compline he passed under the bridge that crossed the canal near the building in which the Condesa lived. If there was any news the little Zapotec maid would be there to tell him.

On June 9, 1690, she was there. The rains had been unusually heavy, with bad storms in the mountains, and the canal was so high that there was no space left under the bridge. He saw her shadowy figure standing near one end of the stone arch, and approached quickly.

"*Señorita* Barbara want to see you, Don Luis," the maid said. "Josefina, she wait inside the gate an hour after compline."

"Thanks, Chintule." He pressed her bony shoulder. "Is it good news?"

"I do not know. The Condesa . . . she say be careful. An informer of the Holy Office . . . she has recognize him in the Romita."

"After her?"

"She do not think so. They would have arrest her before this. She say . . . just be careful."

Barbara was waiting in the tower room. Her dress was black, and the long nun's sleeves of her bodice hid her arms. Her hair was loose and full, shimmering in the candlelight from a vigorous brushing with long-handled brushes that still lay on the table. She wore a pair of earrings with flat twisted gold dangles. In Santa Fe they had been called coquettes.

After his greeting he moved past her, and he heard the door close behind him and the key turned in the lock. Coals smoldered in the three-legged brazier and filled the room with incense. He saw that there was a tray on the table bearing a silver pitcher of frothy chocolate. She glanced at him curiously and crossed to pour a cup for him. He accepted it and stood waiting. She stirred uncomfortably under his gaze.

"Well, I suppose I had better tell you," she said. "The Crown honored the memorial of the Marqués de Gallegos—"

"He's going to lead the reconquest?" Luis could not keep the shock of disappointment from his voice.

"No," she said. "It's not exactly—what I mean is, the Marqués asked an *encomienda*, larger than any grant he ever held before, as a reward for his services. You know how the Church has been fighting *encomienda* since the revolt. Apparently the king succumbed to pressure at the last moment. The appointment for the governor of New Mexico has arrived from Spain. It is to be Don Diego de Vargas—" She broke off as she saw hope color his face. She touched her lips, went on almost too swiftly. "The viceroy will make the appointment official soon. Vargas will be leaving for El Paso. Luis—"

She stopped again, and he asked, "What?"

She touched her mouth once more, and this time the gesture had meaning. He saw the helpless confusion in her face, and it told him everything he needed to know. He looked at the chocolate. He put it down and crossed to a chair and sat down. He leaned back and closed his eyes. Exhaustion was like a drug in his mind. His knees and elbows ached, and he knew he had been sleeping in the open too long. It would be nice to find a room somewhere, a warm room where he could relax, where he would be safe, where he could sleep for a year. He felt indescribably old.

He heard the whisper of her gown and realized she was moving to his side. The scent of her mingled with incense. It was disturbing, perfume, powdered flesh, woman. He opened his eyes and saw her standing above him. Her lips were full and red and heavy.

"Luis—" She put a hand on his shoulder. "Try to understand. Vargas went as far as he could without actually revealing that you were alive. It became obvious that no pardon would be issued in absentia."

"I thought so. I thought it would come to that."

"Please . . . this new inquisitor, Father Zarate. He has been appointed on the wave of Church feeling against our systems of Indian labor. Vargas sounded him out. In Zarate's opinion a man defending the Indians of his *encomienda* against illegal impressment by the Holy Office is not committing any act of heresy."

"And what will that opinion be worth when the board of qualifiers gets through with it?"

"He is the senior inquisitor——"

"Do you think that is the only article? Do you know what I said at Nazario's that night?"

"You were drunk."

"And denounced everybody from the Pope on down. Do you think Toribio will not use it? Anything to protect himself——"

"Very well. Blasphemy. Others have repented. You are no heretic. There are a hundred people from Santa Fe still alive who would testify to that. They can be brought from El Paso. There is a vast difference between a heretic and a blasphemer. Zarate is a moderate. I know him. A fine, just man——"

"In the Holy Office?"

"The Tribunal has been cited by the Pope for its justice and mercy. In Vargas you have one of the most powerful men in the New World to appeal for you. It has been years since anyone was burned."

"Or garroted on the scaffold, or driven insane with the *trampazo*."

"A man suffers such things only if he will not repent. Do you believe your denunciations?"

"Against the Holy Office? Every word."

"Then it is more pride than fear."

He stood up, his face growing hot. "What?"

"The Inquisition—you hate it so. But what can you do about it? In our time what can you do? Nothing. You know it. For all your denunciations, you know it. It is too big for you, just like the problem of a hundred thousand beggars in Mexico City is too big, or the Spanish love of gold."

"Barbara, I——"

"All that fine talk . . . a man cannot move the world, realizing it now, everything burned out, everything but wanting to go back to Santa Fe . . . just that one thing, wanting to achieve something between the Spaniards and the Indians. What was burned out? Anything? You will still not face reality. You will never do it, Luis. You will never go back. Because you will never make the compromise. It would mean going to the Holy Office, humbling yourself before them. That is what you fear. Not the *trampazo* or the torture. Maybe you could do this one thing. Maybe if each man did that, maybe if he did the one little thing he was capable of the world would get better. Maybe that is the way it has to be. But you will not do it. You do not want to go back to Santa Fe as bad as you think."

"What do you know about wanting to go back."

"Maybe more than you think. Can you guess how often I remember the Jornada? Beauty in cruelty—you said that once. I found something there, Luis. I have never felt it since. Not here . . . I have waited, hunted, even prayed. But not here. I do not even know what it is I am hunting. I would have to return to understand. I would have to feel pain and see death and know fear. I smell the *enebro*, Luis. At night, do you know, I wake up and smell the *enebro*—"

She put both hands up and pressed them to her cheeks. She stared at him, wide-eyed, as though surprised at the passion of her whole outburst. He took her wrists and pulled her hands away from her cheeks.

"Do you?" he said. "Do you really smell the *enebro?*"

She did not answer. Her lips were parted and there was a shining look in her eyes, like tears, or fear. She was still breathing heavily with emotion and he could see the shape her breasts made as they lifted against the black bodice. He could see the shape her whole body made beneath the dress, with the bodice pointed in front and shaped over the hips. The gold dangles on her earrings tinkled softly as he pulled her to him.

She came against his body in heavy, silken acquiescence. Her lips were stiff and unyielding, like a woman who had never been kissed before. Then a shudder ran through her body, and her lips parted and the feel of their hot moist shape sent a shock of passion through him. Her hands were against his neck, his face, clinging, digging in, and she was pleading incoherently with him.

"Luis, I was wrong, I was wrong. I had no right . . . we cannot ask that of you. Do not surrender yourself—promise—if there is the slightest chance. . . . Torture, punishment . . . I could never forgive myself—"

She stopped as he kissed her again. Through the rustle of her body moving spasmodically against him, through the little crying sounds she made, the knock on the door sounded very far away. It came again, louder.

She pulled away. Her eyes had a blind look. She pressed her hands to her flushed cheeks so hard that the fingers made white imprints in the flesh. She said something that he could not understand and turned and went to the door. There was a pounding throughout his body, like a single great pulse. There was a sickness in his stomach. It had not been that strong since Kashana.

Barbara's hands were shaking, and the key rattled in the lock as she sought to turn it. She opened the door and Luis saw Josefina beyond. The maid's voice was shrill with fright.

"At the door, *señorita*—the constable, Bartolome Ordonoz. The Holy Office, *señorita*, the Holy Office——"

CHAPTER THIRTY-EIGHT

THE cathedral dominated the Zocalo, Its immense pile of stone and marble rose like an overwhelming shadow into the night sky at the north edge of the plaza. The edifice had been almost a hundred years in the building. Begun in the classic period its walls were as austere as the barefoot Franciscans who had watched them rise. But the baroque had overtaken the church before it was finished. The twin towers—corniced and columned and carved and topped with bald round domes —blossomed like strange flowers from the massive severity of lower walls.

They had named its great bell Doña Ana. It was ringing as Luis emerged from the Street of the Silversmiths and lost himself in the crowd of beggars packed against the cathedral. The whole square seemed to shudder with each brazen clang. The miniature yellow moons of Chinese lanterns bobbed and swayed on the ropes strung between the stalls that lined the Zocalo. The church wall shivered against Luis as he stood with his back to it, looking out into the sea of faces.

There were processions everywhere. Men belonging to the silversmith's guild marched in a solemn line from the cathedral, carrying an embroidered banner of silk and satin on a long pole. Beyond the fountain men from the brotherhoods of Rosario de Animas forced their way through the crowds, their tinkling bells entreating a Pater Noster for some deceased soul. A roar of laughter rose from the square as another procession appeared in the Third Street of the Clock. It was made up of students from the College of San Pedro and San Pablo, dressed in ridiculous disguises. Four of them were harnessed to a coach that bore on its roof a pyramid with lions and castles at its corners and on its apex a throne. Crimson velvet cushions rested on the throne, supporting a crown and a scepter. At the foot of the pyramid were figures representing Carlos II and his new queen.

It made Luis realize that it was the celebration announced for June 9 to honor the marriage of Carlos and his second wife, the Austrian princess, Mariana of Neuberg.

Luis looked over his shoulder toward the Street of the Silversmiths. He still did not know if he had been followed. While Barbara had met the agents of the Holy Office at the front door, Josefina had let Luis onto an alley that ran behind the stables. If they had known he was in the house surely they would have all the routes of escape watched. Yet he had reached the plaza without seeing anybody wearing a green hat of the Inquisitional police. It gave him the hope that they had simply been making a routine investigation. His relationship to Barbara in Santa Fe was known. If they were looking for him it was inevitable that they should get around to her sooner or later.

Luis left the wall of the church and started through the mob.

The palm-thatched stalls edging the plaza were filled with exotic banks of color. The cult of flowers flourished as vividly now as it had when the Aztecs ruled Tenochtitlan. Magnolias made pale splashes against purple masses of bougainvillea. Ravenflowers and orchids and roses of Castile filled the air with a scent that swept overpoweringly against Luis. He felt drowned in perfume.

And ulcered beggars crouched among the flowers, maimed and crippled, clutching at his clothes with leprous hands.

"Pordiosero, señor, for God's sake, pordiosero, kind sir . . ."

It brought back Barbara's words with new impact. *It is too big for you . . . just like the problem of a hundred thousand beggars is too big.*

Was she right? How much of it was pride, and how much fear? The thought of surrendering to the Holy Office, of humbling himself before a system he loathed so much filled him with a seething humiliation. He had to admit it.

In her way she was telling him the same thing Tyame had. The parable of the coyote and the bear. Not all black and white. As many wolves in the sunlight as in the shadows. Too many to kill them all. But he could tell them apart from the rocks. He would live a long time.

Well, Barbara had named his wolves. The Holy Office, the beggars, the Spanish flaws. They were the things he could not change. What good were all those years if he could not accept it? What good were the fires of the rebellion, his new understanding of the Indians, the humility learned through the degradation of the gutters?

Luis saw the green hat.

The man stood near the gibbet. He wore boots wrinkled up about his thighs and a cup-hilted rapier studded with rubies and a scarlet-lined cloak of black velvet. It could be no simple informer. Only the official police would dress so richly. Luis knew it must be the constable. Josefina had called him Bartolome Ordonoz. The feather plume in his green hat bobbed and swayed as he turned his dark face from side to side, looking through the crowd.

Ordonoz had not yet seen Luis. But he blocked off the route Luis had meant to take toward the palace. Luis wheeled and plunged into the crowd, crossing toward the Streets of the Clock. A new procession was coming from the church. Ecclesiastics were everywhere. A Benedictine passed in his black habit, absently blessing the beggars that held their contorted hands out to him. There were Jesuits in black with their horned and fluted caps, Fernandines in coffee-colored cassocks and tonsures, a Franciscan legate in his blue robes. Luis let their procession carry him along till he had almost reached the First Street of the Clock.

He saw Matarife.

The hunchback stood in the mouth of the street, his cloak open to expose the quilted leather *esquipile*. The nearby Chinese lanterns cast a weird saffron light across his simian face. Fingering the misericord at his belt, mouth lifted in a dreamy smile, eyes half closed, he was looking idly around the square. When he saw Luis his expression did not change. He began to walk forward.

Luis quickly backed toward the center of the plaza till the crowd once more hid him. He was cut off from the north and west now. He began to elbow his way through the mass of people toward the south. Most of the Indians were drunk and the smell of raw *pulque* was so strong that it made his eyes water.

The viceroy and his family had appeared on the balcony of the palace and a student stood in the plaza below, shouting to be heard as he tipsily read a poem dedicated to the Count of Galve. Other students were cavorting through the crowd in their striped capes, drinking and pinching womens' rumps and stealing fruit from the stalls.

Luis saw Toribio.

The half-breed stood in the Portal of Flowers at the head of the steps leading down to the canal. Toribio had on black boots pulled to the hips and a deerskin doublet with the green cross on its breast. A torch was socketed on the wall above his head. Its flickering light made a black stippling of the pockmarks on his gaunt face. He stood aloof from the crowd, never seeming to become a part of it no matter how close they surged.

Touched with a sense of panic, Luis backed once more toward the center of the square. They had him bottled up. There must be a dozen more he could not recognize, stationed around the square, covering all the exits.

Once more Doña Ana began to ring. At first Luis thought it was another part of the celebration. But there was something insistent about the shivering sound that brought a change in the crowd. He saw many of them stop their drinking and merrymaking, to look up at the tower. Then he recognized the pattern of the ringing.

"*De rogatives*," somebody said. "*De rogatives*."

There was fear in the voice. *De rogatives* were rung only in some extreme emergency. The crowd began to surge back and forth. The shouting roared up about Luis and he could hardly hear the bell. He saw a stall topple. A mounted soldier loomed above the crowd, coming from the cathedral and shouting to be heard above the tumult.

"Calm down, you *rumberos*, calm down. There is no immediate danger. The storm in the mountains has flooded a section of the city, but there is no danger——"

All the crowd heard was the part about the flood. They took up the cry and it spread panic swiftly. There was a rush to leave the square. Beggars were trampled and more stalls went down and one of them caught fire from a broken lantern. Men scrambled away from the blaze and a fight broke out along the Puente del Palacio.

Seeing how he could turn the panic to his advantage, realizing it was his last chance of escape, Luis ran directly toward Toribio. The man saw him. Luis pretended not to see Toribio till he was but a few feet away, then veered aside and ran down the Puente del Palacio, the sidewalk adjacent to the Portal de las Flores.

It drew Toribio after him, following at a run. When the fight was between them Luis cut back toward the Portal.

Toribio tried to follow, but a dozen fighting men were between him and Luis. The half-breed was caught up in the struggle, his hat knocked off, his doublet ripped. He could not get free before Luis reached the head of the stone steps and ran down them to the canal. At the bottom a dozen canoes were moored. They were made from the hollowed trunks of giant *ahuehuetes* and some of them were still buried beneath their loads of exotic flowers.

Luis jumped aboard one, shoving off with a foot. The Indian in the stern ran toward him, shouting and waving his arms. He almost tipped over the canoe. Luis pulled his knife and stepped toward the man. "Paddle," he said sharply. "Just paddle as hard as you can."

The Indian's mouth gaped. He dropped to his knees and scooped up a paddle. The canoe whispered through the garbage and refuse that littered the water. Luis saw Toribio's black figure run down the steps, pause a moment, then jump into another canoe. More men followed him, calling to one another, some commandeering canoes, others running along the sides of the canal.

The tumult of the crowd and the ringing of Doña Ana faded behind. There were no lights now except for the occasional yellow rectangle of a window or opened door in the buildings flanking the canal. Luis stood over the Indian, keeping his knife against his back. The man paddled till he was sobbing for air. Luis could hear the men in the canoes behind shouting to each other, the clatter of running feet on his left. He knew he could not outdistance them. And if he stopped the canoe they would know where to take up the chase.

They passed beneath a bridge. The flood had raised the canal so high that he had to duck his head. The next bridge he knew would be that of Espiritu Santo. He saw its shadowy stone arch ahead.

He put his knife in his teeth, waited till the last moment, jumped. His hands caught on the coping of the wall and he hung, legs kicking, while the canoe glided beneath the bridge. He was in darkness and the runners did not see him hanging there. But at the end of the bridge of Espiritu Santo was a lamp set in a niche beside a saint's statue. Its beam flickered across the water on the other side of the bridge and illuminated the canoe as it glided from beneath the arch. The runners saw it and kept on going, shouting to those in the canoe behind.

With the running men past, Luis swung himself up onto the wall of the bridge. He was lying there on his belly when the first following canoe glided beneath him. It was so close he could have reached down to touch Toribio on the head.

He waited till two more canoes whispered by and then could hear no more. He dropped off the low wall and ran down the bridge toward the street. He was almost to the niche with the light when he heard more running feet. A pair of laggards coming down the side of the canal. He tried to turn back but he was too late. The light revealed him.

"It is the one," a man shouted. "Pronto."

The first one rushed up the bridge. He saw that Luis had only his knife and it made him overconfident. Luis feinted him into a lunge.

At the last moment Luis dodged aside. The man's sword made a silver flash going past him and the man stumbled heavily into the wall beside Luis.

Luis caught him by one leg and flipped him over the wall.

The man struck the canal with a heavy splash. Luis wheeled to see the second one running at him. It was Matarife, sword out, and he would be tricked by no feint.

Luis rushed him. Matarife stopped, both surprised and wary. His blade was on guard. A foot from it Luis tore off his serape and whipped it across the man's face. The long folded blanket wound itself about Matarife's head, blinding him, and its weight made him take a staggering step backward.

Matarife whipped blindly with his sword, tearing at the serape. When the blade reached the end of its wild arc Luis went for the man's legs. Matarife could not see to thrust, and Luis tackled him.

Matarife went down with Luis sprawled across him. The man awkwardly tried to bring his sword into play. It lifted his arm, exposing one of the vulnerable spots in the quilted *esquipile*.

Luis plunged his knife into the armhole.

Matarife screamed and doubled over. Helplessly he hugged the stiletto buried to its hilt in his armpit. Luis got to his feet. He was shaking and gasping. He could hear the shouting men running back toward the bridge along the canal. He left his knife, scooping up Matarife's sword, and ran down off the other side of the narrow bridge. He ran into the night.

CHAPTER THIRTY-NINE

HE knew what he had to do now. Moving back through the dark streets, stumbling over the beggars that sprawled in drunken stupor in the gutters, heading northward toward the Romita, Luis came to his decision.

Toque de la queda was ringing from the cathedral. He knew how dangerous it was to be found out after curfew. All suspicious persons were arrested and disarmed and taken to jail. He followed back alleys and the edges of stinking canals and finally reached the Romita. He crossed the bridge and walked the block to the long building and knocked softly at the third door.

Luis heard a muffled stirring inside, and finally the door was opened a crack. He knew it would be Chintule, and he whispered his name. He heard the Zapotec gasp, and then the door was pulled wider and he saw the shadowy shape of the Condesa behind the maid.

"I must see you," Luis said. "The Holy Office——"

"They are after you?"

"They tried. I do not think they followed me. We will be safe for a short time."

"Chintule," the Condesa said. "Go to the other side of the bridge. If you see them coming warn us."

The maid passed Luis in a scurrying run. The Condesa pulled Luis aside and shut and bolted the door. Then she lit the stub of a candle on the table. The flame spread the rancid smell of tallow and bayberry through the room and showed him that the woman wore only her chemise. The mattress was unrolled from the edge of the floor, and a single ragged blanket lay crumpled upon it. She saw the cut on his face, the torn shirt, and made a smothered sound.

"Toribio," he said.

She pressed her hand to her lips. "I should have known. He has been acting so strange. That informer I saw in the Romita. Chintule told you? I am sorry, Luis. We both should have known. It was too dangerous. You should have left the capital. Where did they try to arrest you?"

"It was not arrest. They were trying to kill me."

Her eyes widened, puzzled at first, then knowing. Knowing what he knew. The Inquisition was not above killing in secret. But, if only from the standpoint of policy, such a murder in Luis's case made no sense. He had defied the Holy Office. If he was to die for it the Inquisition had every reason to want such punishment public, an official Act of Faith, an example of what happened to a man arrogant enough to challenge the Inquisition, another awesome warning to those children of the Church who might be wavering in their devotion.

Luis said, "Matarife, this constable named Ordonoz, the other vermin—all Toribio's men. The Tribunal was never meant to hear about it. Toribio probably did not even have a warrant for my arrest."

"Luis . . . why?"

"What would happen if the Holy Office found this out?" Luis asked. "One of their own officers, taking it into his own hands, killing a fugitive, depriving the Tribunal of its ordained function."

"It would be serious—a defiance——"

"Then Toribio would be no different from me, truth? What would they do to him? Punishment? Prison?"

"Undoubtedly," the Condesa said.

"And questions. They would want to know. Why should an officer of the Inquisition try to do away with a fugitive in such a manner? What was Toribio hiding? Why was he afraid to have the fugitive fall into the hands of the Tribunal? And if Toribio would not tell—would he be treated any differently from another who defied them? The trestle, the thumbscrew, the boot——"

"The truth, Luis. But I do not see——"

"That is what he risked, Condesa, trying to kill me."

"But you know why. If the Holy Office got you—if you told about Toribio and me——"

"Would I betray you?"

"How can you know? When they get you on that rack—when they do those things——"

He nodded. "That is why you must get away before I give myself up."

"Luis—no!"

"It is all I have left. Vargas could not help me. I cannot go on living like a jackal. This is the only way I will ever get back to Santa Fe. Barbara de Cárdenas made me realize it. I must throw myself on the mercy of the Holy Office."

"Mercy? You saw their mercy tonight," she said.

"That was not the Holy Office acting officially. It was what decided me. It was what gave me a little hope. If Toribio is this desperate to keep me out of their hands, perhaps I would have more chance with the Tribunal than I think."

She clutched his arms. There was no illusion left to her face this close. He could see how papery and brittle the flesh was from a lifetime of cosmetics. He could see the traitorous wrinkles netting her eyes and the lines like tiny claw marks about her mouth.

"If I thought there was any other way out, I would not ask this of you," he said. "But we both face it now. They know I am alive now, and sooner or later, one way or another, they will get their hands on me, and then you would face the same thing that you do now. How much torture can a man stand? I think I would not betray you. But I am only human. And you would not know until too late. Now at least you know. You have time to escape."

"Luis, I beg you—loving Jesus—do not do it——"

She was clinging to him with her whole body. She was working against him with a frantic insistence. He saw that there was more than a plea in her face. Her head was tilted back and there was a drooping shape to her mouth and a blind look to her eyes. It was a familiar expression, a look he had seen in Kashana's face so often. How could emotion do that? How could anger or fear or hysteria change into this one thing?

He had been away too long. There had been too many desolate days in the desert, too many starving nights in the Romita, in the gutters, alone, lost, womanless. The moment with Barbara had started it. Now he could not stop it. He did not want to stop it. The look in the Condesa's face and the fervid movement of her body against his had achieved something that a million words between them had failed to achieve.

It was not like kissing Barbara. The Condesa knew how to use her lips and they took instinctive shape from a thousand former kisses, and what she did with them was the end of his thinking.

The candle had almost burned down. It was a pool of greasy yellow wax in the tin sconce on the table. Its fading yellow perimeter of light washed against scrofulous mud walls. Luis looked at his clothing strewn across the floor. He looked at the Condesa.

She had rolled over and was lying on her stomach with her face hidden. He looked at the hips. They were magnificent hips. If he looked only at the hips he could still believe in the old illusion.

"You told me once that the ancient Greeks worshiped the buttocks," he said.

"They worshiped many parts of the body."

"In a religious way?"

"Yes. In a religious way."

She sighed heavily. At last she turned on her side to look at him. Her hair had come unpinned and made a tumbled black mass beneath her head. He could see the streaks of gray in it that had always been hidden by her careful coiffure. Her cheeks were flushed and strangely puffy and it made her look sullen. But he knew she was not sullen. He had a guilty feeling and he looked away from her.

She said, "I always wondered . . . before, why you did not do it."

"So did I," he said. "Maybe this is why?"

"What?"

"Must you be hurt?"

"Luis, you did not hurt me."

"And you did not feel pleasure."

"No woman could ask for more."

"We never lied to each other before."

"I say the truth, Luis."

"No. I gave you no pleasure. Admit it. I gave you nothing."

He got up, depressed with his sense of failure, still curiously guilty. He walked over to his clothes and stood staring emptily at them.

"We could try again," she said.

"I could not hurt you. I could not hit you or crush your breast with my hand."

"Luis—stop—I hate it when he does that—I hate him."

"But you always go back."

She made a muffled sound. She turned her face toward the wall.

He remembered the shadowy barrier that had always stood between them in Santa Fe, that had always held him back. Could this be the failure he had sensed? Could a man feel such a thing without really knowing what it was?

He began to dress. He felt embarrassed now. He heard her stirring but he kept his back toward her. When he had everything on but his sandals he sat down on the chair and slipped his feet into them. He saw that she was sitting up on the mattress and had slipped on her chemise.

"Well," she said. "Are we not burros—with them out there—as though we had all the time in the world."

"Of course. I was not thinking. Thousand pardons."

"Do not apologize. It was my fault too." She pushed at her hair. The puffy look was gone from her face now, and the forced smile. "You are still going to do it?"

They sounded like strangers talking to each other. He said, "I have met some people while I was in the Romita. There is a man at the Plaza de Santiago who has a brother in Vera Cruz. This brother makes false passports. If you could get to Europe——"

She waved it away. "Do you think I have not looked forward? Escandon will help me."

"The *zambo* who owns the tavern?"

"Yes—that one. He comes from a place in the mountains, up beyond Amecameca. I wanted to keep it as a last resort."

"Condesa——"

"No. You were right. The thing is closing in on us. I would have to do it sooner or later. It is better that I act now, while I still have control of it."

She locked her hands in her lap, staring at him intensely. "The Holy Office—when you go there—you have one thing in your favor, Luis. This new inquisitor, this Father Zarate—he has been appointed on the new surge of Church feeling against the abuse of the Indians. Gain Zarate's favor and he might give leniency on other charges. But you cannot do it by defending your action at Tesuque. It does not matter that you were protecting your Indians against Toribio. There are too many others in the Holy Office who do not share Zarate's philosophy. They will protect Toribio. Try to defend yourself and you will be trapped. Admit your crime. Confess. Repent. Wait for Zarate to question you about New Mexico. He is bound to do it. Answer all his questions. You know more about what went on up there than anybody in the capital. Your information may be the weapon Zarate needs against *repartimiento, encomienda*. As for the rest, no matter how absurd the charges, confess. If they accuse you of spitting on the Cross, Lutheranism——"

"I am no heretic!"

"Luis, Luis, can you not understand what I am saying? It will do no good to defend or deny or fight. They will twist you, confuse you, trap you. It is when you fight that the torture comes. All they want is confession. You must give it to them—beat them at their own game. The first thing to do is request writing materials. Write your confession. Every time you did not attend Mass, every confession you missed, every blasphemy you made. And if you read any books on the Index. God knows I showed you enough prohibited books. Bruno, Descartes, Galileo. Confess and repent. And they will ask you to denounce all the people you know to be heretics. This is the most important thing. It is one of their main sources of information. You must have someone to throw to the dogs. If not it will mean the trestle. Start with me—"

"Condesa—how can I?"

"You must, Luis. This is meat and drink to them. How can you do me any harm? You can tell them nothing they do not already have on file. One more testimony against me will not matter. And I will be gone by the time they question you. But you must make it convincing. Do you understand? Speak of throwing yourself on their mercy—this is what it means. Do you want to go back to Santa Fe that bad? Grovel before them. On your knees. Your belly. Like a dog. Like Andres Rodrigo. Like something you have never been and could never dream of being. Do you understand what I am saying, Luis?"

"I understand," he said. He stood up. She stood up. They faced each other awkwardly, still conscious of what had happened. He pulled at his serape. He ran a hand through his matted beard. He said, "Well . . . companion."

The word sounded strange now. Companion. It had no meaning. He felt the same way he had when he and Bigotes met at Acoma for the last time. Something changed between them, something that no amount of words could bring back. Something broken that could not be mended.

She made a muffled sound and came to him, reaching out to him, taking his hands. She was crying unashamedly, and her lined face was wet with tears.

"God help you, Luis," she said. "God help you."

CHAPTER FORTY

Toribio had extinguished the candle in the saint's niche at one end of the bridge of Espiritu Santo. It left him in darkness as he crouched beside the canal called the Street of the Canoes. The constable named Bartolome Ordonoz knelt beside him. They were both looking at Matarife who lay sprawled on the stone coping beside the canal.

Toribio had pulled the knife from Matarife's armpit and had taken his own shirt off to wad it into the wound. The shirt was soaked with blood. Curfew had long since stopped ringing. The only sound was the soft lapping of the flood-swollen canal and the strained breathing of the wounded man.

"Listen," Bartolome said. "We cannot stay here any longer. Somebody will come or something. Why can we not take him to the palace? Or at least let the others go."

Toribio glanced at the other men, standing in a group against the wall of a building. The one Luis had thrown in the water was still wringing out his clothes and cursing softly.

Toribio looked bitterly at the black chasm of the street across the canal into which Luis had disappeared. It had been half an hour since the fight. Toribio had dragged Matarife off the bridge and had waited with him while the constable and his men searched the adjacent neighborhood.

"Very well," Toribio said. "Tell them to go."

"Shall I get the priest?" Bartolome asked.

It was curious, Toribio thought, how these scum of the earth who had violated every sacrament still could not think of dying with‹ out their priests. "No," he said. "I will get the priest. Return to the palace. I will see you there."

Bartolome joined the others, and they disappeared down the canal. Toribio looked at Matarife. It was a fatal wound. Toribio was certain of it. How long did it take a man to die?

A man he had known all his life.

The memories moved like fitful shadows through his mind. Tlascala. The bitter years of his boyhood. The escape to the mountains after confronting his true mother. Mexico City. The degradation they had known during those first years in the capital.

They had lived in the Zocalo with the other beggars, eating the garbage the fine people threw from their second-story windows, sleeping in the gutters and beneath the bridges, pandering, scavenging, doing things to stay alive that would shame an animal. Such a depraved existence only deepened Toribio's bitter hatred of his origins, of the quirk of fate that had made him beggar instead of king. It only intensified his obsession to assert his Spanish blood and rise above the cesspool.

Mexico City was haunted by the unpaid spies and informers of the Holy Office. Toribio soon saw the fear they instilled in the people, the power they held. He started gathering what scraps of information he could pick up in the Zocalo, ferreting out the heretics and Judaizers and schismatic philosophers in the back alleys of the city. Soon he had made enough denunciations to gain .official appointment as informer for the Inquisition. Finally came the day when he had enough documentation to denounce a judge of the audience. The man had long been an enemy of the Gallegos family, a bitter opponent of the crusade they had carried on against the Crown policies concerning Indian labor. It was a victory for them and put Toribio in the favor of Don Gómez . . .

Matarife groaned feebly. "Hermano . . . you said the priest."

"Soon, little brother, soon."

Mary, Joseph and Child, Toribio thought, how can you hang on so long? There could be no priest. Bartolome Ordonoz and the others had worked for Toribio a long time. They knew that what they had tried to do had no official sanction from the Holy Office. They would keep quiet. But a priest could not be silenced.

Toribio could not afford to have the Holy Office discover what had happened. The Tribunal jealously guarded its functions. Even a sheriff who usurped their authority by arresting a fugitive without a warrant would be subject to punishment, removal from office, perhaps even prison. What could happen to a mere informer who committed such a violation?

Once it was known, no explanation he could give would cover it completely. There would be too many questions . . . an investigation . . . sooner or later the Tribunal would find out why he had done it. A faint tremor passed through him at the thought.

Matarife sighed and said something in Tlascalan. The soft wheeze of his breathing stopped. Toribio put his hand on Matarife's heart. Then, slowly, he reached up and closed the eyes. He could not stand to have them open, even though it was so dark he could not see them.

Few save the constables of the night watch were abroad after curfew, and they seldom ventured this far from the Zocalo. Undisturbed, Toribio stripped the bloody clothes from the body. He found a pair of large stones that had broken loose from the side of the canal. He cut the clothing into strips and made a sling, tying the stones to Matarife. Then he rolled the corpse off into the water.

Toribio threw his bloody shirt into the canal. He washed his hands and rose, pulling his cloak around his naked torso, and started back toward the Zocalo. He felt strange. He felt emotionally spent. Dead inside. Was this grief? He could not identify it. He had never felt grief before.

And he had not gotten the priest.

Why should it haunt him so? Why did he see those eyes? He had closed them. They could not look at him now.

The palace of the Inquisition was a group of massive buildings near the Zocalo. A sinister guardian of the faith, its somber walls and narrow windows brooded over the plaza in a sleepless watch for the slightest deviation from orthodoxy among the cringing hordes of the city. Toribio was passed inside by a guard at one of the side entrances. He descended a stone staircase into a dank and dripping corridor that led to the guardroom. Here he found Bartolome Ordonoz and another of his men drinking at the table. No other guards were present.

Toribio looked directly at the fox-faced constable. "You understand the need for silence."

"Have I not attended to these private matters for you in the past?" Bartolome said. "It is not my silence you will have to worry about. I was just talking to the *alcaide* of secret prisons. He said Luis Ribera has surrendered himself."

Toribio felt a little twitch occur in his face, a little twitch, by his mouth or in his cheek, he did not know exactly where. The room was very small. The room was too small. He was suffocating. He had to get out. He could not let them see what this did to him. He said something. He did not know what he said, but his lips moved and some words came out and then he turned and went into the hall.

Toribio reached the stairs and began to climb. How could he have been such a fool? All these years. Like a drug . . . knowing all the time how dangerous it was, knowing this moment would come, inevitably. Going back to her . . . going back, like a drug.

He stopped in the upper hall and stood turned to a wall with his eyes shut. He had to break free now. He could not be dragged down with the Condesa. If Luis talked . . . It was time, and there was only one way to protect himself. But he could not do it. He struck his fist against the wall. He could not do it. . . .

He looked stupidly at his fist and saw that the knuckles were cut and bleeding. He turned and walked to another stairway that led to the top floor, where the inquisitor's chambers looked across the square toward the viceregal palace. In an anteroom he found an attendant and made his request. In a few moments the attendant returned and admitted him. The junior inquisitor was at his desk studying the book of Membretes in which was filed every scrap of information given the Tribunal by their informers and spies.

"I would like to report a fugitive in the city," Toribio said. "My informers have seen one Luis Ribera——"

"He has already surrendered himself," the inquisitor said.

"Ah?" Toribio said mildly.

He had only reported it to cover himself. Now there was the other. He would say that in Santa Fe there had been none who knew her, and he had been misled by false evidence that she produced. But in Mexico City there had been men to identify her. As soon as he discovered her presence he had contacted them. He would deny everything she said or Luis said. False accusation against the informer was a common thing. The Tribunal always discounted it. The Tribunal protected its own. And there would be no proof. She would have no witnesses. If she claimed Toribio visited her she would have to be specific. For every time and place she cited, Bartolome Ordonoz or any one of a dozen others would swear that Toribio had been with them in another part of the capital. He could refute any claim Luis Ribera made. After all, was he not the one who turned her in?

"I would like to report another fugitive," Toribio said. "I would like to report the presence in the capital of La Condesa de Zumurraga."

CHAPTER FORTY-ONE

LUIS had a cell on the bottom level of the palace of the Inquisition. It was a cramped, narrow chamber with a tiny barred hole near the twelve-foot ceiling.

The floor was already wet on the first night he entered the cell. Through the following days it continued to rise until he was wading over his ankles. He could hear the roar of steady rain outside and gusts of changing wind poured water through the barred hole.

Remembering the Condesa's advice, he requested writing materials and began to write his confession.

There was no escaping the water. Lying, sitting, standing, he was always in water. After a few days his joints began to ache intolerably. He soon had chills and fever. Before he had been in the cell a week he was in delirium.

When he became lucid again the water was gone. He was lying on his soggy pallet, so weak he could not rise. His body ached all over as though from a vicious beating, and it was a constant struggle to breathe. He wondered what miracle had kept him alive.

From snatches of conversation between the guards Luis found out what had happened. Two days after the first slight flood, which had come on the night he surrendered, the heavy rains had moved down out of the mountains. For eleven days almost without interruption it rained. The valley was inundated. The capital was so flooded that it was impossible to tell the canals from the streets. The beggars climbed the roof tops around the plaza and squatted there like hordes of strange vultures silhouetted against the dark sky. Communication with the surrounding country was cut off, and there was fear of starvation in the city.

When the rain finally stopped news reached the city that with the receding flood waters had come the dread *chiahuiztli*, an insect that attacked the roots of the wheat and destroyed it. To make matters more desperate the flood had washed away many of the maize fields in the valley. It was the staple of the natives, the very basis of their economy, and the viceroy took drastic measures to prevent famine and disaster.

All the maize that could be found was seized and deposited in the public granary for rationing. Deprived of their grain by the seizures the people descended upon the capital to beg for their food.

Luis finally managed to regain enough strength to crawl around the dank cell and to keep down the slops they threw him.

All he had now was the patience he had acquired at Acoma, sitting chained on the roof top for so many years. He marked off the days, waiting for the first interview with the Tribunal. It was on San Geronimo's day that he had his visitor.

He heard the footfalls echoing hollowly in the vaulted corridor outside. There was the husky murmur of voices and a key rattled in the lock of the heavy, iron-studded door. He was sitting on his pallet and he rose, standing against the wall because he was still weak. He had not bathed since he entered the prison, and his clothes hung in filthy rags from his emaciated body.

The door opened and one man entered. He was not as tall as Luis. He was slender without seeming fragile. He moved with a measured, self-conscious grace. The richness of his satin cloak and ermine-edged doublet were a mockery in the filthy dungeon. Luis saw his eyes squint as the stench struck him. He stopped just within the door, and it was closed and locked behind him. He looked at the single barred window, high above a man's reach. He looked at the dripping walls. He looked at Luis.

"Permit me." His Castilian was precise, lisping. "Don Gómez de Gallegos."

Luis was not surprised. "You look like your brother, *señor*."

Luis watched Don Gómez warily. His queued black hair was so thickly pomaded that it seemed wet. It was hard to judge the man's age. His face was unlined, unnaturally smooth, each expression carefully calculated as though he was afraid to disturb the waxen surface.

Don Gómez said, "We have another mutual friend. Toribio Quintano." Don Gómez paused, as though for some reaction. When Luis did not respond Don Gómez tilted his head and ran a finger across his glossy hair. "Toribio told me you were singularly uncompromising."

Don Gómez squinted faintly again and his patrician nostrils grew pinched. He pulled his cloak around him as if trying to shut out the smell. "Well, Don Luis, we get older. We get wiser. We learn that no man can get through life without compromising. Now you have surrendered voluntarily to the Holy Office. This indicates something to me . . . something a little different than Toribio's conception of you."

"Does it?"

Don Gómez seemed amused by Luis's wariness. "As you know, the inquisitor is empowered to call upon the judges of the royal audience to sit as consultors in the consultation of Faith. I have joined the board of qualifiers on your case." Don Gómez put his hands behind him, under his yellow satin cloak. "Now, on this charge of defying the Holy Office at Tesuque—how will you plead?"

"I will tell the truth."

"Well, now." With his hands still clasped behind him, Don Gómez transferred his gaze to the barred window high above. "The senior inquisitor, this Father Zarate—perhaps you thought that could save you. The problem of Indian labor—a fetish with Zarate. Once opened—he would pursue it relentlessly, in all its aspects. A man could curry favor. Gain clemency. Feed Zarate information he has been trying to get for years concerning the conditions of *repartimiento* and *encomienda* in New Mexico . . ."

Don Gómez looked at Luis. The impact of his eyes was bright and glittering. "Of course, Don Luis, the inquiry on the revolt in New Mexico was closed a long time ago. Governor Otermin took the declarations and depositions of countless witnesses and put them into his Acts and they comprised a report of many folios. The opinion among the ecclesiastics was that perhaps the governors had been a little harsh with the Pueblos, and the feeling among the secular authorities was that perhaps the Church had been a little too demanding . . ."

And none of it, Luis thought, really revealed the basic causes of the revolt. He began to understand. Don Gómez was afraid of what he knew. They had worked too hard to cover it up. They could not afford to have the abuses of the Marqués de Gallegos and the other *encomenderos* in New Mexico made public. They could not give Zarate a weapon that might reopen the whole case, might destroy their chances for a return to the old systems in the event of a reconquest.

"The trouble is, Don Luis, that acquittal on this one article would not mean freedom. There are eighty-eight other charges against you, Don Luis. You could be burned for any one of them, should the qualifiers decide against you. And there will inevitably come a turning point, Don Luis, a charge on which one man's vote can decide the issue."

"Your vote?" Luis asked.

Don Gómez pursed his lips. He seemed to look more like the Marqués every moment. It was coming to Luis now, something else, a worm crawling into his mind. In trying to kill Luis, had Toribio been acting in interests beside his own? It was known that the Gallegos' were Toribio's patrons. Obviously Don Gómez had as much reason to keep Luis from falling into the hands of the Tribunal as Toribio. There was no other answer. Luis was facing the man who had ordered his death.

"There is one way of avoiding all these complications," Don Gómez said.

Luis did not respond. He was thinking that what he had sensed before was now a certainty. He had been right about surrendering to the Holy Office. He had tied their hands. The very organization that threatened him now also protected him. Don Gómez was afraid to make another attempt on his life within the walls of the Inquisition— even if it could be arranged. Killing him now would not close the issues that his surrender had reopened. His death would cause too many questions, bring too many sleeping dogs awake.

"When you are taken before the Tribunal," Don Gómez said, "simply do not bring the question of *encomienda* into it. Admit you did wrong. Admit you are not qualified to question the Inquisition's authority in the case of the Indians. Give one answer to all Zarate's questions. You impeded the Inquisition. You confess your crime. You ask forgiveness. Avoid his traps. Deny all knowledge of labor practices in New Mexico."

Zarate may be your only hope, the Condesa had told Luis. *Answer all his questions. You know more about what went on in New Mexico than anyone in the capital. It is your only chance, Luis.*

Don Gómez saw the bitter refusal in Luis's face. Don Gómez took his hands from behind his back. The cloak fell about his legs with a soft rustle. The flesh of his cheeks looked pasty, dead, unwholesome in its lacquered smoothness.

"I do not often stoop to bargain with someone in your position, Don Luis. Refuse my propositions and you will destroy yourself."

"And who else will I destroy?" Luis said.

CHAPTER FORTY-TWO

IF Father Zarate had any special interest in Luis's case there was no evidence. It was months after the visit by Don Gómez that Luis finally got his first interview. He merely appeared before a junior inquisitor, gave statements about his ancestry, education, religious training, a brief story of his life, was given his first formal admonition, and then returned to his cell. More months passed before the second and third admonitions.

Finally, in November of 1691, he was taken from his cell for a fourth time. The chains were put on him as before, and he was taken down dripping corridors and up narrow staircases to the audience chamber on an upper floor of the palace. The room was as tall as a cathedral nave with narrow windows that revealed the immense thickness of the stone walls. At a long table bearing the green cross of the Inquisition a clerk sat writing. Though the Dominicans had established the Holy Office in Europe, it was the Franciscans who officiated in the New World. The clerk was of the Order of Saint Francis, as were the two fathers seated on the dais. They were Fray Isidro Capoz, and Fray Juan Nuñez, the two junior inquisitors who had presided at the preliminary hearings. Between them was an empty chair, massive as a throne. At the table beside the clerk sat the fiscal, who acted as a prosecutor, and the episcopal ordinary who always sat with the qualifiers on the consultation of Faith.

There was an air of hushed expectancy about all the men. There was a sound in the corridor, and the fiscal hissed warningly. The clerk stopped his whispering, and everyone turned toward the door.

Four *mestizos,* naked to the waist, bore the sedan chair into the room. In it sat a shriveled husk of a man in the white robes of inquisitional purity. Luis knew immediately that it was the senior inquisitor, Father Medina Zarate. Light streaming from the windows focused on the bald dome of his skull with a glow like fox fire. His face had the yellow waxiness of a very old candle, and his deep eye sockets were dark with a stain that was more than shadow.

Two of the half-breeds lifted Zarate bodily out of the sedan chair and carried him to the throne. He held rigidly to the arms of the massive chair after they had seated him. His translucent eyelids were closed like fragile blue shells over his eyes. His strangely sculptured lips were compressed so tight that they had turned white. It was a look of religious ecstasy, or infinite pain. With one hand he raised his crucifix to his lips, kissed it, and murmured a soundless prayer. Then he said:

"The prisoner will stand before the Tribunal."

His voice was startling in the hush. It was hollow and ringing like a bell. It made disturbing melodies in the room. Chains clanking, Luis stepped forward. The guards bowed and left the room. The four bearers carried the sedan chair out. The door was closed.

"Prisoner," Zarate said, "you have received your three preliminary admonitions and have been given time to search your soul. Is there anything more you would like to confess before facing accusation?"

"I have written all I could remember, Your Reverence."

Zarate opened his eyes. They were startlingly large in his gnomelike face. They were intensely black and luminous.

"In your written confession you make no denunciations," Father Zarate said. "How can a penitent not wholly cleansed be reconciled to Mother Church? Surely a man cannot be tainted by so many heresies and blasphemies without having gained the knowledge from others."

Luis bowed his head. He had prayed. He had hoped against hope that he would not be called upon for this. But why should the Condesa have been mistaken about it when she had been so right in everything else?

"I wished to make such denunciations to you in person, Your Reverence," he said. He heard the faint stir in the room. With his head still bowed and his eyes closed, he said, "I denounce the woman known as the Condesa de Zumurraga. She is really Lupe Mariscal, from Granada, whose mother was a *morisco.* She had many books on the Librorum Prohibitorum and was conversant with the heresies of Luther and Erasmus."

"Do you know her whereabouts now?"

His throat closed up. He could not. If they burned him he could not. "No, Your Reverence."

The clerk's quill scratched the answer. The silence after that became so protracted that Luis had to look up. Zarate was studying him with an undecipherable expression on his face. The papery eyelids had folded into a net of miniature pleats about the lustrous black eyes. It gave him the look of benign cunning, or of an old man's gratification that such an important revelation had been withheld for his ears alone; Luis could not tell which.

"*Ad mayorem Dei Gloriam,*" Father Zarate said. "Will the clerk now read the formal accusation?"

The clerk read from a thick folio full of yellow paper heavy with wax seals and marked by scrawled signatures. After a short preamble he reached the specific articles.

"One: That upon the night of September 3, 1679, at the tavern of Nazario Aguilar, the accused, Luis Ribera, was overheard to make the blasphemous declaration that fornication between the unmarried is no sin."

"The prisoner has admitted the charge in his written confession," Father Capoz said.

Zarate nodded in agreement and told the clerk to proceed. Without interruption he was allowed to read through the charges that Luis had already confessed to.

Luis was stunned at the things that had been reported. Had everyone in Santa Fe been an informer? He saw that even Zarate was surprised at how many he had already confessed to. But there were many Luis could not possibly have foreseen. The clerk's voice droned on interminably. Luis grew exhausted. His eyes ached and his voice was hoarse from answering so many questions. The worst was obviously being kept till the last. Finally it came.

"Eighty-nine: That the accused, on August 6, 1680, did impede and offend the Holy Office of the Inquisition, insulting and threatening one Toribio Quintano, the then *alguacil mayor* of the Holy Office in the province of New Mexico, to wit: That when the said sheriff did attempt to engage a number of Indians from the *pueblo* of Tesuque for necessary work, possessed with the required permit, signed and sealed by the then governor of New Mexico, Don Antonio, the permit having been taken out *in absentia* in the name of Don Felipe Manzano, the accused did impede and prevent the sheriff from carrying out his duty. . . ."

Luis felt his face go hot. There had been no permit. He was certain of it. Toribio would have taken malicious pleasure in flaunting it at him. Then they must have forged one later, to cover themselves. And Governor Otermin would undoubtedly attest to it. Either they had threatened him or had shown him the forgery and convinced him he had signed it. A royal official had an overwhelming mass of paper work. How could he remember one document out of dozens he might have signed on a certain day ten years ago?

"The prisoner has made a partial confession to this charge," the fiscal said. "But there are many questions remaining unanswered. He has not explained why he made no mention of the permit."

Luis glanced sharply at the man. Up to now the fiscal had taken little part in the proceedings. He was an enormously fat man. His eyes were shrewd slits in a beefy face, and with one sausage of a finger he kept wiping sweat from the deep creases flanking his nose.

Luis knew it would do no good to deny the permit. Don Felipe Manzano had been an *encomendero*. If the permit had been in his name, even *in absentia*, Toribio was in effect acting for him and not the Holy Office.

"In my zeal to repent," he said, "I overlooked a mention of the order from Governor Otermin."

"Then you admit the order?" the fiscal said.

Why should it be the fiscal? Why was he making such a point of it?

"I do not remember seeing the order," Luis said.

"You mean you forgot that you saw it."

"Yes—I—that must be it—I forgot."

"This means you admit seeing it."

There was a pattern forming in the room, closing in, a pressure; Luis could feel it. He was floundering, trying to guess all the implications.

"I—I do not know—that is I did not say that I did see it—"

"A man cannot forget seeing what he did not originally see." The fiscal turned to the Tribunal. "Your Reverences, I submit that if the prisoner admits seeing the permit he must have known the sheriff was acting legally. Therefore, if he knew this, the prisoner must have been impeding the sheriff on some other grounds than the fact that he was employing Indians illegally."

Luis saw the pattern now. The trap. The point the fiscal had been trying to establish was purely a legal one and had nothing to do with matters of faith. It was a maneuver that would come from a lawyer's mind, and not a priest's. And was not Don Gómez Gallegos the most eminent lawyer in New Spain? Was the fiscal his man?

Father Zarate said, "If you were not impeding the sheriff on legal grounds, prisoner, what was your motive?"

Still Luis could not answer. He could see now how inextricably he was caught between the conflicting ambitions of Don Gómez and Zarate. Perhaps Zarate did not even know the permit was a forgery. Perhaps the whole thing had been prepared by Gallegos. Zarate's voice was growing rusty with irritation.

"Prisoner," he said, "in the publication of witnesses you will learn that many of those testifying against you mentioned the trouble you caused the governors and the *encomenderos* and even the priests at Santa Fe. In the testimony there are many hints that this trouble was over their abuse of the Indians. Is this connected with what happened at Tesuque?"

Luis began to tremble. It was not fear. It was outrage. He realized that in admitting the existence of the permit he would be absolving the Holy Office of any illegal action and would be putting himself in the position of impeding the Holy Office in its lawful duty. But there was another reason for the fiscal's insistence on establishing the point. Luis could see the threat it contained. Don Gómez was giving Luis his chance for the last time. If Luis ignored the threat, if he insisted on telling Zarate what he wanted to know, the fiscal could lead Luis step by step into the trap, back down the long list of heresies and blasphemies already confessed to, where an unfavorable vote on the board of qualifiers would doom him.

Zarate was gripping his crucifix tightly. "Your last chance to speak, prisoner. What was behind this trouble at Tesuque? Were the *encomenderos* abusing their privileges in New Mexico? Was the governor involved? If such things existed I must know."

On your knees, the Condesa had said, *your belly . . . like a dog.* And Luis had thought he understood.

"Your Reverence," he said, "I can only plead blind, youthful arrogance in each case. If I defied the governor it was when I was drunk. If I caused the *encomenderos* trouble it was because I would rather carouse at a tavern than take my rightful duty on a military campaign. If the priests complained about me it was because of my escapades with women. How could such a dissolute young fool know anything about *encomienda* or *repartimiento?* I hardly ever saw a field or a plough. I doubt if I could tell you how corn is planted. And I know now that Sheriff Quintano was acting within the law. I had no right to question the authority of the Holy Office. I confess all these things and ask absolution. I throw myself on the mercy of your holy wisdom and Mother Church."

After Luis had finished the only sound was that of the clerk scratching with his quill. Zarate had leaned back in the chair. His eyes were closed. His lower lip began to tremble uncontrollably, and he lifted the crucifix and pressed it against his lip to stop it. He looked like a very tired old man.

The fiscal watched him closely until Zarate's head moved in a barely perceptible nod. The fiscal turned to Luis, smiling triumphantly.

"The prisoner will sign the protocol," he said.

Luis went to the table and took up the quill. He signed below the last line of the proceedings. He saw that the shadow of his arm and the fiscal's arm lay across his name. The shadow made the shape of a cross.

CHAPTER FORTY-THREE

IN the Cárdenas house they followed the usual custom of eating their heavy meal of the day at two in the afternoon. The ill-assorted family gathered in the dining room with its austere whitewashed walls and its immense cypress beams and its massive table and its formal chairs with their high backs and their seats of polychrome leather and their fringe of gold bullion lace.

On the first week of January 1692, they assembled for such a meal. Barbara de Cárdenas sat at the head of the table, removed from the others, eating silently while Nuno and Aunt Ramona prattled and quarreled among themselves.

Barbara was thinking of Luis.

It seemed she could never think of anything else. How many months now? How many years since she had seen him? Or even heard anything about him.

She knew he had surrendered to the Inquisition. She knew that much. The knowledge had come only a few days after he had turned himself in, over a year and a half ago.

Don Gómez Gallegos had told her. The man rarely discussed his business with the Inquisition. Barbara was never quite sure of his motives in telling her as much as he did. Yet it seemed to come out casually enough in the course of a conversation. Don Gómez mentioned remembering that Barbara had known Luis Ribera in Santa Fe. Don Gómez thought she would be interested to learn that Luis was still alive and had turned himself over to the Holy Office. Don Gómez told her that the Condesa had been arrested too. The woman had slashed

her wrists in the cell on the night of her arrest and had bled to death.
Barbara knew her face turned white. She began to tremble. She
wanted to cry. She couldn't cry: Her whole body began to shake, and
she rose from her chair and walked away from Don Gómez.

She thought of the little comb with the knife blade in it, hidden in
the Condesa's abundant hair. She thought of the look on the Condesa's
face when she had showed Barbara the comb. That one moment when
her soul was stripped bare and Barbara could see the true shape of the
terror the Condesa had lived with all her life.

"How . . . how did they get her?"

"Some informer, I suppose. He had told them a lot. When they
found her room empty they knew enough to go to some tavern—the
Renegade, or something. They found this Condesa in the loft. The
innkeeper was hiding her till he could get an Indian to take her to
Amecameca."

Barbara stood at the window, holding tightly to the drapes. Why
had Don Gómez told her? Of course his brother, the Marqués, would
have informed him of her friendship with the Condesa at El Paso. Did
it go farther than that? Did Don Gómez suspect how much more there
had been?

Yet she could no longer dwell on the Condesa. She had to know.
"The man . . . Luis Ribera. I did know him in Santa Fe. I would
like to . . . to help in some way . . ."

"What do you know about him?"

"He is a good Catholic."

"Are you certain? How long did you know him?"

"Well . . . a few weeks."

Don Gómez seemed to restrain a smile. "You would do him no good,
Barbara. A character reference of such vague, general nature is value-
less. Best to stay out of it. The case has too many ramifications. It
would be too dangerous."

Was it a warning? She tried to read his face, but the waxen cheeks
and bland eyes held nothing, and he soon changed the subject.

In the following months she had asked him about Luis as often as
she dared, but he could tell her nothing more. She knew the Holy
Office guarded its proceedings jealously and she had been lucky to hear
as much as she had. She struggled with the impulse to ask help from
Don Gómez, to take him into her confidence. But she knew how deeply
Luis's case was involved with *encomienda*. She still trusted Don Gómez
in her personal relations, yet she feared what his attitude would be
toward Luis. It might do Luis more harm than good.

The months dragged by interminably. She felt responsible for Luis's decision. It filled her with a deep sense of guilt. She spent much time in prayer. She bought a little statue of Luis's patron saint and burned a candle before him constantly night and day. She wrote dozens of letters to Vargas. Busy as he was on the frontier he promised to do what he could. She prayed . . .

"*Patróna.*" It was Josefina's voice, wrenching her from the past again. The Tlascalan maid was by her chair, curtsying. "Don Gómez and Jorge Paz, they have called upon you. They are in the patio."

Nuno and Doña Ramona were quarreling about something and did not even seem aware that Barbara excused herself. The door of the dining room opened on the patio. She closed it behind her and crossed toward the two men by the fountain.

Jorge Paz sat on one of the marble benches, immobile as a dark statue. He was the manager of Barbara's estate, a Nahuatl Indian from one of the free villages. He had a Neanderthal look, glowering, primitive, but she knew him as shrewd and loyal. That he should come with Don Gómez puzzled her. Don Gómez saw the questioning glance she sent the Indian and after his punctilious greeting said:

"I fear we have come with bad news, Barbara."

She frowned, waiting.

"Well—to begin with——" It was the first time Barbara had ever seen Don Gómez at a loss for words. He would not meet her eyes. He adjusted his satin cloak uncomfortably. "You know how much of your corn land was washed away by the floods eighteen months ago——"

She looked at her manager. "Something has happened to the dikes?"

"They are almost finished," Jorge said. "That is not it."

"This *chiahuiztli,*" Don Gómez said. "Just a speck to the naked eye. Myriads of them on each ear of wheat, spreading with astonishing rapidity."

"You are saying they have spread to my wheat?"

"Everybody has suffered," Jorge said. "The wheat has been destroyed on a dozen estates around us."

"But they still have the land," Don Gómez said. "Next year something can be done, perhaps. They can plant again."

"And I cannot?"

"You will not have the land next year," he said. "You know what you had to do to get that last mortgage, after the flood. All your notes will come due before next planting." He stepped closer. "You have only one chance left, Barbara. I do not have the capital to cover the notes. But my personal guarantee would hold the foreclosure another season. I would be glad to give it if you agree to go back to the old methods—bring Fecundo Rascon back as manager, let me oversee the operation."

She could not see Don Gómez. She was looking right at him but she could not see him. There was a coppery taste in her mouth. She was thinking of what the Condesa had told her about a woman alone. She was remembering the fear she had seen in the Condesa, the corrosion, thinking of what she had been forced to do simply to remain alive.

Then there was another memory. It was the red missal ribbon dangling from the waist of the Indian who said Fray Bernal had been killed. And the bodies, scalped and mutilated, lying naked in the ditches, marking every mile of the Royal Highway from Santa Fe to the Jornada. She closed her eyes, shaking her head from side to side.

"Barbara," Don Gómez said. "You must go back to *repartimiento*. You are ruined if you do not. Even this house is mortgaged. You will have nothing left."

She locked her hands together. She opened her eyes. She saw that Don Gómez was watching her closely. He reached out and took her hand in both of his. There was a strange look on his face, a search, a lonelines.

"Barbara, you know my feelings about *encomienda*. But with you— how does it say itself—we are all such a mixture of bad and good——"

"I have always trusted you, Don Gómez."

"My brother thinks I am weak . . . letting you provide such an example."

"You are a different man than your brother."

"Well, we have all committed our sins." Color touched his cheeks as though he were embarrassed at revealing so much of his feelings. He smiled wryly. He patted her hand. "At the same time, I can think of no other way to save yourself than to take my offer. Think it over. Your creditors need not know for a while." He let her hand go, still watching her. "There is something else, Barbara. I thought you would like to know. The Holy Office held an *auto particular* in the Jesuit church yesterday. Luis Ribera was one of the penitents who received sentence."

She could not hide her reaction. Her eyes widened and her hand went to her throat.

"None of them will be executed," Don Gómez said. Barbara made a soft moaning sound of relief. Don Gómez was looking at her closely. "Ribera is to lose all titles, patents of nobility, *encomiendas*, and any other beneficences granted by the Crown. He is further condemned to the *sanbenito* for five years."

She crossed herself. She closed her eyes. But it would not blot out the picture. She had seen too many victims of the Holy Office wandering through the streets, shunned like lepers, branded by their *coroza* and *sanbenito*—the penitent's crown of yellow pasteboard and the linen holy sack plastered with the red crosses of Saint Andrew that made even the beggars crawl out of the way and pull their filthy rags aside.

"When will they release him?" Barbara asked. "When can I see him?"

"It is too late. He has already been released."

"You do not understand!" She had not cried in a long time. She felt the hot tears in her eyes. "Don Gómez, I love him——"

For once a strong expression broke the lacquered smoothness of the man's cheeks. She could not tell if it was surprise. She could not tell if he had known. Finally he said, "Barbara—pity of God. Ribera is gone. He has been banished from New Spain for life."

CHAPTER FORTY-FOUR

By January of 1693 Don Diego de Vargas had been at El Paso almost two years. It had been a trying time, a time of exasperating delays, official procrastination, plans disrupted by new uprisings among the Indians around El Paso. Even after they were quelled the area had to be policed. General Vargas often rode with the patrols.

One evening late in January he brought his squad back to the mud-walled *presidio* overlooking the Rio Grande, turning his horse over to an Indian and sending for Antonio Valverde. The Secretary of Government and War reported to Vargas in his own quarters. The general dictated the details of the scout while Valverde transcribed them in the daily journal Vargas kept.

After Valverde left, Vargas stood in the open doorway looking across the dusty parade ground. The diffused light of a dying sun came redly through the salenite windows. It gave a varnished glow to the general's strangely colored cheeks. It made prismatic flashes against his brilliant eyes and against the single emerald studding his rapier hilt. It turned the alkali in the creases of his boots to a chalky white spiderweb.

He was wondering how much longer it would be. How many more of these maddening rides in a circle before he could once more start northward? He still had not been able to gather the number of colonists he felt necessary to resettle Santa Fe. And though the viceroy had authorized the enlistment of a hundred soldiers he had been unable to fulfill the quota. Why should troops enlist when they could not be paid? In November of last year the royal audience had voted Vargas over twelve thousand pesos. It was already gone. It had not begun to pay for the supplies needed to move a thousand settlers northward. The viceroy had promised more money but it had not come yet.

Tiredly he turned into the room. He saw that his secretary had left the journal open on the table, the pen aslant against the well of guizache ink. He closed the journal and put it neatly on top of the ledgers. He cleaned the pen and placed it in line beside the other quills. He turned the chair until it was in precise relation to the vargueño upon which lay the pens and books.

He crossed the room and sat down in another tall chair. He leaned his head back and closed his eyes. His hands were placed on the knees of his horse-stained boots, still wrinkled high about his thighs.

"Andres," he called.

In a moment he heard the Negro slave's bare feet on the floor. Without opening his eyes, he lifted his feet to let the slave pull off his boots. He stretched and curled his toes. They got cramped in the stirrup after a day of riding. He remembered the time when he could spend a week in the saddle without getting a cramp.

"The wine before the shoes," he said. "Pour yourself a glass too." He heard the slave rise and start toward the trastero. He said, "Do you not put the boots away?"

"I meant to clean them first, patrón."

"Of course," Vargas said. "Am I getting worse about this, Andres? It seems I cannot bear to see the slightest thing out of place."

"The mark of a good soldier, patrón."

Vargas heard the gurgle of poured wine. Andres handed him a milk-white goblet from the glassworks of La Granja. Vargas was still exercising his feet. The slave knelt to massage them. Vargas took a drink of the wine. He held it in his mouth, savoring it for a carefully measured moment. He had an aristocrat's taste for fine things. It was a grave, austere taste, fulfilled by the nutty wines from the earthenware tinajas of Montilla, the lean and nervous horses from the plains of Cordoba, the sinewy fire of the gypsy wenches from Granada.

His wife had been like that. And the woman in Mexico City, who had borne him children. And Barbara de Cárdenas . . .

Well, not sinewy, exactly. There was too much flesh on her to call her sinewy. It had always been a matter of curiosity to him how deceptive some women were, seeming so slender and fragile, yet at the right moment assuming a certain position, turned a certain way . . . he smiled and took another sip of wine.

He had so often wondered about Barbara, so often known the impulse to . . . but how could it work out? She was not that kind of a woman. Whatever he proposed would have to be honorable. And how could he make it honorable, with his wife still alive in Spain and his alliance in Mexico City known? Was that what had held him back? He wondered if it would have restrained him twenty years ago. His blood had been hotter then. His feet did not cramp in the stirrup, and he had not learned so many painful lessons.

There was a knock on the door. Andres waited for Vargas to nod and then crossed to open the door. Francisco Alaya stood outside. He was corporal of the guard, an emaciated husk of a man who irritated Vargas with his constant hawking and spitting.

"A man, Your Excellency. He wished to see you."

"What is his name?"

"Luis Ribera, Your Excellency."

Vargas started to stand. Then he realized he still did not have shoes. Andres was already scurrying to get them from the chest against the wall.

"At the moment—bring him in."

The corporal stepped aside. Andres was kneeling before Vargas, slipping on his red-heeled shoes, when Luis entered. Vargas realized how tightly he was gripping his wine goblet.

Luis stopped just within the door, and there was a moment in which neither spoke. Vargas could not deny the shock.

Luis still wore the *coroza* and the *sanbenito*. But the yard-high crown was battered and broken and the tattered holy sack was bleached to a chalky color by abuse and weather. The tangled hair showing beneath the pasteboard crown was entirely gray, and gray variegated his waist-length beard. Its remarkable collection of twigs and thorns made it appear like a mat of curly mesquite transplanted to his chest from some impenetrable brushland. His clothes beneath the holy sack were nothing but filthy rags.

They revealed the pitiful emaciation of his body. His bare arms and bare legs were almost black with sunburn and dirt. They were as bony and fleshless as an old man's. His face had the hollow hopelessness Vargas had seen in the starving hordes of the capital. His eyes were sunk deep, as from a great sickness, and so filmed and vacant that Vargas could not tell if they were focused on him.

After that first moment Andres had Vargas's shoes on. He rose, without apology. "God give you good days, Don Luis."

"And you, Don Diego."

Luis's voice was feeble, husky. The effort made him break into a weak cough. He held his side and wheezed for breath. Vargas motioned to the chair and Luis slumped into it, still bent forward and coughing. Vargas made a signal to Andres, and the slave poured another glass of amontillada, taking it to Luis.

"I think the next thing will be food," Vargas told Andres. "See what you can do at the kitchens. Nothing too solid, by the looks of him."

Andres left, closing the door behind him. Luis had managed to conquer his coughing and was sipping at the wine.

"*Señorita* Cárdenas wrote me as soon as you were released," Vargas said. "Of course it takes weeks for the mails to get here. You must realize our efforts to find you—"

Luis nodded, his eyes closed. "They gave me no chance to see Barbara. They took me out of the city immediately. They were afraid—"

"With good cause. You must have heard of the corn riots after you left."

"In June, yes. It was bound to come."

"But things are under control now, and you are welcome here, Don Luis. What I have learned these last two years has proved your value. I suppose—coming north—you heard that I have already made a reconquest."

Luis quickly looked down at his wine. But he had not kept Vargas from seeing the deep disappointment in his eyes. Vargas could appreciate what a blow it must have been to learn that the reconquest had already been made. It in no way altered Luis's goal of returning to his homeland. But the reconquest had become a symbol of that goal, a symbol for which he had suffered and sacrificed so much. By sharing in it he could return to usefulness and value and identity with his people. To have it snatched from his hands just as his trials were ended was like cheating a man of his rightful inheritance. A soldier himself, Vargas knew what a hollow triumph it would be to accept victory from someone else's hands.

"Do not look so downcast, man," Vargas said. "There is still much to do."

Dully Luis said, "The *entrada*—the entrance—I did not hear the details."

"I made the *entrada* in August of last year. I took the men you had recommended into my confidence, Tupatu, Tyame, Juan Ye. By December I had gained a peaceful submission of all the tribes along the river. New Mexico is once more a royal province, and it did not cost us a man."

"Why did you not stay?"

"It was only a military conquest. I had to return for the colonists."

"And you left no men at Santa Fe?"

"I barely had two hundred men, including the Indian allies that went from here. Too small a force to divide. I needed every man in my trip back. I circled west to get the submission of Acoma and Zuni and the Moqui villages."

"At Acoma—did you happen to see—Kashana was her name."

"She asked me personally about you, Don Luis. I told her all I could."

Luis was leaning forward. The dull look was gone from his eyes. It was the first life Vargas had seen in his face since he had entered.

"There were boys—sons——"

"I saw one. Migenna?"

Luis leaned back against the chair. He was looking beyond Vargas now. "They are my sons, you know," he said. Vargas did not answer. Luis said, "Was there talk . . . did she say . . . was there anything about another man?"

"Do you mean a husband? I could not say."

Luis was silent a long time and then said wonderingly, "And they submitted at Acoma. No fighting."

"Not a blow. I dealt with the old *cacique*, Tyame. You were right about him. He said if you would give your word about me he knew there would be peace. You were right about many things. Perhaps you heard—while I was in the Moqui country I passed through the region of Sierra Azul. I took ore from the region where the mines were supposed to be. The assay did not prove out. There was no sign of silver or quicksilver."

Luis was silent for a moment. Then, "I am sorry."

"Be honest. It was what you told me in the beginning. You should feel vindicated."

"You are still going back. It is all that matters."

Vargas felt almost disappointed that he could not strike sparks from Luis as he had at Mexico City. The man's attitude toward gold seemed affected to him, hypocritical. Vargas was a man of his times. Slavery was an unquestioned fact in his life. His devotion to the Catholic faith was sincere and unshakable. The Holy Office was an absolute necessity to keep the Faith pure. The fever of treasure and conquest seemed as natural to him as the excitement over a woman. How could Luis question it? Could he not see that discovery of Sierra Azul would mean more than personal enrichment? It would be a boon to New Mexico. It would make a first-class colony out of a beggarly province.

Vargas turned to regard the statue of La Conquistadora in the wall niche. She was patron saint of the reconquest. Every year he gave her new azure robes and a fresh veil. Every night he knelt before the china-white serenity of her face and said his prayers. She had accompanied him to Santa Fe on the first entrance last year, and he firmly believed that he would not have succeeded without her help.

Our Lady of the Conquest. She seemed to epitomize his nature. He was impelled by far more than the lure of mythical treasure. It was the restless, questing, Spanish chemistry in his blood, the heritage of Cortez and Pizarro, that drove him. Life had been going stale at Tlalpujagua. He had experienced everything—honors, titles, wealth, women, fame. And now, nearing fifty, he had come to the dead end of it all in the ragged little mining town in the barren mountains north of Mexico City. Appointment as administrator of the royal quicksilver had been a signal honor—but it had soon grown meaningless.

There were no new worlds left to conquer. Spain was decaying, and the retaking of New Mexico would probably be the last big chance for glory and conquest that would come to him in his lifetime. Could Luis not appreciate that? Was he not Spaniard enough to understand the call?

Vargas shook his head angrily. He rarely felt called upon to explain his actions to anyone. Why should he want to justify himself to this young man? He saw that Andres had allowed La Conquistadora's veil to become slightly misplaced and reached up to straighten it.

"What about the Pueblo leaders?" Luis asked. "Did you execute Po-pe?"

"Po-pe is dead."

Luis looked incredulous. "You are certain?"

Vargas turned. "All the Indians swear it. I saw no sign of Po-pe. Tupatu is generally accepted as their ruler now. The story I got was vague. It apparently happened several years ago. I talked with Pedro de Tapia. He said it happened at Acoma. Po-pe's body was found at the foot of the cliff after a big rainstorm. He had been stabbed. They could not prove who had done it. For a while there was talk of retaliation against Acoma, but nothing was ever done. I think most of the Pueblos were glad he was killed . . ."

Vargas stopped talking. Luis was looking beyond him, toward the north. There was a strange look on his sunken face, almost as though he had stopped listening.

Andres entered with the food. There was a big bowl of the steaming gruel they called *atole*. There was a silver pitcher of chocolate. Andres insisted on making Vargas's chocolate himself. It was his pride. On a heated *metate* he ground up the cocoa beans and stick cinnamon and pecans and sugar and made them into a paste, and when it dried he cut the paste into cakes. The cakes could then be cooked with thick whole milk and vanilla and a secret spice that Andres would not reveal.

The slave set the tray on a table and helped Luis move the chair over. Andres poured two silver beakers of the chocolate, serving one to Vargas. Luis began to eat the *atole*. Vargas saw sweat break out on his forehead.

"It seems to me your fortune has been better than it would appear," Vargas said. "Señorita Barbara wrote me of the number and nature of the charges against you. In Spain you would have been burned."

A bitter smile touched Luis's face. "A matter of politics."

"Don Gómez Gallegos?" Vargas asked. Luis glanced at him in surprise and Vargas said, "I have been in the New World long enough to know its politics, Don Luis. And the Marqués de Gallegos has been here for some months."

Luis sipped at the scalding chocolate. "Then perhaps you understand. In the hands of the Inquisition I constituted a danger to the Gallegos'. Don Gómez had the power to influence my sentence in either direction. He offered me a bargain. He forced me into a position where I had to accept it."

"Does that end your danger?"

"They tried to kill me to keep me from the Inquisition. I do not think it will make them any happier to have me tell you what I know."

"Did they follow you?"

"I think one of their men tried to. I could not swear to it."

"You have friends here as well as enemies, Don Luis. You will have protection."

"There is much you should know——"

"You are too exhausted for much more talk. You must rest first."

"I should report to the commissioner of the Inquisition."

"He is Father Salvador de San Antonio," Vargas said. Luis glanced at him in surprise. Vargas smiled gravely. "Is he not the one you suggested?"

Luis made a vague gesture with his hand. He seemed at a loss.

"Just so," Vargas said. "Your advice was sound. Father Antonio has made a fine administrator. He will be the father president at Santa Fe. Did you think I was joking when I said you could be of value?"

Luis bowed his head. Vargas could see he was on the point of collapse. He told Andres to take the young man to the mission. Vargas stood in the doorway, watching them cross the parade ground.

He thought of the pride he had seen in the provincial aristocracy here. If anything they were haughtier than the Spanish-born *gachupines*. Had Luis been such a one? Vargas tried to think what it would take for a man like that to swallow pride, humiliate himself, degrade himself, grovel, for the sake of a dream. He wondered if he would have the kind of courage it took.

CHAPTER FORTY-FIVE

ANDRES waited outside the mission while Luis reported to Fray Antonio. The commissioner made Luis welcome and confessed him. Throughout his long journey north Luis had found this acceptance from the priests. They exemplified the mercy promised by Mother Church to her penitents. It was the people who shunned him.

He had seen the penitents stumbling miserably through the streets of the capital in their hideous holy sacks, avoided by even the beggars. But until his trip north he had never realized how complete their ostracism was.

He had held some thought of trying to see Barbara de Cárdenas for a last time, to thank her for what she had done. But the Inquisition had given him no chance. All the banished penitents had been hurried through the Zocalo by a squad of guards and taken to the city gates. Commanding the squad was Bartolome Ordonoz, the constable who had been with Toribio when they had tried to kill Luis.

Luis did not think they would attempt anything in the city in broad daylight. But it let him know what to expect. Once in the open country he would be fair game.

Ordonoz did not return to the city with the other guards when the prisoners were released. Luis was not sure that the man followed him, but he managed to lose him in the scattering of hovels surrounding the city. He had hidden in an abandoned corn granary until nightfall. He headed north, avoiding the obvious route of the Royal Highway, moving through the wilderness west of the road. It had taken him months to get out of the mountains of central Mexico and into the

barren plains in the North. It was a return to the struggle for survival
he had known after escaping Acoma. He found that the dread of the
Holy Office was even greater in the small villages than in the capital.
The Spaniards were afraid to offer him food or shelter of any kind.
Only in a church or mission or among some of the Indians could he
find help.

But north of Zacatecas the settlements began to dwindle. The missions were hundreds of miles apart, and there were vast stretches completely uninhabited. Luis was reduced to grass and cactus pulp and
rodents that he spent whole days trapping. His feet became so swollen
that he could not walk. He did not know how many days he spent
crawling on all fours. He lost count of the times he fainted by the
roadside.

Near Parral he went into a delirium. Weeks later he came out of it
in the hovel of an Indian family. For a month he did not know if he
would live or die. When he was able to walk he began his pilgrimage
again . . .

After confessing to Father Antonio, Luis went back to the *presidio*
with Andres. He drank in the dry smell of the desert. It was sulphurous
as an ignited firelock, so different from Mexico City, so evocative of
Santa Fe and all that lay ahead. They passed through the gate in the
walled *presidio*. The adobe buildings took shadowy shape in the silvery
twilight—the stables with their bear-grass roofs, the mud-walled corrals,
the long barracks studded at ceiling height with the inevitable vigas.
Near the gate a group of artillerymen lounged about the *pedrero grande*
and the *pieza de bronza*—the two cannons that had already been up the
river once with Vargas.

Luis recognized Captain Roque Madrid talking with the men. His
reckless handsomeness was gone. All that remained of his black hair
was a graying fringe that crept hesitantly around the egglike dome of
his head. His lean jaw had turned to jowl, fleshy and furrowed, and a
thickening belly strained at his broad silk sash. He stared at Luis,
mouth open in surprise, in recognition. A dull red color crept into his
slack cheeks.

In the awkward silence one of the artillerymen ran around Madrid.
Luis was caught up in a whirlwind of pounding fists and flying arms.
As he was swung around in a crazy dance he saw the red kerchief tied
about the man's head and the big brass earring spinning against his
gypsy cheek. It was Emilio.

"By the five wounds, Luis! Adam's navel. They told me you were
alive. Holy cloth that sopped the blood! I almost deserted and rode to

the capital. Thirty pieces, why did you not bring me a suit like that. We would not have to fight the Apaches any more, we could scare them to death!"

Shamed by Emilio's spontaneous joy, Captain Madrid stepped forward and grasped Luis by the shoulder. "Don Luis, forgive me. Why must we *hidalgos* possess such stiff necks?"

Luis grinned down at his bizarre costume. "I do not blame you, Don Roque. This clown suit comes as something of a shock at first."

"I admire you, Don Luis. I do not think I could joke about it."

Madrid and Emilio took Luis to the nearest barrack. It was a long, featureless coffin of a building with narrow windows and a sagging door. It had the cold, dank odor of ancient earth peculiar to these adobes. A candle in a wall niche cast a feeble circle of light at the far end of the single room. Cuirasses lay like grotesque metal tortoise shells on the floor, and other equipment was hung from wooden pegs in the wall. A half dozen men sat on their straw pallets beneath the candle playing monte.

"This is Don Luis Ribera," Captain Madrid said. "Many of you will remember him."

Men dozing on nearby pallets were awakened by the voice. They rolled over, cursing, or came up on one elbow to peer at Luis. The group at the end of the room made no move.

Emilio put scarred fists on his broad hips. "Listen, you whoresons, if it had not been for the warning of Don Luis at Santa Fe you would not be alive today——"

"No importance, companion," Luis said. "It is something you will have to get used to." He turned to Captain Madrid. "And you might as well both get used to something else. I am a don no longer. It is just plain Luis Ribera."

Madrid was still embarrassed and seemed glad to take his leave. Emilio took Luis down the room. On a pallet near the end Luis saw Emilio's German mace—the short handle and the length of chain and the spiked iron ball.

"The bed beside me belonged to a soldier killed in the last fight with the Mansos," Emilio said. "It is yours if you can stand the stink."

Beyond the empty bed, against the corner of the room, was the last pallet in line. A man occupied it, lying on his back. He was barefooted, but he still wore his breeches and a sleeveless *esquipile* of quilted rawhide. He had a sly face, full of sharp angles and secret shadows. He stank of garlic and onions, and his eyes glittered like knife points.

"I sleep beside no heretics," he said.

"Then move," Emilio said.

"I move for no blasphemer."

Emilio picked up his mace. "How would you like a Hapsburg crack in your skull, L'Archeveque?"

Luis put a restraining hand on Emilio's arm. "Bowels of Judas, Emilio, can you not see that this is no man of violence. He would rather sit quietly in some corner and philosophize with me. Come now, L'Archeveque, let us discuss Luther and Calvin . . ."

L'Archeveque's eyes dropped to the yellow holy sack Luis wore. Sweat made little silver beads on the bristles of the man's week-old beard. A haunted look touched his face, the same dread Luis had seen in so many Spaniards coming north. With a strangled sound L'Archeveque gathered up his gear. He walked down the barrack, taking a pallet as far away from Luis as he could get.

"You should not say such things, even in jest," Emilio told Luis. "If you are denounced again it would mean the stake for sure."

"I know, companion. But sometimes it gets too much to bear." Luis looked after the other man. "L'Archeveque. It sounds French."

"This expedition is drawing many strange birds," Emilio said. "Does the name La Salle mean anything to you?"

"Was he not the French cavalier trying to establish a colony for France somewhere on the gulf?"

"It is believed now that his real goal was the wealth of our rich mines in Nueva Viscaya. After establishing his colony he planned to march west and conquer our northern provinces for France. His whole mission failed, and he was killed somewhere inland. This L'Archeveque was involved in the murder. One of our expeditions came across him and another Frenchman living with the Indians. L'Archeveque spent some time in our prisons. How he got free is a mystery."

"Maybe he convinced the viceroy that killing La Salle really served Spanish interests."

"In a way it did," Emilio agreed. "This L'Archeveque is a simpering, fawning, smirking lackey who could squirm his way through any situation. He has already ingratiated himself into the favor of the Marqués de Gallegos."

"Then I was not so rash after all," Luis said. "I would not get much sleep with a Gallegos man at my back."

CHAPTER FORTY-SIX

LUIS spent the following weeks at the *presidio*, resting and regaining his strength. He could not forget Toribio's attempt on his life before he had surrendered himself to the Inquisition. He could not forget Bartolome Ordonoz following him outside the capital's gates. He knew that he could never relax his guard now. L'Archeveque was one of the men he watched. Emilio had said that the Frenchman was a Gallegos man. And L'Archeveque had already been involved in one murder.

Most of the soldiers, even the ones Luis had known at Santa Fe, would have little to do with him. He was a pariah, with only Emilio to alleviate his loneliness.

It was from him, during the first few days, that Luis heard about the first *entrada*. In August of 1692 Vargas had started upriver with his handful of Spaniards. The *pueblos* north of the Jornada were deserted.

Not until they reached Santa Fe itself did they meet any resistance. The Indians had fortified the town and were prepared for war. But after a parley and a show of Spanish strength they agreed to surrender. They insisted that Vargas give proof of his peaceful intentions and his promises of pardon by coming into the capital unarmed, with only the father president and six soldiers to accompany him.

"It was there that I saw the greatness of the man," Emilio said. "We were outnumbered hundreds to one. We might have been able to take Santa Fe, but General de Vargas knew how many of us would die storming those walls. He looked at us and said, 'He who takes no risk to win an immortal name accomplishes nothing.' He dismounted and took off his armor. He prayed to the Virgin with the priest. He walked into that villa without so much as a knife in his garter. There were thousands of them, Luis. The walls were bristling with spears. They could have killed him like you step on an ant. I think it was his performance more than anything else that gave us back New Mexico without the loss of a soldier."

Luis could appreciate what a profound effect such a daring act would have upon the Indian mind. He could not fail to be impressed himself. It was either a flamboyant gesture or a calculated risk taken by a man devoted to his cause and convinced of its righteousness. And Luis could not conceive of the grave, thoughtful Vargas being flamboyant.

"Emilio," Luis said, "do you think it will stick? Will we go back without a fight?"

"I know what you are thinking, Luis. I am suspicious too. It was too easy . . . much too easy."

Luis was silent a while. Then he asked, "When you were up there . . . Bigotes . . ."

"I talked with Antonio Bolsas, the war captain at Santa Fe. He nad heard that Bigotes went north to marry a Yuta squaw. But that was many years ago . . ."

When Luis was stronger he was put to work. There were the usual details, gathering wood along the river, cleaning the stables, guard duty. Later he was assigned a mount by Pedro Arbalos who had charge of the horses. The animal was a cinnamon-red named Canelo. He did not have the Castilian pace so dear to the heart of the Spaniard, but he had a *sobre paso* that set him trotting with his hind legs and galloping with his front and covered ground with surprising speed.

There was little of the indolence Luis remembered at Santa Fe under Otermin. There was too much for the small garrison to do and Vargas was an exacting commander.

The restless Mansos and Jumanos still had to be kept under surveillance, and the patrols were always out. In April the royal audience issued Vargas the promised thirty thousand pesos with which to purchase more supplies and recruit soldiers and colonists for the trip to Santa Fe. Captain Hurtado was in charge of the colonists and it fell on his shoulders to enroll the settlers. One morning before dawn Sergeant Ruiz de Castros tramped through the barracks kicking awake half a dozen men. Luis was one of them. He learned that he was assigned to a squad Hurtado was sending south to meet a party of colonists coming from Zacatecas.

After a hurried breakfast the men assembled on the parade. Spring heat was already sucking the putrid smell of bottom mud and the syrup of white brush from the river. Horses stamped and fretted under their heavy equipment. An Indian led a *grullo* from the stables, striped like a zebra on the hind legs. Its Moorish saddle was set with silver and pearls, and heavy bronze shoe stirrups turned and flashed in the rising sun. Luis knew that it belonged to the Marqués de Gallegos.

The Marqués came from the officers' quarters with General de Vargas and Captain Madrid. Instead of a morion the Marqués wore an old-fashioned cabasset for a helmet, the engraved cheek pieces clasping his fire-scarred jaws. The haughty self-possession Luis remembered at Santa Fe was gone. Luis had seen the same change in many of the others who had survived the horror of the revolt. The Marqués moved with an agitated hop that made Vargas hurry to keep up with him. The nervous claws of his hands were never still, adjusting the hang of his sword, fussing with the clasps of his cuirass. Furtive little changes of expression passed through his face, squinting his eyes, pulling at his mouth.

A lackey held his stirrup. The Marqués was in the saddle before he saw Luis standing beside his horse on the other side of the squad. The Marqués's face turned so dark that the scars from the fire stood out like patches of chalk on his cheeks.

"General Vargas," he said, "I will have no heretics in my command."

Luis could not believe that Vargas would give him duty with the Marqués in command. It was Hurtado who had assigned him to the squad. It was Hurtado's mistake. Or was it a mistake?

"He is no heretic, Don Desidero," Vargas said. "He has repented and has been absolved."

"He is still in *sanbenito*. I will not have such a man infecting my troops."

"I have received special dispensation from the Holy Office to use him," Vargas said. "With so many out on patrol he cannot be replaced in this squad."

"Remove him or get another officer," the Marqués said.

It was the first open clash that had occurred between Vargas and the Gallegos factions. An apprehensive stir passed through the soldiers, rustling cloaks, rattling armor. A horse stamped fretfully. It was silent.

"Don Desidero," Vargas told the Marqués, "Luis Ribera will stay with this squad. I order you to carry out your mission at once."

The Marqués let out a waspish sound. He turned his blue horse and lifted it to a Castilian pace across the parade. Luis felt tension crawl through his shoulders as he waited for Vargas to call him back, to reprimand him. Vargas did not speak. He was perfectly immobile. The strange color of his face looked almost yellow in the early morning light. It showed no anger, no humiliation, nothing. When the Marqués had reached his quarters he stepped off the horse and stalked inside.

Vargas turned to the sergeant. "Castros, can I trust you with this mission?"

The sergeant saluted. "With certainty, Excellency."

Luis turned to tighten his cinch. He did not want to look at Vargas. He felt a bitter disappointment. Though Vargas had not actually backed down about Luis, the Marqués had made the whole thing seem like a defeat for Vargas. Luis felt that Vargas should have ordered the Marqués back, reprimanded him, should have taken some immediate action. In the eyes of the troops it made him seem afraid to take issue with the Marqués. Was this the man who had walked unarmed into an army of hostile Indians?

The Royal Highway led the squad southeast along the Rio Grande. A league and a half from the Pass and the *presidio* stood the Spanish town built by Otermin's seventeen hundred refugees. It was named La Plaza de Armas de San Lorenzo in commemoration of that awful tenth of August, that day of Saint Lawrence which none of them would ever forget. A league farther east, on the north bank of the river, were the three mud villages built by the Pueblo allies who had come south with the Spaniards in 1680. Beyond them the Camino Real turned southward into the barren plains. The soldiers were to meet the colonists at the edge of the El Paso district and escort them back through country still made dangerous by the restlessness of the local tribes.

Luis had made sure there were no Gallegos men in the squad and felt comparatively safe. Though the men had become used to his weird figure accompanying them on patrols the insidious barrier still remained. He was usually last in line, and he might as well have been riding alone.

On the evening of the third day they reached the caravan. Three heavy wagons and a two-wheeled cart were camped on a waterless plain beside the road. Half-naked boys herded the stock beyond camp. Fires made yellow blooms in a silver dusk. The soldiers passed a mounted guard and rode into camp. The smell of chile and beef rose from copper stew kettles. The shadowy figures of women passed back and forth at their cooking chores. One woman was crouched at a wagon wheel making soap.

It was something Luis had seen a hundred times in Santa Fe. It brought back the memories with such vivid nostalgia that he slowed down to watch. Sergeant Castros was hunting the captain of the caravan and led his squad on without realizing that Luis had dropped behind.

The soap jelly was made from animal fat, and the woman was skimming it and straining it through a piece of fine swiss. When it was clean and white she added a pinch of salt and then some ground melon seeds and bran and *romero* weed to give it texture. Luis let his fretting horse drift nearer. He knew the yellow chamiso blossoms would come next, and perhaps some juniper juice. When the soap cakes dried in the sun they would be the color of lemons and would smell piny as junipers on a rainy night.

There was something distinctly peasant about the woman as she worked, something of the earth. All her motions were strong, rhythmic. Her long sleeves were rolled to the elbow. Firelight burnished the ripple of muscle in her arms. It shimmered wetly across the black chain of her braids. She heard the horse and turned to look.

It was Barbara de Cárdenas.

Luis pulled his horse to a halt. The surprise was like a shock, tingling through his whole body. Barbara stood up. Her eyes were wide, and her lips were parted and damp and shining. She was barefooted. She had on a heavy wool skirt and a *camisa*—the white cotton blouse of the poor, which was pleated around the yoke so that the pleats gathered across the breasts and turned them to soft and tantalizing cones.

He dismounted and she came toward him. He did not understand the look on her face. He remembered when he had first seen her in her house at Mexico City and her eyes had been so lustrous they seemed touched with tears. They had the same look now. Only they could not seem to see him. They were staring at him, but the tearful luster made them look blind and he had the feeling that she could not really see him. How could there be tears? She was smiling. She was smiling and lifting her hands toward him, as though she would touch his face or take it in her hands. Her hands were so close that he could smell the perfume of the juniper juice.

"Well," he said. "Barbara." He felt like a fool. He did not know what to say. He took her hands. Was that what she wanted? "This is insane. What happened? What are you doing here?"

Her throat convulsed. She seemed lifted toward him. "Vargas wrote me you were here, Luis. It was all I had waited for. I knew that if you were alive you would come to El Paso. Luis, when I heard—you have no idea—I could not stay in Mexico City. The floods, the *chiahuiztli*— there was nothing left. All I had was the house and it was mortgaged.

I made a bargain with Nuno. If he would relinquish his claims to the property of Uncle Celso in Santa Fe I would sign over the house to him. Luis . . ."

"Listen," he said. "Are you crazy? Don Celso's property——"

"The land is still there. It was rich land. The Crown is supplying each settler with a little money, stock, supplies to start over again."

"But a woman . . . like you . . . alone . . ."

"Alone?"

For the first time her parted lips closed completely. The odd expression of blindness left her eyes. They narrowed and darkened and seemed to move to every corner of his face as though searching for something. He knew what it was now; there could be no mistaking it —he understood her expression, the parted lips, the breathlessness, the uplifted hands. He held them rigidly against him.

"Barbara, listen, the truth," he said. He wondered how it could have taken him so long to understand. "You would have come anyway. Of course. You told me. The way you woke up at night, smelling the *enebro*, the thing you found up here, how you hunted for it in Mexico City, waited, even prayed. You would have to return to understand. Remember? You would have to see the Mountains of the Blood of Christ."

"You were here," she said stubbornly. "I knew you were here."

"But you cannot think—you did not think——"

She drew her hands from his. They were still clasped together and she let them drop until they were pressed against the folds of her heavy skirt. The excitement and the eagerness and the waiting were completely gone from her face. There was a sort of a dread in her eyes.

"What else was I to think?"

"A man," he said. He made a helpless gesture. "How do you think it was? Out in the desert, months, a year, and the Romita, the gutters, for how long? And then—a woman like you——"

"Is that all it meant to you?"

"No. I am trying to tell you. What do you mean *all*? It just happens. How can anybody know? A man and a woman, that is all——"

He shook his head angrily. How could he explain it when he didn't understand it himself? How could she make so much of it? Had it really been that much? He remembered how he could not forget it. He remembered how guilty he had felt. A man did not feel guilty that long over just a kiss. But that was not the core of it either. There was no use skirting it any longer.

He said, "I should have told you . . . if I had told you in Mexico

City . . . you must remember the girl named Kashana. At Acoma——"
He hesitated. "At Acoma I took her as my wife."

He saw the shock in her face before she looked down at her clasped
hands. He saw how desperately her hands strained at each other. She
made no sound. She turned and walked away from him.

She stopped by the wagon. He stood where he was a moment, helplessly, and then followed her.

"Go away," she said. Her voice was taut, strained, filled with unut-
terable humiliation. Her head was bowed and her shoulders were
pulled together and he thought he saw her whole body trembling. "Will
you please just go away?"

"I should have told you. I know I should have told you. But it seemed
like I did not really get a chance."

She did not answer.

"You can go back," he said. "You must go back."

"To what?" The words sounded squeezed from her, thin and desperate.

"Surely some of your family, Doña Ramona, even if you had to go
to Spain——"

"I would rather be with the Condesa."

"You cannot go there. It would be too dangerous."

"I can very easily go there." Hysteria lay just beneath the surface
now, giving an odd singsong cadence to her voice. "All it takes is a
little blade, just a little blade in a comb. . . . She told me it did not
even hurt much——"

Fear made him catch her shoulders. "Barbara, what are you saying?
Tell me—tell me—the last time I saw the Condesa she was leaving for
Amecameca."

"She never got there. She killed herself in a cell——"

She broke off, cringing and gasping softly with pain. He realized
how cruelly his fingers were digging into her. He released her. He felt
sick. He felt guilty and deeply sick. It seemed a long time before he
could speak. His words sounded far away, dead.

"How did it happen so soon? I know they did not follow me to her
place that night. I know it. Somebody had to denounce her. Was it
Toribio? Did Toribio betray her?"

"Nobody knows. A dozen people could have denounced her. Who
knows? Ask Toribio. He is here——" Her voice broke. She put her hands
to her face and it was hard to tell if she was crying or not. "For the
love of God, will you please go away? I do not want to see you any
more. I do not want to talk with you——"

He stared emptily at her back. Her body looked so slender and vulnerable in the heavy clothes. How had it ever looked peasant to him? He had never felt so helpless. In the prison of the Inquisition he had never felt so helpless. Miserably he turned and went to his horse. He led the animal toward the fire of the wagon captain, where Sergeant Castros and the squad had already dismounted and were unsaddling.

She had said Toribio was here. Out of the rest of his misery and guilt that was the one clear thought he could find. He began looking at the people who passed by, their shapes, the way they walked. He realized his hand was on his sword.

He was still twenty feet from his own squad when he saw the man. A tall, narrow silhouette crossing before a fire. He passed a woman and she glanced up at him without speaking. He seemed oblivious to her. No other man had ever possessed an aura of such complete loneliness.

The firelight glittered on his cuirass and cast a linty shine on his green hat. He wore a handsome satin cloak and his rapier was hung in a stiff taffeta baldric that sparkled with jewels. They were not the shabby clothes of the informer that Luis had seen him wearing in Mexico City.

Toribio was crossing the camp somewhat ahead of Luis and did not recognize him till he was almost past. He stopped and turned. Luis kept walking till he was two feet from the man. Toribio revealed no surprise. The shadowy pits of the smallpox scars looked like some unwholesome corrosion on his face.

"I must admire your tenacity," he said. "Most men would be ashamed to return to their people in such a costume."

There was something strange about the man. His voice had a hollow, dead sound. There was no emotion in it. There was no expression on his face. Luis remembered the hunger in Toribio's eyes. He could not see it. His own emotions were too chaotic to analyze it or understand it or even wonder about. He was filled with a return of the sickness and outrage he had known when Barbara told him about the Condesa. Had this man done it? An ache filled his hands. If he only knew for certain. He thought he was capable of killing the man with his bare hands if he knew for certain.

"What about the Condesa?" he asked.

"What about Matarife?" Toribio asked.

"You sent him into it," Luis said. "Did you send the Condesa into it?"

"You know who sent her into it. They told me you gave a complete denunciation of her."

Luis flushed. His throat closed up, a thickness, a pressure that made it hard to speak. "It was months later. I gave them nothing they did not already have—" He broke off. He made an inarticulate sound. "Someday I am going to find out, Toribio. Sooner or later I am going to find out—"

"I do not have to wait that long," Toribio said. "I already know who is responsible for Matarife. You are going to make a mistake, señor. One day, tomorrow, or a month from now, you are going to make one little mistake. I will be waiting."

"You will wait a long time. Do you think the Gallegos' will let you put me back in Zarate's hands?"

Toribio looked at the yellow holy sack. "I do not mean that kind of mistake," he said.

CHAPTER FORTY-SEVEN

LUIS spent most of his time on the trip back outriding or scouting or night-herding. It gave him little chance to see either Barbara or Toribio. During the brief periods that he was in camp Barbara avoided him.

He wanted to talk with her again. Yet what good would it do? Her sudden appearance renewed the miserable confusion he had known in Mexico City. Kashana seemed very far away again, a dream figure in another life. Yet he remembered a time when he had wanted her, vividly, completely, without any doubts. Could a man's needs change? Could time and distance make that much difference?

It was not until the caravan got back to El Paso that Luis heard why Toribio had come. He was to be the new sheriff of the Inquisition for the province of New Mexico. The incumbent had been accused of accepting a bribe to let a denounced illuminist escape, and was to answer the charge in Mexico City. Luis had no doubt that the Gallegos' were involved at both ends. It would not be hard for the Marqués to arrange the bribery charge. And Don Gómez had already shown his power with the Tribunal. And their protégé once more occupied a key position in the provincial heirarchy.

The new colonists settled at San Lorenzo. Barbara and her maid, Josefina, moved in with the Artiagas. Juana Artiaga had served Barbara's uncle, Don Celso, in Santa Fe, and she welcomed Barbara as one of the family.

Within a few days Luis was once more riding with a squad, this time under Captain Hurtado, to recruit colonists from Fresnillo. The response was meager. Despite Hurtado's work, he had brought in only twenty-seven new families by the end of summer. Luis went on a last ride to Sombrerete and returned to San Lorenzo on September 20. As he rode into the square with the pitiful handful of colonists they had managed to gather he saw a dusty crowd gathered around a crier. The man was reading a proclamation by Vargas that had been posted on the wall of the *cabildo*.

". . . the settlers are residents and natives of the said kingdom, whom, in virtue of another cited command, I require and summon . . . to go to populate another kingdom where I shall supply them with meat, maize, and wheat . . . and likewise for their transference I shall transport and keep them in the greater part, loading in the wagons the women and children. . . . Likewise I shall assist them in the repair of their nakedness and anything more I can possibly do. . . . I shall give them in the other kingdom their lands, sites, and haciendas which they had and left at the time of the uprising of the nations of the other kingdom, also extending to them the privileges, honors, and prominences which as such conquerors of His Majesty (may God spare him) may concede and grant through his royal name."

At El Paso, Luis found that preparations were already under way for the *entrada*. Vargas could delay no longer. He had run out of money again, did not have half the troops he needed, and was bitterly disappointed at his failure to get more colonists. The viceroy had promised further help and had written that sixty-seven additional families were on their way from Mexico City. But Vargas was at the end of his patience. If he waited any longer it would be winter and the entrance would have to be put off till next year.

On October 4, 1693, the caravan assembled at the Pass. Eight hundred colonists, a hundred soldiers, scores of Indian allies, eighteen friars. Three carts for the brass cannon, eighteen rumbling wagons loaded with supplies, a thousand mules and two thousand horses and nine hundred cattle. Nobles and peasants, convicts and mercenaries, farmers and vagabonds, gentlewomen and half-breed Indians, Luis Ribera in his yellow holy sack and Toribio Quintano in his green hat and the barefoot superintendent in his rough blue robe and a French renegade who had murdered La Salle on some distant prairie.

At three in the afternoon they left the Guadalupe mission to the sound of buccinal music and flags fluttering at lance tips. Luis was assigned to the cattle guard. They rode with the herd five leagues ahead of the colonists to break trail for the main caravan. One by one they passed the familiar names, Salineta, Estero Largo, Yerba del Manso,

the camp sites along the Royal Highway that had been known to the
Spaniards almost a hundred years now.

Riding with the herd ahead of the main column, Luis had little
chance for contact with Toribio or Barbara. On October 22 a halt was
called at San Diego de Tesuque, the last *paraje* before the Journey of
the Dead Man. The herd was held there until the rest of the caravan
caught up. As soon as camp was pitched Luis was asked to see General
Vargas.

It seemed to Luis that time had stood still. He had ridden through
this same camp thirteen years ago. There were the same animals bray-
ing and whinnying and kicking up the choking clouds of yellow dust,
the same dusty faces, dull and gaping with exhaustion, the same weary
people sprawled beneath the same halted wagons or beginning to
gather in long lines at the cook-fires. He dismounted before the general's tent of heavy Michoacan cloth, pitched at some distance from
the confusion of the main camp. Beside the tent was the cart devised
especially to carry Vargas's patron saint, Our Lady of Conquest. A sentry announced Luis and he was told to enter.

Candlelight made a yellow glow against the tent. The father president, Salvador de San Antonio, knelt beside Vargas, who lay on his
pallet. The general's face was pale, gleaming with sweat. His usually
brilliant eyes were filmed and feverish.

"You will have to put up with me, *señor*," he told Luis. "I am afraid
I caught the chills in the river crossing. I wanted to know how you
fared with Corporal Francisco Alaya."

"I can take care of myself," Luis said. "It is the cattle you should
worry about."

"Explain."

"Alaya is driving them too hard and too dry and then letting them
bloat at the water holes. Half a dozen died before Roblero, and I have
seen too many others with colic."

"Alaya reported no deaths."

Luis hated to be a bearer of tales, but he knew Vargas was faced
with too many insidious threats to split moral hairs. "It is my opinion
that Alaya should not be given such responsibility, Excellency. In Santa
Fe he worked sometimes as a sheepherder for the Marqués de Gallegos."

The priest looked sharply at Luis. Candlelight caught silvery glints
in the ragged gray hair fringing his bald, yellowish dome. His snuff-
colored cheeks were dry and rutted as the desert in which he had spent

his life, and the wisdom in his piercing eyes was at once beneficent and shrewd.

The sentry pushed aside a tent flap and spoke from behind Luis. "Your Excellency, a group of your captains is assembled outside. They ask an audience."

Vargas muttered something beneath his breath. He wiped at his face with a lace-fringed Rouen handkerchief, sodden and soiled with his sweat. Then he sighed heavily and lifted an elbow.

"For favor, Señor Ribera. This tent will not hold all of them."

Luis took his elbow and helped Vargas up. He could feel that the man was shaking. Vargas closed his eyes, and his lips compressed to a gray line. He leaned heavily on Luis. The curious sallowness of his face gave him the look of jaundice. He gathered himself, freed his elbow, and walked outside.

It was a large group. There was something ominous about its silence. Luis could see that all the captains were there. Roque Madrid, José Arias, Antonio Jorge, Lazaro Misquia, Rafael Jiron, Juan Godoy—it was like a roll call of the old *encomenderos*. It was hard to believe that most of them came from noble houses, had once possessed estates so vast they had been unsure of the boundaries. They looked more like a ragged group of tough mercenaries. None was dressed as handsomely as Vargas. Most had suits of leather or buckskin, chalky at the elbows and knees from age and use. If a man wore a cloak it was faded and patched, lifted behind like a tattered peacock's tail. Beneath the cloaks the cuirasses were tarnished, and every morion bore the dents and scars of past battles. Their faces were hard, unyielding, darkened by a lifetime in this upland sun. Roque Madrid with his cavalier handsomeness gone to jowl and pate, Godoy with a patch over his left eye, Antonio Jorge with a scar on his cheek like a puckered purse mouth.

Their cloaks rustled softly. Their armor clanked. The Marqués de Gallegos stepped forward. Beneath the rim of his cabasset the edges of his powdered wig were chalk-white against his dark face. A nervous tic made his cheek flutter as he spoke.

"For favor, Excellency, we have come to make a petition."

"Make it, Don Desidero."

The Marqués unrolled a stiff piece of paper, his fingers quick and spiteful as an old maid's. He began to read in his nasal, lisping Castilian.

"The captains of the army, the corporation, magistrates and councilmen of the *villa* of Santa Fe, who are today at the camp site called San Diego de Tesuque, in the name of all the inhabitants residing in the province of New Mexico and its districts and jurisdictions, appear before Your Excellency in form of supplication, and as may best suit the rights of the community. We do hereby appeal and contend that when Don Juan Onate colonized New Mexico in 1598 he made a contract with the viceroy, approved by the Crown, which gave him the right to dispense *encomienda* through three generations. Many of us, as the third generation, still possess title to those *encomiendas*. It is therefore our contention that the promise of privileges extended to us in the proclamation of September 20, 1693, has not been fulfilled."

"The proclamation," Vargas said, "merely promised you privileges and honors which the king might concede and grant through his royal name. Nothing was mentioned of *encomienda*. The proclamation was superseded by a far earlier decree of the Crown, to which you were all made privy. This decree was very explicit that by sharing in this campaign you earn the title of *reconquistadores*, your houses and lands should be returned to you—but no *encomienda* lost in 1680 shall be recovered, either by you or your heirs. No Spaniard is to regain his old right of annual tribute from an allotted number of subjugated Indians."

The Marqués went on reading as though Vargas had not interrupted. "Be it known that there is no article in any royal decree specifically revoking the Onate contract. It is our contention that this invalidates any ruling which denies us our *encomiendas*. It is our further contention that even though we do not accept the validity of the said decree, by its very wording it allows us to retain our grants. It states that no *encomienda* lost in 1680 shall be recovered. We submit that we did not lose our *encomiendas*. The land and the people are still there. The decree recognizes this in restoring our estates."

Vargas swayed slightly. "It seems we put different interpretations on this decree, my good Marqués."

Vargas must have realized the trap he had walked into as soon as he spoke. Luis saw his back stiffen. The Marqués squinted his eyes.

"Then the captain general admits that it is his interpretation and not the decree itself which denies us our privileges. In such a case, is it not your legal duty to put it to a vote before your captains and the corporation?"

Vargas did not try to hide the contempt in his face for such sophistry. Luis was standing close enough to see the tremor shake the general's body. He wondered if it were weakness or sheer outrage.

Vargas said, "A corporation may have been formed, *señores*, but you are still under military rule. As such you are all subject to the final authority of your captain general."

There was a stir among the men. With tense, nervous movements, the Marqués rolled up the petition. The stiff paper made a mocking crackle.

"We have decided we cannot go on until this is decided."

Vargas did not show the violent reaction Luis had expected. He seemed to have trouble holding his head up, and his eyes looked heavy-lidded, sleepy.

"I will discuss it with my Secretary of War. If necessary we will request a clarification from the viceroy."

The Marqués tugged at his cloak. "By that time it will be winter."

"Then we will wait till winter. Is there anything else?"

The men stirred uncertainly. Luis looked at Roque Madrid. The captain flushed and looked at the ground. The Marqués squinted. The nervous tic made a flutter in his cheek. With a quick motion he stuck the scroll out to Antonio Valverde, the Secretary of Government and War, who accepted it without comment. The Marqués turned and stalked off. He had an agitated, bridling stride, like a spooky horse ready to shy at the first puff of wind. The captains drifted after him, silent, self-conscious.

Luis was watching Vargas. The man was sweating heavily, and his jaw was clamped with the intense concentration of holding himself on his feet. It made hard ridges of muscle in his yellow cheeks. The Marqués could not have chosen a better time for his first attack, Luis thought. And he had the same sinking disappointment he had known when Vargas had allowed the Marqués to defy him at the Pass.

Vargas swayed and Luis caught his arm. Vargas saw the expression in Luis's face. His heavy-lidded eyes widened, and a feverish brightness glowed through their dull film for a moment.

"Would we have any reconquest if I put all my captains in irons?" Vargas asked acidly.

Luis did not answer. It was the closest Vargas had ever come to revealing his motives. Luis understood his dilemma. Yet he still could not help a sense of creeping disillusionment. It was too reminiscent of the blunders Otermin had made, too much like the vacillation and procrastination which had brought disaster on him.

"Sooner or later you will have to quit fencing with the Marqués de Gallegos," Luis said. "It would be dangerous to let him choose the time and place."

Vargas took a deep breath. "On the contrary, Señor Ribera . . . the

Marqués may think it is his time and his place, but it will be I who have done the choosing." The general's head began to sink. He jerked it up, eyes blank, like a man suddenly awakened. His teeth chattered uncontrollably.

"You should lie down, Excellency."

Vargas gripped Luis's arm tightly. He seemed to gather himself, speaking and thinking with great difficulty. "First . . . I did not see . . . I did not see the captain of the colonists in this group. What is his name?"

"Hurtado. I do not think he has been disaffected yet."

Vargas began to shake. "It was he who put you in the squad commanded by the Marqués at El Paso."

"At the time I suspected him," Luis said. "Now I think it was simply a mistake. He did not understand the situation."

"And the colonists—has the good Marqués infected them?"

"I have no doubt he has men at work among them. But I think you can still count on them."

"Just so. Fetch your Captain Hurtado. I will order his colonists across the Jornada first. Does not Captain Madrid have a family with the colonists?"

"And many of the other captains."

"Just so." Vargas was shaking uncontrollably now and the sweat was pouring off his face. "We will see how long the *encomenderos* can sit here with the rest of their people moving north. We will see if the Marqués can really give the glory of retaking Santa Fe to the peasants he despises."

CHAPTER FORTY-EIGHT

BEFORE dawn the caravan moved out of San Diego. Barbara de Cárdenas walked with her maid behind one of the creaking wagons. There had been a rumor of a clash between General Vargas and some of his captains over the question of *encomienda*. Before the train was out of camp a group of the old *encomenderos* appeared at its head in an argument with Captain Hurtado. They were apparently trying to halt the march, but Hurtado would not do anything without direct orders from Vargas.

Some of the captains took their families out of line. But the common soldiers who had wives and children in the column were under Hurtado's command, and their people remained. Then Antonio Jorge and Lazaro Misquia and some of the other captains rode among the colonists and tried to get them to return to camp. But the people were indifferent to them. Andres Artiaga expressed the feeling of all the peasants.

"What do we care whether they get back their *encomiendas* or not? Will it make any difference to us? The peon never got anything out of the system. He would be better off without it. I have waited thirteen years to get back, Barbara, and I am not going to give it up now just because the *hidalgos* are as greedy as ever."

The column moved on, and the frustrated captains finally dropped behind, disappearing in the murk of dawn. Plodding behind the wagon, her shawl across her face to keep out the dust, Barbara began thinking about Luis again. It seemed she could think of nothing else. She knew it was pointless to let it torture her, but she could not drive it from her mind.

Luis's confession of his marriage to Kashana had been a stunning blow. It had left Barbara completely at a loss. That night after Luis had told her, still seething with bitterness and humiliation, she had tried to decide her course. The alternatives had whirled through her mind—the Cárdenas family in Spain, Doña Ramona's invitation to live with her in Peru, even a convent.

But something in her had rebelled. The independence she had known was rooted too deeply. She could not subject herself to the bondage and the blind authority implicit in any such return. Was Luis right? Would she have come to New Mexico even if she had not thought she was joining him? He was only echoing her own thoughts. Something had been calling her back long before she knew Luis was alive. She remembered the restlessness in Mexico City, the dissatisfaction, the boredom.

As the cruel gateway to New Mexico took shape before the marching column the forces that had been at work within her for thirteen years seemed to take focus. It was as though she saw the land through new eyes, loving its overwhelming savagery as well as its limited goodness. She could understand the passion of a *penitente* now, dreading the suffering to which he returned, yet drawn irresistibly by the ecstasy it gave him.

Barbara had thought that this late in the year the heat would not be so unbearable. Yet during the noon hours the Mameluke bits and bronze shoe stirrups and metal cuirasses were too hot to touch. And at night it grew so bitterly cold that a man froze to death in the first camp north of San Diego.

For such a host, facing the eight or nine days of dry desert, there was no way of carrying more than a bare minimum of water. At the Alivio *paraje* Captain Hurtado prohibited the use of water for cooking. At the Perillo camp site the supply had diminished so alarmingly that everyone was rationed a pint of drinking water a day. The wagons were limited to freight, and only the sick or the maimed or the very aged could find a place to ride. The rest walked.

At Cruz de Aleman a woman of sixty died. They said it was her age. Barbara knew it was exhaustion and exposure and thirst.

North of the Penuelas camp site the landmarks began to appear. Barbara visited them like shrines. She counted them like beads on a rosary. She passed the spot where she had given the Condesa water. She found her mother's headstone still lying in the little graveyard at

Cross of Anaya, and she knelt for a long time in the pale blue twilight and prayed and asked for guidance. At Las Tusas was the lava flow where the Condesa had given Barbara strips from her blanket to wind about her bloody feet. North of the lava flow she passed the spot where the Condesa had shamed Barbara into giving her mother her place in the cart.

By the end of the Jornada thirty people had died from hunger and exposure, and they were out of food and water. They camped at the ruined hacienda of Luis Lopez. A few Indians visited them from the inhabited *pueblos* upriver, and the Spaniards sold them horses and even arms for some grain and wheat. There was not much to be had, however, as a plague of locusts had recently attacked the Indian grain fields.

Juana Artiaga was sick from the harrowing march, and Barbara prepared the supper for the family that night. The *metate* was placed at an angle in the crude box. Into the hollowed grinding stone the corn was poured. On her knees Barbara ground the corn in the *metate* with the stone *mano* held in her hand. Wrapped in a blanket and seated against a wagon wheel, Juana clucked her tongue at Barbara.

"Not so hard, little one. You will grind half the *mano* off into the corn."

Barbara was flushed and breathing hard. "Can it be helped? Mother used to say everybody eats a *metate* and four *manos* in their lifetime."

"The truth." Juana sighed. "I would give my Manila shawl for a stone hard enough to keep sand out of the *tortillas*."

"I must learn, Juana. I must grow strong and learn it all. It is different now, you know. I am not a great lady any longer."

"You would be a great lady if you worked in the fields all your life. Do not worry, Barbara. You will learn how to live in this country . . . if they give you the chance."

Something in the woman's voice made Barbara look at her. Juana was looking toward one of the campfires. Her husband, Andres Artiaga, was squatting around the blaze with half a dozen others. Barbara recognized Francisco de la Mora and the Frenchman, Jean L'Archeveque.

"That troublemaker," she said. "What is your husband doing with him?"

"There has been bad talk. The people say General Vargas had no right to send us ahead without the protection of all the soldiers. They say he planned the entrance badly—not enough troops, not enough food or water——"

"Nobody has ever solved the water problem on the Jornada," Barbara said. "And how could he get any more food without money?"

"Did not the viceroy give Vargas over forty thousand pesos? They say he only spent seven thousand on us and kept the rest for himself."

"Pity of God! Do you know what it costs to supply a caravan like this? How much do you think they charged him in Parral for those wagons? Enough corn to feed a thousand people all winter and seed the land next year—what kind of a fortune do you think that cost? And the horses, and the cattle, and the soldiers— Do you realize his treasury was so empty that he had to advance each soldier a hundred and fifty pesos out of his own pocket to get them paid?"

Juana sighed. "I only say what I hear, Barbara. The general cannot seem to control his captains. The Marqués de Gallegos defies him openly. The people say that perhaps the Marqués is right—perhaps Vargas is too weak a man for the job. Maria de la Cruz says her husband is talking of desertion . . ."

Barbara looked again at the men around the fire. Captain Hurtado should be warned. After the meal she went to his quarters. He was staying with some of the other officers in the ruins of the house that had once belonged to Luis Lopez. As she approached the crumbling, fire-blackened walls, she saw two men talking near the sentry at the gate. One was Hurtado. The other wore a tattered holy sack.

Barbara stopped. There was a little prickling across her scalp, a little needling that spread quickly into her face. There it became a flush. She could feel its heat in her face. A heat that moved through her whole body. But she was cold. She shivered violently, and when she pulled her shawl tight she could feel the frantic flutter of her heart against her ribs.

Stupid to feel this way. Stupid. It was all over now. She hated him. She did not want to talk with him.

No, she did not hate him. She did not know what she felt. That was stupid too. She had to stop going around in circles. She remembered how long she had hated him after that first time he had humiliated her in Santa Fe thirteen years ago. She could not be that childish about it now. He was not really to blame. The truth. In Mexico City, if he had suspected how she felt about him, he surely would have told her about Kashana. He had been given no chance to mention it. On his first visit to her house he had just started telling her of his life on Acoma when Vargas arrived. And after Vargas left they had quarreled. And the second time the Holy Office had interrupted them.

The second time he had kissed her.

She flushed again at the thought. How naïve he must think her. A man had kissed her and she had chased him across half the New World. Humiliation made her sick. It was not Luis she hated. It was herself.

Her eyes were still fixed on him. There was implicit respect in the tone of his voice and in the way he stood as he talked with Hurtado. It made her think how much he had changed. With a touch of nostalgia she remembered the hotheaded young rebel of Santa Fe.

Now he no longer seemed to take delight in ignoring the flowery amenities of greeting or parting. He had begun to adopt some of the painstaking formalities observed by the Spaniard in the smallest detail of his life. He called Vargas Excellency. He bowed and removed his hat to Father Antonio. If he disagreed with one of the corporation he did not embarrass everyone with a hotheaded denunciation before the whole town——

She bit her lip. Such thoughts were too possessive. They were too fond and too possessive, like those of a . . . a lover . . . or a wife.

Luis turned to leave Hurtado. He saw Barbara. He hesitated, then crossed to her. Her hands began to ache. She realized how tightly she had been gripping the shawl.

The tatters of his patched, faded holy sack flapped against his bare calves. Beneath the bizarre garment he wore only a rough shirt and rawhide knee breeches.

Pobrecito, she thought, is he not frozen?

He stopped before her, looking very tall and angular and awkward. He had cut off his thorny beard and had left only a short goatee, streaked with gray. He took off his coronet. He no longer showed any self-consciousness about it. He bowed gravely.

"*Buenas tardes, le de Dios, señorita.*"

"God give them good to you," she murmured.

She saw that he was tying his hair in a queue once more. It was gray at the temples but still black on top. Only thirty-five and so much gray, she thought.

"You were with Vargas," she said. "Does this mean he has rejoined us?"

"I came with the cattle. The captains and remaining soldiers are right behind. They only stayed at San Diego two days after you left. Then they realized how cowardly it would seem—the captains and most of the troops staying behind while the women and children went ahead. There are too many good soldiers among those old *encomenderos* to let such a story get back to the Crown."

They had been talking awkwardly, self-consciously, glancing at each other, quickly looking away. Luis flushed.

"I wish you would not feel bitter, Barbara. I feel guilty and I wish I could undo it in some way, but you must know I did not intend it."

"I am trying not to feel bitter," she said. "I will tell you what I am trying to feel. I am trying to accept it realistically. I am trying to see you as just a man now, with nothing to separate you from all the other men I see every day, except perhaps that we have been through so much together, the things that happened in Santa Fe and Mexico City, and that we could not forget even if we wanted to, and when we meet I do not want to hold anything against you simply because something did not work out, and we should be able to talk about it like two friends, without embarrassment."

"I like that," he said. "Without embarrassment."

"Let us put ourselves to the test, then. Tell me about . . . about Kashana. Was she a good wife?"

"In many ways."

"Were there children?"

"Two boys."

"You must look forward to seeing them."

"I do. I have wanted to go hunting with them. I think a lot about hunting with them. I even dream about it. My father never went hunting with me."

"Will you live in Santa Fe?"

"Oh yes."

"Will she . . . will Kashana want to?"

He looked down at the penitent's crown, turning it in his hands. She remembered when it had been hard to tell whether he was angry or amused. There had been something about the shape of his face . . . but it had changed now, or was not so distinct. Perhaps it was the beard, or the receding hair, or age. It was easy to see that he was disturbed, and there was no humor in it.

"I am sorry," she said. "Perhaps we have talked enough about personal things the first time. There is something else . . ."

She told him about the feeling among the colonists, Francisco de la Mora and Artiaga and the others who were talking of desertion.

"Perhaps they have a point," he said.

"Luis, surely you do not still doubt Vargas?"

"Did you hear how he walked unarmed into Santa Fe during the first entrance?" he asked. "It almost convinced me . . ."

"Luis——"

"You must know how I felt when I first heard we were going back without *encomienda*. Now I know it was merely a matter of policy with Vargas, rather than principle. He is not so far removed from the Marqués de Gallegos as we would like to think. The slaves he owns, the *encomienda* he still holds in Mexico——"

"He is a man of his times, Luis. Is it not enough that he sees the necessity of going back without the old systems of labor—whether it is policy with him or principle?"

He looked past her into the night for a long time. Then he said, "I came with the advance guard. Vargas may not get here till tomorrow. I will tell him about Francisco de la Mora and the talk of deserting. But there is no proof of anything. You cannot put a man in irons for grumbling. Our good general will probably be as helpless with this as he was with the captains." He bowed. "That you go with God, *señorita.*"

CHAPTER FORTY-NINE

GENERAL VARGAS was over his fever when he joined the settlers at Luis Lopez. The weather was turning bad. The column moved upriver against a bitter attack of frost and wind and snow. In four days they only made sixteen leagues. On the twelfth Vargas sent two Tanos Indians with a letter and a rosary to each of five governors in the northern villages, asking them to meet the general at the ruined hacienda of Cristobal Anaya.

The next day Vargas and fifty soldiers left the line of march and crossed the river to the pueblo San Felipe. The Indians made friendly overtures, and Mass was said and many Indians baptized. Reassured of allegiance, Vargas returned to his column. On the fifteenth the Spaniards reached Cristobal Anaya. On the next afternoon the five governors arrived from the north bearing the rosaries Vargas had sent them. Their leader was Tupatu.

He had long been a great man among the Indians and commanded the respect of both the Spaniards and his own people. He was from Pecuris and had been governor of that large village at the time of the revolt, but now he was governor of San Juan. The mantle of leadership had fallen on his shoulders with Po-pe's death, and last year Vargas had appointed him governor of all the Pueblos. He appeared on a horse Vargas had given him then, a handsome *moro*, blue as a Toledo blade. He was a big, imposing man in his middle fifties, wearing a mother-of-pearl shell as a crown on his head and dressed in the Spanish style with a cuirass and knee breeches of black deerskin. He acted as spokesman for the five governors.

He said that things were bad. They were not good. He said that things had changed since last year. Many villages now did not want to admit the Spaniards. They wanted war. They did not want peace. He said that people were troubled. People said Vargas did not mean to keep the promises he made last year. He did not mean to give pardon to people. Vargas meant to execute all the leaders of people who fought in the war thirteen years ago. For every Spanish child killed in the war Vargas would behead a child of people. Wherever a Spanish priest had died the village would be destroyed.

Vargas asked: Who said these things?

Pedro de Tapia, the Tano interpreter, said these things.

Vargas answered that Pedro de Tapia had lied and deceived them. Vargas said that if Tupatu found Pedro de Tapia he was to bring the traitor to Vargas who would prove that Tapia lied and would then execute him. If Vargas had meant to execute the leaders of people would he not already have done so at San Felipe? Antonio Malacate was there, and the war chief Sebastian of Jemez. They were not executed. They were pardoned. They were given absolution. Their children were not beheaded. Their children were baptized. Spaniards became their godfathers. There were prayers and rejoicing. And if Tupatu feared execution why had he presented himself thus, with so few followers and so poorly armed?

Because Tupatu trusted the word of Diego de Vargas.

Then, Vargas said, Tupatu should be living proof of that word. If Vargas wished to execute them he surely could do it now. When Tupatu returned to Santa Fe unharmed, pardoned, and absolved, would not people believe Vargas?

It would be a strong sign, Tupatu said. But many would still waver. There was Juan Ye.

Vargas was reminded that Juan Ye was suspected of killing Fray Bernal, the superintendent of the missions, in the revolt.

Tupatu said there was no proof. It was just a thing the Spaniards said.

Then Juan Ye should be given fair judgment, Vargas said. If there were no witnesses who saw the deed and no other proof and if Juan Ye solemnly denied it in the presence of the Holy Cross he could not be condemned. If Juan Ye was innocent he would surely be pardoned.

The five governors were pleased and said they would carry these fine promises back to Santa Fe.

One of the men was Domingo, from Tesuque. When Luis had known

him he was the finest maker of *katsina* masks of all the Tewas. Now
he was the governor of Tesuque.

Luis asked him about Bigotes.

The Mustaches? Domingo smiled at memory of the rogue. No, he
had not seen Bigotes in many winters. Bigotes had not been at Tesuque
for a long time. All Domingo knew was what he heard from a Taos
hunter. The Taos hunter had told Domingo that Bigotes was dead.

It was bitterly cold that night in the Spanish camp. The shivering
colonists sat huddled in their blankets as close to the campfires as they
could get. Toribio Quintano did not join them.

He sat alone in the darkness. His back was against the crumbling
remains of what had once been the west wall of the Anaya house.
The handsome cloak with which Don Gómez had outfitted him in
Mexico City was now shabby and tattered with travel. His legs were
crossed and in his lap sat the plate, little more than a slab of wood,
upon which he had heaped his ration of corn and beans and meat.

He was not eating.

He was remembering a time when none of his hungers could be
assuaged. Food and drink and women and ambition had been the ap-
petites that gnawed him during the day and made so many nights
sleepless. That had been the time when he resented the chinks in his
armor, when he had thought that a man's strength could lie only in
standing completely alone, devoid of feeling. Well, the chinks were
gone now. He stood alone.

*You have a disease inside you. It is that you do not believe in any-
thing. It will eat away at you from the inside until there is only a shell
left, and then that will crumble.*

He closed his eyes. He remembered when she had said that. How
did she know? What could the Condesa have known about his beliefs?
He believed in himself. He believed that the blood of Spain ran in his
veins and that he was as good as any *hidalgo* and that someday he
would be Don Toribio Quintano, sheriff of the Inquisition in Mexico
City.

Why had the Condesa been so stupid? They would not have burned
her. They did not burn Luis Ribera, did they? Penance, perhaps. The
sanbenito and the penitential psalms. Perhaps even banishment. But
certainly not death.

He saw the eyes.

He opened his eyes quickly and looked around, seeing the familiar
glow of campfires, the shadowy silhouettes of the shivering people. He

should have known better than to close his eyes. He always saw the eyes then. He saw them when he slept too. He dreamed of them. Matarife's eyes, hurt, accusing, because he had not gotten a priest.

Chingada! Why must it haunt him so? He should exult that they were gone. They had been his weaknesses. The Condesa and Matarife. Now there were no chinks in his armor. He could never be hurt again.

He saw a man picking his way through the ruins. He had his sword held against his side, beneath his cloak, so that it would not hold the cloak out behind and let in the cold air. He stopped above Toribio. He had not been long out of the saddle, and the nitrogen pungence of a horse still clung to his boots. It was the Marqués de Gallegos.

"You told me once," he said, "that a man who had known real starvation could never get enough food."

Toribio glanced down at his untouched food. The Marqués tugged restlessly at his cloak.

"Are you ill?" he asked.

"I am never ill," Toribio said.

"You have been acting strangely these last weeks. It seems to me you have lost quite a bit of weight. You do not hear sometimes when you are spoken to. Even the commissioner has commented upon it."

"I am touched by your concern."

"My concern is only that of a man whose tool has grown dull, Toribio. If he cannot sharpen it again he discards it."

The Marqués watched him narrowly, waiting. When Toribio made no move the Marqués looked down at his boots and stamped them to restore circulation in his feet. He could never seem to remain still very long. He circled Toribio restlessly. Little spasms of expression kept altering his face.

"Pedro de Tapia sent word by an Indian that he would meet us at Santo Domingo tonight," the Marqués said. "But Vargas has called a council of his captains. I would be missed. You must go to Santo Domingo alone."

Toribio did not answer. He mistrusted this arrangement with Pedro de Tapia. The Indian had contacted the Marqués the year before when the Marqués had come north on the first entrance with Vargas. Tapia had made certain overtures. He protested that he had always been loyal, always working in Spanish interests. It was simply a question of which Spanish master he chose to serve. Tapia had seen the jealousy and hatred the Marqués bore Vargas. Could not some arrangement be made? If it happened that Vargas failed in the conquest and the Marqués were appointed captain general in his place, would not the Marqués be in a position to reward a man who had been instrumental in the downfall of Vargas?

"Apparently Pedro de Tapia has kept his bargain," the Marqués told Toribio. "From what Tupatu said, Tapia's talk has swung half the villages against us. Now it must become more than talk. The Indians must have final proof that Vargas has lied to them. You will tell Tapia that the proof will come from Vargas himself. They will see Vargas break every promise he has made."

"How can you be sure?"

"We will make it sure. They will find babies beheaded. They will see the leaders in the revolt die. You know how Tupatu is respected by them. Can you imagine their outrage when he is killed? You know what an exalted position Juan Ye holds among them. Can you conceive of their fury when he is executed for the murder of Fray Bernal at Galisteo?"

"Vargas will never do that. There is no witness to the killing."

"We will produce a witness. Was not Pedro de Tapia himself at Galisteo?"

"He would not dare."

"You do not know the man, Toribio. He has always played both sides against the middle. He has always ridden with the winners. And now he thinks the Spaniards are the winners again. If the reward is big enough he will do anything."

"What reward is big enough to make him risk such a lie?"

"Tapia has long sought to be the governor of Pecos. With Juan Ye dead, who would stand in his way? It is what you will tell him tonight. Do this, and under Spanish jurisdiction Tapia will be governor of Pecos."

"What Spanish jurisdiction? If they rise up again we will be lucky to get back to El Paso alive."

"We will return. And when we do there will be a governor general in command who knows how to treat these beasts. Every warrior over thirty must have taken part in the revolt thirteen years ago. I will chop off their left hands. Each village will produce the men personally responsible for killing its priest. If they refuse the town will be razed, their fields sowed with salt, and every tenth person executed, man, woman or child. The captains shall be reinstated in their *encomiendas* and shall receive the full tribute of their Indians for every year that they were absent. Those families who cannot pay the tax will be sold into slavery."

The Marqués's eyes glowed and his mouth twitched spastically. Toribio studied the scarred, fanatical face. Somehow it was not the man's vicious need of revenge that disturbed him. He could understand that, in a way. His whole life had been a revenge. He was thinking that there were only a hundred Spanish soldiers. Otermin had possessed half again as many, and the walls of a city, and still the Indians had driven him out. How many Spaniards would die this time? Why should it bother him, the sight of a man betraying his own people for the sake of his personal ambitions?

"When you were an *encomendero*," Toribio said, "when you were the *alcalde* of the San Juan jurisdiction and lived up there in that big house with all the land you needed and all the people in the world to work for you, what did you want?"

The fixed look left the other man's eyes. He frowned at Toribio. He squinted nervously.

"Did you want to be governor?" Toribio asked.

"I gave it some thought."

"After that what would you want?"

The Marqués stared at Toribio suspiciously. His imperious nostrils were pinched and white.

"I am not being sarcastic," Toribio said. "I would really like to know. When you have everything, when you get everything you want, then what is there?"

"I do not know. I never really considered it." The Marqués stamped his boots, peering at Toribio curiously. Then he said, "You will go to Santo Domingo."

Toribio turned and walked toward the horse lines. He remembered his food, but he did not turn back. He could not feel hunger. He thought of the Marqués and his talk about discarding a dull tool, but he could not feel anger. He was alone and the night felt very big and very dark and very empty.

CHAPTER FIFTY

THE report that many villages had become hostile again made
Vargas realize that he could not by-pass the *pueblos* remaining between
him and Santa Fe. He did not want an army forming behind him and
falling on his rear. Much as he hated the delay, he knew he would have
to make a tour of the towns and test their temper and if possible
regain their allegiance.

Leaving the main body of Spaniards at Cristobal Anaya, he visited
Cochiti and Santa Ana and Sia and the mesa at Cerro Colorado and
Jemez. He found signs of growing suspicion and hostility everywhere
but was able to placate the Indians and reassure them of his intentions.

It took Vargas many days to consolidate his position. He returned
to find that on December 3 Francisco de la Mora and four other soldiers
had deserted, taking a hundred and eighteen of the best horses. With
them had gone Andres Artiaga and his wife Juana and many other
settlers.

It was a severe blow and Vargas knew he had to get his people on the
move before any more dissension weakened them further. Just beyond
Santo Domingo they ran into a blinding snow storm and had to make
camp at the ruined estate of Captain Roque Madrid, only two leagues
south of Santa Fe. When the storm had subsided a deputation of Indians came from Santa Fe, led by Domingo, the governor of Tesuque.
Domingo said that the promises Tupatu had carried from Vargas had
reassured people and the Tanos in Santa Fe were willing to let the
Spaniards enter their old capital in peace.

On December 16, 1693, near the noon hour, the Spaniards marched into the town they had left so long ago. The main body of colonists was camped on the snow-powdered plain south of Santa Fe. Vargas led a representative column of soldiers and settlers and priests into the capital for the ceremonies. Ahead appeared the familiar adobe buildings, so close to the earth in color and shape that they seemed like geometric mud banks standing beyond the shivering aspens on the banks of the miniature river. Behind the town the overwhelming mass of the Sangre de Cristos rose to the pale winter sky. On their slopes the bold white streaks of deep drifted canyons broke the solid black mantle of timber. High above was more snow, so white and glaring that it made the eyes water, splashed like a virgin's helmet on each peak.

General Vargas led the mounted column of his captains and the town corporation, followed by Father Salvador de San Antonio and his fifteen priests who chanted hymns as they walked. Luis rode near the standard-bearer, Don Bernardino Chavez, who bore the same royal colors Onate had carried when he first colonized New Mexico almost a hundred years before.

That first sight of the town came as a distinct shock to Luis. He had left a Spanish city. He was returning to an Indian *pueblo*.

Most of the buildings in the Analco were in ruins. Fire-blackened beams angled crazily skyward from crumbled walls in a charred and bitter reminder of the terror so long ago. The roof of San Miguel had fallen in. Cattle were corralled in the chapel's littered nave. The surrounding fields, once so green with Spanish wheat and melons and grapes, now were nothing but patches of gray winter weeds. The silvery threads of water were gone from the bottoms of the irrigation ditches and they were choked with debris.

As they crossed the river the frigid air carried the clink of accouterments ahead of them like the tinkle of a thousand distant sanctus bells. They climbed to the Alameda—the shaded trail that had once followed the high north bank of the Rio Santa Fe. Luis looked eastward till he saw the ruins of the house the Condesa had occupied. He touched his cross and murmured a prayer for her.

Ahead lay the city wall, breached in a score of places. The Indians were shadows moving among the ruins, peering at the Spaniards from behind heaps of adobe. Luis could not help touching the hilt of his sword. He saw tension in every bearded Spanish face about him.

Vargas rode through the broken wall, very tall and straight in his saddle, looking neither to right nor left. The column was among the ruins now. More Indians drifted through the rubble on either side.

They were wolf shapes in their buffalo robes and winter furs. They did not speak or come near. The only sound was the furtive rattle of their bare feet through the crumbling adobe.

The remains of the church of San Francisco appeared ahead. The roof had collapsed, leaving the nave open to the sky, and the bell towers had crumbled. Luis saw the shattered heap of adobe and burned beams that had once been the Ribera house. Beside it the Indians had erected one of their terraced communal houses.

Hundreds of Tanos thronged the plaza, the men on one side, the women on the other. Luis could see that beehive ovens studded the square behind them. A *kiva* had been built against the wall of the palace. The only thing that seemed to remain unchanged was the portal. The cedar posts still stood like a rank of age-silvered sentries, supporting the roof that formed the shadowy arcade all the way across the front of the palace.

A cross had been newly erected where the gibbet had once stood in the center of the plaza. Before it, waiting to greet Vargas, Luis saw a group of Indian *caciques* and governors. He recognized Domingo from Tesuque, and Tupatu, and Antonio Bolsas, who was now war captain for Santa Fe, and Joseph, its governor.

Vargas halted before them. He stepped off his horse, giving the signal for all the Spaniards to dismount. The soldiers formed two ranks, between which the friars marched barefooted to the cross. The Indians watched silently, a dark sea of impassive faces, the opaque glitter of their eyes fixed on Vargas. Father Antonio gave the order for all to kneel. The Te Deum was sung. The solemn ceremony was concluded with the Litany of Our Lady.

When the litany was finished the people stood again. Luis saw the Indians nearby staring at his faded yellow holy sack and his bizarre crown. Curiosity was in their faces, and awe. He could not help smiling. He bet himself a *peso* that they thought he was part of the show and would perform a dance for them.

In a long speech the general officially restored the spiritual command of the province to the priests. He restored the possession of the town to the corporation, saying that they should give him, the said captain general and governor, testimonials of having taken the same. Finally he spoke to the Indians. He repeated what their lord the king had sent on the news of their surrender last year. He said that with the report of their surrender all the king's displeasure had vanished and he would call them again his children, and for that reason he had sent many priests in order that they might be Christians as they were, and that likewise he sent the general with soldiers for the purpose of defending them against their enemies. He promised them that these were his sole objects in coming.

"In conclusion," Vargas said, "if you have among you any bad and malicious Indian, you should tie him up and bring him to me to ascertain the truth of what he has said, and in case of falsehood I will order his instant execution. In this way only can we live as brothers and be very happy."

There was a pause. It was hard for Luis to believe that such a vast crowd could be so utterly still. A little wind whispered from between the buildings and ruffled the general's cloak. The pale sun shimmered on his engraved cuirass.

Finally Tupatu turned and lifted an arm. The Indians gave way, forming a path through the midst to the palace gate. A pair of men dragged a struggling, protesting figure down the path. It was Pedro de Tapia.

His arms were tied behind his back. There was a smear of blood on his forehead. Sweat leaked like melted lard from the fat creases of his Mongoloid face. His rabbitskin robe was torn down the front to expose his stomach, naked and swollen as the belly of some obscene Buddha.

Tupatu said, "Last night the traitor was found and captured and I now deliver him up to you."

Tapia stumbled and the two men released him and allowed him to fall to his knees before Vargas. All the bracelets encircling his arms jingled and rattled as he struggled at the rawhide bindings.

"Good General, Your Excellency, most revered representative of His Most Holy Catholic Majesty, Carlos the Second, why should I be treated thus?" Spittle formed at the corners of Tapia's thick lips. He got to his feet with difficulty, fawning and bowing like a court fool. "I have been a loyal servant, I have only sought to serve the best interests of all, I have been accused falsely——"

"I have heard the lies you spread," Vargas said. "Where are the beheaded babies you promised? Where are the destroyed villages? I say now that if there are any leaders of the revolt who have not yet received their pardon and absolution they should step forward."

There was a stir in the crowd. For a moment Luis thought nobody would appear. Then Juan Ye stepped out.

Though he must have been in his fifties now his hair was still black, clubbed in a chongo behind his muscular neck. Stout, bowlegged, he had a limp that made him move like a gouty old man. He wore a claw necklace and a buffalo robe to the knees. It was full of bot holes and so old and rotten that it kept shedding tufts of hair that floated behind him like dark feathers in a wind. The robe was hung with many tiny bells from Mexico. They made an eerie tinkle as he walked.

He passed Pedro de Tapia and stood in the open, ten feet from Vargas. The voice of the Marqués de Gallegos broke the unnatural silence.

"How can you give pardon and absolution to the murderer of Fray Bernal?"

"There has been no proof of his guilt," Vargas said.

Luis saw Toribio talking earnestly with the father president. Fray Antonio turned to Vargas.

"I am told that there is a witness to the murder. I am told that Pedro de Tapia saw it."

Juan Ye looked at Tapia. His eyes glittered. The little bells on his robe made a copper clatter.

"Is this true?" Vargas asked Tapia. "Why did you not speak last year?"

Tapia smiled nervously. The fat moons of his cheeks seemed to swallow the slits of his eyes. Then he looked as though he would cry. He glanced fearfully over his shoulder at the Indians. A series of little hops took him nearer the Spaniards. He tilted his head to one side, fawning.

"Naturally, I feared reprisal," he said. "I wanted to be sure of protection—"

"A traitor asks protection?" Vargas said coldly.

"You must give him protection," the Marqués said. "Is not the crime of Juan Ye far greater than his?"

"I will give him nothing but the gibbet," Vargas said. "And that today instead of tomorrow if he does not answer immediately about Juan Ye."

The Marqués turned to Fray Antonio. "Then perhaps the good fathers will intercede. Here is one of your flock repenting and seeking absolution. Would Mother Church deny him the mercy she has promised?"

"The truth." Tapia licked thick lips, smiled nervously, bowed to the father president. "If I said General de Vargas did not mean to keep his promises I was merely repeating what hundreds of others were saying. Is it a crime to doubt a man until he has proven his integrity? Did not Tupatu himself doubt the general? Did he not express those doubts before all the captains at Cristobal Anaya? If I am to be executed for such words then must you not execute him also?"

There was an agitated movement among the priests. Their dusty robes stirred and settled. They whispered urgently to each other. The father president seemed oblivious to it. The pale winter sun made a yellow dome of his bald skull. He looked at Vargas.

"The man is right. Mother Church cannot discriminate in her mercy. If it is a capital crime to doubt you then some of your own people would face execution."

"If you show this traitor mercy then perhaps you will also show mercy to the murderer of Fray Bernal," Vargas said.

"And let the Indians think they can murder our priests at a whim?" the Marqués asked disgustedly.

"The truth," Fray Antonio said. "The crime of Juan Ye is of a different nature. Does not the Holy Office hand impenitents over to the secular arm when the sentence is death?"

The Marqués said, "If you do not make Juan Ye pay for this crime, General Vargas, you are sacrificing the life of every priest in this mission field on the altar of your stubbornness. What will happen if they see they can murder our priests without punishment? If you will not offer the witness protection then it is up to the Church."

It amazed Luis how moveless Vargas could remain, how cold and expressionless he could keep his face. Luis knew the anger and frustration that must be seething through him. It was the same kind of trap the Marqués had set for him when they had demanded a return of *encomienda* at San Diego. He would create bitter enmity by either choice. Luis knew a bitter disillusionment. He had watched Vargas walk, step by step, down the same path that Otermin had taken. This clash with the ecclesiastics was only one more repetition of the mistakes that had led to such a complete destruction of Spanish authority thirteen years before. When it became obvious that Vargas would not speak, the father president turned to Pedro de Tapia.

"In the name of the Most Holy Trinity, and the undivided Eternal Unity, Deity and Majesty, Father, Son, and Holy Spirit, I promise you the sanctuary of Mother Church, her mercy, and her protection."

Tapia's thick lips twitched spastically. Luis could not tell whether it was a smile or a grimace. The sweat had leaked into the Indian's eyes and the sting of it made him blink frantically. He sent a covert glance at Toribio, at the Marqués de Gallegos. He licked his lips.

"Yes," he said. "I saw Juan Ye kill Fray Bernal."

A startling roar swept from the horde of Indians. Fury made Juan Ye's face diabolical.

"It is a lie," he yelled. "The fat pig lies!"

The first lines of Indians surged toward Tapia. He scuttled into the Spanish ranks so hurriedly that he tripped and fell on his face at the father president's feet. Captain Madrid gave a shouted order to close up and the soldiers formed a cordon that held the Pueblos back. The Marqués de Gallegos pulled his sword and pointed it at Juan Ye.

"General de Vargas, I demand the arrest and execution of this murderer!"

Juan Ye shouted something in Tano and wheeled to plunge into the crowd.

"Get him," the Marqués shouted. "Sergeant Tellez, Captain Madrid —after him!"

"Stand your ground!" Vargas's voice pierced the din like a trumpet. "Not a man will move without my order."

It was obvious that any Spaniards sent into the crowd after Juan Ye would be torn to pieces. The Indians surged back and forth at the point of violence. Their voices made a roar that deafened Luis. The wild eddies of the throng threw the Spaniards back on their inner ranks and they had to close up tight. Tapia was on his knees, buffeted back and forth, and the father president had to hold him up.

Vargas raised both hands. The sight of them, empty of weapons, finally quieted the Indians. The captain general waited for the voices to die out. His face was a frigid mask that hid whatever lay inside.

"The matter of Juan Ye is not at an end. He will be judged fairly and will be given justice. In the meantime you are once again children of the church and vassals of the king. This is once more a Spanish villa. We will give you time to return to your villages. We will retire until the town can receive us."

CHAPTER FIFTY-ONE

THE Spaniards made their camp on a hill northwest of town. That night it was bitterly cold and a new snow storm swept out of the mountains. When Luis woke at dawn he was shivering violently and he saw that each soldier in the sleeping line beside him was half buried in a miniature drift. The people huddled in miserable circles around their breakfast fires, more interested in the feeble warmth than their food. Luis heard that two children had frozen to death during the night.

The Indians gave no indication of leaving Santa Fe during the following days. The colonists demanded that Vargas eject the Tanos by force if necessary, but the general knew his precarious position and wanted to avoid open warfare if possible. He requested corn for his destitute Spaniards. The Tanos gave him a hundred sacks. It was soon gone. He asked for more. The Indians refused.

The Indians said that Vargas should prove his promise of bringing the Christian religion to all by distributing the Franciscan priests among the *pueblos* as it had been done before the revolt. But the friars had been deeply offended by the general's apparent defense of the man they thought had murdered their former superintendent. They presented a formal protest against the distribution among the villages. They said that they were willing to sacrifice their lives if necessary for the Faith, but were unwilling to go rashly and unnecessarily to their deaths.

Vargas sent some of his Indian allies to Pecos to sound out Juan Ye. The governor of Pecos thought he had been betrayed and said that if the other villages attacked the Spaniards he would join them. He would not see Vargas, either in Pecos or in the Spanish camp. By the end of the week fifteen Spanish children had died of exposure and cold.

Through the trying days Luis cut wood in the mountains and labored at the flimsy brush shelters for the colonists and stood guard duty and fought frostbite and suffered hunger pains with the rest of them.

On the night of the twenty-third he was coming off guard duty when a soldier said the general wanted to see him. He wrapped his thin holy sack about him and climbed the slope through the deep fallen snow. He had wrapped strips of blanket around his feet, but they were so numb that no amount of stamping would bring back any feeling. Vargas was pacing between a fire and his Michoacan tent, a blanket about his shoulders. The general saw Luis shivering in his holy sack and called for his slave to get a blanket out of the tent. He put the blanket over Luis's shoulders himself and led him to the fire. The two of them stood as close to the blaze as possible, wreathed in the pungent smoke.

"Señorita Cárdenas told me that once I smelled the *enebro* I could never forget it," Vargas said.

"There are many things here one cannot forget, Excellency."

The general gazed silently into the flames. His face was usually a mask of precisely chiseled aristocracy that rarely revealed the man. But tonight there were cracks in the mask. The jeweled brilliance of the eyes was dulled by a silvery film. Luis wondered if his own eyes had looked as lifeless in the depths of his disillusionment. The lips appeared shriveled and gray, like the lips of a tired old man. Vargas roused himself with a distinct effort.

"As you know, Luis, some Tanos were among the Indian allies who came with us from El Paso. I left several in Santa Fe. They now tell me that the feeling in town has turned completely against us. This incident about Juan Yc was perhaps the turning point. The hostility is spreading to San Felipe and Sia and the other Keres villages. Word has been sent to Acoma also. Is it not the largest Keres town?"

"When I was at Acoma they could muster about four hundred warriors," Luis said.

"Just so. The feeling in Santa Fe is that Acoma will send its warriors and that they will tip the balance. All our work among the Keres villages will be destroyed. We will face a hostile army outside the capital as well as inside."

He paused. The disaster was plain to Luis. The Spaniards would be caught between three prongs—the Tanos in Santa Fe, Juan Ye and his Pecosenos on their east, the Keres on their west.

"If Acoma stayed out of it," Vargas asked, "would it neutralize the rest of the Keres?"

"The big towns have always been the keys. Without Acoma the Keres would lose half their fighting men. I think it would hold them back."

Vargas looked thoughtfully at Luis. They both knew what remained. Vargas could not afford to send any of his soldiers to Acoma.

"What do you propose to do about Juan Ye?" Luis asked.

For a moment he thought he saw irritation in the general's eyes. Vargas said, "The priests demand that I arrest him immediately. But I am sure that would precipitate open fighting. Do you believe Pedro de Tapia actually saw Juan Ye kill Father Bernal?"

"I would believe nothing Tapia said."

"My own feeling," Vargas said. "Tapia has tried to make too many deals with us before. It is unnatural that this has not come up till now. But Tapia has played a sly game. He knows I cannot violate the protection of the Church."

"Did you consider that the Marqués de Gallegos might be involved in this, Excellency?"

"I had not overlooked the possibility."

"Whatever undermines you works in their favor."

Vargas nodded. "I am trying to locate other Indians who were at Galisteo during the uprising. Their testimony might prove that Tapia lies."

"Juan Ye will not wait forever."

"You are right, Luis. Time is precious." Vargas glanced shrewdly at Luis. The film was gone from his eyes again. They glittered with a disturbing brilliance. "You could not do much traveling tonight, at any rate. Will you give me your answer in the morning?"

Luis bowed his head. "Excellency."

He took his leave and moved through the snow toward camp, confused, torn with conflicting emotions. Had Vargas sensed his doubts? Why else would the man leave the question unspoken between them, give Luis so much time to decide?

There was a wagon ahead, its wheels half buried in white drifts. A cloaked figure stood by its dropped tongue. As he drew near he saw that it was Barbara. She had apparently been watching him all the way down from the general's tent. She hesitated, then picked up her cloak and crossed to him.

He could still not help feeling awkward with her, confused. It angered him. She seemed to be handling the situation better than he.

But there was still a touch of the might-have-been about it. Whenever he saw her he could not help remembering the feel of her body in his arms, the blind look of passion in her eyes. Yet he knew it would be gone when he saw Kashana again.

"Did General Vargas ask you to go to Acoma?" she said.

He was startled for a moment. But he knew how swiftly word passed through the camp. The people probably knew all about the threat of hostility from the Keres. When he did not answer, she said:

"Luis, you must have faith in Vargas."

"Barbara," he said, "the whole thing hinges on convincing Acoma that Vargas can be trusted. I could not hide anything from that old *cacique* at Acoma. Tyame would see how I really feel. I wanted to have faith in Vargas. Do you think I would have gone through all this? But I cannot help what I have seen——"

"What did you expect, Luis? Some magic that would do away with problems that have afflicted men from the beginning of time? In Mexico City—when Vargas asked you if there was a key to the reconquest, what did you say? Three things. First, there must be no *encomienda*. Has that not been fulfilled?"

He was looking at her closely, and he did not answer.

"Second, that the Church must be more lenient. You recommended Father Salvador de San Antonio as *custodio*. Do you know what a fight Vargas had to put up to get him?"

Still Luis did not speak.

"Third, that Vargas must keep faith with the Pueblos. Has he broken it yet? Did he not do all that was humanly possible to keep his word about Juan Ye? Did he not defy his own priests in refusing to convict Juan Ye by accepting the word of a traitor?"

"But none of it is settled yet—the question of *encomienda*, of Juan Ye's guilt——"

"You asked for faith, Luis. Do you think any governor will ever solve all the problems of this country? Is not the courage and integrity with which he meets them the thing that matters? Has not Vargas kept faith with you? Would Otermin have stood against all his captains down there at San Diego over the question of *encomienda*? Has not Vargas kept faith with the Indians? Would Otermin have defied the Church to defend an Indian he thought was being unjustly accused? Can you ask for more than that?"

Slowly he turned to look up at the lonely Michoacan tent on the hill. Barbara's voice had become strained toward the last and he thought he knew why. It struck him as bitterly quixotic of her that she could plead so passionately for a cause that would send him out to the woman she thought stood between them.

CHAPTER FIFTY-TWO

VARGAS could not spare a squad but he offered Luis a companion. Luis chose Emilio. It took them two days in that bitter weather, wading their horses to the knees in the snow much of the time. It was almost evening when they came upon Acoma. Emilio drew rein, gaping in the same awe Luis had known the first time.

In the dying light the whole mesa looked like a ruined city, the broken towers and slender minarets and crumbling ramparts tinged with crimson by the sunset. As they drew nearer the sunset faded and the immense rock towered black and forbidding against an amethyst sky. The weird totems leered down from their dizzying heights. The broken pillars of rock ringed the base of the cliff like the destroyed idols of a vanished race staring forever into the north.

Luis stopped at the foot of the ladder trail. The Spaniards had already been sighted, and he could see figures lining the edge of the crag above. Struggling with the half-forgotten Keres words, he told them who he was and asked to come up. After a long while a man answered, giving him permission.

"Stay down here," Luis told Emilio. "Take the horses a mile west and do not let anybody but me approach you. If I am not back by noon tomorrow go to Santa Fe."

"Luis, I will go up with you——"

"Somebody has to watch the horses, Emilio. And if something happens Vargas should be warned. There is really nothing to worry about. Many here are my friends."

He clapped the scarred convict on the back and began the ascent.

As he climbed the finger-and-toe holds up the sheer face of the cliff the wind howled out of a deep bay and almost tore him off. It struck the rock wall in a shivering boom. It slid away with the oily hiss of a receding wave. He remembered the wind.

It was almost four hundred feet to the top. When he reached it he was so exhausted he could hardly stand. A crowd of men waited for him, muffled in buffalo robes and rabbitskin mantles. The faces came back to him. He saw Tsiki, with the scars like pale clawtracks on his copper face. He saw Kashana's uncle, Pesana. He asked where Tyame was.

"Tyame is dead," Pesana said.

For a moment Luis could not speak. It was more than a blow to his hopes. He had felt the same bitter sense of loss at the grave of Don Bernabe, or kneeling over his father's dead body. He bowed his head and told them of his deep sorrow. He asked who was *cacique* now.

"I am *cacique* now," Pesana said.

Luis had thought it was the wind at first. But it was too rhythmic for the wind. The mesa seemed to tremble with a pulse of its own. Somewhere, in one of the *kivas*, they were beating the *tombe*.

"You will want to see your wife," Pesana said.

"I came to see her," Luis said. "But I also came as an ambassador with Vargas. A year ago in his presence you swore renewed fealty to the Spanish king and once more embraced the Cross. Now we hear bad things. We hear that the *hoinawe* is danced again on Acoma."

A murmur ran through the crowd. Pesana frowned thoughtfully. He had grown heavy. His smooth brown cheeks were cleft with two deep lines that ran from his flat nostrils to the corners of his lips. His hair was gray.

"This is talk for the long house," he said.

Moving toward the village beside Pesana, Luis was torn with a strange conflict—an overpowering urgency to see Kashana, a perverse reluctance to face her. Yet he knew the talk had to come first. It was their way. The warriors would be unable to understand a man allowing his feeling for a woman to interfere with the council and ceremonies of the long house. He could not afford to offend them. As they walked Pesana spoke in a low voice.

"Tsiki is no longer war chief, but he still has great influence. It is much the same as when you left. The young men for war, the older ones against it."

It was almost night now. The wind pulled at their fur robes with capricious hands. The wind roared down the chasm beneath North Row and Middle Row. Luis looked about him at the ghostly tiers of buildings, the men shuffling along like figures from the stone age.

He was filled with a frightening sense of unreality. It was an illusion. It could not be grasped. It was a dream. He remembered when he thought he could be content here, living among these reserved, ceremonious people, cut off from the rest of the world. Now he realized how impossible it was. He could not step back in time a thousand years. He could not spend the rest of his life in a dream, always struggling to wake up.

A few lights showed in the long rows of communal buildings, and Luis had the sense of furtive movement on the roof tops. They reached the long house near the ruined church. Coals already glowed in its center fire pit, and the smoky warmth was a relief after the freezing weather outside. Luis saw a plate of blue wafer bread near the fire. The acrid scent of cedar brew stung his nostrils. He knew what it meant. The wafer bread fed the dancers and the cedar tea purged them. They were dancing the *hoinawe* in some *kiva*. The drum was beating for the warrior dance. And he would not win until the drum stopped.

The men crowded into the long room and sat on the stone benches against the wall and on the floor. Luis stood before them in the middle. They stared curiously at his tattered holy sack as he told them of his mission.

Tsiki rose and threw aside his robe so they could see the proud scars on his body. He asked how they could know that the Spaniard would keep his promises and protect them from their enemies?

Matthew stood. He was one of the war captains. He said how the words of Tyame were still with them. Tyame had said how they should have proof that Vargas would keep his promises. Tyame said how they should see that Vargas could make his own people keep them.

It was the test Luis had dreaded. Pesana was not as shrewd as Tyame. But he knew Luis well and would be able to see if Luis did not really believe in his own words.

"I will tell you a story," Luis said. "One of the promises Vargas made was that Juan Ye should be pardoned and absolved if there was no proof that he had killed Fray Bernal at Galisteo. But Pedro de Tapia said he saw Juan Ye kill Fray Bernal. And all the Spaniards demanded that Vargas arrest Juan Ye and execute him. And even the priests have demanded it. But Vargas knows Pedro de Tapia is a traitor. Vargas has refused to arrest Juan Ye or execute him."

A murmur ran through the crowd. He could see how it impressed them. It was the terms they dealt in, like one of their allegories, like the parable Tyame had told him about the coyote and the bear. It gave them a dramatic example, something far more tangible than his mere promise that Vargas could be trusted.

Pesana got up and said this was a good sign. It was not bad. Would they not think one of their own leaders a man of great honor if he stood against the will of his own people and even his *caciques* in order to keep his word?

Tsiki said it proved nothing. Had Juan Ye been pardoned or absolved? That was the promise Vargas had made. Had he kept it?

The debate went on interminably. Luis had been twelve hours in the saddle, and it was torture to fight off sleep. Finally Pesana told him that he would take Luis to Kashana. The talk might go on all night and Luis had said all he could. It was up to them to decide now.

It was the same room on the third level of North Row. Light edged the door and he knew she had been waiting. Pesana knocked and the two men stood leaning against the wind, shivering in the cold, till the door was open.

Kashana was silhouetted by the light of a fire dying on the hearth. She stood demurely in the door, her face turned down, looking at him from veiled eyes. She wore a black mantle over her cotton dress, and white buckskin boots over the thick cotton wrappings of her legs.

"Welcome, husband," she said.

He might have been gone a day. Luis felt stiff and restrained in Pesana's presence. He did not know what to say. Why was he always so bad at these reunions? He remembered how foolish he had felt when he first saw Barbara in Mexico City. Kashana turned aside so he could see into the room.

"Your sons have stayed awake." Her voice was husky, barely audible. "Perhaps they can join Pesana's household tonight."

Migenna stood against the wall, staring at Luis as though he were some curiosity like a bird caught in a trap or a new kind of food. Bare toes peeped from the bottom of his buckskin breeches, and Luis saw them curl under and make random little marks in the floor. Migenna had hollow temples and a face of many tilted angles that made it hard to tell if he was smiling or angry.

"It must be this holy sack," Luis said. "If I took it off you would remember me."

"I remember you," Migenna said. "You are the *cashtira*."

"Yes," Luis said, "I am the Spaniard. But I am also your father."

"Our mother said you were probably dead," Hoshken said. "She said you probably died in the desert."

Hoshken was shorter. He was so heavy in the torso that he looked almost potbellied and he was distinctly bowlegged. His face was flat and his nostrils were splayed broadly against his bland cheeks. It was impossible to find any traces of Spanish blood in him. Luis wondered if he was Kashana's favorite.

"You are both good hunters," Luis said. "I can see it."

"We do not get to hunt much," Migenna said. "The Apaches would kill us."

There was an awkward silence. Then Pesana said:

"You boys will come with me. Your father and mother have not seen each other in a long time."

Luis wanted to touch them as they passed. He wanted to reach out and put his hand on Migenna's shoulder. When they were gone he followed Kashana into the room. She closed the door. In the wall were many little chambers meant to be sealed with adobe so they would be airtight and contain the piñon nuts and dried plums and soapweed pods that were used as famine food. He saw how many of them were open now and empty.

Kashana sat on a mat. She kept her head bowed and was not looking at him. He saw how she had gained weight and how she looked so much like the other Pueblo squaws. He thought how a Spanish woman would be in his arms, crying, clinging, after having been parted so long.

"Well," he said. "I have been away a long time."

"Yes," she said. "You have been away."

"Well, I suppose it has been hard for you, raising the boys, without a husband to help."

"I suppose it has been hard for you too."

It made him think of how he had sat with Bigotes in this same room and how awkward it had been, saying so many things and not saying what they wanted to.

"Well," he said, "it would interest me to know what happened after I left. Did they look to see if I was in the grave?"

"No. They were too upset over the death of Po-pe. They forgot about you. They threatened to punish us but there were not enough of them."

"Who killed Po-pe?"

She did not answer. Her bowed head kept her face hidden from him.

Luis said, "In the graveyard, when Pesana let me out of the matting, he told me the women had lured Tapia and the other Tano warriors away. He said if Po-pe appeared you would lure him away." He paused, waiting for some reaction. She was silent. He said, "Did Po-pe appear?"

Still she did not answer. The coals were dying and it was almost dark in the room. It frightened Luis to think about it. Vargas had told him that Po-pe was found at the foot of the cliff after a big rain storm. Po-pe had been stabbed. The implications filled Luis with a strange excitement, but it frightened him too. How could she look so demure? How could she look so soft and shy and virginal? It was impossible. She couldn't have done it.

"Well," he said. "The fire is almost out."

She did not answer. There was something submissive and very Oriental about her bowed head. He had the feeling that he could get no farther with words. Words had never played a very big part in their relationship. He remembered how much of the time they had spent together without speaking. He had not felt uncomfortable. He had thought it was sufficient. Perhaps she understood it better than he did. She had been the first one to stop talking now. She was waiting, simply waiting. It was very apparent. It was the role of the wife when the husband returned from a hunt, or a long journey.

It was the way they accepted everything, birth and death and summer and winter, quietly and very ceremonially. Sitting on the floor with her black hair undone and her eyes downcast and waiting so movelessly, she looked like a woman occupied in an ancient rite.

He went to the fire and scattered the coals. He returned and found her in the darkness. He could not arouse her. He undressed her and kissed her breasts and caressed the sensitive places of her body, but she would not respond.

He wanted her to fight him. He remembered how deeply it had disturbed him, how he had hated it, the clawing and biting, her hands pushing him away and pulling him to her at the same time. But now he wanted it. He labored with growing desperation. If he could have nothing else he wanted her to fight him, because it had been a sign of her passion and had always ended in her ecstasy.

"*Yo-ko,*" she said. He felt her tremble beneath him. Her hands gripped his shoulders. "*Satsi ish kaw! Sy himatsh! Noy-a-kwich skumia . . . yo-ko. Satsi ish kaw,* Luis, *satsi ish kaw, satsi ish kaw!*"

The town crier awoke him. He opened his eyes and saw that it was dawn and heard the *kahera* making his rounds in the streets below, jingling his little bells.

Luis had a drugged feeling. He began to shiver with cold, trying to gather the sluggish thoughts in his mind. He had thought his frustration and his sense of failure would keep him awake. But the exhaustion of his ride had been too much for him.

It was not the same failure he had known with the Condesa. He knew Kashana had finally shared his pleasure. He could still hear her voice, shrill and strained as an old squaw's, and the senseless words, telling him to go away, calling him lover and devil in the same breath, saying she did not understand.

He had known women to say many strange things at the height of their passion. It had not bothered him before. And she had not fought. He kept thinking that. She had not fought him. He rolled over to look at her.

She was gone.

Her pallet was empty. He sat up, looking for his shoes. They were not beside him. Neither were his weapons. He shuddered violently. It was more than the freezing chill. It was the panic of a trapped animal. He lunged to the door, pushing it open. His shoes and his lance and his holstered firelock lay in a neat pile beside the door.

They were half buried in a snow that was still falling, a million white feathers drifting softly to the earth. He shook the snow out of his shoes and put them on. Like distant shadows he saw Pesana standing before the doorway of his house talking with Matthew and Chotika, one of the ancient medicine doctors who had prepared Luis for his sham death in the *kiva*. Luis picked up his weapons and went to them.

"Go ua tzimo," Pesana said. "Zatse gacha guh we."

Luis was too upset to observe their unhurried formalities. Without returning the greeting or agreeing that it truly was not hot today, he said, "Is she in your house?"

Pesana looked at Luis's shoes. His voice was not unkind. "My boy, the village has seen your belongings outside her door."

"I must talk with her."

Pesana was still looking at the shoes. "Has she not said it all?"

Pesana's broad body blocked his narrow door. Luis stared helplessly at him. Was the man right? Could it end that simply?

The snow descended, piling into little drifts on their shoulders, making miniature white hedges of their brows. And Luis knew he was wrong. There was nothing simple about the ending. It was only a culmination of something that had begun long ago, when he was here before, when the first exaltation they had known at Yapashi began to fade, to degenerate into confusion and misunderstanding, when he had begun to realize that he could not spend the rest of his life in this dream city. If he had not been forced to escape then there would have come a morning when he woke to find his belongings outside the door.

"But there is more——" Luis said.

"How can there be more? No Spanish priest was here. You were never really married in the eyes of the Church. You are free, *cashtira*, in the eyes of your people as well as mine."

"But the boys——"

"Kashana wants to keep them here," Pesana said.

"She has no right. I will take them to Santa Fe. At least I can do that."

"In your world they would be *mestizos*," Pesana said.

A wind swept through the snow, caking it against their faces with stinging force. Luis was thinking of Mexico City. He was thinking of the breeds squatting against the cathedral wall in their rags while the passing Spanish horses kicked dust in their faces. He was thinking of how he and all the other young men had looked upon Kashana when he had first known her in Santa Fe. Perhaps that was what had contributed to the failure more than anything else. The two bloods in her, ever in conflict, belonging neither to the Spanish world nor the Indian world, hating him as a *gachupin*, hating herself for wanting him, fighting against the want.

And last night she had not fought. She had submitted as a duty and had even taken her pleasure as a duty, because she had learned in that moment that it was over, that the gap could never be bridged, that she had joined a people Luis could never join, and the want was gone, and there was no need to fight any more.

"I know how much you love your sons, *cashtira*," Pesana said. "That is why you will leave them here."

Luis thought of Toribio, twisted, hating, hungering for something he could never have. Here it is not so, Tyame had said. Here the child will receive equal affection from all. . . . Love is given us by the gods, and therefore we have no right to divide it or question it or say how it shall be parceled out.

The snow fell and there was no sound in the world. It was something Luis had been too upset to notice before. The drums had stopped beating.

CHAPTER FIFTY-THREE

LUIS and Emilio returned to Santa Fe on the twenty-ninth of December. It was before dawn but the Spanish camp was already stirring. Just inside the sentry posts they saw artillerymen polishing the *pedrero grande* and the *pieza de bronza* until the two brass cannons had a translucent green shine in the firelight. They passed Sergeant Tellez scouring his halberd, patiently rubbing sand over the steel beak on one side and the ax blade on the other and the lance point at the top. They rode through long lines of cloaked and shivering soldiers who waited patiently in the crusted snow for their turn at the field confessionals.

"By all the Spanish saints," Emilio said. "It looks like we have returned just in time."

Luis found Vargas before his tent, conferring with his adjutant general and Captain Hurtado. The general was dressed in plain armor with a heavy cloak over his cuirass and his boots pulled to the hip. He immediately ordered some food and hot wine for the two newcomers and then asked for the report.

"Pesana and the older men are still friendly," Luis said. "Your defense of Juan Ye impressed them. They had stopped the warrior dance when I left. But they would make no promises. Some of their men are among the Tanos now. If they cannot carry the news back that you have pardoned Juan Ye and given him absolution I think Acoma will come against us."

Vargas stroked his minute goatee with one lean finger. "It is still a stalemate. I have been unable to find witnesses that could refute Tapia's story."

"These preparations for battle——"

"We attack the town. My patience is at an end. Twenty-two people have died of cold and starvation out here. I ordered the Tanos to leave Santa Fe yesterday. They gave me open defiance. They closed the gates. They said the devil could help them more than God and Mary. They said nothing but defeat could be our fate, and we would be reduced to slavery and finally killed."

"What of Juan Ye?"

"Still at Pecos. The reports are that he is still ready to join the Tanos if we attack."

"Pecos is an even bigger village than Acoma. You cannot afford to have that kind of force coming up on your rear."

"Then we must take Santa Fe before he arrives. If you are not too exhausted, *señor*, you will join Captain Madrid after you eat."

Luis and Emilio ate hurriedly and then crossed camp to Madrid's squad gathering near the artillery. With his Negro manservant, his secretary, and the adjutant general, Vargas was inspecting his army. He did not miss a man. He stopped to talk with each one, yet managed to show none special preference. There was a gravity about him, an austerity that set him apart. He rarely smiled, yet his comments often drew a grin or a laugh from one of the men. It was almost sunrise. The chaplains had finished confessing the troops.

In the frozen gray dawn, before the whole camp, Vargas went to the cart holding the statue of La Conquistadora. He knelt before the moving shrine that had brought the patron saint of the expedition all the way from El Paso. The little army went to its knees in the snow. With the father president and the other priests Vargas prayed to Our Lady of Conquest and asked her to protect each man in battle and give success to the cause.

Luis was on one knee beside his tired horse, shivering uncontrollably in the cold. He glanced up the slope to where the dark mass of women and children stood before their miserable brush shelters. He could not see Barbara. He knew a sudden wish that he could have had time to see her before the battle. But there was no time. And what good would it do to tell her what had happened? He still didn't know himself. He still didn't know.

Vargas rose from his prayers and asked his captains to join him for their final orders. One by one the men left their squads and walked through the snow. As they gathered Luis looked down on the town. In the dim light the buildings were like a haphazard collection of gray coffins and odd-shaped boxes threaded by a labyrinth of narrow streets and crooked alleys. The outer wall was breached and crumbling and in many places had fallen away into heaps of rubble. Luis had no doubt that the cavalry charge could carry it and drive the Indians back to the citadel at the center of town, the walled fortress of the palace, and the royal houses.

Luis became aware of a man edging toward him in the ranks. He saw that it was L'Archeveque. Emilio stepped closer to Luis, scowling at the Frenchman.

"Do not let him get behind you in the charge," Emilio said. "If they have been waiting for a chance this battle is it. Who could swear where a shot came from?"

Luis did not answer. But he took careful note of Toribio's position, and of all the other Gallegos men on either side of him. All the captains had joined General Vargas now. It was the Marqués de Gallegos who spoke first, raising his voice for all to hear.

"General Vargas, you have not yet made an official and proper reply to our petition concerning the return of our *encomiendas*. We have decided that the decision must be made today. We will ride into battle as *encomenderos* or we will not ride into battle at all."

It was impossible to see any reaction in the general's face. It was rigid with cold, and the lips were distinctly blue. Slowly his eyes passed over the assembled army behind the captains. Many of the soldiers in each captain's squad had been men-at-arms for that captain in the old days, when he was an *encomendero* at Santa Fe. They had been in his retinue for a lifetime, an integral part of his household, and their allegiance to him undoubtedly went far beyond their allegiance to Vargas. The captains would not have taken such a stand unless they were sure their men would back them.

A horseholder stood near the general with his mount. Vargas turned silently and walked to the horse and put his foot into a bronze shoe stirrup and swung aboard. His cape swirled and settled against the saddle as he wheeled the spirited animal to face the army.

"I will give you my official and final reply now," he said. When he raised his voice the tone carried like a trumpet. "Those who follow me into this battle will go as *reconquistadores*. Before this colony they will renounce their claim to *encomienda* for now and evermore. Those who do not follow me shall be known to Spain, to the king, and to God, and by them will be judged."

He wheeled his horse to face the town. He pulled his sword and raised it.

"*Santiago!*"

The horse responded to the ancient battle cry without any need of spurs. It broke into a Castilian pace that took it through the sentry lines and into the open ground before the town.

"Bowels of Judas," Luis said.

He swung into the saddle. He spurred Canelo into a gallop after the general. Emilio was right behind.

"*Santiago*, you whoresons," the convict shouted. "Come on, you bastards. That man will die out there alone and you know it. Can you face your women after this day? Can you face your confessor?"

Captain Madrid could bear it no longer. He looked at the Marqués, his face strained and white. He turned and ran for his horse, shouting for his squad to mount. They were in the saddle as he swung up, and Luis could hear the wild crackle of crusted snow behind him as a dozen horses broke into the charge.

Most of the other captains were running for their horses. There were too many good soldiers among them to hold back now. They knew the shame that would be attached to their names if they failed to follow Vargas. His audacity had defeated them. But Luis knew it was more than audacity. He knew that Vargas had looked forward to this moment ever since the day the captains had presented their petition. *The Marqués may think it is his time and his place, but it will be I who have done the choosing.*

It swept the last doubts from Luis. He knew Barbara was right. He knew he could follow this man anywhere now. It took him back to that moment thirteen years ago when the exaltation of battle had joined him in spirit with another man, when he had stood back to back with his grandfather on this same battlefield.

The charging squads closed up, forming the Spanish wedge that had swept the Moors from Granada and had shattered the feathered hosts of Montezuma half a world away. They were only sixty men but they made the earth tremble like six hundred. The hill flattened out. They were crossing the tilted fields north of town. The running horses kicked up snow till it lay behind and above them in a powdery white haze.

Luis could look back and see the infantry following, the two dozen arquebusiers under Lieutenant General Granillo trotting down the hill with their clumsy guns, the column of armed colonists under Captain Hurtado who were to act as reserves. Higher on the hill he could see more colonists and the Pueblo allies from El Paso, fanning out in a skirmish line that would protect the Spanish against a surprise attack from the northern villages.

The outer limits of the town was before them now, a gray mass of broken walls and charred buildings. The early morning sun made a mica glitter against the snowdrifts banked high against every standing surface. Luis could see the scurrying movement of dark figures among the ruins, ants beginning to swarm from their heap. The cannons opened fire from the hill.

The crash of the *pedrero grande* was followed by the lighter cough of the *pieza*. Luis saw smoke belch skyward like a puff of dust kicked up by a peevish child. The walls crumbled in two places.

A shower of arrows filled the air. Shafts clanged off cuirasses, struck helmets with a tinny rattle. An arrow pierced Luis's holy sack, catching and pulling at him so strongly that he was twisted around in the saddle.

The Tanos had some Spanish arquebuses, and the Spaniards were met with a startling burst of gunfire. The man beside Luis coughed and pitched off his horse. Gunpowder drifted in a thickening cloud across the scene, black and greasy. It stung Luis's eyes and turned everything to a shadowy nightmare.

Figures seemed to burst from the sooty veil. A screaming Tano appeared before Luis, and he barely got his lance up in time. The man took it in the throat and almost tore Luis from the saddle before he could free the blade.

The whole battle at the outer defenses was as brief as it was savage. The Tanos could not stand against the armored cavalry. They broke and scattered back through the littered streets. Luis was near enough to Vargas to see him raise his sword and shout:

"After them—at the gallop. They must establish no new defense short of the palace."

The order was passed through the milling cavalry and each man responded without trying to re-form on his captain.

Luis followed three Indians who ran down a narrow alley south of the convent. It was littered with wreckage, some of it half buried under the white snowdrifts. The Tanos clambered over a heap of logs and adobe rubble and disappeared beyond. Luis saw that it was a barricade, too high to jump. He had to rein his horse savagely to stop in time.

Canelo almost went to his haunches, squealed, and pivoted. Facing the other way, Luis saw that only one man had followed him. The rider galloped his horse a few feet into the alley and brought it to a halt. He had a firelock in his hand, the match burning. The man was Jean L'Archeveque.

They faced each other for but an instant. They were only ten feet apart. Luis had no time to react. He saw strain pull the Frenchman's mouth into a macabre grimace.

Then there was a clatter on one flank and General Vargas appeared in the ruins of the convent north of the alley.

L'Archeveque glanced that way, wheeled his horse around, and galloped back out of the alley. Vargas shouted at Luis, and Luis turned his excited animal through a breach in the crumbling convent wall and joined the general.

"Get back to the lieutenant general," Vargas said hurriedly. "He is not bringing the arquebusiers up fast enough. I want them deployed at the north corner of the church. They must clear the palace wall by the gate before we put the storming ladders up."

Luis found Lieutenant General Granillo and his twenty-four arquebusiers just coming through the outer wall in a double file. Luis gave Granillo the general's order.

As the arquebusiers double-timed it around the convent Luis rode through the ruins toward the re-formed cavalry. A pair of men in Captain Misquia's squad led two extra horses on which were tied the cedar storming ladders. Across the plaza Luis could see the horde of Indians on top of the royal houses and the palace walls. Their war cries sounded like a pack of coyotes wailing and yipping at the moon.

The first rank of arquebusiers stepped into view. Each man had his heavy gun at his shoulder. He knocked the ash off one end of the burning cord clamped to the breach of the arquebus by a metal serpentine. He blew on the cord till it glowed. Granillo lifted his sword.

"Fire!"

A dozen fingers squeezed their triggers. A dozen serpentines pivoted, dipping the burning end of the matches into the pan. The flash of ignited powder ran down the rank like a chain of lightning. A dozen guns roared, kicking the arquebusiers back a foot.

The figures seemed to melt away from the walls above the palace gate. As the first rank of arquebusiers dropped back to reload, the second rank moved forward. There was another shattering volley. Luis saw Indians pitching head foremost off the palace. Vargas raised his sword.

"Santiago, y cerra España!"

A hoarse cheer rose from the cavalry, and they followed Vargas into the plaza at the gallop. They deployed into a long line that crashed across the empty square and swept against the palace like a breaker on a beach.

The arquebusiers were still firing, trying to keep the wall cleared above the cavalry. But more Indians crossed the roofs of the royal houses to take the places of those who had fallen. A robed shape loomed above Luis, bowstring drawn. Luis sidled his horse against the wall and drove high with his lance. Steel bit flesh. The Indian dropped back, his arrow popping skyward.

Misquia's squad had dismounted, unlashing the ladders and leaning them against the wall. Luis saw that Rafael Tellez was the first to start climbing. The mounted men gathered on either side, firing at the Indians above, hacking with their swords, driving their lances at the screaming, painted Tanos.

A pair of squaws came into sight above Luis. He saw the kettle they carried and tried to wheel Canelo from under it. But the boiling water splashed over him. He shouted helplessly, dropping his lance. He could feel his panicked horse rear and almost pitch him off. He was blinded. He knew he was burned but he could feel no pain. He fought the horse, pulling his rapier. When he could see again he drove Canelo back into the battle.

The Indians had pushed the ladder off and it toppled into the cavalry milling beneath the wall. A pair of soldiers fell with it.

The arquebusiers had moved up now and their devastating fire once more cleared a place on the ramparts. The ladder was raised again and Vargas swung off his horse to be the first one up. Sword under one arm, agile as a boy, he clambered toward the top.

Beneath a rain of rocks and boiling water and arrows, the cavalry held their horses at the wall, standing in their stirrups to hack and thrust at the Indians above. When Vargas neared the parapet the arquebusiers had to shift their fire to avoid hitting him. A swarm of Indians rushed Vargas.

Fighting below, Luis had a glimpse of the general's lean Spanish figure, cuirass glittering dimly in the smoke, hacking savagely about him in an effort to get on top of the wall. But a blow from a *macana* stunned him, and the ladder was pushed back. The general and the men on the lower rungs had to jump to save themselves.

Luis raced to the spot, but Vargas was already getting to his feet. A horseholder brought his mount, and he swung into the saddle again.

Luis lost count of the times the ladders were raised in a vain attempt to scale the walls. The *kiva* in the plaza was finally captured, and a squad of arquebusiers was put inside to hold that point. But the Spaniards could not gain the ramparts. Luis was still milling around beneath the walls with the others, so exhausted he could hardly lift his sword any more, when the trumpeter sounded retreat.

The cavalry streamed back across the square in a disorganized mob, leaving the arquebusiers in the *kiva* and in other strategic spots among the ruins. Upon reaching the convent, Luis slid off his horse and threw himself flat on the ground behind a protecting heap of rubble.

He made little sobbing sounds with the effort to breathe. His face was smeared with blood and powder and sweat. He ached all over, and the burns were beginning to hurt.

He heard a rattle nearby and reluctantly lifted his head. Toribio was climbing over the heap of broken adobe bricks. He had a sword in his hand.

Luis sat up, his hand on his own sword. Toribio slid down the pile of rubble and ended on the ground in a sitting position. He stared glassily at Luis. He looked down at the sword in his hand. He made an unintelligible sound and let it slip from his fingers to the ground.

"Well," he said in a dead voice, "there goes the day." He raised his eyes, and they gazed emptily at each other. Luis could hear the dim clank of armor all about him in the ruins, the groans of men wounded or exhausted, the whimper of spent horses. The Tanos were chanting on the walls and taunting the Spaniards. Shreds of smoke still drifted above the battlefield. The snow was trampled and furrowed in the plaza, and the broken ladders lay impotently at the base of the scarred palace wall.

Toribio looked out at the desolate scene. He passed a hand across his face. The fingers made white streaks in the grime. He looked strangely at Luis. He made a sighing sound.

"Do you ever pray for her?"

"What?" Luis asked dully.

"The Condesa."

Luis looked more closely at the man. He blinked, trying to clear the fog from his mind. How could they sit here and talk of such an irrelevant thing, two enemies, too exhausted to hate each other. But somehow it was not irrelevant.

"I pray for her every night," he said. "I pray for her soul in Purgatory, that it be forgiven her sin, because it was really not her fault, and it should be her murderer who is sent to hell."

"No," Toribio said, "you could not wish that on anybody."

"No. I could not."

"And you really mean it when you pray? You really believe the prayer is heard?"

"Yes, Toribio. I believe that."

Luis was staring curiously at the man. He remembered seeing the same expression in Toribio's face when they had met in the wagon camp that night, south of El Paso, the hunger gone out of the man's eyes, the life gone. He had gotten hints of it since and had been bothered by it. But now it was stronger. Toribio's cheeks looked sunken, grooved, shriveled. His eyes were dead and glazed. It was more than exhaustion. Luis had a weird sensation, the feeling of looking at a husk, something crumbling inside, something going to pieces, turning to dust, the hungers and the passions and the ambitions and the bitterness, until only a hollow shell was left.

"Is it on your conscience?" he asked. Toribio looked at him, eyes glazed. Luis said, "Does it bother you at night, does it come to you in your dreams, do you see her face, do you see it the way it must have been in that cell at Santo Domingo, before she used the little knife in the little comb, do you know what it is to be that afraid now . . . ?"

He broke off as Toribio came to his knees. It made a startling rattle in the debris. Toribio's nostrils were pinched and white and his eyes glowed. It was a return of his old bitterness. But he could not hold it long. He sank back, breathing heavily, as though the effort had exhausted him.

"Talk," he said. "Go ahead and talk. Words will not help you. They will not save Vargas. You will not have your patron much longer, Luis."

"The battle is not yet done."

"Closer done than you think. Why do you suppose Vargas sounded retreat?"

He turned his head. Luis followed his look. He could see antlike movement on the slopes of the mountains. At first he thought it was the skirmish line of colonists and Tano allies. But they were too high on the slope, and they were too many. It took him back to that dread day when Otermin's besieged Spaniards had stood within the palace walls and had watched the swarm of Tewas gather on the same mountain slope. It could only mean the same thing today. The Tewas of Tesuque and Nambe and San Juan and San Ildefonso and Santa Clara had come to join the Tanos in the palace.

"Well," Luis said dully, "you got what you wanted."

Toribio studied him with narrowed eyes.

"You and the Marqués de Gallegos," Luis said. "But it is a strange achievement, Toribio. How do you expect to get out alive?"

CHAPTER FIFTY-FOUR

LUIS found Vargas with his captains behind the church. He had already ordered Roque Madrid and Antonio Jorge to move their squads in support of the skirmish line on the hill. They were going through the ruins like sleepwalkers, collecting their spent men. The Marqués de Gallegos was quarreling with Vargas.

"I demand that you move out of this untenable position, General. This new report that Juan Ye is coming to join the Tewas on the mountain means that we will have an overwhelming force at our rear. This pathetic excuse for a rear guard will never hold them. We are in a nutcracker, Your Excellency. You cannot expose the whole colony to another massacre——"

"Your solicitation for the colony is admirable, Marqués," Vargas said. "But the skirmish line must stay where it is to protect the colonists. And with Juan Ye coming from the east the only route of escape is right through here. We must hold this position until the withdrawal is effected."

Powder and blood streaked the general's haggard face like war paint. His eyes were glazed with exhaustion. One of them was bloodshot and inflamed, and he kept rubbing it with the back of his grimy hand. He noticed Luis waiting and turned to him with a questioning frown. Luis asked to see Vargas alone. The Marqués de Gallegos scowled suspiciously as Vargas joined Luis.

"Juan Ye must have six or seven hundred warriors," Luis said. "If they were with us we could stop the Tewas and hold our position."

"He is not with us. Our Tano allies brought the word."

"Pedro de Tapia is still the key. He is in a dangerous spot and he knows it. He is a man who changes with the wind, Excellency. If we could put enough pressure on——"

"What kind of pressure?"

"A talk with him would show you. I would like you there, Excellency, and some of our Tano allies."

Vargas studied him thoughtfully. He massaged his sword hand. Then he nodded, called for his horse, and ordered the lieutenant general to take command till he returned. Luis mounted with him, and the two Tanos who had brought word of Juan Ye followed them up the hill.

They passed the artillerymen, swabbing their steaming guns with melted snow water. One of them told Vargas that he was afraid the *pedrero grande* would blow her breech if she did not get a rest. Vargas told them to hold their fire till further orders. Beyond the artillery Father Juan Alpuente was administering last rites to one of the soldiers wounded in the battle at the walls. Higher on the hill the colonists surged about Vargas and the air was filled with their babbling. He merely held up one hand to silence their questions and moved on through them. His face was composed and grave now, and he gave no sign of the devastating defeat they faced.

Outside one of the brush and earth shelters used by the priests they found Pedro de Tapia. He sat before a fire wrapped in a blanket. He did not offer to rise. His sly smile made his cheeks bulge, creating deep slits into which his eyes seemed to slide until they were hardly visible.

"God give them good to you, Your Excellency. I trust we are winning."

Before Vargas could answer, Fray Geronimo and the father president appeared. Luis dismounted and spoke respectfully to the father president.

"The general has allowed me a few words alone with the prisoner."

"He is no prisoner," Fray Antonio said. He turned to Vargas. "He is under the protection of the Church. I will not allow him to be threatened or coerced."

The priests made no move to leave. Luis tried to hide his frustration. He could not threaten Tapia openly in their presence. He stared hard at the Tano. He could not believe the man felt as smugly secure as he appeared. Tapia must realize what a precarious position he had put himself in. The Indian began to stir uncomfortably. He pouted and looked around at the other men.

"Acoma!" Luis said sharply. Tapia started visibly. Luis said, "You must have heard I was at Acoma. They told me a strange thing there.

They said how you killed Po-pe. They said how you were jealous of Po-pe and wanted to take his place——"

"A lie, a lie," Tapia said. It had wiped the bland smile from his face. He gestured violently, and it threw the blanket off his fat body. "They say this to protect themselves. They killed Po-pe. It was that girl—Kashana——"

"You know there are many followers of Po-pe still among the villages," Luis said. "Are not Jaca and Francisco still alive? Would they not take vengeance on the murderer of their leader? Would the murderer be able to sleep at night, or turn his back on any man, or walk openly on the road——"

"Fray Antonio, stop them," Tapia said, turning toward the father president. The Indian grabbed the blanket and pulled it up around him again with agitated jerks. "Can you not see he is threatening me?"

"I only repeat what I heard at Acoma," Luis said. "Of course Pesana, the *cacique*, and Matthew, the war chief, and the council of elders at Acoma all have great honor among the Keres people. What they say will be held as truth——"

Pedro struggled to his feet, wheezing with the effort. The blanket dropped off again and gathered in folds about his ankles. Sweat shimmered greasily in the deep pleats of his face, and the sour smell of him reached Luis on the frigid air, the smell of fear.

"Calm yourself, my son," the father president said.

"You do not understand," Tapia panted.

"Exactly," Luis said. "Only an Indian could understand."

He was looking intently at Tapia, and he knew the Tano understood his threat. Tapia undoubtedly still questioned whether Luis was telling the truth or bluffing. But the possibility of being branded Po-pe's murderer had shaken the man even more than Luis had hoped. Vargas got off his horse and stood beside Luis. He understood what Luis was doing now and was adding the weight of his disturbing eyes to the pressure on Tapia. The two fathers glanced in confusion from Tapia to Luis, apparently sensing the hidden implications without really understanding them.

"Let us say that General Vargas was defeated and had to return to El Paso," Luis said to Tapia. "Let us say that this failure caused a new captain general to be appointed. The next logical man. The Marqués de Gallegos. Do you think the Marqués could protect you against Jaca and Francisco and all the other men who remain loyal to Po-pe?"

"You cannot do this," Tapia said. He turned to the father president.

"You promised protection—you must go to Acoma—stop them from saying these things——"

"You know he cannot go," Luis said. "You know it would not be enough if he could. Only someone the Acomas know could influence them . . . someone who had lived among them and had held their trust. . . ."

Tapia wiped sweat from his face. His fingers left white tracks in his flushed jowls. "You will make them stop this talk," he told Luis. "You will make them tell who really killed Po-pe?"

"Perhaps I can," Luis said. "But that is only my half of the bargain. Let us say you made a bad choice, Pedro. You sought the patronage of a man who was not really as strong as he seemed. You were in a tight spot and had to make a quick decision and made the wrong one. But now you have a chance to change it."

Tapia's lower lip trembled. He pressed fat fingers against it. He looked at Vargas. His voice came from him in a breathless rush.

"No punishment—there shall be no punishment!"

"How can you ask that?" Vargas said.

Luis turned to the general. "It is a sacrifice you must make. It is the only way."

Grudgingly Vargas nodded. "Very well. I shall not punish you."

"And protection," Tapia said. "Swear it—the Two Majesties."

Vargas said, "By God and by His Most Catholic Majesty, Carlos the Second, I swear that you shall not be punished and you shall have protection."

Tapia pouted at them, frowned, put a finger to his eye. He looked like a little-boy on the verge of crying. He turned and waddled away, slapping the back of his neck. He waddled back, clasping his hands before him.

"Well, good fathers——" He stopped, moistening his lips. He was shivering and his breath steamed on the air. "Well, señores—how does it say itself—to begin, when I saw this Indian kill Fray Bernal at Galisteo the Indian had a red missal ribbon at his waist. When Juan Ye appeared in Santa Fe later with the missal ribbon I naturally thought it was he who killed Fray Bernal. But I have been thinking— yes, the truth, thinking—and I finally remembered that I saw Juan Ye near Galisteo after Fray Bernal was killed, and Juan Ye did not then have the ribbon. So he must have been given the ribbon by the killer, truth? And the killer must have looked very much like Juan Ye, which caused me to make this very natural mistake, no?"

Tapia pressed his fingers into his jowls. His eyes darted around at the men, as if gauging the effect of his words. He was gaining confidence. His sly smile returned. He tilted his head to one side like a coy elephant.

"Of course. That all makes sense, truth? Anyone can be mistaken. And who looked very much like Juan Ye? Why, the Pecos war captain named Zubia, of course. Enough to be brothers. Unfortunate that Zubia is dead now, but, yes, it is the truth, it was Zubia, and not Juan Ye, who killed Fray Bernal. It is a coincidence that you came to me at this moment, just when I was going to tell the whole thing to the good fathers."

Luis felt disgust, the sickness of reaction to a long chance paying off. It was impossible to tell what Vargas felt. He turned gravely to the priests.

"If you do not give absolution to Juan Ye now, how will the rest of these people ever trust the mercy of Mother Church?"

Fray Antonio was looking at Luis. His shrewd eyes mirrored many things, confusion, doubt, a growing suspicion. But he was too wise to make an issue of a thing that threatened the lives of the whole colony. He touched his cross and closed his eyes. Luis knew he was praying for guidance. At last he said:

"If Juan Ye will come in and confess, I will give him absolution."

Vargas turned to the Tanos who had accompanied him. "Will you take this news to Juan Ye? His name has been cleared of all guilt. The father president promises him absolution, and the captain general promises him pardon, in the eyes of God, and all people."

CHAPTER FIFTY-FIVE

THE Tewas were already testing the skirmish line above the Spanish camp, and the sound of arquebuses was like the brittle crackle of broken sticks when Juan Ye appeared. The *cacique* of Pecos and the council of elders was with him, and a guard of fifty men, painted for war and heavily armed. They stood restlessly at the edge of camp while Juan Ye went into one of the brush shelters with Fray Antonio. The confession took fifteen minutes. Then Juan Ye reappeared, and in an impressive ceremony before the whole Spanish colony Vargas gave the Pecos chief official pardon and amnesty. To show his good faith Juan Ye announced that he would join the Spaniards against the Tewas on the hill.

The cavalry and arquebusiers remained in the town to hold the Tanos within their palace walls. Six hundred Pecosenos joined the Spanish infantry and their Tano allies on the hill. With two squads of cavalry in support they closed with the Tewas.

All afternoon long the war chants and the rattle of gunfire echoed through the timber and the smoke drifted into the sky or lay in thin gray patches over the deep-drifted canyons. With sunset the blood of Christ once more seemed to tinge the mountains. The Tewas broke and retreated before dark. But their threat was not entirely removed and the Pecosenos remained on the hill with the Spaniards.

Only then did General Vargas return to his cavalry in the ruins about the palace. The night was bitterly cold. The men built fires behind the crumbling remains of the convent walls and huddled about the meager warmth eating their starvation rations. A wind swept out of the

Sangre de Cristos, sharp with the smell of wet pine and winter earth. An hour before dawn Vargas woke and inspected the sentry lines, a serape wrapped tightly about his body. He still could not stop shivering, and the ague of exhaustion was an insistent ache throughout his whole body. After the inspection he dismissed the officers who had accompanied him and stood alone in the darkness by a broken wall, staring at the *villa*.

The Royal City. It had an ironic ring to him now. Beside Mexico City, Rome, Madrid, all the glittering, cosmopolitan capitals he had known, this town seemed nothing but a miserable crossroads hamlet of destroyed hovels. He could understand the disdain and indifference of former governors. For Otermin it had been only a steppingstone to some higher post. Cruzate's main interest had been the military fame of a reconquest. The memory of his early enthusiasm returned to mock Vargas. He remembered how he had wanted to explain it to Luis. Heir of Cortez and Pizarro, the last chance for glory in his lifetime, the Spanish chemistry in his blood that turned new lands and new treasures into mere symbols for the real rewards of conquest—it made him smile bitterly.

And this ragged excuse for an army, this handful of lazy, untrained ruffians scraped from the bottom of every barrel in New Spain, these arrogant, stubborn provincial captains, indulging in their petty jealousies, endangering the whole expedition by their constant quarreling and their selfish ambitions. He thought wistfully of the crack guardsmen he had commanded in Naples. With a squadron of them he could have conquered this whole vast territory.

His sword hand ached and he massaged it absently. His joints felt swollen and arthritic, and cramps caused little spasms in his numb feet. He thought longingly of the woman he had left in Mexico City. What had possessed him to come on this fantastic adventure? He was nearly fifty. A man needed the comfort of a woman in his old age, and sons to honor him. What if he should die in battle tomorrow, without having provided for them?

He should not have had that *expediente* executed last year, should not have given his wife in Madrid such sweeping powers of attorney. It had left too many loopholes by which the children of his woman in Mexico City could be deprived of their bequest. He would draw up a new *vihuela* tonight, a new will. He would legitimize Juan and Alonso and Maria. They would have the annuity from the salt works at Ogana, the olive orchards and entail in Tordelaguana——

He tried to check himself as he realized how disordered his thoughts had become. A man should not allow himself to think after sunset. It was only in the dark, cold hours of the night that he knew how pitifully small and weak he was, that panic and defeat could crawl in through the chinks of his armor.

He stalked back to his quarters in the ruined church. The fire was still going and he stood over it until he could stop shivering, trying to plan tomorrow's battle. He realized that in his mind he had not been prepared for this fierce resistance. He had allowed the easy success of last year to deceive and lull him. Today had proven a bloody lesson. It was obvious that the palace could not be taken by direct assault.

He looked up as a commotion started somewhere out in the darkness. He heard voices and then the rattle of feet in the crumbling ruins. The sentry at the door of the church gave the challenge. It was answered, and a shadowy group of men entered the roofless nave. As they came into the circle of firelight Vargas saw Roque Madrid, the captain of the guard from vespers to midnight, and a pair of sentries who held an Indian between them.

"We found this man in the Arroyo de los Saises," Madrid said. "He is a Tano from inside the palace. He was trying to get through our lines."

Vargas spoke to the Tano in Castilian and got no answer. Vargas told Madrid to fetch an interpreter. As he waited the general studied the sullen, dirty Indian. He knew these spies had been passing back and forth through the lines, learning the Spanish plans, carrying word of their pitiable condition back to the Indians, taking messages to the outlying villages. But this was the first one he had caught. And the Spaniards had not discovered how the Indians got out of the palace without being seen by the Spanish sentries.

Madrid returned with Pascual. He was one of the Tano allies who had distinguished himself by service to the Spaniards ever since the first entrance the year before.

"Is not the mouth of the Arroyo de los Saises just above where the ditch begins that takes water into the palace?" Vargas asked. Both Madrid and Pascual nodded. Vargas said, "Then perhaps that is how they are getting out. Tell this man that if he does not talk I shall have to execute him as all spies are executed in wartime."

After hours of haggling and cajoling and threatening the Tano finally talked. Pascual translated. "He says it is true that he got out by the water ditch. He was going to Juan Ye. He would tell Juan Ye that if Juan Ye did not desert the Spaniards the Tanos inside the palace would kill Juan Ye after they killed the Spaniards. He says how he was to return tonight with the answer of Juan Ye."

Vargas walked away from them, stroking his small goatee. It seemed to crystallize an idea that had been forming vaguely in his mind since they had failed to storm the palace. He woke his adjutant and asked him to assemble some men. The names he gave included the most trusted captains who had served under Otermin and a dozen other veterans of the revolt. Luis Ribera was one of them. The Marqués de Gallegos was not.

The men soon gathered in the church, shivering and sleepy. Vargas noticed that Emilio was the only one who sat close to Luis Ribera. Though Luis had fought beside the others, starved with them, suffered with them, they could never forget the holy sack.

"I have called you because you know the royal houses best," Vargas told them. "We have seen the futility of storming the walls. But we have a squad of arquebusiers in that *kiva* next to the palace. Would it not be possible, in the darkness, to lift the ladder through the trap in the roof of the *kiva* and place it against the palace wall?"

"We would meet the same thing we did before," Captain Arias said. "It is the very place the Indians will be watching most closely. Their guards would raise an outcry. We would have the whole garrison on us before there were enough Spaniards on the wall to hold it."

"What if there were no guards to meet us?" Vargas asked. He saw the surprise on their faces, and said, "One of the Indian spies is expected back tonight. He meant to use the water ditch and the hole by which it passes through the wall."

"There will be guards at the hole."

"But they expect the spy. What if it were one of our Tanos instead, and he convinced them he was the spy? And what if there were some Spaniards behind him, and they overcame the guards at the hole and took the guards on the wall by surprise from behind?"

None of them spoke for a moment. Then Captain Madrid stepped forward. "There is a chance it could be done. I would like to command the squad."

Luis stepped out after him, and Emilio. When Madrid had eight men the others were allowed to leave. Pascual volunteered to take the place of the spy.

So that there should be no clanking metal the men removed their spurs and exchanged their cuirasses for leather *esquipiles*. They surrendered their pistols so no shot would give the attack away too soon. Madrid complained that the chain on Emilio's morning star might clatter but Emilio wrapped it in his kerchief and persuaded the captain to let him keep it. Padres Zavalete and Bahomonde were awakened. They confessed the men and then prayed over the kneeling group.

Vargas promised that as soon as there were sounds of fighting on the walls and it was obvious that Madrid had been discovered, he would attack with the whole army. He walked with them to the spot where the water ditch began, a point on the Santa Fe River just above the spring of Rio Chiquito and below the mouth of Arroyo de los Saises.

"That you may go with God, *señores*."

The ditch was deep enough in most places so that a man could crouch on all fours without showing his rump over the top. Deep snowdrifts and the tall pink winter weeds provided an additional screen that gave them partial cover from the palace. The moon was down and the stars were dying, and in the darkness the Spaniards squirmed their way through the cornfields and the charred ruins.

At a turn Madrid halted his squad and sent Pascual ahead. What little water lay in the bottom of the ditch was frozen now. It did not matter to the Pueblos inside the walls. They had plenty of snow to melt. It was why Vargas had not tried to force their surrender by blocking the ditch.

As he lay against the ice, shivering uncontrollably, waiting, Luis could not help wondering at his feelings. He remembered how bitterly reluctant he had been, during those first few days of the revolt so long ago, to meet the Pueblos in battle. He remembered the torture it had caused him, knowing that sooner or later he would have to make his choice.

Yesterday he had known no such conflict. He had gone into battle automatically, as a thing to be done. He had killed. He could not think of the Indians inside the palace as individuals. They were simply The Enemy, a faceless, nameless mass that stood in the way and had to be removed. He realized that most of the Tanos inside were from Galisteo, and he had known few of them personally. But it went deeper than that. It disturbed him. There was something numbed in him that would not respond as it once had.

The men stirred restlessly. Behind Luis lay Mathias Lobato. He came from a family of peons that had settled the land with Onate. He had known Luis all his life and had gone through the revolt with him. He lay farther back than was necessary. On the march north he had never spoken to Luis unless he had to. It was the same reaction they all gave a man in the holy sack.

Pascual returned and in a hoarse whisper reported to Captain Madrid that the guards on the wall were walking back and forth. When they reached the west tower it cut them off from sight of the ditch for a short time. It would give the Spaniards a chance to crawl unseen from the turn in the ditch to the corner of the wall.

The last stars were fading, and the town was shrouded in the intense darkness before dawn. Luis could barely see Madrid, two feet ahead. On their bellies, their breath choked off by the slightest sound from the palace, the squad crawled the last twenty feet. They gained the wall.

The entrance was only a few feet ahead. Again Pascual crawled away from them. Luis began to sweat. He was shivering uncontrollably with cold but he was sweating. He was sure the Indians inside the walls could hear his teeth chattering. His palm was clammy against the wire-wrapped hilt of his sword.

He stiffened at the sound of Pascual's voice, ahead. The Indian spoke in Tano. Luis could not understand. There was another voice, from within the walls, muffled and indistinct. Then a grating sound. They would be pulling aside the rocks that blocked the hole. The voice inside came again, clearer. Pascual answered in a whisper. Then there was a rustle, a grunt, the sounds of a man crawling through the hole. Apparently Pascual had convinced the Tanos inside he was the spy.

Luis held his breath. He began to count. How long did it take to get through the hole? The palace walls were four feet thick—

Captain Madrid crawled down the ditch and squirmed into the hole. Luis followed. The opening was barely big enough to permit the passage of a man's body. One of Madrid's feet kicked Luis in the face. The captain had gotten out of the hole when Luis heard a surprised challenge in Tano.

Luis rammed himself on through, scraping cloth and hide from his shoulders. Then his head was in the open. He saw Madrid jumping to his feet and lunging at the four shadowy figures that stood to one side of the ditch.

One of the figures was Pascual. He was already plunging his knife into a Tano. A second tried to lift his war club. Madrid's sword closed the gap. The Indian gasped and doubled up with the blade in his middle.

The rocks used to block the ditch were lying in a heap just beyond the hole. Luis was trying to scramble over them and get to his feet when he saw that the third guard had started running away. Luis had his knife out, and he let it go in the quick sidearm throw that Torres had taught him when he was a youth. The Tano got out one shout before the knife struck him between the shoulders.

But that shout was enough. As the Spaniards squirmed from the hole behind Luis, there was the sound of a guard running along the wall somewhere above. He called in Tano. Pascual answered. The sound of running stopped.

"I said how it was nothing," Pascual whispered to Madrid. "I said how a man stumbled into the ditch and hurt himself. It will give us a minute."

"Along the wall," Madrid hissed. "There must be a ladder against the palace——"

The palace extended along the south side of the enclosure. Hugging the rear wall of the building, the Spaniards ran until they found the first ladder leading to the roof. It was so dark that the guards could see only the vaguest movement below them and apparently still thought it was their own men. But the shout had aroused others in the compound. A door opened in the royal houses a hundred yards distant. A candle burning within turned it to a yellow rectangle, silhouetting a figure. Someone called softly from a great distance.

The ladder creaked and swayed beneath the Spaniards. As they reached the top Madrid gave each man his duty. The last man up was to wait at the parapet and throw down the ladder as soon as he felt Indians start to climb it. He was to stay and hold the post as long as he could. Two others were to run down the rear of the palace and throw off any other ladders they found. The rest crossed the roof with Madrid.

They were almost to the parapet at the front of the palace when they heard the ladder fall to the compound behind them with a heavy crash. There was immediately a wild shouting from the ground. The guards on the wall reacted in confusion, yelling at each other and at those below, running back and forth on the four-foot parapet.

Luis jumped onto the parapet. He saw a shadowy shape before him and thrust with his sword. He missed and plunged heavily against a robed body. The Indian stumbled backward and pitched off the wall.

Luis caught himself, dropping to one knee to keep from falling after the man. The savage battle was going on all along the parapet. A foot from Luis a pair of figures reeled, locked in a struggle. One of them tripped and fell off the parapet onto his back on the roof below. The second one jumped after him, straddling his downed body, knife upraised.

"*Madre de Dios,*" the downed man gasped.

Luis jumped after them and put his sword through the one with the knife before he could use it. He pushed him off and grabbed the fallen man by an arm, helping him to his feet. The Spaniard's pawing hands found the holy sack. Only one man among Spaniards wore a garment as flimsy and long as that.

"Luis," the man said. It was Lobato's voice.

Luis did not wait to answer. He heard more Tano guards coming from the direction of the east tower. He leaped back onto the parapet. A shape startled him, seeming to appear from nowhere. He started his lunge.

"*Santiago,*" grunted the man.

Luis barely checked his sword in time. There was no mistaking that voice. "Excellency!" he said.

"Save your steel for the Tanos, *señor,*" Vargas said. "We put the ladder up as soon as we heard you fighting."

More Spaniards appeared. Their figures seemed to take solid shape in front of Luis, streaming onto the wall, and he realized that the first faint light of dawn had come.

Vargas issued quick orders. Captain Jiron led a squad to join Madrid near the west tower, quickly subduing the guards that remained. Captain Arias led his squad toward the east tower, meeting the Tanos who had been running from there. The Indians put up a savage fight, but there were only half a dozen of them. The Spaniards soon overwhelmed them and moved on. A third squad under Captain Jorge deployed across the palace roof to support the three men Madrid had left at the rear parapet.

As the pearly streaks of dawn broadened in the east they revealed the line of Spaniards silhouetted along the walls of the *presidio.* They had captured the two towers at either end of the palace and were now moving northward along both parapets of the walled enclosure. They had smothered most of the Indian resistance on the parapets and were deploying out onto the roofs of the royal houses and the other buildings.

Hundreds of Indians swarmed in the courtyards below, their wailing war cries and husky shouts making an unintelligible welter of sound. Bowmen and a few Indians with guns were firing at random. Their shafts made a futile clatter against morions and steel helmets. The Spanish arquebusiers answered with a shattering volley from the walls.

The Indians went down like wheat before a scythe. They broke in panic, running in every direction. But they were hopelessly exposed and there was no escape. The arquebusiers kept up their murderous fire. Knots of yelling Tanos jammed up in narrow doors, trying to regain the safety of the royal houses. By the time they had all found shelter the patios were littered with bodies.

The Spaniards held every wall now. Vargas ordered the Indians to come out empty-handed and surrender. None of them appeared. Standing on the palace roof, Luis could already see more Spanish cavalry crossing the plaza outside, accompanied by Juan Ye and a big body of painted Pecos warriors. With them they had the *pedrero grande*. A daring pair of Spaniards dropped off the wall and gained the safety of the *zaguán*. They opened the battered gates, and the bronze swivel gun was set up in the tunnel-like entrance.

Through a Tano interpreter, Vargas told the Indians below that the *pedrero grande* was now trained on the royal houses. If the Indians did not come out and surrender he would open fire.

The Indians knew they were helpless. The heavy cannon balls would shatter the flimsy doors of the buildings. The grape and canister that followed would turn the narrow rooms to a slaughterhouse. A moaning wail came from the rooms, and then they began to drift into the patios.

The first strong light of the rising sun glittered against the armored Spaniards lining the walls. They leaned tiredly on their swords and arquebuses. Black beards brought their faces to Satanic points beneath the battered brims of their morions. They talked in low voices, cursing the cold, stamping numb feet softly, watching the miserable Indians gather below. Looking along their ranks, Luis saw Toribio. The half-breed was watching him intently. His pocked face looked gray and sunken in the early light. It made Luis look elsewhere. He could not see L'Archeveque.

When the Indians filled the patios Vargas brought the Spanish cavalry and Juan Ye's warriors from the plaza to guard them. The horsemen clattered past the royal cannon, herding the Indians into little bunches against the wall. Juan Ye appeared. From above, made top-heavy by the bulk of his shaggy buffalo robe, he looked like a gouty, bowlegged gnome.

He was near the palace with a group of his warriors when he stopped and stared at something. Then he pointed at the main door, shouting up at Vargas.

"There is smoke. Somebody has set a fire."

Vargas did not need to issue an order. The Indians were already at the door, trying to get it open. But it was apparently bolted.

"A battering ram," Vargas shouted. "See if you can find a loose beam in the stables."

The mob of Tanos began to mill excitedly. The Spanish cavalry circled them, pressing them back, beating at them with the flats of their swords. Luis knew it would take too long to batter the doors open. He turned and ran along the edge of the roof till he reached a *viga* extending from the wall at ceiling height just above a window. He bellied over the two-foot parapet edging the roof, straddled the rafter, threw one leg off. It swung him down, hanging from the *viga* by both hands. He let go while he was still swinging and his feet crashed through the salenite window. The jagged edges of salenite ripped at his holy cloth, tore his face. He struck the floor inside in a heap.

The room was full of smoke. He could barely see the high tester bed, and knew he was in the bedroom formerly used by the Spanish governor. Luis had lain on the same bed when he had first come to warn Otermin of the uprising, and Dr. Roybal had treated the wound Bigotes' knife had made in his arm.

Beyond the bed, half hidden by the clouds of choking smoke, a man was hanging by his neck on a rope. The rope was tied to a rafter and the man twirled slowly from side to side. Coughing, choking, Luis stumbled toward him. He almost tripped on a captured Spanish halberd lying on the floor. He reached the dead man and identified him as Joseph, the governor of the Tanos in Santa Fe. Luis doubted if his own people would hang him. He had committed suicide.

Across the room, flames made eerie red flashes in the choking smoke. Stumbling toward them, Luis saw that they came from *enebro* faggots heaped against the wall. The drapes had caught fire and were blazing toward the ceiling. Once they reached the rafters and herringbone pattern of willow saplings that supported the earthen roof, the whole building would be doomed. Luis kicked the burning cedar faggots into the mud floor at the center of the room. He heard somebody else drop through the window but the smoke was too thick to see. He burned his hands and twice his holy sack caught fire and he had to beat it out against his body. But he got the blazing drapes down before they could ignite the wood of the ceiling.

There was a sulphurous pain searing his lungs and he was coughing violently. Pawing at his watering eyes, barely able to see, he groped toward the door of the anteroom. He did not trip on the halberd and realized that it was gone from the floor. He heard an echoing crash as the Indians outside finally broke through the outer door. They ran into the corridor and Luis could hear Juan Ye's unmistakable voice calling him, husky and grunting as a bear.

"Don Luis . . . Don Luis . . ."

It was not Luis who answered. It was someone in the anteroom ahead of him. "In here," the man said.

Mystified, Luis slowed down. He found the anteroom door. Ahead of him, little more than a shadow in the smoke, he saw the man with the halberd.

In the same instant another man plunged through the door from the office beyond. Even in the smoke Luis recognized that it was Juan Ye. His squat, burly figure, moving with its gouty limp, was unmistakable. The halberd descended. Juan Ye seemed to see it in the last moment, tried to dodge. It struck him a glancing blow and drove him to his knees.

Luis was near enough now to see that it was Toribio with the halberd. The half-breed lifted the weapon to drive it through the stunned Pecos chief.

"Toribio," Luis shouted.

It made Toribio wheel toward him. Luis was pulling his sword. Toribio shifted his grip on the halberd and drove it at Luis like a spear.

Luis wheeled aside. The halberd went past him so close that the beak on its triple-duty blade ripped his holy sack away from his chest. Luis was already thrusting.

Toribio did a strange thing. He made no attempt to lunge back. He looked curiously down at the blade as it came at him. There was an odd expression on his face, the same look Luis had seen when they had crouched together in the ruins the night before, a mask with all the life gone from it, the brittle emptiness of a shell with nothing left inside.

The reflexes of long training made Luis free the blade immediately and step away. But Toribio fell neither backward nor forward. He put a hand to the wound. His mouth opened and his eyes were blank with shock.

"Condesa," he said.

It was a little child crying for his mother. It made the blood bubble up in his mouth. He choked on it. He held his hand out before him, all smeared with blood, pawing for something his blind eyes could not see. He started walking toward the wall. He pitched over on his face.

Juan Ye had gained his feet. More Pecos warriors were crowding in behind him. Juan Ye shook his head dazedly, looking with glassy eyes at Toribio.

"It seemed almost like he wanted you to do that," Juan Ye said.

Luis wiped his mouth with a hand. He did not want to think about it that way. Condesa, the man had said.

Shakily, Luis said, "It was their last attempt to discredit Vargas."
Juan Ye understood. He said how it was a bad thing. He said how
Vargas would never have had honor among the Pueblos again if the
Pecos warriors had found Juan Ye dead here with a Spanish halberd
beside him.

"Get somebody to Tupatu," Luis said. "Did he not return to San
Juan? Say how he is to keep guards about him at all times. Say how he
is to receive no Spaniard until he meets with Vargas here. This may
not be finished yet."

Juan Ye nodded and went into the corridor with his men. The smoke
was thinning, an acrid gray veil in the anteroom. Luis looked at the
dead half-breed again. How many men had he killed since the fighting
began? Why should this one shake him so?

It was like opening a boil. All the emotion he had been unable to
feel swept through him in a poisonous wave. He began to shake violently. He thought he was going to be sick.

He heard Emilio in the corridor calling for him. He could not answer immediately. He saw a chair and went to it and sat down. He
put his head down and covered his face with his hands.

CHAPTER FIFTY-SIX

THE royal banners of Castile once more flew over the Palace of the Governors. Squads of soldiers moved through the storerooms and the royal houses, sacking the Indian stores of maize, beans, vetch, and lentils, for the use of the starving Spaniards. Almost four hundred of the captured Tanos, men, women, and children, had been herded into the stable area. They were to become slaves of the Spanish colonists. Seventy others, including the war chief Antonio Bolsas, stood bound in the main courtyard. They were listening to a sermon by Fray Juan Alpuente. After that they would receive absolution. Before the whole Spanish garrison they would be shot.

Luis crossed the courtyard, joining the group of officers around Vargas. He waited till Fray Alpuente's sermon was over, then reported that the last of the food had been gathered.

"Captain Madrid is taking his squad to escort the settlers into town," Vargas said. "You will join him."

Luis hesitated. He was looking at the Marqués de Gallegos, who stood nearby. The Marqués was staring vindictively at the bound Indians. He fiddled nervously with his sword. He grimaced. He tugged at the edges of his wig beneath his helmet. Vargas must have sensed what Luis was thinking.

"If there was a conspiracy," the general said in a low voice, "do we have enough evidence to present a case before the Crown?"

Reluctantly Luis said, "No."

"Just so. And for the same reason I could not justify any action I took against the Marqués personally. We won a battle today—not a war. There will always be men like the Marqués de Gallegos."

Luis knew he was right. They could prove nothing against the Marqués. They could not prove Toribio's connection with him, could not even prove that Toribio had tried to kill Juan Ye. He might easily have mistaken Juan Ye for an enemy in that smoky room. It made Luis think of the other wolves a man could not kill. The Marqués and what he stood for seemed to take his place beside the Holy Office, the Spanish flaws, the beggars in the Zocalo. They would not last forever, and he had done what he could today.

He went toward the horse lines, grateful to get away. He did not want to see the Indians executed. It was true they had broken their allegiance for a second time. It was true they had caused the death of twenty-two Spaniards on the hill, most of them children, and more in the battles. He was tired of trying to decide. Tired of trying to judge a man, separate his greatness from his human failings, his vision from the limitations imposed upon him by his times.

He mounted Canelo. As he passed the Tano prisoners in the stable-yard he saw one who had known Bigotes. He stopped and asked.

No, the Tano did not think Bigotes was dead. He thought Bigotes had gone to the west. Bigotes had gone to live with the Zunis or something.

Luis crossed the patio. Near the *zaguán* Mathias Lobato and Sergeant Tellez stood among the Spanish guards. As Luis passed Lobato seemed about to step out. Luis almost stopped his horse. He knew Lobato was thinking about that moment when Luis had saved his life on the roof.

But Lobato did not move. His eyes dropped from Luis's face to the holy sack. He turned red and looked at the ground. He wiped his hand across his mouth.

Luis rode out the gate. In time, Lobato, he thought. In time. He could not feel bitter. He could not feel anything. He was sick with exhaustion. He wanted to lie down somewhere and sleep for a year.

He looked northward toward the mountains. The Tewas were still up there, undefeated. The Spaniards faced a dreary series of campaigns. Perhaps they would have to subdue each village, one by one. But the back of the confederation was broken. The Keres were friendly and the Tanos were defeated, and the Cross and the sword were back in the land to stay.

The colonists were already coming down from their miserable camp on the hill. Luis held his horse at the edge of the plaza, watching the long plodding line of shivering people move slowly through the ruins.

When he saw Barbara and Josefina he dismounted. Barbara came out of the line to meet him. A heavy black wool shawl was draped over her head and shoulders, shadowing her face. The slender shape of her body was obscured by voluminous skirts.

"I heard you were back from Acoma," she said. There was intense restraint in her face. "I have been praying for you."

"I wanted to see you before this," he said. "The fighting kept me from it."

She saw the rip the halberd had made in his holy sack and the blisters the boiling water had left on his grimy face. She lifted one hand toward him. She let it drop back.

"I wanted to tell you," he said. "Kashana . . . Kashana would not come with me. She would not let me bring the boys."

"Luis——"

"I have been trying to decide——" For a moment he could not go on. It would make it too final. How many tortured hours had he spent since leaving Acoma? When he finally spoke his voice sounded hollow and distant, like someone else saying the words. "I think . . . I think it is better. You know how the boys would be looked upon here . . . how they would be treated."

"But you can go to see them."

Again he could not say the words. She saw the expression in his face and put her hands together as though praying and made a soft sound of pain and compassion.

"No," he said. "They should . . . they should forget me now. I could not damn them by making them half one thing and half another. Kashana has made them Indian. She is Indian. She has made her choice for all of us. She could not come to me and I could not go to her. It is over."

Barbara closed her eyes. She lifted both hands to put them against his chest, holding on to his torn holy sack. He covered them with his hands.

"I will walk with you to the palace," he said. "They have begun to cook some food. Can you smell the *enebro?*"

She smiled, and tears were coming from her eyes. "Yes, Luis. I can smell the *enebro.*"